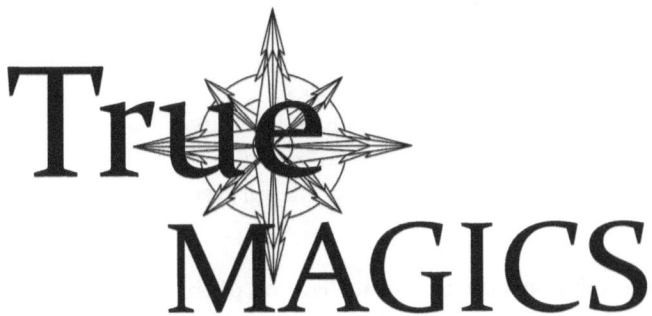

True MAGICS

Erik Buchanan

www.dragonmoonpress.com

True Magics

Cover Model: Erick Fournier

ISBN13-p 978-1-897492-84-0

Printed on acid free paper

www.dragonmoonpress.com
www.erikbuchanan.ca

True MAGICS

Erik Buchanan

Acknowledgements

Like the two books before it, True Magics was written amid more life changes than I ever expected. And like the others, it could not have come into fruition without the help of a great number of people. I owe a great deal of thanks to:

- Gwen Gades and Dragon Moon Press, who waited for the third one far more patiently than I could have hoped,
- Gabrielle Harbowy and Jamie Wyman, whose amazing editing work made the book far better than it was when it started,
- Marie Bilodeau, Katie Bryski, Gabrielle, Katrina and everyone else at the Dragon Moon Press table at Ad Astra who helped me brainstorm the title, (special thanks to Katie, who came up with the title, and who is one of the best writing partners ever.)
- Daniel, Kirsten and everyone down at Rapier Wit, who keep me sane and swinging swords (and knives, axes and whatever was at hand),
- And Maggie Buchanan and Katrina Guy, who put up with me while I was writing it and, worse, while I was editing it.

There are many more of you who helped by listening, by reading, by encouraging, by occasionally browbeating, and by being inspirations. I thank you all.

Dedication

For Katrina.

Dearest Father, Mother and Brother,

The war in Frostmire is over. Eileen, George, Henry and I are back in Hawksmouth, unhurt. We arrived last night, and I am writing this letter before my breakfast. There's going to be a celebration at the Academy this morning to welcome us back and to honour the eight who did not return. It will be rather bittersweet.

As I am sure Lionel has told you, the Church's guards destroyed our last apartment. Given all that occurred there, Henry and I have no desire to go back. We are renting new rooms and I will send you the address as soon as I may.

George and Eileen are staying in the city until the spring at least. They could manage the roads, but all of us are all tired of travel and the cold and wish nothing more than to stay in place for a while. Also, here in the city George and Eileen will have the protection of the Academy, should the Church of the High Father try to move against them.

Beware the Church, all of you. It was they who forced Eileen and George to go north with Henry and me, and I am worried that they may come after you to get at us. This afternoon we will go to the Master of Laws to ask the Academy to take court action. Henry will also appeal to the king. We will not let them hurt us or those we care about anymore.

I fear none of us are the same as we were before we the war. But we are unhurt and I am sure that, once the winter has turned and the days grow longer, we'll find ourselves and become whole again.

I must go. I will write again soon. I love you all.

Your obedient son,
Thomas Flarety

1

"Proof!" Thomas shook the sheaf of papers above his head and banged his other hand on the lectern. "Copied from the Academy's records! For over one hundred fifty years it happened! And was the Academy destroyed in that time? No! We are still here!" He pointed at the two students sitting on the far side of the stage. "With this proof, I challenge—no, I *defy* my opponents to find a single honest reason why the Academy should not once more admit girls!"

Half the audience in the Academy Assembly Hall erupted in cheers, the other half in boos and catcalls and a rousing chant of "Down with him! Down with him!" Their voices echoed off the decorated plaster of the ceiling and their stomping feet shook the wooden floors and the long benches on which they all sat. From the front row, the sixteen survivors of the Academy's Expeditionary Company chanted, "Captain! Captain! Captain!"

Thomas stepped away from the lectern, bowed, and took a chair beside Henry on the left side of the stage. Henry dug an elbow into Thomas's ribs. "Nice work."

"Glad you thought so," said Thomas. "Let's see what they do to top that!"

"Doesn't matter what they do," said Henry, lowering his voice as the noise died down. "Our best argument is still waiting in the wings."

Thomas looked. "I don't see 'our best argument.'"

"Well, there was some mention of needing to vomit..."

On the other side of the stage, Keith Rolston rose to his feet. Like Thomas and Henry he was in his fifth year of law at the Academy. He was stout and strong and known in law class for the skill with which he destroyed his opponents' arguments. The sneer on his lips conveyed both superiority and disdain as he looked at the booing students. He walked slowly to the lectern and aimed his sneer at Thomas and Henry.

"Try to keep a straight face this year," said Henry, just loud enough for Keith to hear.

Keith didn't acknowledge him at all. Instead he shook his head back and forth in long, slow swings. "Shame!" Keith pronounced, his deep voice rolling from the stage and filling the auditorium. "Shame, shame, and shame again!"

Thomas resisted the urge to chew on his lip and tried to look confident. Out of the corner of his eye, he could see Henry putting on the half-smile he wore when he didn't want anyone to guess his feelings.

"Shame on my esteemed opponent," Keith continued, "for taking up the valuable time of the Royal Academy with so unworthy a topic. For what could be less worthy than the suggestion that a *girl* could fill a place among this learned company?"

Polite applause and mild booing greeted his opening. Keith nodded as if the entire Academy had agreed with him. "I know full well that girls had a place here. But I say that they lost that place! And they lost it for good reason!"

Keith let them all hang on his words a moment before continuing. "Two hundred years ago, King Darren the Third laid out in no uncertain terms what it is to be a student. And there is not a girl in the world who has the qualities that his Majesty put forward on that day!"

Graham Silvers, a tall, thin philosophy student, whose shock of brown hair never seemed to lie down properly, stepped out of the wings with a thick sheet of vellum embossed with the school's coat of arms. He raised it high for everyone to see and walked with slow, deliberate steps across the stage.

"Look upon the proclamation!" roared Keith. "Look upon the words of King Darren the Third!" He pointed to the first line. "Let it be known that our students are to comport themselves with the highest possible standard of behaviour!"

That brought a loud laugh, and rolled eyes from the professors.

"No points scored with that one," said Thomas. Henry grinned.

Keith smiled in spite of himself and let the laughter die down a bit. "They are to swear their fealty, bravery and loyalty to their king and his Academy! They are to swear fraternity, hospitality and charity to their fellow students! They are to conduct themselves with dignity, with decency and with courage, and defend the honour of the Academy above all things, even to the point of arms!"

Keith paused to let the words sink in, then repeated, "Fealty! Loyalty! Bravery! Hospitality! Charity! Few *men* possess all these qualities, let alone *girls*. And what of fraternity? Can you name a single girl whom you would turn to and say, 'You are my brother'?"

The "against" side laughed and cheered. The "for" crowd grumbled. Keith raised his voice over them all. "And let us not forget the most important of all matters: honour! How can a mere girl defend the honour of the Academy? She can't even defend her own honour, save that she has a man to do it for her!

"Thus I say, no girls should be admitted to the Academy!"

Thunderous applause from the "against." Thunderous booing from the "for." Keith bowed and took his seat.

Henry rose, sauntered over to the lectern, and leaned on it while the noise died down. When it had, the "for" side were sitting on the edge of their seats, hoping Henry could turn the balance their way.

"I am supposed to rebut this argument." Henry's voice was not deep and resonant like Keith's had been, but Henry had been a captain in his father's armies since he was fourteen and was trained to be heard over the clamour of battle. "Unfortunately, my opponent's argument is not worthy of a rebuttal!"

The "for" side laughed. Henry raised his hand for silence. "Instead, I will yield the floor to one who is not a student, but who, through worthy action, has been given the honour of freedom of the grounds and the right to join us in this debate!"

Henry stepped back from the lectern. A slim figure wearing a too-long robe, with red hair tied back with a leather thong into a short ponytail, stepped from the wings and walked across the stage to the lectern.

Come on, Thomas urged silently. *You've done harder things than this.* At the first sign of weakness, the "against" side would start jeering and the entire debate would be lost.

"You know me as Alexander Gobhann!" The words came out clear and steady, and filled the now-quiet hall. "I am not a student, and there are some of you that may think that this precludes me from speaking here today. After all, what person who is not a student could possibly know loyalty, bravery, fraternity and honour?"

Alexander's eyes swept the room. "I can."

One slim hand pointed to the Student Company. "Bravery and fraternity I learned fighting beside the Academy's Expeditionary Company in the frozen streets of Frostmire!" The hand swung to Thomas. "Loyalty I showed when I helped rescue Captain Thomas Flarety, kidnapped by treachery most foul and given up for dead." Alexander's hand slammed down, flat and hard, on the lectern. "And those who tried my honour found that I would fight for it with fist, knife and rapier, and they have the scars to prove it!"

Alexander undid the string that held back the ponytail. Hair fell in curly red rings around a suddenly feminine face.

"When I returned to Hawksmouth with the Student Company, I was asked what reward I should be given for my service. I wanted only one thing: to be allowed to sit the exams and *earn* my way into the Academy."

Alexander started undoing the buttons on the robe.

"My words were greeted with cheers. I was promised that, should I pass the exams, I would be given a full scholarship! And for three months I have been treated as a guest. I have been able to sit in the lectures and study in the library! All so that I may take the exams and prove myself worthy to be a member of the Academy!"

The robe fell to the floor. Five hundred students and their masters stared in disbelief.

Eileen Gobhann stood tall and straight in the black puddle of the robe, wearing a dress that was the orange-red colour of freshly fallen autumn leaves. It was tight and low-cut in the bodice, fabric clinging over her hips before flaring out into the skirts. She smiled. "So what difference does it make that I'm a girl?"

In the deep, pregnant silence, Eileen curtseyed, picking the robe from the floor in the same motion, and walked to stand beside Thomas and Henry.

The place went insane.

If the building was shaking before, the clamour that was rising now threatened to bring it down. Students shouted and screamed in amazement and anger and glee and disbelief. Graham and Keith were both staring, mouths open. Keith's face was bright red. Students yelled at the stage and at one another. Some began pushing and swearing at each other.

Aldrick Thornton, Master of Rhetoric, dashed down the centre aisle and up the stage steps to the lectern, calling for order as he went. Even his magnificent voice went practically unheard over the arguing and fighting until the rest of the masters and professors rose to their feet and demanded silence.

When the audience was finally back in their seats and the howls of outrage and glee reduced to muttering and chortles, Master Aldrick turned his eyes on Thomas, Henry and Eileen. The three braced themselves but, to their surprise, the master said nothing. He didn't even look angry. He looked... curious. He turned back to the audience, who were now holding their breaths to see what would happen next.

"Well," The Master of Rhetoric said, "In twenty years of debates, I can say that this was the most surprising argument that I have seen."

Nervous laughter came from both sides.

"Enough of this!" Macklin Revus, Professor of History was still on his feet. He leaned on the bench in front of him, his round, florid face practically beet-red with anger. "Are we to let this farce continue?"

"Farce?" the Master of Rhetoric's face was impassive and his tone gentle, but something in his bearing made the entire assembly fall silent.

Professor Revus didn't notice. "Yes, farce! To let a girl into the Academy! To let her participate in a debate... it's a mockery!"

The Master of Rhetoric's left eyebrow rose a measured quarter-inch. "You're taking the "against" side, then?"

Another nervous laugh rolled through the room.

"This is not a joke!" snapped Professor Revus.

"It most certainly is not!" said Master Aldrick, his voice now loud enough to fill the room. "It's a debate! And I, for one, am anxious to hear how our audience will weigh the arguments that we have heard here today!" He looked to Keith and Graham. "Do you have more to add?"

"We do not," said Keith, his voice tight and furious. Graham, beside him, just nodded.

Master Aldrick bowed formally to Keith and Graham, then again to Henry, Thomas and Eileen. "Both sides have finished their arguments!" he announced. "And now, students of the Royal Academy of Learning, it is up to you to decide who will be the victor!" His held out his hand toward Thomas, Henry and Eileen. "Let those who think that the 'for' side has won their argument convincingly, rise to their feet!"

The Student Company were on their feet in an instant. The others around them—all friends—rose next. Then more and more stood up until two-thirds of the students in the hall were on their feet. For a moment the room was silent as everyone watched.

Then pandemonium broke out again.

"The 'for' side has won!" declared the Master of Rhetoric, his words drowning in cheers. "It is therefore the opinion of the Royal Academy of Learning that girls should be allowed to attend!"

Henry and Thomas rose to their feet and bowed, Eileen dropped into a deep curtsey. Master Thornton shook the hands of all three. "You do realize there will be grave consequences to this," he said, raising his voice to be heard.

"We do," said Thomas.

"But not today!" added Henry as cheering students swept onto the stage. All three were raised high on shoulders and paraded around the hall. Eileen, Thomas saw, was being lifted by members of the Student Company, who were being quite careful both about where their hands were and who was allowed close to her.

Then Thomas had to duck as they carried him out the Assembly Hall and into the bright sunshine of the cold, early spring morning. Behind him, Eileen squealed as the near-freezing air hit her bare arms. William from the company tossed her robe up and she wrapped it tight around her shoulders. The cheering students took them once around the Academy's common before letting the three of them down. There was more cheering and many handshakes and much backslapping. Someone produced a flask of whisky and each of the three got a swallow before it was passed out of their reach.

"Excellently done," said Mark, a lieutenant in the Student Company. He tossed Eileen her cloak and coat, then Henry and Thomas theirs. "I didn't think we'd actually win! Good work, Eileen!"

"Great work!" said Marcus, who'd been one of Thomas's runners during the battles for Frostmire.

"All we won was the debate," warned Thomas, hurrying into his coat. "Next step is the petitions. After Festival we start collecting signatures, demanding they change the rules and let Eileen into the Academy. Then we go to council and that's where things will get difficult."

"By the Four, this is the easy bit?" Eileen shook her head. "I should have stayed in the north!"

The students around her laughed. Thomas smiled. "And what would I have said to your parents?"

"They've got to let her in after that performance," said Charles, who had lost his right hand in Frostmire's streets.

"They don't have to do anything," said Eileen as she buttoned her coat then pulled the cloak tight around her shoulders. "After today, they don't even have to let me into the grounds."

"They may not even let *us* back in," said Henry.

"They can't ban us without speaking to us first," said Thomas.

"Which they can't do if we are not here," said Henry. "And since the Festival of the Rains is tomorrow..."

"We need to go somewhere and get good and drunk before we go in the water!" declared Wilson, another member of the company. "We'll not survive it otherwise! To the Quill!"

The crowd cheered and shuddered at once. The Festival of Rains was the second of the spring festivals, only two weeks after the Equinox. It was a festival of defiance; a show of strength against winter and faith in the coming spring. And in Hawksmouth, capital city of Criethe, the Festival of Rains was celebrated by walking to the beaches and immersing oneself in the ocean as the sun broke the horizon.

For students of the Academy, it was a matter of honour to go in first, a matter of pride not to sleep the night before, and a matter of practicality to be somewhat less than sober.

They flowed out of the Academy grounds and poured into the streets of Hawksmouth in a stream of black cloaks and high spirits. Thomas grabbed Eileen's hand as they went and squeezed it hard. Eileen raised her voice above the clamour. "I have to go home first and tell George!" she called. "We'll meet you there!"

"Don't be late!" called Marcus. "You need as much alcohol as possible!"

Eileen pulled Thomas onto a side street, then grabbed him and kissed him thoroughly. "It worked!" she nearly shrieked when they broke apart. "It actually worked! We did it!"

"*You* did it, you mean," said Thomas. "You're the one who gave the speech."

"Which was my idea," said Henry, making them both jump. "Does that mean I get one of those?"

Eileen hugged Henry hard, then reached up and kissed his cheek. "You're a fool, Henry Antonius."

"*Lord* Henry Antonius to you," said Henry, hugging her back.

"I am so proud of you," said Thomas. "You were amazing."

Eileen blushed. "You wouldn't have said that if you saw me before the debate. I wasn't sure if I was going to throw up or pass out."

"Good thing you didn't," said Henry. "I had money riding on it." He pushed her away. "Now let's tell George. I want to be at the Quill before the food is gone!"

The Street of Smiths was a fair distance from the Academy, down two major streets and across a market square filled with people, wagons and carriages. Eileen practically bounced the entire distance, with Thomas and Henry hard on her heels.

George's small house was at the end of the Street of Smiths. Henry's brother John, who was now Duke of Frostmire, had rewarded them all generously for fighting in the north and George had used his money to rent a smithy. The small house had been run down when George took possession, but it had a forge on the main floor with a kitchen and sitting room directly above, and two bedrooms on the third floor, just below the roof. George had repaired the forge and opened it for business in less than a week. The rest of the house had taken most of a month for George to fix up, but now it was snug and cozy.

The sign above the wide doors of the smithy read "Sir George Gobhann: Blacksmith and Bladesmith." Henry had suggested adding George's title, claiming a little nobility never hurt a business. It seemed to have worked. In two months George had built a steady clientele of carters, soldiers and housewives asking for horses shod, weapons sharpened or fixed, and pots repaired.

The doors to the smithy were wide open and George was inside, working shirtless under his apron despite the cold. Where Eileen was the image of their mother, George was built tall and wide like their father, with Lionel's brown hair and eyes.

A tall young lady with pleasant curves and a length of blonde hair braided into a ponytail down her back was watching him repair a pot, though she seemed far more interested in George's bare arms than the work he was doing. For his part, George was doing a remarkable job of simultaneously fixing the pot and flirting.

"Who's the girl?" asked Thomas.

"Linda Gatron," said Eileen. "She's been coming over for about a month, now."

"She must have a lot of pots that need mending," said Henry.

"I doubt it," said Eileen. "Her father is the head of the Smiths' Guild."

"He is?" Henry sounded impressed. "George is moving up in the world."

"Why did I not know about this?" asked Thomas.

"Because you haven't sat down to talk to George once in the last five weeks," said Eileen.

"I have tried," said Thomas. "He won't go out. Says he's too tired or too busy."

"And now we know who he was too busy with," said Henry, watching George hand back the girl's pot. Their fingers met on the rim and stayed there as they chatted. "He is smooth, isn't he?"

"Be nice, you," warned Eileen. "George! We won the debate!"

"You did?" George's face lit up. He spoke a quick word to Linda and hurried out to the street. "Good for you!" He swept Eileen up in a huge hug, spun her around twice and dropped her solidly on her feet. "And what about you two? Are you still students?"

"So far," said Henry, shaking George's hand. "After Festival we'll find out if we're all out on our ears."

George's eyes narrowed. "You're far too cheery about that, Henry." He let go of Henry's hand and shook Thomas's. "What happens next?"

"Petitions," said Eileen. "Then the Council of Rules, if we get enough signatures."

"Which we will," said Thomas. "We're going to the Quill to celebrate—"

"After I get changed," said Eileen, heading for the door of the smithy. "If I go dressed like this they'll think I'm the entertainment. Be right back." She waved a greeting at Linda and dashed up the stairs. Linda smiled and waved back.

"Come with us, George," said Thomas. "It'll be fun."

George shook his head. "No, you don't want me there."

"Yes, we do," said Thomas. "When's the last time the four of us got together?"

"Too many students," said George. "Too much noise. I'll meet you on the beach."

"Because it will be all sorts of quiet there," said Thomas.

"Quieter than the Broken Quill."

"George, come with—"

"No." His expression darkened, like a sudden cloud covering the sun, and for a moment he looked almost angry. He blinked a few times, as if something had gotten into his eyes. Then he shook his head and the darkness lightened a little. "Thank you. Just no."

"All right," said Thomas. *What is going on?* "Another time."

"I'd best get going," said Linda. She smiled at George. "I'll see you at the beach in the morning?"

The cloud over George vanished and he smiled. "You will. Give my regards to your father."

"I will." Linda smiled back at him and walked away.

Henry watched her go. "Nice girl. And the daughter of the head of the Smiths' Guild, too, I hear. When are you going to introduce us?"

"Never," said George. He pointed a warning finger at Henry. "Keep away from her, you."

"Not to worry," said Henry. "Sure you won't come with us? There will be much drinking."

"I'm sure," said George, turning back to the forge. "You can wait for Eileen in the kitchen."

"We'll do that," said Thomas.

***

The *Broken Quill* was the largest pub in the student quarter. It was a solid stone building, three stories high, and had been there as long as Hawksmouth itself—perhaps longer, if the stories were to be believed. The pub seated more than two hundred and, from the noise coming from within, it was already full. Just inside the wide, open door sat Fenris and Marcus, a pair of nearly identical, very tall, very large men with equally large iron-studded wooden clubs. One was watching the street, the other, the customers inside.

"Good evening..." Thomas stopped and studied the man in front of him, "Fenris?"

Fenris smiled. "Very good, Master Thomas. How are you this evening?"

"Very well, Fenris. Is there room for three more?"

"There is," said Fenris. "In fact, your friends have saved a spot for you by the fire." He smiled at Eileen. "And here is the cause of the debate. Does this mean we get to learn your real name, now?"

"Fenris, Marcus," said Thomas formally, "Allow me to introduce Miss Eileen Gobhann."

Marcus looked back over his shoulder. "You do look much better as a girl," he said. "You've caused something of a stir."

"I know," said Eileen. "I hope it hasn't caused any trouble for you."

"Only minor, so far," said Fenris. "Let's hope that doesn't change with your arrival."

The inside of the Broken Quill was awash with noise and smoke and the smells of roast pork and mulled wine. Twenty long tables filled the big hall and most of them were overflowing. More people stood along the rail of the balcony running the length of the second floor. There were ten private rooms above, and students and their girls were wandering in and out of them. The room was loud and rowdy, and everyone was arguing about the debate. Thomas led the way to the Student Company's table.

"I take it things have been tense," said Thomas.

"Some people aren't happy," said Mark. "A lot of them think you pulled a dirty trick."

"You did pull a dirty trick," said Keith, coming up behind them. Graham Silvers stood right behind him.

"You're just grumpy that you fell for it," said Henry.

"Everyone fell for it," said Eileen, smiling at Keith, "not just you. Doesn't Professor Dodds say that the obvious isn't what's in front of you but what's out of place?"

"Don't quote Dodds at me," snapped Keith. "You shouldn't even have been in that class."

"But she was," said Henry. "She was, we won, and you owe me money."

Keith growled in disgust, but pulled out his pouch and after some fussing, tossed some coins on the table.

Eileen stepped forward. "I'm sorry you thought it was a dirty trick," she said. "But we had to do it. We had to make a case for girls in the Academy if I'm going to get in." She held out her hand. "Friends?"

"Get in?" Keith's eyes went wide. "You're not getting in! You won't even be let in the grounds after Festival."

"That's for the Headmaster to decide," said Thomas.

"No it isn't! Girls don't go on the Academy grounds!"

"This one does," said Henry. "By invite of the Headmaster, in fact."

"But she can't go back! She doesn't belong!"

"She *is* going back," said Eileen, her smile gone and a sharp edge on her words. "And she will be taking the exams and going to the Academy if she passes."

"We're doing petitions starting after Festival," said Charles. "Will you be signing?"

Keith's face alternated red and white for a pair of moments, then he turned and stalked away.

"He took that well, didn't he?" said Henry.

"By the Four, are they all going to be like that?" asked Eileen.

"Some," said Thomas. "Not all of them."

"He's just sore," said Graham, who was still standing there. He handed over coins to Thomas. "And so am I. That was a dirty trick you pulled and you and Henry should be ashamed of yourselves." He turned to Eileen and stuck out his hand. "Good debate."

Eileen, bemused, shook it.

"See?" said Thomas as Graham went back to his table. "Keith will come around, I hope."

"He'd better," said Eileen. "I've come too far to stop now."

She took off her coat and cloak and laid them on the bench. She was wearing her green skirt and bodice with a white blouse beneath.

"You do look better as a girl," said Jonathan.

"But we'll all miss the sight of you in pants," said Henry, earning a swat. "Now, hands up everyone that won a bet on this."

Every member of the company raised his hand.

Henry grinned. "Then let's celebrate in style!"

***

Five hours later, the midnight bell rang and the students spilled out of the pub, filling the streets with laughter and song. Plans and promises to meet on the beach were shouted back and forth as they split up to gather their supplies. Eileen and Thomas, hand in hand and smiling, with Henry right beside them, went to Thomas and Henry's apartment. They fetched blankets and a basket of food and wine that Henry had organized that morning. Then they walked through the city, across the harbour and out the land-gates.

They followed the curve of the bay that protected Hawksmouth from the ocean down to the mile-long gravel beach. The path to the beach had been lined with torches, and hundreds of people were already walking to the shore, their lanterns and torches making a twinkling procession. Beyond the beach, the water rolled in small, foam tipped waves that reflected the lights of the fires and the lanterns. The breeze coming off the ocean was strong and cold and wet.

For Thomas, who could also see the inner lights of the people on the beach, it looked like a thousand small lights were dancing in the wind.

"Thank the Four it isn't raining," said Henry. "Or snowing. Remember two years ago? We nearly froze before we even got to the water."

"I still don't understand why you have to go in," said Eileen. "We never did this back home."

"You weren't by the ocean back home, were you?"

"Thomas! Henry! Here!"

Michael was beside one of the many beach fires, jumping up and down and waving his arms. A great store of wood was put away every fall for the Festival of

Rains, and fires had been built down the length of the beach. The students from the Academy traditionally gathered by the royal pavilion to show their support and respect for the king. Nearby, a stage had been set up for the Archbishop to lead the prayers for the festival.

"There's George!" Eileen pointed to another fire. "I'll be right back." She dashed up the beach to where her brother stood amidst a group of young men and women. Linda was on his arm. She hugged Eileen and smiled.

"George better be careful," said Henry, "or he'll end up settling down here and marrying that girl."

Thomas shook his head. "He hates the city."

"He used to hate the city," said Henry. "I'm guessing he likes it much better now."

Thomas, seeing the smile on George's face as he looked at Linda, found himself agreeing. Linda reached out, took Eileen's hand, and let Eileen lead her toward Thomas and Henry. She also held tight to George's arm, forcing him to come along.

"Sir George!" Henry stepped forward and bowed. "So good of you to join us. You must introduce me to your lovely lady."

George's eyes narrowed, but he said, "Linda Gaston, Henry Antonius."

Linda curtseyed. Henry took her hand on the way up and brought it to his lips as he bowed. "Lord Henry Antonius," he corrected. "And I am very charmed to meet you."

Linda laughed. "I see what you mean about the students, George."

"He's one of the worst of us," said Thomas, taking her hand from Henry and bowing over it. "Thomas Flarety, at your service."

"Hardly fair," complained Henry.

"But so true," said Eileen. "We just got here. How has it been?"

"Cold," said Linda.

"Well, we can fix that," said Henry. He raised his voice loud enough to echo down the beach. "A drum! A drum to dance and stay warm! Who has a drum?"

"A drum! A drum!" A dozen voices took up the call, then a hundred more. Above the clamour, the first drum struck, hard and fast in a dance beat.

"Dance with us!" yelled Henry, grabbing Linda by the hand. "Who will dance with us until the dawn?"

Linda giggled and grabbed George by the hand. "We will!"

"I will!" shouted a girl.

"I will!" The cries went up and down the beach, and soon dozens joined hands in a long chain of men and women, Henry in the lead. With a yell he jumped in the air and led the line forward, singing at the top of his lungs. George stumbled on the first two steps, and Eileen, right behind her brother, laughed at him. He growled at her, then turned back and found the rhythm.

Thomas, holding Eileen's other hand, frowned. George was usually the one who enjoyed parties the most, not the least.

More people joined in as the line of dancers snaked their way down the beach. Others sang and clapped their hands and. People danced in groups large and small on all sides.

The line wended down and back the length of the beach, with dancers joining in and falling out as they went. After the second round, George and Linda dropped out. Henry dropped out on the third and came back with a girl on the fourth. On the fifth trip, James, sitting at a fire with a buxom young woman on his lap called out, “Hey, Thomas! Someone’s looking for you!”

“Who?” Thomas asked, raising his voice to be heard over the singing.

“Don’t know. Three of them. Said they had business.”

Three? “What did they look like?”

“Like they had sticks up their backsides.” James pointed. “You’re dancing right toward them.”

The dancers kept moving up the beach, carrying them towards the royal pavilion. Eileen called to Thomas, “Who do you think it is?”

“No idea.”

“There’s Thomas Flarety,” called Lord Cormac, son of a baron of Frostmire, and once co-conspirator with Lord Richard to overthrow and murder the duke. His voice was loud enough to carry down the beach. “There’s the duke’s personal witch!”

2

Thomas felt his stomach drop and all the blood rush away from his head. He staggered and for a moment thought he would collapse. The front of the line of dancers stumbled to a halt and broke apart. The back of the line kept going, weaving around them. Thomas looked for other members of the company. None were nearby.

Lord Cormac had a beard now, as did his two companions, Lord Anthony and Lord Ethan. All three were richly dressed in thick, wool coats and white fur capes, with tall boots on their feet. All three were smiling at Thomas and Eileen.

"And here's Eileen as well," said Cormac, just as loud as before. "Is she as free with her charms here as she was in Frostmire?"

Thomas caught Eileen as she started forward, her face white with rage. "It's Festival," hissed Thomas. "You fight, you get flogged." He raised his voice, "As I am sure these cowards know."

"I'm sure she is," said Lord Ethan, who had a bend in his nose from when Eileen had broken it in Frostmire. "Just as I'm sure we'll get a second opportunity to sample them."

Eileen lunged at Ethan. Thomas wrapped both arms around her and hauled her back again.

"Rapist!" Eileen spat. "Dogs! All three of you!"

"Such harsh words from the witch's lover," said Cormac, keeping his voice loud. "It's a good thing Lord John—now the Duke, since his father died and he arrested his own brother—had Thomas. Otherwise those raiders would have put the whole Dukedom to the torch. But this one stopped them dead. Threw lightning right out of your hands, didn't you, Thomas?"

A rumble of disbelief went through the people around them. Half shook their heads and turned away. The other half stared at Thomas, as if expecting him to throw lightning on the spot.

Thomas felt his teeth clenching. He hadn't even known about magic until the past summer, let alone that he could use it. And in the same day Thomas had discovered it, Bishop Malloy tried to steal the magic from him. By the end of summer, Thomas had lost two friends to the bishop's plotting, learned how to summon power from the earth, and killed more than a dozen men with lightning and steel. And when he and Bishop Malloy came face to face the last time, Thomas had taken the man's magic and then killed him in cold blood.

Which was why, when raiders attacked the Duchy of Frostmire with magic, Lord Henry, the Duke's youngest son, asked Thomas to come north. And when the raiders in Frostmire had called fog down to blind the Duke's men and fire to burn the city, Thomas had answered with lightning.

And now this idiot is yelling about it to everyone.

"What's he talking about, Thomas?" asked one of the students. "You never said anything about witchcraft in the North."

"There's no such thing as witchcraft," the words came out of Thomas nearly of their own accord. He made his brain rally around them. “Everyone knows it.”

“Really?” said Lord Anthony. “Did ‘everyone’ see lightning fly from your fingers?”

“No,” said Thomas. “And neither did you. Any of you.”

“We were there when the palace was attacked,” said Lord Anthony.

“Not during the fighting,” said Thomas. “Lord Richard had you all safely out of the way when he let the raiders into the castle. Was that so you could help him murder his father?”

A new buzz went through the crowd, and all eyes turned to the three men.

“We were misled,” said Lord Cormac, without the faintest trace of remorse. “Lord Richard was the rightful heir and we followed his instructions. We cannot be blamed for that. Whereas you, Thomas, well, you knew exactly what you were doing, didn’t you?”

“I was fighting the raiders,” said Thomas. “Me, the Student Company, and all the decent nobles in your Dukedom. Unlike all of you.”

“You’re a fine one to talk of decency,” said Ethan. “You practice witchcraft. Your girl dresses as a boy and throws herself at any man she fancies. Is it true she slept with Baron Goshawk? He never did answer that.”

The growl that came out of Eileen was more animal than human, and Thomas barely managed to restrain her. “How very brave,” Thomas ground out through clenched teeth. “Trying to start a fight at Festival, where fighting is forbidden.”

Ethan spread his hands wide and put on a look of innocence. “I’m merely telling the truth,”

“Truth?” spat Eileen. “Fine! You’re a coward. You’re a rapist. You’re a traitor.”

“But not a witch,” said Anthony.

“You have no friends here,” warned Thomas. “And Festival ends tomorrow, so shut up or be prepared to answer for it.”

“And what a pity we can’t,” said Cormac. “Unlike you, we’re dedicated to keeping the King’s Peace. In fact, when we met with the king this morning we told him of your propensities towards violence and witchcraft.”

“The King’s Peace,” repeated Thomas, suddenly understanding. “The Duke banished you.”

Cormac’s eyebrows went up. “We’ve decide to pursue our fortunes elsewhere.”

“The King’s Peace is the surety that an individual will conduct himself with exemplary behaviour for as long as that individual remains in the country and is only given on the condition that the individual agrees that he will leave within the fortnight,” recited Thomas. “You’ve been banished from Criethe and you’re in Hawksmouth on the king’s sufferance. Probably until better weather for a long sea voyage.” Thomas stepped closer to Cormac. “Get out of here.”

“Of course,” said Cormac, his voice calm and as cool as the night air. “After all, I’d hate for you to throw lightning at *me*. Gentlemen, shall we?”

The three walked straight forward, shoving Thomas and Eileen aside with their shoulders. Thomas didn't bother shoving back. Eileen glared daggers at them, her fists clenched. Thomas stepped between her and their retreating backs. "Let's get out of here."

Eileen, her jaw tight, nodded.

They'd covered less than twenty yards when a man in his middle years stepped in front of them. He was dressed in long robes and had a thick fur collar on his cape and a gold pendant around his neck—all symbols of a well-to-do merchant. "Thomas Flarety?"

Thomas stopped. "Yes?"

"I think I need to beg your forgiveness." The man bowed to Eileen. "Both your forgiveness."

Thomas, who had been prepared for a number of things from questions about witchcraft to calls for his arrest, was caught flat-footed. "Pardon me?"

"Those young men came south on one of my ships," he said. "I do business with their fathers, and am providing them with a line of credit." He looked in the direction of the young nobles and shook his head. "They said they knew you in Frostmire and wanted to speak to you. They said you were a student, so I brought them here where I knew the students would be. I had no idea they would..." The man shook his head. "I am truly, deeply sorry for their actions. Had I known..."

"It's not your fault," said Thomas, stepping around the man. "If you'll excuse me."

"But it is," said the man, again blocking Thomas's way. He held out his hand. "My name is Malcolm Bright. I'm a merchant."

Thomas really wanted to get away, but the man was only being polite and Thomas wasn't about to behave like the young nobles and walk through him. He took the man's hand and shook it. "Merchant Bright, there is no need to—"

"It's just that when they told stories about the magic they had seen, I became intrigued," said Malcolm Bright, quickly. He leaned in close to Thomas and dropped his voice. "I've always loved the idea of magic. I had no idea they would be so disparaging of it. Calling it witchcraft..." Malcolm released Thomas's hand. "Please, let me make it up to you."

"That's not..."

Malcolm reached into his coat. "Are you aware that this festival originally lasted three days?"

"Did it?" asked Thomas, his eyes on the man's hand.

"Today, tomorrow—well, yesterday and today, to be correct—and the next day." Malcolm pulled from his coat a very thick piece of paper, folded and sealed with wax, and held it out. "My family keeps the old custom, and we would be honoured if you would join us."

"Ummm..."

"It would be an opportunity to meet with others with similar... *interests* as your own. People who know what it's like to be blessed."

Thomas eyes narrowed at the words, unsure and suddenly suspicious of the man. Malcolm was still smiling a warm and friendly smile that Thomas didn't trust for a moment.

"You don't have to come," said Malcolm. "But do take it."

Thomas took it.

Malcolm's smile grew wider "It was good meeting you, Thomas Flarety." He bowed slightly. "And you, Eileen. I hope to see you tomorrow night. And if not, I am glad to have made your acquaintance, despite the circumstances."

The man stepped away and was soon gone. Thomas stared at the invitation, then put it into his coat. He looked at Eileen, unsure of what to do next.

"Thomas! Eileen!"

They turned and saw Henry, George, and the rest of the Student Company charging toward them.

"I was behind you in the dancing," gasped Wilson when he reached them. "When I saw the lords I ran for the others. They were all over the place. Are you all right?"

"I'm fine," said Thomas. "Eileen?"

"Fine," she snapped. "Just fine."

"What happened?" asked George, his eyes on his sister and his face darkening. "What did they say?"

"Not here," said Thomas. "Come with me, all of you."

He led the group away from the crowded fires and the beach to the rocky land above it.

"Are you all right?" asked Henry. "What did they want?"

"Revenge," said Thomas. "They told everyone I did witchcraft in the north and insulted Eileen so we would pick a fight with them."

"Witchcraft?" George practically spat the word out. "I thought we were done with that!"

"So did I until those idiots started shouting about it!" snapped Thomas. He forced himself to take a breath and calm down. "It will probably all just blow over."

"Blow over?" repeated George. "How can it blow over? What if they go tell the Church? Will we have to run away again? I have a business, Thomas! I can't just leave!"

"We won't have to leave!"

"We will if the Church comes after us!"

"The Church will not come after us! Those idiots can't tell anything to the Church because they didn't see ANYTHING!" Thomas pulled his voice back down from top volume. "They weren't in any of the fighting, remember? All they have is hearsay and the Church won't go against the king for that."

"You're sure of that, are you?"

No. "Yes. Just watch what you say and we'll all be fine."

George growled something Thomas couldn't hear and turned away. He stared at the people milling about on the beach for a time. At last he said. "We'd better be fine. And now, if you'll excuse me. I have to go explain to the Smiths' Guild why I had to run after my sister in a panic."

Thomas shut his mouth and kept it that way as he watched George go. When he was calm enough, he turned to the others. "They're just three spoiled little lordlings who are bitter about being banished. No one is going to pay any real attention to them."

"What if they do?" asked Marcus. "What if they just keep showing up everywhere you go, talking about witchcraft?"

It was a good question, and Thomas was still thinking up an answer when Henry said, "Hearsay means nothing. It will be 'I heard' this and 'someone said' that. If they can't say they saw it with their own eyes, no one is going to believe them. Unless you lot let something slip."

"Us?" Michael sounded deeply offended. "Why would we say anything?"

"Because you all drink too much and try to impress girls in taverns," said Henry. "How many people heard?"

"At least a hundred," said Thomas. "Probably more."

"Then there's going to be questions. And the answer to all of them is 'they weren't there.' Got it?" He turned to Eileen. "Are you all right?"

"I'm fine," said Eileen, her voice still blazing with anger. "I'll gut them if they come near me again."

"I'll help," said Henry. Heads nodded, but no one in the company looked happy.

"And now we should get back," said Henry. He looked east, where the deep blue of pre-dawn replaced the black of night. "Someone has to show them how to go in the water without crying."

"Look there," said Wilson. "Here come the rest of them."

Thousands of people were making their way down the path to the beach, led by a flock of priests of the High Father, all dressed in grey robes to honour the Festival of Rains.

"All the ones who were too lazy to stay up all night," said Michael.

"You mean too smart," said Marcus. The others chuckled a bit and trooped together down to the beach. Thomas, Henry and Eileen followed behind.

Thomas took Eileen's hand and squeezed it tight. "It will be all right. They'll be kicked out of the country and this will all be done." Eileen didn't say anything. Thomas turned to Henry. "On the bright side we got invited to a party."

Henry's eyebrows went up. "What?"

"A merchant named Malcolm Bright," said Thomas. "One of his ships brought Cormac and the others, and then he led them to the beach. He was 'appalled' at their behaviour and invited me to his party tomorrow night to make it up to me."

"Really," said Henry. "That's...odd."

"Apparently it's a place where I can meet others with similar 'interests'."

"That sounds vaguely foreboding," said Henry. "Interests in what?"

"I'm guessing magic," said Thomas. "Malcolm was very excited about magic—and he called it magic, not witchcraft."

"Interesting," said Henry. "I take it you're not going?"

"Not even if it would get me out of exams," said Thomas.

The first bell sounded from the city, then another. On the beach, priests of the High Father began ringing bells they had in their hands. Soon a multitude of bells — high and low, sharp and dull, loud and soft—were ringing out.

Thomas, Henry, and Eileen followed the company to where the rest of the students—nearly a thousand of them—had gathered. George was nearby, with Linda on his arm, surrounded by men whom Thomas guessed to be the other members of the Smith Guild. George still had a pair of lines in his forehead where his brows were drawn together in anger. Linda was smiling and laughing, and Thomas guessed George hadn't explained what had happened.

"Hey," Keith yelled. "Get that girl out of here!"

"You're joking," said Eileen, looking around to see where he was. "Here? Now? Really?"

"Keep walking," said Thomas. "He doesn't have a say in this."

"Oh, I'll keep walking," Eileen said, mayhem in her voice. "Right over him if I have to!"

The Student Company reached the edge of the crowd, and Keith and a dozen others blocked their way. "She doesn't belong here!" said Keith, his loud voice carrying down the beach. "Not with us!"

"I'll go where I like!" said Eileen.

Henry stepped until he was nose to nose with Keith. "Move."

"Why don't you make me?" said Keith, glaring at Henry.

"It's Festival," said Henry. "Otherwise I already would have."

"I'd like to see you try!" Keith turned on Eileen. "You'll never be one of us!" said Keith, spitting the words at Eileen. "Girls don't belong at the Academy!"

"Speak for yourself," shouted another student. "Some of us like girls!"

"Gather round and listen!" The Master of Rhetoric called. "For those who are doing this for the first time and those drunk enough to need a reminder," he said, bringing chuckles from the students, "we will go into the water in groups, twenty five wide and two deep. Into the water, head under the water, and then out! No one gets ready until the priests have said their words! No one goes in until the king has gone in!"

Henry stepped forward the moment the Master of Rhetoric had finished, shoving Keith aside with his shoulder and leading the company toward the water.

The priests, meanwhile, had reached the beach and were spreading out and ringing their bells. And wherever the bells were heard the people went silent, waiting.

Thomas craned his neck and saw Archbishop Culverton and his retinue.

Like the other priests, the Archbishop wore a grey robe, though with his bright red cloak of office over top. The bell in his hand was gold, and Thomas could hear its clear tone above the others, even though he was a good fifty yards away from it. The Archbishop climbed up the steps to a small stage and stood, his eyes toward the east and the lightening sky over the ocean.

Thomas turned to the east as well, and felt Eileen wrap her fingers in his. The beach fell silent as everyone watched the horizon grow brighter and brighter, as around them, the priests continued the slow, steady ringing of their bells.

The sun broke the horizon.

The bells stopped, and for a moment there was no sound save the winds and the waves. Then the Archbishop raised his voice, leading the people in prayer and song. Across the beach, hundreds of priests did the same, bringing the people together to celebrate the end of winter, and the coming of the spring rains that would cleanse the snow from the earth and make way for new life.

The singing stopped, and all eyes went to the Archbishop.

"It has been a long winter," said the Archbishop, and all down the beach his priests echoed his words so that everyone there could hear his sermon. "And for some of the people in our country it has been a very difficult one." He looked to where the students stood. "In the north of our country, in Frostmire, there was a war."

Thomas felt his throat close.

"And though it was a brief war, it was no less tragic for the people who lived there than any other conflict," the Archbishop said. "A group of raiders attacked Criethe's northernmost duchy, and they did so using the vilest instrument the Banished give to those who usurp nature! They used Witchcraft!"

A murmur of disbelief rumbled down the beach. The students around Thomas and the rest of the Student Company all stared at them.

Archbishop Culverton raised a hand for quiet. "I know it is hard to credit," he said, "but it is true nonetheless. They called fogs to hide their action and called flames to burn down the towns they seized. Hundreds of men, women and children died. Our own envoy and the twenty good men he took north at the call of the Duke were slaughtered in an ambush."

The Archbishop lowered his voice. "And as horrifying as that is, there is still worse news. The witchcraft that so decimated our northern duchy did not die with the raiders." He searched the beach with his eyes. "For those who went north to fight these raiders also used witchcraft, casting spells against them. Witchcraft that they have brought with them back to Hawksmouth!"

And as he spoke those words, the Archbishop found Thomas.

"Our priests, who minister to the families of this city, who care for the sick and the poor, and who guide your souls to the High Father, have heard disquieting rumours," he said, his eyes locked on Thomas's. "Rumours of those who would use powers beyond those granted mortal men. Rumours of those who would endanger their souls by engaging not with the High Father, but with the Banished!

"So when we show our defiance to the winter," Archbishop Culverton declared, "when we show our refusal to submit the frost and when we use our faith to send the cold away, let us also think of those in Frostmire, whose faith and defiance cast off the shroud of witchcraft that hung over that land! And let us renew our own faith, and renew our strength, that we may resist the siren call of the Banished, and bask instead in the glory of our High Father!"

The Archbishop stepped down from the stage and made his way to the water while his priests led the people in prayer. Thomas mouthed the words along with the others, but they were like ashes in his mouth. Eileen's grip on his hand would have been painfully tight if Thomas had been able to feel anything.

Instead, he stood there, numb and horrified, as the Archbishop walked toward the water and went in up to his knees, as ceremony required.

3

"So," Evan's voice was bitter. "All going to blow over, is it?"

Thomas couldn't find words, could barely move. His eyes fixed on George, who was standing rigid, his face a mask of fear and anger. *He can't let the smiths see him like that,* Thomas realized. He shook himself out of his stupor. "Eileen. Get George. Tell him he's jumping in with us. Hurry."

Eileen took one look and then ran to her brother. She grabbed George and Linda's arms and started pleading with them. All around the Student Company, people were looking their way. Thomas could see the questions in their expressions. *Thankfully now is not the time.*

"The king is preparing to go in!" said the Master of Rhetoric. "Students, make ready!"

Thomas craned his eyes to the royal pavilion. He could just see the king, wearing a long white robe and flanked by guards and courtiers, step out onto the beach.

"Student Company!" yelled Henry. "Let's be first after him! Sir George! Hurry!"

Eileen and Linda pulled George toward the rest of the company. George, already red with suppressed anger, turned a shade darker on hearing his title. He sped up, though. Soon, the entire company were together.

"Well, don't just stand there!" shouted Henry, pulling off his cloak. "Student Company! Make ready!"

"Stand back," Thomas warned Eileen. Linda caught Eileen's hand and led her to one side.

"Why?" asked Eileen. "What are you going to do?"

Thomas didn't bother answering, just started taking off his clothes. Around him, hundreds of other boys and young men were doing the same thing, to the cheers and laughter of the girls and women around them. Eileen stood there, her mouth open with amazement. Then she started laughing as well, though it had a near-hysterical edge to it.

"How far down do we go?" demanded George, watching the others tossing off cloaks and shirts and breeches.

"To the braies," called Michael. "Have to keep a modicum of decency, you know."

"But only a modicum!" said Henry. "Faster, boys!!"

Thomas was down to his own braies in a matter of moments, the rest of the company soon after. Together they started pushing toward the water's edge. All around them girls and women cheered. Then Keith Rolston's voice rose up above the others. "Not so keen on being a student now, are you, *girl?*"

Thomas spun. Keith and a gang of students had come up behind Eileen and Linda. All were in their braies, and all of them were glaring at Eileen. Linda had her hand over her mouth and was at once turning red with embarrassment and glaring at Keith for being so rude.

Eileen stepped forward until she was nearly chest to chest with Keith. "What did you say?"

"Students go in the water," said Keith. "Don't see you getting ready to go in!"

"Don't be ridiculous!" said Linda, before Eileen could reply. "Girls aren't allowed."

"Gentlemen!" A priest pushed into the crowd. His face and tone were both severe. "This is not a time or place for arguing."

"Is there a rule against girls going in the water, Father?" asked Keith.

The priest, caught completely off guard, stood there with his mouth open until Keith prompted him. "Well?"

"Umm... no. No, there's no rule," stammered the priest. "It isn't done, though. Not here, anyway."

"That's because we've more sense than the men," called one of the women in the crowd, bringing laughter all around them. "Now leave that poor girl alone!"

"Hey, Thomas!" called one gloriously drunk student from the side. "Your girl is causing trouble! Magic her off the beach!"

"What?" said another, right beside him.

"Didn't you hear? Thomas is a magician!" He began repeating Lord Cormac's story, loudly, while he slowly got his clothes. Thomas felt panic and anger rising inside him, but the drunk fool was five rows back and there was no way Thomas could reach him and shut him up.

"Eileen doesn't want to be a girl," Keith yelled, ignoring the drunk. "She wants to be a student. So be a student and go in, *little girl.* Or get off the beach!"

"Now, that's enough of that, young man," said the priest. "She has as much right to be here—"

"No, she doesn't!" snapped Keith. "If she wants to stand here with us, she can well go in with us!"

"Fine!" Eileen shouted. "You want to see me go into the water! You just watch me!"

Linda's eyes went wide. "Eileen, you can't!"

"You watch my things and make sure the *little boys* don't take them!" Eileen snapped. She turned toward the water and stripped off her cloak. Thomas swore and pushed harder, forcing a path toward her.

"Eileen!" George was furious. "You are not going in there!" Eileen ignored him, unbuttoned her coat and threw it on the ground by her feet. George grabbed at her arm. "You will not do this!"

Eileen twisted her wrist out of his hand and shoved her brother, not moving him at all. "Don't you tell me what I can't do!" She spun to face Keith. "Any of you!"

George turned even brighter red. He growled, "You are embarrassing me."

"The only embarrassment here is Keith!" yelled Eileen, pulling off her sweater then unlacing her bodice. Several of the students started whistling. George's head swivelled like a bear scenting prey. The boys nearby stopped.

Eileen's bodice hit the ground, followed quickly by her blouse. Her boots, stockings and skirts followed in short order. The whistling, cheers and laughter grew louder as Eileen stood, barelegged and shivering in her short shift and drawers. George was steaming. Keith just stared at her, fuming.

"What?" demanded Eileen. "Never seen a girl's underthings before?" She stepped up to Keith and poked his chest hard with a finger. "You want me in the water? You watch me go!"

She turned her back on him and stomped toward the shore. The students parted in front of her. When she reached Thomas, she grabbed his hand and kept on going. The rest of the Student Company stood, gawking.

"Right," said Henry. "Student Company, Sir George! Make ready! We're ALL going in together!"

The students of the company looked unsure. Henry yelled. "Follow *Captain* Thomas and *Lieutenant* Eileen! Now! Sir George! Hurry!"

Michael found his tongue first. "You heard him! Let's go! The Academy!"

"The Academy!" echoed half of the company, and charged for the water's edge. The rest followed a moment later. Wilson punched Eileen in the shoulder on the way by, yelling, "All together! Come on!"

At the water's edge Thomas wrapped his arms around Eileen. "You shouldn't have done this," he whispered.

"I had to," Eileen whispered back, huddling close to him. "There's no way I'm letting that loudmouth Keith say what I can or can't do!"

Thomas shook his head. "By the Four, what a mess."

"No fair!" called Winston. "The rest of us don't have anyone to cuddle!"

"The more fool, you!" Eileen yelled back, but she let Thomas go and stood beside him, her fingers entwined in his and looked out at the cold, grey water. "How bad is it going to be?"

"Oh, very," said Thomas. *But I'm thinking it will be worse when we get out.*

George stomped up beside Thomas and Eileen. He was still red with anger, and the expression he gave Eileen left no doubt at whom.

Behind them, the last lines of men came together across the beach. Most were young. Some were older, a few actually elderly. All stood tall and proud against the incoming wind. For a moment, the beach was silent as everyone waited for the call to go forward.

The priests began ringing their bells again. Slowly at first, then faster and faster until the ringing was continuous then, together, then stopped.

All the people on the beach called out, "In the name of the High Father, let our faith, our strength and our will to drive the winter back!"

"In the name of the High Father!" shouted the king, dropping his robe. He wasn't young anymore, but he was still powerfully built. He charged into the freezing water without hesitation, his legs breaking through the surf until he dived, head first, into the waves.

"Students forward!" the Master of Rhetoric called. "For the honour of the Academy!"

"The Academy!" roared a thousand students. Thomas, Eileen and the company charged for the water. A cheer broke out from thousands of throats along the length of the beach and the first wave of men and boys charged into the sea.

Oh, gods! Thomas felt the breath rush out of his body the moment his legs touched the freezing water. He kept running, yelping when the water reached his groin, then dove forward and under. For a moment he couldn't move, couldn't draw breath. He forced his legs to work, got his feet under him and pushed his head back above the surface. He let out a strangled yell when he surfaced. Eileen came up a moment later, screaming and shaking in the cold. He grabbed her hand. "Out! Now!"

They ran back to the beach, dodging the ones rushing in. Around them, hundreds of men and boys, all soaked and freezing, their braies plastered to their bodies, dashed up the beach toward their clothes. The crowd cheered and applauded, and the women on shore laughed and yelled at the sight of them. The boys caught sight of Eileen and did the same.

Eileen looked down and turned bright red. She crossed her arms over the front of the now see-through shift and drawers that clung tight to the curves of her body. Thomas charged ahead to their blankets. He grabbed the closest one and wrapped it around Eileen before taking the other for himself. They rubbed at their freezing flesh, drying themselves as best they could. Then Thomas stepped close and wrapped his blanket around them both, pulling her up the beach to their clothes. Her cold, wet skin pushed against his, and he could feel her shivering.

"By the Four, Thomas!" she said through chattering teeth. "I don't think I'll ever be warm again!"

"It gets worse," said Thomas. "You have to take off your shift and drawers before you freeze."

Eileen's mouth dropped open. "What?"

"You'll never warm up, otherwise." Thomas stepped away and wrapped his blanket around his waist. With some struggling against the cold wet fabric, he managed to free himself from his braies and let them drop onto the beach.

"Thomas!" Eileen's hand went to her mouth and she started laughing even as she shook. All over the beach men and boys were the same thing all to the cheers of the watching women. Thomas pulled on his breeches under the blanket and laced them up. "Do it or you'll freeze! Stand over your clothes."

Eileen's blush grew even brighter, but stood over her clothes and struggled with holding the blanket while pulling at her shift. Thomas wrapped his blanket around his shoulders, then grabbed the edges of hers and held both up, forming a makeshift screen.

"Pray George doesn't see us! He's angry enough already!" Eileen said as she wriggled and pulled her way out of her shift and tossed it aside. Every boy who could see cheered his approval. Eileen rolled her eyes. She pointed a finger at Thomas. "Not a word out of you!"

Thomas didn't say a thing.

She disappeared under the blanket again and a moment later her drawers hit the sand, too. Another round of cheers and whistles came from the students. Eileen raised one hand in a rude gesture before using the blanket to rub the parts of her that were still wet. She grabbed her shirt up from the ground and for a moment arms and cloth waved above the blanket as she pulled the shirt over her head. She disappeared again, grabbed her skirt from the sand and a moment later pulled the blanket from Thomas's hands. "Done!"

"Good!" said Thomas, stepping away to grab his shirt while Eileen tied her skirt and started on her stockings. A couple of boys gave half-hearted, shivering whistles, but by now most of them had hit the water and were too busy getting themselves dried off. Thomas hurried into his coat and cloak, and grabbed his braies off the beach while Eileen quickly struggled into her bodice. "M-m-my hands," she said. "Th-th-they're shaking too bad to do up the laces."

Linda elbowed her way to Eileen. "Here," she said, taking the laces and deftly pulling them tight. "Is your brother as wild as you?"

"N-n-no," said Eileen. "He's the calm one in the family."

"B-but not the s-smart one," said George, who was standing in his braies, still dripping water. He was shivering now, and turning blue, but he didn't look any less angry. "Otherwise I'd have g-guessed you were g-going to d-d-do that and b-b-brought you your own b-b-blanket."

"George!" Eileen grabbed up her blanket and threw it over George's shoulders. "I'm so sorry!"

Thomas tossed his blanket over George's shoulders as well. "Get yourself dry. Hurry!"

George wrapped one blanket around his waist and struggled out of his braies while Linda dried his shoulders and back with the other. Thomas noted that her father did not seem at all distressed by her actions and wondered just how far along their relationship was.

"Thomas!" Eileen's call brought him back from his thoughts. "What do we do next?"

"Breakfast!" declared Mark, coming up beside her. "Hot breakfast and mulled wine! And cheers to Eileen for going in!"

Eileen managed a smile as the Student Company cheered, slapping her back and shaking her hand. Keith, still in line to go into the water, ignored them entirely.

"I always said you had lovely legs," said Henry clapping a hand on Eileen's shoulder. "Thanks for showing everyone I was right."

Eileen punched his chest. Her cheeks were bright red, and not just from the cold. Thomas wrapped his arm around her shoulders. "You were amazing. Now let's get out of here."

Eileen nodded and leaned against him as Thomas led them all off the beach. Most of the students had girls with them, and Linda was walking arm-in-arm with the still-furious George. Everyone was shivering, and their wet hair was turning to ice

"To the Quill for breakfast!" declared Henry.

"The Smiths' Guild is coming to my place," said George, "I'll be making breakfast for them all. Eileen, you need to be there to serve. Thomas," George looked angrier than before. "Don't come."

"George," Linda sounded very disapproving. "That's not nice. Thomas is your oldest friend."

"I want to stay with Thomas," Eileen said. "If he can't come, then I can't come."

"You've caused enough trouble for one day," said George. "You need to come home."

"I wasn't the one causing trouble."

"No, you were the one naked on the beach."

"No more than you!"

"Be fair, George," said Thomas. "She wouldn't have done it if it weren't—"

"For you?" said George. "I know! None of us would be here if it weren't for you." Sarcasm and anger laced his voice. "But maybe, just once, we can make this not about you!"

"George!" Linda's tone was sharp. "What's going on here?"

"Thomas Flarety?"

Everyone turned to look. The voice belonged to a thin, weather-beaten man wearing the blue and white livery of the king. He rode the most magnificent horse Thomas had seen. "Is one of you Thomas Flarety?" he asked.

"I am," said Thomas.

"The king requests your presence in the palace," he said. "And yours, Lord Henry."

"Of course he does," said Henry.

"Immediately, if you please."

"But... why?" Eileen's voice shook. "Why does the king want you?"

"One guess," muttered George, earning him another sharp look from Linda.

Thomas swallowed his anger and took Eileen's hand. "It's fine. I'll be back soon, I'm sure." He kissed her hand, and then her lips. "Go home. I'll see you tonight, and we'll go out to dinner."

"And try not to scandalize the Smiths' Guild any more than you already have," said Henry, stepping out of Eileen's reach. "At least not until we can watch."

"Follow me, gentlemen," said the messenger, turning his horse and walking it back up the path toward the city. Thomas and Henry fell in behind him, walking quickly to keep up.

"I don't suppose you brought us horses, too?" asked Henry.

"No."

Thomas looked back over his shoulder. Eileen saw and waved. She tried to smile but just looked worried and scared. Thomas tried a smile of his own but couldn't manage it. Then the crowd closed in around Eileen and he lost sight of her.

The length and events of the night and the chill of the water all washed over Thomas at once. His legs began shaking with cold and exhaustion and Thomas could feel his strength running out like the tide. He rubbed his face hard with the heels of his hands, trying to scrub wakefulness through his skin.

"How are you doing?" asked Henry.

"Oh, badly," said Thomas. He let his hands fall. "Everyone is going to know now, aren't they?"

"Everyone is going to hear," said Henry. "Not everyone will believe."

"I should have known," Thomas shook his head. "I did know. I knew everything would come out eventually. I just hoped..." Thomas began swearing; quietly, viciously and for a very long time.

Henry waited until the words stopped. "Done?"

"No," said Thomas. "I just ran out."

"Well, let me know when you've got any new ones. I'll take notes."

Thomas tossed a weary, rude gesture in Henry's direction, and kept walking.

4

They followed the messenger past the harbour and through the outer city. The streets were mostly empty and the silence was almost unnerving. It took an hour to reach the wide-open gates of the old city walls. The messenger nodded to the guards and led Thomas and Henry inside. The streets here were pristine, the businesses fancy, the houses large and the residents wealthy. And in the middle of it all sat the royal palace.

It had been a true castle, once, and the walls and towers of the old keep were still visible beneath the newer wings that grew at right angles from the original buildings.

It had been five years since Thomas and the rest of his class were brought to court to give their formal pledge of allegiance to the king and the Royal Academy of Learning. The place had been packed with courtiers and soldiers, and the king had been in full regalia—fur cloak, crown, rich red robes, the queen on the seat next to him and pages standing to either side.

Thomas, who had never been anywhere larger than the nearest town before his arrival at Hawksmouth, had been completely stunned and overwhelmed by all the pomp and ceremony. He had thought the palace was magnificent. Now, the building felt ominous and imposing, like the weight of it was going to crush him at any moment.

They passed through the gate in the low outer wall and into the courtyard. A pair of guards wearing swords stood in front of the large, ornamental main doors. The messenger announced, "Thomas Flarety and Lord Henry Antonius, summoned to the king."

The guards nodded. One said, "This way," and opened the door.

The hallway on the other side was wide with polished, white marble floors and smooth plaster walls painted with murals of the kingdom's history. Large windows let in the light from outside. It was ornate, immaculate and terrifying. Thomas wondered if they were ever going to be allowed out again.

Don't be stupid, he told himself. *If he wanted to arrest us we'd already be in chains.*

Thomas really hoped he was right about that.

They stopped at a small door with two more guardsmen standing at it. These were older, with a bit of grey in their beards, but they stood just as straight as the others. The man escorting Thomas and Henry saluted. "Thomas Flarety and Lord Henry Antonius to see the king."

"Of course," said the guard at the door. "He'll be here eventually. You two stand and wait."

The first guard saluted and left. Henry shrugged and leaned against the wall. After a moment, Thomas joined him. Neither of the guards looked impressed, but neither said anything. Thomas took in the grain of the polished stone on the floor, the murals painted on the wall and the lacquered shine of the wood in the door. By the time an hour had crawled by, he had also calculated the cost of the guards uniforms, if they were to come from Thomas's father's warehouses, the cost of the steel of the weapons, if George was to make them, and how far he could run before the guards chased him down and arrested him.

Another guard approached, saluted the two at the door and said, "His majesty is ready."

"Excellent," said Henry. "And is his majesty in a good mood?"

"You'll find out soon enough," said the guard, opening the door. "Go in and turn—"

"Don't bother," said Henry. "I know the way. Come along, Thomas."

They walked past the guard and through the door to the throne room.

"Now what?" Thomas asked out of the side of his mouth.

"Walk forward until you're in the middle of the floor, turn left, and bow," said Henry. "And let me do the talking."

The throne room had black marble columns running down the length of it, with a balcony all around. Thomas and Henry's boot steps were sharp and hard on the green marble floor and echoed through the mostly empty space. Tapestries on the walls depicted battles and hunts. Windows along the length of the balcony let in a dull, grey winter light. Someone was arguing, though it stopped as soon as Thomas and Henry came into sight.

They reached the middle of the room, turned left and bowed. And waited. And waited.

"Rise, Thomas and Lord Henry," said the king. "And approach."

They straightened.

The king sat on a silver throne on a dais the same colour as the marble on the floor. His hair was still damp from the beach and he wore a plain white jacket and breeches—certainly rich but by no means close to full regalia. Save for the purple of his cloak and the gold circle on his head, he could have been a simple noble. His face held no expression whatsoever, which made Thomas even more nervous.

Three men stood below the dais. One wore a plain grey jacket and breeches. His expression was as neutral as the king's. The second wore the red robes of a churchman and a sneer on his thin face.

The third, wearing black and leaning on a walking stick, was Father Alphonse.

Thomas felt his heart stop, and then tear into motion again, beating far faster than it should.

Father Alphonse was an Inquisitor, part of the Church's defence against witches. In the fall, he had chained Thomas to a cell floor for two days, questioning him relentlessly about witchcraft. He had also followed them north, and at Lord Richard's request, tortured Henry's brother John. When Thomas and his friends had left Frostmire, John had said that he was looking forward to making the man die very slowly and very, very painfully.

Henry pushed Thomas from behind. Thomas stumbled forward, caught his balance and tried to make his stride normal. Father Alphonse smiled. Thomas focused on keeping his breathing steady as he walked. It calmed him a bit, and helped with the trembling. He wished desperately for his rapier and dagger.

I won't let him take me in for questioning again, Thomas swore to himself. *I'll kill him first.*

The thirty feet to the dais seemed unreasonably long. Their footsteps, measured and careful, seemed too small to cover the distance. Thomas wished that his clothes were cleaner, and that he didn't have a pair of wet braies stuffed inside his jacket. He hoped his hair wasn't a mess and that he wasn't tracking mud across the floor.

Henry, much to Thomas's annoyance, looked sublimely unconcerned.

Up close, the king had a fair bit of grey in his hair. He looked much more severe than he had running into the water on the beach.

Of course he does. He's dressed. Everyone looks more serious when they're dressed.

Can I think of anything that isn't stupid?

I hope my hands aren't shaking.

Thomas and Henry reached the throne and bowed again. "Your Majesty," said Henry as he straightened. "Good to see you again. And Inquisitor Alphonse," Henry nodded at him. "I'm surprised to see you alive."

"The High Father smiled upon me," said Father Alphonse. His voice was hoarse, as if he had screamed so much he'd destroyed it. Thomas wondered what, exactly, John had done to the man before letting him go. Father Alphonse shifted his weight against the walking stick he leaned on, and groaned at the effort. His gaunt face was lined and twisted with pain.

"He must have," said Henry. "Last I heard my brother was going to flay your feet and leave you for the weasels."

"That will be enough, Lord Henry," said the king. "Thomas Flarety?"

Thomas swallowed hard. "Yes, your Majesty."

King Harold Plastine had brown eyes, surrounded by wrinkles, in a round face. He was not much taller than Thomas himself, but much wider, both in the shoulders and the stomach. "Your teachers say you are one of their brightest—possibly *the* brightest. They say you managed to catch up in your classes and maintain your grades despite being gone... was it two months?"

"Around two, yes, your majesty," said Thomas. *Why is he being nice to me?*

"And studying both philosophy and law," said the man in grey. He was distinctly average: neither tall nor short, a plain face and brown hair. His eyes were also brown, and they bored into Thomas's eyes like a pair of drills. "Very impressive."

"I thank you," said Thomas, wondering who the man was. "I'm sorry, I don't know how to address you, sir."

"How foolish of me," said the king. "Lord Henry Antonius, Thomas Flarety, may I present Sir Walter Deehan."

Henry nodded politely at the man. Thomas bowed, though not as low as he had to the king. "Sir Walter."

"And Father Leopold," said the king. "The Archbishop's representative to the king."

Father Leopold had a sneer on his face as he waited for Thomas to bow. Thomas met the man's eyes and stayed upright. *I will not bow to him; I will not show fear to him,* Thomas thought, *no matter what happens.* Thomas watched Father Leopold realize it and saw the man's lips go into a hard, angry line.

"And I believe you know Father Alphonse," finished the king, after the pause had gone on long enough to be awkward.

"Yes, your majesty," said Thomas, still staring down Father Leopold.

"Are we through with the pleasantries?" demanded Father Leopold. "This boy stands accused of witchcraft."

"Without evidence," said Sir Walter.

Before Thomas or Father Leopold could protest the king raised a hand for silence. "We have heard some rather strange tales of what happened in the north, Thomas."

"From Lords Cormac, Ethan and Anthony?" asked Henry. "The ones who didn't actually see anything?"

"They talked to those who did," said Father Alphonse. "And they heard tales of witchcraft. Of men throwing fog and fire." He smiled at Thomas. "And lightning."

"Those who serve the Banished cannot be allowed freedom!" said Father Leopold.

"You have no evidence of the Banished," said Henry. "You have no evidence of anything. Just hearsay."

"We have evidence enough to question Thomas Flarety," said Father Leopold. "And we demand that he be turned over to us. At once."

"Demand?" repeated the king, a flicker of annoyance coming into his voice.

"We cannot allow the Banished control over men's affairs," said Father Leopold. "We *will* not allow such things to happen."

"You have no evidence," said Henry. "You have no authority, and you have no right to be making demands of the king!"

"The king must answer to the High Father in matters of the spirit!" Father Leopold quivered in righteous anger. "Thomas, by his actions, gave us the authority!"

"Actions for which you can't produce a single witness!"

"Gentlemen!" Sir Walter's voice cut through the room. "This is not a Court of Law and you will not practice your arguments here!"

"Thomas has been very silent," said Father Alphonse in the silence that followed. "Thomas? Why are you not speaking?"

"Because I have not been asked a question yet," lied Thomas. *Because I cannot lie to the king. I swore an oath.* "And I should very much dislike to speak out of turn."

The king smiled again. "Law students. Always cautious with their words. Did I not say as much, Sir Walter?"

"You did, your Majesty," said Sir Walter. "Though Lord Henry seems to lack that quality."

"Then I'll ask a question," said Sir Alphonse. "When did you start practising witchcraft, Thomas?"

For a moment Thomas was back in the cell under the Church's buildings, chained to the floor and staring at four soldiers ready to beat him senseless while Father Alphonse sat behind his little desk, droning questions over and over.

Thomas blinked and was back in the throne room. Father Alphonse was leaning on his staff and waiting for an answer. Thomas forced in a pair of breaths, forced all fear and anger out of his voice. "I never practised witchcraft," said Thomas. "There is no such thing."

"There is," said Father Leopold. "I have seen it."

"Really?" asked Sir Walter. "What have you seen?"

"I have seen the Beudlean tribes to the south using powers they raised from prayers to the Banished to fight the soldiers of the Church," said Father Leopold. "I have seen men die under flame and the earth shake." His eyes went to the king. "It is this that we must protect true believers from, your Majesty. It is for this that you must—"

"Did you actually see them praying to the Banished?" interrupted Henry.

"I did not need to *see* it," said Father Leopold. "Only the Banished could grant such powers."

"Funny," said Henry. "Because when your Bishop Malloy prayed to the Banished for power, it didn't work at all."

"Father Malloy was not praying to the Banished," said Father Alphonse. "He was praying to the High Father when Thomas *murdered* him."

Thomas felt himself bristling. "Bishop Malloy," he said through clenched teeth, "was cutting the throats of children and offering their blood to the Banished to give him power." He forced in a breath and stared into Father Alphonse's eyes. "And it didn't work because there's no such thing as witchcraft."

"That is enough, gentlemen," said the king, his voice soft.

"It is indeed," said Father Leopold. "This *boy* must face the question, so that we may have the truth out of him!"

"I already faced the question," said Thomas.

"Enough," said the king again, his voice no louder, but the command in it unmistakable. "I will not have anyone calling my students liars."

"They are liars," said Father Leopold. "They lie, they brawl, they engage in debauchery at every opportunity, and now they are engaging in witchcraft."

The knight stepped uncomfortably close to the envoy. "Watch your tongue," he said, his eyes boring into Father Leopold's. "You are speaking to the king."

"And *you* are speaking to the Archbishop's personal envoy," said the priest, not budging an inch. "The envoy of one who answers to the High Father, to whom even kings must bow. I will not be threatened by the likes of you. And I *will* have this one in my custody."

Thomas felt himself begin to tremble again and this time he couldn't control it. *I will not go back.*

The king rose to his feet and stepped down. "We are aware of the Archbishop's *request,*" the emphasis on the last word was deliberate and unmistakable, "and we once more remind you, the students are *ours*. They are servants of the king, and answer only to the king's law in all matters."

"Then arrest him, in the name of the king's law," said Father Leopold. "Arrest him and hang him for witchcraft."

"The king's law requires proof," said Sir Walter. "And you have provided none."

"And until you do," said the king, "no actions will be taken against Thomas. Or *any* of those who fought in Frostmire. By anyone. Under pain of my displeasure. Have I made myself clear?"

Father Leopold's back grew straighter, as if the rod planted there had been pushed upward. "The Archbishop will not be swayed by threats."

"Nor will I," said the king. "And you may go and tell Culverton that. Now."

Father Leopold bowed, though not low enough to be respectful. Alphonse's bow was lower, and he smiled at Thomas when he came up. "I will look forward to seeing you again. Soon."

The two men backed away, bowed again, turned and left. Thomas's knees nearly buckled in relief. No one in the room spoke until Father Alphonse and Leopold stepped outside of the room and the door swung shut behind them.

"You did that very well, young man," said the king.

Thomas swallowed. "Thank you, your Majesty."

"Unlike you, Lord Henry," said the king. "Must you fight with everyone?"

"It's what I was raised to," said Henry, blithely. "Please accept my apologies."

"I would if I thought there was the slightest bit of sincerity in your words." The king stepped back up on his dais and sat down again. "It was quite the mess in Frostmire. Though thankfully short."

"Yes, your Majesty," said Thomas and Henry together.

"The death of Duke Antonius was most unfortunate," said Sir Walter. "As were the actions of his son, Richard. Who killed Richard?"

"Baron Goshawk," said Thomas, wincing a bit. Richard had been Henry's favourite brother, before the war. "With a throwing axe."

"A nasty bit of business," said the king.

Thomas remembered the axe slamming into Richard Antonius's chest and suppressed a shudder. "Yes, your Majesty."

"How do you feel your brother will be as Duke?" asked Sir Walter.

"Devious," replied Henry. "And probably fair and decent to the common people." He looked thoughtful for a moment. "The ones he doesn't flog for his amusement, anyway. John was always worrisome in that respect."

"So I've heard," said the king. "Now, Lord Henry, perhaps you could explain exactly why you lied to me about the nature of the events in Frostmire?"

The silence that followed that was so full of tension that is was practically visible, coiling around them like a snake squeezing its prey.

Henry swallowed, and then said, "Not so much lied as omitted details that would not be believed without proof."

"The Archbishop believed them," said the king. "Father Alphonse certainly believed them, to the point of being ready to torture them out of the pair of you. My spies came back with several stories that I was planning to ask you about in a more subtle way had the Archbishop not announced it to the entire city. So tell me, Lord Henry, was witchcraft used in Frostmire?"

Henry smiled. "No, your Majesty."

"Then where do these stories of fire and fog and lightning come from?"

"Oh, people used those," said Henry. "They just didn't use witchcraft."

The king turned bright red. Thomas swallowed his nerves and stepped forward. "Please, your Majesty, may I speak?"

"Yes," the king said, his eyes still on Henry and the threat of mayhem in his expression. "Quickly."

"Witchcraft has a very specific definition under the law," said Thomas. "It requires the user to offer his or her soul to the Banished in exchange for powers beyond those of mortal men."

The king's eyes narrowed with annoyance. "You throw lightning from your hands, if the stories are true," said the king. "If it isn't witchcraft, what is it?"

"Magic."

"And what, exactly, is the difference?"

"For a start," said Henry, "the Church can't hang you for magic."

"The Church would disagree," said the king. He cast a speculative eye at Thomas. "So if your powers don't come from the Banished, where do they come from?"

"I was born with it, I think," said Thomas. "I mean, I was born with the ability to see magic, which I didn't realize until I saw Bishop Malloy using it. The other things—lightning, fire—I learned how to do those. And the power I took from Bishop Malloy when we stopped him from murdering the children but..."

"Enough," said the king.

"Yes, your Majesty."

"Show me."

Thomas hesitated. "I don't think lightning would be wise here, your Majesty. It's loud, and last time I did it indoors I nearly started a fire."

The king's eyebrows went up, "Can you do other things?"

"Yes, your majesty." *I just can't think of any right now...*

It wasn't as though Thomas knew a lot of magic. He'd really not been practicing or searching magic out since he'd come home from Frostmire. He'd been too busy studying and planning for Eileen's entry into the Academy. *I need to do something, though...*

Light the candles? He looked around and saw no candelabras.

Thomas's mind flashed back to the first time he'd shown his friends magic. Then, he'd only been able to fill a cup. Now, though...

Thomas took a deep breath and concentrated, reaching out to the water in the air. *Good thing we're in a seaport and not the desert.*

A thought brought the water together. Another lowered the temperature of the room enough that the water became vapour, then...

"By the Four," said the king, looking at the thick, swirling white fog rising off the throne room floor. "Are you doing this?"

"Yes, your Majesty," said Thomas, though he kept his concentration on the fog. The cloud grew larger and thicker, until the entire room was full and no one could see more than a foot or two in any direction.

"I think that's enough, your Majesty" said Sir Walter.

"Yes," said the king. "I can't see a thing. I assume everyone is still here?"

"Light up the room," whispered Henry to Thomas. "With your ball of light."

Or I could have just used the ball of light in the first place. Thomas fought down the urge to smack himself in the head. He raised his hand and brought a small, swirling ball of blue and yellow light into being. It barely penetrated the fog at all.

"What's that?" asked Sir Walter. "What are you doing?"

"Light," said Thomas. He focused on it and it grew brighter and brighter until it pierced through the fog like a beacon. Thomas heard boot steps, and the king appeared out of the fog. Sir Walter was only a step behind him. The king stared at the ball of light, his jaw hanging open. "That is... it's..."

"Magic," said Sir Walter.

"Amazing," said the king. "Can all magicians do this sort of thing?"

"They can learn," said Thomas. "But I have a lot more power than most."

"Power you took from Bishop Malloy?" asked the king.

"Yes, your Majesty. He'd taken it from others and I took it from him."

"When you killed him?"

"No," said Thomas carefully. "I took the power first. Then I killed him."

"Why?" asked Sir Walter.

"He said he was going to have us all hanged," said Thomas. "I couldn't let him do that to my friends."

The king shook himself, like a dog shedding water from a light rain. "I think that's enough, Thomas. Put out the light and get rid of the fog."

Thomas doused the light, then looked around, uncertain.

"Is there a problem?" asked Sir Walter.

"I never actually learned how to get rid of fog," said Thomas. "I could try to summon some wind, maybe..."

The king snorted. "No, thank you."

"It's already starting to lighten a bit," said Henry. "If you opened the windows, maybe?"

"I think we will leave it," said the king. "Come with me, please."

The king disappeared into the fog in the direction of the small side door. Thomas hurried after, as much to keep from getting lost as anything else. The two guards snapped to attention the moment the door opened, and the king walked through. If either of them had an opinion about the fog that rolled out of the throne room, they didn't give it.

"We are hungry," said the king. "We'll need breakfast for four in the private library, please."

"Yes, your Majesty," said the guard. He saluted and left at a fast pace.

"Excellent," said the king. "This way, please."

The king led them through two hallways, up a staircase and down a third hallway to a small, plain door. The king opened it and the musty scent of old paper and dust hit Thomas's nose immediately. The room was filled with shelves of scrolls and books, with several comfortable chairs and a table in their midst. The king took one of the chairs and said, "Please, sit."

The other three did, and no one said anything more. The king seemed contemplative, Sir Walter inquisitive, Henry calm and Thomas hoped he didn't look as nervous as he felt. The room stayed silent until servants arrived at the door with mulled wine and trays full of fruits, cheese and bread. The king helped himself and gestured for the others to do the same. The smell of the food made Thomas realize he hadn't eaten since dinner the night before. He filled his plate and wolfed half of it down almost at once.

"Better, I take it?" asked the king, once all the plates were empty.

"Yes, your Majesty," said Thomas. "And thank you. It's been a long night."

"I usually don't bring food in here," the king said. "Too likely to spill it onto the books."

"It's a very nice collection," said Thomas.

"Thank you," said the king. "I keep this one mostly closed. All the books in it are on the Church's forbidden list."

Thomas's eyes went wide and he looked closer at the volumes. Henry whistled appreciatively. "Impressive. Does the Archbishop know?"

"One suspects he does," said the king, "though he never mentions it."

The king stepped over to one of the shelves and pulled down a thick book with a worn leather cover. There had been gold filigree on it once, but it had faded to near-invisibility. He held it out to Thomas. "What do you think of this?"

Thomas took the book and gently opened it. The script was old-fashioned and hand-written, and on the first page were the words, "Spells of divine guidance and learning, for the worship and service of She who protects us all."

Interesting. Thomas turned to the first spell inside. It was prettily written, and very poetically described how one could make contact with the Mother and ask her for her protection and guidance. Unfortunately, it was not magic. Thomas turned the page, then the next, and the next. Finally he leafed through the book front to back.

"It's beautifully written, your Majesty," said Thomas. "But there's no real magic in it."

Sir Walter peered over Thomas's shoulder. "Really? They looked like spells to me."

"They look like spells," agreed Thomas. "But they're just words."

"And you're certain how, Thomas?" asked the king.

I will have no secrets left, when he is done. "Spells glow. Blue ones are beneficial. Red are harmful. This book has nothing."

The king's eyebrows went up. "Where did you first learn that?"

"In the library beneath the Theology building," said Thomas.

"Law students aren't allowed in that library," said the king.

"No, your Majesty."

"Should I ask what you were doing there?" The king raised his hand while Thomas struggled to find an answer. "Don't worry, I won't. What sort of spells did you find?"

"Everything from straight cutting of wood to warding off vermin, your Majesty. And I have one book with the sort of magic that you hear about in stories."

"I see," said the king. He looked around at his library. "And how long would it take you to go through these books and tell me which ones have magic?"

Thomas looked over the room. The books ranged from beautiful to tattered, from thick tomes to slim volumes. He suspected he could pleasantly spend a week there. But to find magic? "A few hours, maybe. I'd have to look through each one."

"Not today, then, I think." The king sat down in another chair and rubbed his chin with one hand. "Tell me, Thomas, can you tell when someone has magic?"

"Not to look at them," said Thomas. "People with magic look the same as everyone else."

"Then how did you know who had it?" asked Sir Walter. "In Frostmire, I mean."

"I saw them using it," said Thomas. "Or felt them using it, when they had me in the caves."

"And was Frostmire the first place you noticed the magic, Thomas?"

"No, your Majesty. I saw it first back in Elmvale," said Thomas, "when I went home for Fire Night last spring. A juggler made a ball of light appear in his hand."

"I think I should like to meet this juggler," said the king.

Thomas remembered watching the life fleeing from Timothy's eyes as he bled to death under his own overturned wagon. "He's dead, your Majesty. Bishop Malloy killed him to take his magic."

"Is that why you went after Bishop Malloy?" asked Sir Walter. "Revenge for the juggler?"

"No, sir. The Bishop was after my family, sir."

The king cocked his head to one side. "For magic?"

"Yes, your Majesty."

"I see." The king sat forward in his chair, leaning his elbow on the arm and his chin upon his hand, the very picture of studious thought. "How many others with magic are there?"

"I..." Thomas had never thought about it. "I have no idea, your Majesty."

"Why not?"

"I've never looked," said Thomas. "I was too busy hiding my own from the Church."

"Look now," said the king. "I want to know how many there are with magic in my city."

"Yes, your majesty." Thomas said. After a moment he added, "May I ask why?"

"The Church of the High Father is not happy," said Sir Walter. "They have not been happy since last summer, and they are less happy now that stories are going around of how a... *magician...* managed to defeat the enemies of the kingdom where the Church's soldiers failed."

"And given their current fear-mongering about witchcraft," said the king, "it would be very unfortunate if anyone who can actually use magic were to fall into their hands."

"Whereas if the king knows who they are he can extend his protection over them, should it become necessary," said Sir Walter.

"I suggest you start tonight," the king said. "There are feasts this evening throughout the city. If your juggler was a magician, maybe there are other troubadours who disguise their magic as part of their performance."

Thomas, who'd been hoping to spend the evening with Eileen, managed not to sigh when he said, "Yes, your Majesty."

"Do not trust anyone in this, Thomas," said the king. "Show no one any magic. Not until you have proof of theirs. Consider that a command."

"Yes, Your Majesty," said Thomas.

"And take Henry with you," said the king. "He can consider it part of his punishment for not telling me of this earlier."

5

It was well after lunch when Thomas and Henry reached the Street of Smiths. They'd stopped at home for dry clothes and their rapiers, and to raid whatever food they had left in their cupboard. It yielded some stale bread that they broke in half and crunched on as they walked through the streets. The wind had risen since the morning, and the day had not warmed up at all. The shops were all closed for the holiday and the few folks they saw were walking briskly from one house to another.

Thomas walked fast, both from the cold, and because he was sure Eileen and George were desperate to hear that they were all right.

Or at least Eileen, Thomas thought as they reached the house. George he wasn't too sure of any more. The man had seemed more irritated than anything else when the whole mess had happened.

Thomas hammered on the door of the smithy and called up, "It's us!"

He heard Eileen shout, "They're back!" and then her footsteps pounding down the stairs. The bolt inside was shot back loud enough to hear, and Eileen swung the door open. She wore a plain brown dress and sweater and her hair was a mess. She looked wonderful to Thomas. "You're back!" Eileen wrapped her arms around Thomas's neck. "Thank the Four!" She pushed him back. "What happened? What did the king want?"

"Nothing we can talk about here," said Henry. "Glad to see you, too, by the way."

"Don't be stupid, Henry," Eileen said, rolling her eyes. She gave him a quick hug anyway. "Get in here and tell me what happened." She led them upstairs to the kitchen. "George is just getting changed. He's been invited to the Master Smith's house for dinner."

"*We've* been invited," corrected George, coming down the stairs in a clean shirt and breeches. "And *we* should both be there." He looked over Henry and Thomas. "You're all right?"

"Yes," said Thomas.

"Good." George sat down at the table. "What sort of trouble are you in?"

"We aren't," said Thomas. "I mean, the king was upset with Henry for not telling him the truth about what happened in Frostmire, but he mostly wanted to talk about the magic. So after Father Alphonse left..."

"Alphonse?" George's eyes widened. "The Inquisitor? I thought he was in the dungeon in Frostmire."

"Apparently my brother let him out," said Henry.

"Apparently?" George fumed where he sat. "And now he's after us again, is he?"

"No," said Thomas. "The king told him in no uncertain terms that anyone who went to Frostmire has to be left alone. The Archbishop's representative wasn't happy about it."

"Who?"

"You are doing a terrible job of telling this," said Henry. "The Inquisitor and the Archbishop's representative were there to demand Thomas's arrest, at least in part."

Now it was Thomas's eyes that went wide. "In part? Why else would they be there?"

"No idea," said Henry. "But you don't send a priest whose been fighting the Beudleans just to petition for the arrest of a witch in Frostmire."

"So you didn't get arrested so far," interrupted George. "What did the king want?"

"First, to see magic," said Thomas.

"You didn't cast lightning!" Eileen looked horrified. "Not in the palace!"

"No, I didn't do lightning" said Thomas. "I did fog."

"Think it's dispersed by now?" asked Henry.

"Should be," Thomas had a vision of the court coming into a foggy throne room. "I hope so."

"Because that would be embarrassing."

"And then what happened?" demanded George.

"We had breakfast," said Henry. "In the king's private library. Good breakfast, too."

"Henry..." George growled out the word like a dog about to attack. "What does the king want of you?"

"He wants us to find the other magicians in Hawksmouth," said Thomas. "Henry and I are supposed to go looking for them." He looked apologetically at Eileen. "Tonight."

Eileen's opened her mouth to protest, and then stopped herself. She looked away instead. "That's fine."

"Why does the king want magicians?" asked George.

"To protect them," said Thomas. "Sir Walter said it would be bad if they fell into Church hands."

"Who is Sir Walter?" George sounded exasperated. "No one mentioned Sir Walter before!"

"He was with the king," said Thomas. "I don't know who he is."

"He's the king's chief spy," said Henry. "Which is the other reason I think this was about more than just Thomas." He frowned. "I wonder if the king's appointment with the Archbishop's representative came first, or if they found out about us being summoned and tried to head us off."

"The king's chief spy?" said Thomas. "You didn't think to tell me?"

"Would telling you have made you any less nervous?" asked Henry.

"Does it matter?" demanded George. "The king has put you two right in the way of the Church!"

"I'll go with you," announced Eileen. "Just let me get changed."

George rounded on Eileen. "You are *not* going with them. You can come to dinner at the Master Smith's tonight."

"You don't tell me what to do," said Eileen, poking a finger in her brother's direction. "I'm going with Thomas."

"What about the Academy?" George demanded. "Tomorrow is your first day there as a girl. You want to go there exhausted, having been out all night searching for magicians who may not even exist?" Eileen's resolve faltered. George saw it and pressed his point home. "Or maybe end up arrested by the Church and not get there at all? The Academy is everything you want. Remember? Don't throw it away because these two have a job to do."

"He's right," said Thomas.

"He isn't," protested Eileen, but there was no spirit behind the words.

"We're just starting the search tonight," said Thomas. "We probably won't find anyone anyway. You can help us later on, all right?"

Eileen pouted. "We're not even getting dinner together, are we?"

Thomas shook his head. "Sorry."

"Fine," Eileen tossed her head and looked away. "I'll stay here tonight and study."

"Don't be silly," said George. "Come to dinner."

"No," said Eileen. "If everyone's so worried about me being in the Academy, I'd better make sure I can get in."

"Wish I could help," said Thomas.

"Me, too," said Eileen. "I'm still terrible at Astronomy, and worse at Trigonometry."

"Then you'll never be a navigator," declared Henry, looking sad. "Which is too bad, because I hear it pays well."

"Not funny," said Eileen, getting to her feet. "I'll be in my room. Goodnight."

"Eileen," Thomas started to rise and she caught him in a hug.

"Don't you get hurt or arrested tonight," Eileen said as she crushed his ribs. "You hear me?"

Thomas hugged her back. "I won't. I promise."

"Good."

Eileen went upstairs. George rose to his own feet. "And now I have to get ready to go to the Master Smith's dinner. So if you'll excuse me..."

In the street, Thomas looked up at the light coming from Eileen's room and sighed. "I was really looking forward to dinner tonight."

"Don't worry," said Henry. "You'll still eat."

"It was the company I was looking forward to," said Thomas.

"It was the kissing you were looking forward to," said Henry. "Now let's be off. It's time to look for a magician or six!"

"Say it louder," muttered Thomas. "I don't think the entire city heard you."

"The entire city is getting ready for the feast," said Henry. "We, on the other hand, are going to the docks."

"And why the docks?"

"Because that's where you'll find the most entertainers. Especially now that shipping is open again."

They walked from the Street of Smiths, through the more fashionable districts close to the city walls, and around to the docks. The closer they got, the more folks they saw in the streets, stepping in and out of the taverns. By the time they reached the dock area proper, the place was alive with people. Sailors, beggars, men and women together, and men out on their own, all looking for a place to eat and drink their Festival feast.

A cold wind was gusting hard from inland toward the sea. Thomas pulled his coat tighter and counted himself lucky. The stink from fish and seaweed and offal from the sewers that came from the harbour was usually bad enough to make the unwary gag. Tonight, though, the wind was driving the dock stench before it.

"Here," said Henry, stopping before one of the better-kept looking taverns. "We may as well start at the top and work our way down."

The dinner at the first tavern was quite good, and Henry paid for it, which cheered Thomas up slightly. The entertainment was a singer whose voice, while impressive, was certainly not magical. Thomas and Henry left as soon as they finished eating.

The second tavern had a pair of girls dancing to hurdy-gurdy and drum. The third had no entertainment, but the men there—ships' crews from the look of them—were singing loudly and happily all on their own. Thomas and Henry had a drink and sang a round with them, then left.

There might have been entertainment in the fourth tavern, but the men inside were too busy fighting with one another to listen. Henry suggested they skip it.

The fifth tavern had enough empty seats that Thomas could lead Henry to a table that gave them a view of the door. They ordered a pair of small drinks and Henry scanned the room. "Doesn't look like they have any entertainment." He followed Thomas's eyes back to the door. "Who are you watching for?"

A stout man with a blue cloak and a green coat stepped through the door, looked around, and went up to the bar. "Him," said Thomas. "He's been following us."

"Really?" Henry looked surprised. "I didn't notice."

"I noticed him in the second tavern. Church?"

"Maybe," said Henry.

"Should we ask him?"

"No," said Henry. "If he is, he'll lie about it, report back and get replaced."

"So we just let him follow us?"

"Yes."

"And if he figures out what we're doing?"

"That will be difficult," said Henry, "since we don't even know what we're doing."

"True." Thomas looked around the tavern and sighed. "Is there even any entertainment in here?"

Two taverns later, they found a man performing magic. He was a tall, thin fellow with a long cloak with stars woven into it, and a tall, floppy hat. He claimed the name of Magnificent Martin, which made the sailors chuckle, and he was surprisingly good. He did several tricks with cards and dice and a hat borrowed from the audience that he turned into a chicken drumstick and back again. Thomas watched and listened closely, but didn't hear or see anything that was more than parlour magic.

The stout man in the blue cloak had followed them to each tavern. He watched the magician's performance with interest, too. So much so that he seemed to forget about Thomas and Henry entirely until the show was done.

Magnificent Martin did a second performance of all new tricks then went through the audience betting coppers they couldn't guess which card he had in his hand, or which numbers the dice were on after he hid them with a cup. Thomas bet him three times and lost each one. As near as he could tell, the man used no magic whatever, just slight-of-hand and some excellent patter.

After the magician left, they finished their drinks and headed out into the night. The wind was still blowing and the temperature had dropped. The streets were beginning to quiet down. The remaining sailors going from tavern to tavern were staggering more than walking, and singing loudly and off-key.

"Enough of this," said Thomas, pulling his cloak tight around his body. "Time to go home."

"The dancing girls were pretty at least," said Henry as they walked away from the docks.

"Unlike most everyone else we've seen tonight. Why do so many sailors have missing teeth?"

"They lose them on long voyages," said Henry. "And in fights."

"Well, at least we managed to avoid that," said Thomas. "Unless our friend plans on attacking us." He looked back down the street. "Hmph. Not even here."

"I am unimpressed with his stamina," said Henry. "It was hardly a late night at all."

"Filthy witch!" someone shouted. There was a clatter of something being thrown and missing, then another. The third time there was a *thud* and a yelp of pain. "Father-hating scum!"

"Help! Oh, help!"

Thomas drew his rapier and dagger and ran towards the sound. Henry followed two steps behind, They raced round the corner and found Magnificent Martin curled up in a ball against a wall, being pelted with garbage by a trio of sailors. Martin's hands were over his head and blood streamed from between his fingers.

"Hey!" Thomas yelled. "Enough!"

The sailors turned. They were all burly men, and all of them wore the high father's symbol on their coats. One of them started saying, "Who the—" but stopped when he saw the rapiers.

"You're making a disturbance in the streets of our city," said Henry, stepping up beside Thomas. "Leave."

"He's a witch!" said one sailor, staggering forward. "Fellow saw him turn a man into a dog!"

Thomas rolled his eyes. "No one can do that."

"Fellow said he did. Fellow saw it happening."

"What fellow?" demanded Thomas. "Who?"

The sailors looked around. "He's not here now."

"Then you don't need to care what he said. Now get on with you."

The three sailors grumbled and swore, but they turned and walked away with many glances over their shoulders.

"Keep an eye on them," said Thomas, putting his weapons away and going to the man on the ground. "Martin? Martin, it's all right now."

"Not Martin," said the man, his voice shaking. "Leon."

"All right, Leon. Can you get up?"

"Are they gone?"

"Aye, they're gone." Thomas reached out a hand and helped the man to his feet. He had a cut on his head that bled profusely but didn't look too deep. "You'll be all right."

"We'd best leave," said Henry. "In case they decide to come back with friends."

"I'm not a witch," Leon babbled. "I'm a weaver. I just do tricks for fun. My old uncle taught me. Everyone knows they're just tricks. I don't... I don't know any magic."

"I know," said Thomas. "I know. Come on, we'll help you get home."

***

It was well past midnight by the time Thomas and Henry reached the small square where they rented an apartment.

When they had returned from Frostmire two months earlier, there were no rooms to be had in the student quarter. Instead, Henry found one in a much more expensive neighbourhood nearby. The other tenants were all wealthy merchants and minor nobility. The building had only six apartments and was on a square with its own fountain for clean water. The apartment had large, clean, dry rooms that were free of insects and mice. Henry had paid for it all, claiming that his brother had decided to share the family wealth with him.

Thomas suspected Henry had raided the Duke's treasury before they had left Frostmire.

The apartment had come furnished, with a pair of chairs and footstools and a padded couch in the main room, and comfortable beds and desks in each of the two bedrooms. They even had a stove in the kitchen to cook their own food. They rarely did, since neither had any skill at it, but it was handy for heating tea and soup, and gave them a warm room to sit in during the worst parts of the winter.

Thomas went straight to the dark fireplace when they stepped inside.

"Well," said Henry as he closed the door behind them, leaving them in the dark. "That was exhilarating."

"It was stupid," said Thomas, making a ball of light just bright enough to see the kindling box. He piled a layer into the fireplace. "And useless. We didn't find a single hint of magic anywhere."

"We did keep a man from getting beaten senseless," Henry said, hanging up his coat and cloak on the neat little pegs by the door.

"By idiots who thought he had magic when he didn't." Thomas stared at the kindling pile until small flickers of flame rose up from it.

"Of all your tricks," said Henry. "I think I like that one the best."

"It is the most useful," said Thomas. "Aside from the one keeping out vermin."

Thomas hung up his own coat and cloak, took off his weapons and sat down in his chair. The weariness that he'd been ignoring until then wrapped itself around him like a big, heavy blanket. Henry put a log on top of the kindling and the flames licked and danced around it.

Henry sat in his own chair. "So, now what?"

"I don't know," said Thomas. He rubbed his eyes. "We've been up since when?"

"First bell of yesterday morning."

Thomas yawned. "We should probably get some sleep before class tomorrow."

"Assuming we get to go to class," said Henry.

"Aye, there is that." The heat from the fire began seeping into Thomas's cold limbs. "How much trouble do you think we're in?"

"Oh, lots," said Henry. "Doesn't seem quite so important now, though, does it?"

Thomas shook his head. "It will in the morning, though."

"What's the worst they can do?" asked Henry. "Aside from flogging and expulsion, I mean."

"I was thinking that," said Thomas. "My father would kill me."

"We're star pupils and war heroes," said Henry. "Plus the king likes us. We'll be fine."

"Says you," Thomas grumped. He held out his hands to the fire. "I don't think I've been warm since the beach." A memory from the night before leapt into his mind. "The merchant."

Henry blinked. "Which merchant?"

"At the beach. Malcolm Bright. Invited me to his party to meet others with 'similar interests.'"

"I'd forgotten about him. I take it you're going now?"

"I am," said Thomas. "We are, in fact." He managed a smile. "All of us. Eileen won't forgive me if I don't bring her this time."

6

George was already at the forge when they arrived at the smithy the next morning. The grey clouds had opened in the night, sending a slow, miserable drizzle to fall on the city. The heat from the forge was a welcome respite, and soon their cloaks were steaming from it. George didn't look any happier than he had the day before. He grunted a greeting, but his eyes were on the hot metal in front of him.

Eileen came down the stairs with her robe on, but with a skirt underneath instead of the breeches she usually wore. She was looking wide-eyed and nervous, but managed a smile and a "Hello."

"Good morning," said Thomas, kissing her cheek. "How was studying?"

"Oh, bad," said Eileen. "Between being exhausted and worrying about you and thinking about this morning, I got absolutely nothing done. I don't even remember what books I was looking at."

"Astronomy," said Henry. "And Trigonometry."

Eileen rolled her eyes. "Knowing doesn't help if it won't stay in my head."

"Maybe you can audit a trigonometry class," said Thomas. "Talk to the Master of Mathematics today."

"Thomas, I don't even know if they're going to let me in the gate, today," said Eileen. "Can we worry about that first?"

"I'm sure you'll be allowed in," said Henry. "At the very least to get yelled at."

"You're not helping at all."

"If I really wanted to not help," said Henry, after Eileen said good-bye to her brother and they'd stepped back out into the rain, "I'd ask if you're ready for your first glorious day as the only girl in the Academy."

"Me? Aye. Sure," said Eileen, her tone saying the opposite. They walked out of the Street of Smiths and onto the thoroughfare, dodging people and trying not to slip on the cobbles. "Do you think it's going to be bad?"

"Probably," said Henry, "But not like the young lords in Frostmire. The students have a code of conduct, and flogging is no one's friend."

"Good to know," said Eileen, not looking at all convinced.

"You'll be fine," said Thomas, taking her hand and squeezing it.

"I hope so," said Eileen. She left her hand in Thomas's. "What happened last night?"

Thomas told her as they walked. Despite the drizzle, people were thick in the streets. Men were going to their jobs. Merchants with baskets or boxes hawked their wares. Housewives and old women held their cloaks over their heads and gossiped with the neighbours as they walked to the bustling market square.

The square halfway between the Street of Smiths and the Academy and was one of the largest in the city. It had room for a hundred or more stalls and vendors who were selling everything from winter vegetables, to baskets, to wine. The three wended their way through, moving with the crowds and stopping to buy some pastries for breakfast.

"Don't be fooled!" a man shouted. "Don't be fooled by those who say that there is no such thing! For I tell you they walk among us now!"

The man was standing on a crate near the street that led toward the Academy. He was ragged and dirty as if he only had the one set of clothes and hadn't bothered washing them—or himself—since he'd put them on a year or two ago.

"The witches are everywhere!" The man waved his arms as if they would encompass the entire city. He seemed oblivious to the fact that the merchants and their customers were almost completely ignoring him. "They have attacked our northern realm! They have attacked our neighbours to the south! And they will soon be attacking here! They will try to destroy the Church of the High Father! And what will you do about it?"

"Nice timing," muttered Thomas.

"Perfect timing, in fact," said Henry.

"He doesn't look like a churchman," said Eileen.

"Itinerant preacher," said Henry. "Looking for money and preaching the many words of the gods as delivered to their brain by the Four themselves."

"Except they usually preach opposite what the Church does," said Thomas. "Unlike him."

Eileen looked the preacher over. "You think he's with the High Father's Church?"

"It's possible," said Henry. "Though his appearance isn't up to their usual standards."

"What do we do about it?"

"Nothing," growled Thomas. "There's no law against preaching in public. Especially if you're on the side of the High Father."

"Watch your neighbours," the man ranted. "Watch your family! Beware the witches! Beware the marks of the Banished!"

"Come on," said Thomas. "We've more important things to do."

"We do indeed," said Henry. "Can't miss our scolding, after all."

The rain was starting to seep through their cloaks by the time they reached the Academy gates. Students were hurrying in from all directions, more eager to be out of the rain then to get to class on time.

"Here, now!" called Michael from a side street. "Wait for us!"

The three turned and saw the Student Company bearing down on them. Several looked rather the worse for wear, but most were smiling.

"I see everyone had a good evening," said Henry. "How was the Quill?"

"Much calmer without you lot in it," said Marcus. "No fights, no arguments, just a great deal of food and alcohol."

"Of which you looked to have partaken a great deal."

"I wasn't alone in that."

"Who cares?" Jonathan pushed to the front of the group. "What happened yesterday?"

"If you're losing days you should cut back on the drinking," said Henry.

"This from you." Jonathan turned to Thomas. "Seriously. What happened?"

"The king was annoyed at us," said Thomas. "Especially at Henry."

"And?" demanded Michael. "What happened?"

"We..." Thomas remembered the king's words. "We had breakfast, he forgave us and sent us home."

Michael gave Thomas a look of complete disbelief. "And that's it?"

"That's all I'm going to talk about standing in the street," said Thomas. He pointed a thumb at Eileen. "Besides, we have more important things to worry about."

"Which is why we're all waiting for you," said William. "We've come to escort Eileen to her first day as a girl at the Academy!"

"Cheers for Lieutenant Eileen!" shouted Mark.

The rest of them gave a cheer, though some held their heads as they did. Eileen blushed and beamed at the same time. "Oh, guys! Thanks!"

"Our pleasure," said Mark. "We came early so we could greet you at the gate. Except Charles, the lazy dog."

"Why not Charles?" asked Thomas. "Where is he?"

"No idea," said William. "I saw last Charles at Terrence Miller's place, three sheets to the wind and heading for four. He's either on Terrence's floor or waking up in some alley right now, wondering why he's soaking wet and hoping it's just water."

"Can we get somewhere warm?" asked Marcus, who was one of the ones looking rather the worse for wear. "It's going to be a long day, and I'd rather not spend it wet and shivering."

"Good idea," said Mark. "Escorts for Eileen, fall in!"

"I'm in your mathematics class," said William, stepping forward. "And James is in history class. We'll be your escorts for the first part of the morning."

"Bill, Ronald and I are in with you for Professor Dodds' class," said Mark. "We'll meet you there. And Thomas will meet us for fencing before lunch."

"Assuming I'm allowed to stay," said Eileen. She managed a smile. "Thank you all very, very much."

"No need," said James. "Now let's get someplace warm!"

The troop marched together through the gates, to the amusement of the other students. The Warden at the gatehouse stepped out as they passed "Henry Antonius, Thomas Flarety and Eileen Gobhann are to report to the Headmaster's house immediately upon arrival." His mouth quirked up on one side. "Caught some trouble for that stunt at the debate, haven't you?"

"More than you can imagine," Thomas muttered. Eileen took a deep breath and kept walking. She was shaking slightly, but doing her best to hide it. Thomas took her hand again. She squeezed his but didn't look at him.

The Headmaster lived in a very grand three-story brick house that looked down over the other masters' houses and most of the campus. Thomas had been in it only twice before. Once when he convinced the Headmaster to let him take both philosophy and law at the same time, a second time when Thomas was released from the gaol beneath the Academy the previous summer. The Headmaster, he recalled, had been very pleasant on both occasions. *Which is far too much to hope for today.*

The whole company insisted on going with them. Other students watched with curiosity, amusement, and—in a few cases—downright hostility. Thomas hoped more were friendly than hostile, or the next part of the plan was going to be difficult.

Thomas stopped in front of the Headmaster's porch. "I think we need to go on our own from here," he said. "We'll let you know what happens."

"We're waiting until you come out," said Mark.

"We'll be a while," warned Henry. "The last lecture I had here took the better part of an hour."

"Then it's a good thing we're early for class," said Michael. "Now hurry up and get yelled at so we can be on our way."

Thomas led Henry and Eileen up the stairs and knocked on the door. Matron Marshall, the Headmaster's housekeeper, opened it and glared at the three of them. "Well, about time you lot got here," she said. "The amount of trouble you've caused, I'm surprised you're still students."

"We're surprised, too," said Henry. "But since we are, would you be so kind as to tell the Headmaster we've arrived?"

"Oh, he knows," said the Matron. "Scrape your boots off and get in here."

She sent them into the parlour, which was set up for guests, much to their surprise. There was a steaming pot of tea with cups at the ready, a plate of scones and another of sticky-buns. The smell of it all combined together into something at once sweet and sharp that made their stomachs rumble despite the pastries they'd eaten in the square. It was all Thomas could do to resist reaching for a sticky-bun.

"Now you three stay right here until the Headmaster comes," said the Matron. She waved a finger at them. "And don't be eating anything, either. That's for your betters."

"I admit no betters," said Henry as the Matron left. He stayed away from the food, though.

The wait was short. The Headmaster, a thin man with thinner grey hair and brown eyes that missed nothing, stepped into the room with the Masters of Rhetoric and Laws right behind him. "Oh, good," he said. "You're here."

"Yes sir," said Thomas.

"Excellent," said the Headmaster. "We are here to discuss whether to have you, Thomas and you, Henry flogged and expelled from the Academy, and whether or not we should have the three of you banned from the grounds and the city."

Thomas swallowed. "That seems a bit... extreme."

"You lied to us," said the Headmaster. "For two months."

"Lied?" repeated Henry. "What lie, exactly, did we tell?"

"You know very well," said the Master of Laws, Horus Greyfields. He was a large man with a quiet voice to which one felt compelled to listen. Thomas had watched him in action in the Law Courts, and had seen him almost mesmerize judges as he argued the law to them.

"I don't," said Henry. "No one ever asked if Eileen was a girl."

"A lie of omission," said the Master of Laws, looking down his nose at Henry. "I would expect one of my students to muster a better defense than that."

"I would hate to see you thrown out and disgraced," said the Headmaster, frowning at Thomas. "Imagine what your father would say."

"I have a pretty good idea," said Thomas, remembering his visit home the previous summer.

"Then why were you fool enough to bring this girl onto the Academy grounds?" demanded the Headmaster. He looked down at Eileen. "Young lady, what is your real name?"

"Eileen, sir," she said. "Eileen Gobhann, sister to George Gobhann, the smith."

"Sir George Gobhann," corrected Henry. "Knight of the Order of the White Wolf. And also a smith."

"Miss Gobhann," said the Headmaster, using the proper title for the young female relative of a knight. "You will forgive me if I do not include you in this conversation."

"No," said Eileen. "I won't."

The Master of Rhetoric's lips twitched in what might have been a very well concealed smile. The Headmaster blinked in surprise. "I beg your pardon?"

"You're deciding my future," she said. "I should have a say in it."

"No we aren't," said the Master of Laws, his eyebrows drawing down as he frowned at Thomas and Henry. "We're deciding *their* future right now."

"But rest assured," said the Headmaster, "we will be discussing yours very shortly. Thomas, answer the question."

"Eileen is smart," said Thomas. "She's capable, and I truly believe that this place is where she belongs. And the only way to prove it was to have her here and show what she could do."

"And the fact that you are blinded by love has nothing to do with it?" asked the Master of Laws. "Is her love worth that much to you?"

"Not blinded," said Thomas. "And yes, it is."

Eileen blushed and bit her lip, but said nothing.

"And you, Lord Henry?" said the Headmaster. "Unless you're also madly in love with her?"

Henry smiled. "No."

"Then why did you do this?"

"All the reasons Thomas gave," said Henry. "Save the last one."

"Is that all?"

Henry, for the first time, looked lightly less than completely confident of the situation. "I would rather not say more."

"I would rather you did," said the Headmaster. "In fact, I'll insist on it."

Henry's eyes went to Eileen. "It may be taken the wrong way."

"Right or wrong, you will say it," said the Master of Laws. "You will say it now, or it will weigh very heavily against you."

Henry sighed. "She's damaged."

"What?" Eileen's mouth fell open. "I'm what?"

"You're damaged," Henry said. "You and Thomas and George."

"We are not! I am not!" Eileen was furious. "How can you say that?"

"I hear Thomas's nightmares," said Henry. "I saw you try to drink yourself insensible on the way back from Frostmire. I see the dark circles around your eyes. And how well is George sleeping?"

Thomas, who had thought the dark circles were from her studying, was staring at Eileen now.

"He's... fine," muttered Eileen. "Just fine. You're too nosy, Henry Antonius."

"Yes." Henry squared off with the Headmaster. "They wouldn't be in this condition if I hadn't asked Thomas to come north, and I want them better."

"And you think sneaking her into the Academy was the way to do that?"

"If she were religious, I'd send her to the Sisters. But she isn't. She's a scholar at heart, and this is the best place for her. Just like it was the best place for me after fighting the tribes for four years."

"I'm not damaged," muttered Eileen, though she was looking at her feet.

"I see." The Headmaster looked back to the Masters of Rhetoric and Laws, who were looking inquisitive and highly disapproving respectively. "You have put the Academy and me in a very awkward position."

"There was no other way," said Thomas. "You wouldn't have let Eileen in if you'd known she was a girl and we had to let you see what she could do. Eileen belongs here."

"I *do* belong here," said Eileen. "I love the Academy."

"In point of fact," said the Headmaster, "indeed, in point of law—you do *not* belong here. And all three of you knew that before you began this scheme. You knew women were not allowed to study at the Academy. You knew that bringing a girl onto the grounds was a punishable offence."

"A flogging offence, I believe," said the Master of Laws.

"Only if done for licentious purposes," said Henry. "Which it wasn't. Unless Thomas has been stealing kisses in the library?"

"Shut up," said Thomas.

"Or perhaps the fencing hall?"

"Henry!" Eileen hissed at him. "Shut up!"

"I was just asking."

"Do shut up, Lord Henry," said the Headmaster. "You both lied, as did the other members of the Student Company. And the only reason the entire group of you aren't already out in the street is because you risked life and limb to preserve the integrity of our kingdom. Your actions in Frostmire were heroic and earned you some leeway, but they in no way make up for lying to us about Miss Gobhann."

"What about Eileen's actions?" asked Thomas. "You said they earned her the right to study here and to sit for the exams."

"That was when we thought she was a young man, not a young woman," said the Master of Laws.

"What difference should that make?" demanded Thomas. "She fought beside us!"

"That does not make her a boy!"

"Why are boys so special?" demanded Eileen. "I'm as smart as any of them. Why do they get to be here and not me?"

The Master of Rhetoric looked thoughtful at that, while the Master of Laws looked like he was building up another head of steam. The Headmaster sighed. "Everyone sit down. Thomas, pour us some tea."

The request caught Thomas completely off guard. "Um... Yes, sir."

Thomas poured cups for them all. The Headmaster took a seat on the couch, while the masters sat in a pair of chairs near the fireplace. Each of the three gave a polite "thank you" when they received their tea, but didn't say anything else. The warm smell of the tea made Thomas's stomach rumble. Without being asked, he took up the tray of sticky-buns and offered them first to the masters, then to Eileen and Henry, before setting it down and taking one himself. The Headmaster looked both resigned and irritated.

Thomas, Eileen and Henry sat on the couch directly opposite and waited.

No one spoke. The Headmaster sipped at his tea and nibbled at his pastry. The silence grew long and, for Thomas and Eileen, very uncomfortable. Henry, on the other hand, looked as relaxed as if he were at home, sitting in front of his own fire.

The Master of Rhetoric was finished his pastry first. The Master of Laws downed a second cup of tea. The Headmaster took his time on both. When he finished, he put his cup and plate on the table and sighed. "A decision has been made."

Thomas and Eileen leaned forward in spite of themselves. Henry remained unmoved.

"Eileen may continue her time here at the Academy with whichever masters are willing to teach her," the Headmaster said. "And she may sit for the spring exams."

Eileen clapped both her hands over her mouth to keep from squealing.

Thomas nearly yelled out a cheer as well, but managed to stop himself. Henry nodded and allowed himself a satisfied smile.

"But do not expect to be allowed in," warned the Master of Laws. "Academy rules forbid it."

"We know," said Thomas. "We'll be delivering a petition to challenge the rules by the end of the week."

The Headmaster sighed, "Of course you will." He stood, and the others did the same. "Take yourselves out of here. And let's not have any more foolishness."

Henry and Thomas bowed and Eileen sank into a deep curtsey. Then they fled the parlour. Matron Marshall was standing by the door, glaring at them. She opened it and watched them go by. "Not the decision I would have made," she said as Thomas walked out the door. "Not by a long shot."

"Then we'll be thankful it wasn't your decision," said Henry as he passed her.

For a reply, Matron Marshall closed the door practically on his heels.

The rest of the company was still standing on the grass in front of the house in the cold, grey rain. "Well?" demanded James. "Well?"

Eileen collapsed against Thomas, her breath *whooshing* out of her. Thomas wrapped his arms around her and squeezed tight. "I can stay," said Eileen. "I can't believe it! I can stay."

"Yes!" shouted Mark, and the others cheered. "Time to get to class!"

"Mathematics!" said William. "We'll say we were at the Headmaster and we shouldn't get in trouble for being late. Come on."

"One moment," said Eileen. She turned and kissed Thomas on the lips, catching him by surprise. She smiled wide. "I have been wanting to do that before class for months."

"Me, too," said Thomas, grinning back. Around them, the Student Company mimed gagging and choking as he kissed her again.

"And you," Eileen pointed a finger at Henry. "How could you say that?"

"It was true," Henry said. "Though not necessary, apparently."

"What?" Eileen's voice nearly squeaked on the word.

"They said a decision was made," said Henry, dropping his voice so it wouldn't carry. "That means they weren't the ones making it."

Eileen frowned. "Then who...?"

The king," said Thomas, keeping his voice as low as Henry's. "Why?"

"Well, that is the question," said Henry.

"Hey!" called William. "Stop muttering! We're late enough as it is!"

"Right!" said Eileen. She took a deep breath, put on a smile and said, "See you at lunch!"

"Have a great day," said Thomas.

"I will," promised Eileen. She smiled at her escorts. "Let's go!"

Thomas watched them run to class and tried to ignore the worry that had started gnawing at the pit of his stomach.

***

Halfway through Thomas's morning class on Precedence and Law, someone behind him whispered, "Is it true?"

Thomas ignored whoever it was entirely and tried to pay attention to the lecture.

"Seriously, Thomas. Is it true? What those lords said about witchcraft?"

"Is there something you wish to share with the class, Master David?" demanded Professor Smythe, from his place at the front. "Something so vitally important that it is worth missing how to apply the law when standing before a Ducal Trial?"

"Uhhh... not vital," said David.

"Oh, but it must be. Please repeat it. Loudly, for all of us."

By the Four, please no, thought Thomas.

"Uhhh..."

"Now!"

"I was asking Thomas if it was true what the young lords were saying about him throwing lightning and being the Duke's personal witch," the words came out in a rush with no space for breath between them. There was a moment's silence. Then the class erupted in sniggers and whispered comments.

"Fascinating," said Professor Smythe, his cold, hard voice cutting through the noise in the class. "And Thomas, what was your reply?"

"I didn't reply," said Thomas.

"Oh, surely there must have been a reply. It takes two to converse."

"But only one to whisper irritating questions when the other is trying to listen," said Thomas, glaring at David. "I did not answer him, and had no intention of doing so."

"You were listening?" Professor Smythe smiled. "Then perhaps you can tell me what precedent was set by Duke Clarence the Third."

Thomas could and did, in great detail, until the Professor stopped him and resumed his lecture. All was quiet until the Professor gave them their case for the day. "Sir Roland Greensward vs. Pig-keeper Harris, in which Harris's pigs got into Sir Roland's garden, and Sir Roland slaughtered them. The Pig-keeper brought Sir Roland to court. Who won, why, and should they have won? Break into groups and discuss, then we'll find out whether or not you are right."

Thomas made a point of not being in the same group as David. It didn't help.

"Witchcraft?" said Fred, as soon as their group sat down together. "Really?"

"There's no such thing," said Thomas. "Pig-keeper or knight?"

"Knight," said Billy Randolph. "I heard what those northerners said about you. Why would they say that?"

Thomas sighed.

"The Archbishop said the raiders used witchcraft," said Fred. "And he said someone on the other side used lightning."

"I don't care," said Thomas, keeping his words slow and even. "I care about whose side we are going to argue for, and how we are going to win."

"Maybe you could throw lightning at the Professor," Fred sniggered.

Thomas wiped all expression from his face and stared at the other student.

"It was just a joke," said Fred.

Thomas kept staring.

"It *was* a joke, Thomas," said Billy. "He didn't mean anything."

"Pig-keeper or knight?" Thomas kept his voice soft and as calm as he could make it. "Which side?"

"Knight," said Fred, sounding very nervous. "The pig-keeper will lose because his pigs were the ones that got loose. And one man is nobility, and the other isn't."

"Which is as good a reason to defend the pig-keeper as any, isn't it?" said Thomas. "Now here's what I think..."

Thomas made it through the rest of the class without another incident, and even managed to convince the law professor that, contrary to what had actually happened, the pig-keeper should have won. Those two victories didn't live past the classroom door.

"All right, what really happened up north?" demanded Billy the moment they stepped out of the house. A dozen others were gathered around, looking eagerly at Thomas.

By the Four, how much of this will I have to talk about? "What have you heard?"

"You killed Richard Antonius with a lightning bolt."

Thomas shook his head. *The stories are already getting bigger.* "Baron Goshawk killed Richard Antonius with a throwing axe to his chest."

"The raiders used witchcraft to break into the castle," said David, joining the group.

"They used witchcraft to kidnap the Duke's middle son," said another.

"You used witchcraft to find out who killed the Duke."

"They fought with blades made of fire."

"Enough!" said Thomas, loud enough to silence them. "Lord Richard let the raiders into the castle. No one used blades of fire." He looked at the group. "Sorry to disappoint you. Now, if you'll excuse me, I have to get to fencing."

Thomas was accosted four more times as he crossed the grounds to the gymnasium. He fended off the questions with a curt "late for class" even though he wasn't. Halfway across the grounds he spotted Henry with William, Mark, James, and Wilson. He jogged over to them. "Hey! How did the morning go?"

"Well enough," said Henry, "By which I mean no one asked about Eileen because they were too busy pestering us with questions about witchcraft."

"Pestering is right," said Wilson. "One of the *professors* even asked me if it was true about the raiders throwing fire and you throwing lighting." He shook his head. "I thought everything was going to be about Eileen, today!"

"What did you say?" asked Thomas.

"That you threw candy and the raiders threw flowers, what did you *think* I said?" Wilson rolled his eyes. "The raiders used fire. You never used witchcraft. That seems to satisfy them."

"For now," muttered Thomas, not wanting to think what would happen when they weren't satisfied any more. "Thank you."

"You're welcome. How long before all this blows over?"

"Depends who's doing the blowing," said Henry. "If it's just the lords, that's one thing, but after the Archbishop's speech?"

"Where's Eileen?" asked Thomas. "She should be here by now."

"Professor Dodds' lecture," said Wilson. "Those always go long."

"Dodds likes her," said Thomas. "Or at least, he liked Alex."

"Don't suppose you remembered to bring a lunch?" said Henry.

"I didn't," said Thomas.

"The Green Goose has a good stew," said Wilson. "And it's closer than the Quill."

"Cheap, too," said Henry. "Shall we all meet there after your fencing class?"

"Well..." said Thomas, who was actually hoping to have lunch alone with Eileen, "I was thinking..."

"Thomas!" Graham Silvers was running across the grass, toward them. "Thomas, Come quick! They've got Eileen cornered!"

"Who?" demanded Thomas.

"Keith Rolston and his friends!" Graham slid to a stop on the wet grass. "There's practically a brawl in Professor Dodds' class!" He turned and ran back the way they had come. Thomas took off after him, and the rest followed a moment later.

"I thought you were on Keith's side," shouted Thomas as he chased after Graham.

"Just in the debate!" called Graham over his shoulder. "Thought I'd pay you back for the drubbing I took when we did 'rights of the lord against rights of the people' last year! But this is different!"

"How?" demanded Thomas, putting on a burst of speed to catch the other, taller man. Their boots dug divots in the soaking brown grass and spattered mud and water on their robes.

"I like him," said Graham. "I mean, I liked him, and she's still him, even if she's Eileen now. And it's not fair to pick on her for not being him!"

"That made no sense," said Henry from just behind them.

"Well, neither does this, so hurry up!"

They heard the arguing the moment they stepped inside the philosophy building and followed it to the largest of the lecture theatres. The doors were wide open and several professors were standing outside looking in. One saw them coming and stepped in front of the door. "No one else in there, lads. There's trouble enough already."

"I say she doesn't belong!" they could hear Keith's voice rise about the rest. "She's not a student!"

"I know I'm not a student!" Eileen yelled back. "All I want is the right to take the exam and *become* a student if I pass it!"

Other students jumped into the argument.

"Girls can't be students!"

"Why not?"

"Because it would wreck the whole Academy! No one would get any studying done!"

"Some of us can actually concentrate with girls around!"

"You can't concentrate with a wet sock around!"

There was a crash and dozens of loud voices all started talking at once. Thomas shoved past the professors and charged inside with Henry and the Student Company on his heels. On the floor of the theatre and in the raised benches all around the hall, young men were arguing and struggling, and in a few cases, actively swinging fists at one another.

"Eileen!" Thomas yelled.

"Thomas! Here!" called Bill. Eileen was in the centre of the floor in front of the professor's podium. Roland and Mark had her arms, holding Eileen back from charging at Keith, who was three benches up. There were bodies everywhere in the way, blocking Thomas's path. Professor Dodds had scrambled up on the podium and was demanding decorum and silence.

"Form a wedge!" Thomas ordered. "Push forward!"

"God, it's like Frostmire again!" said James.

"At least no one's trying to kill you," said Henry. "Follow Thomas!"

The seven of them pushed their way into the room. A few students tried shoving back, but the combined weight of the company was too much. In moments Thomas and the company were against the podium.

"Look out!" called someone near the top. "The witch is at the podium!"

The words nearly made Thomas's heart stop.

"And so is her boyfriend," shouted one of the boys near Keith, bringing a roar of laughter and renewed yells and pushing.

"Is that how you snuck in?" demanded Keith. "By bewitching your boyfriend?"

Eileen tried to charge at him again and was once more hauled back by Roland and Mark.

"Don't do it," said Wilson. "You hit him, and he'll use it as proof you shouldn't be here."

"Careful now!" taunted Keith. "Your boyfriend can't toss lightning around in here!"

Want to bet on that? Thomas stepped in front of Eileen. "What happened?"

"That fool, Keith," snapped Eileen. "Class was just about done when he stands up and asks me what the position of the ancients was on the inferior intellect of women." She raised her voice loud enough for Keith to hear it above the din. "Of course, if you'd *read* the ancients you'd know that the Beaudleans spoke of women as equals, the Haperions suggested that women were intellectually superior, and that the Dralfons did not mention women's intellect at all!"

"The Dralfons call women the incarnation of temptation!" yelled Keith.

"That has nothing to do with their intellect!"

"The teachings of the High Father specifically called the followers of the Mother and Daughter feeble in mind!"

"That reference was referring to the nuns who held out against the Church in a fortress on an old volcano," said Wilson. "The poison fumes seeping from the cracks in the earth caused their feebleness of intellect! It's not about anyone else!"

"And a two-hundred-year-old text isn't ancient!" Eileen shouted.

"You would say that! You're a woman!"

"I say that because I'm right!"

A brain-piercing screech filled the room. Everyone's hands went over their ears and everyone's eyes went to the podium. Professor Dodds was blowing hard into an odd-shaped horn whose sound drove into the students' ears like rusty, jagged spikes. He sounded it twice more, then yelled, "Everyone who is in this classroom take a seat and be silent! Now!" When there wasn't immediate action, he blew the horn again. Everyone scrambled for a place, and Thomas found himself squished into a front row seat between Henry and Eileen.

Professor Dodds held up the curved instrument. "This is a Cavlarian war horn. It makes the single most awful noise in creation. This is only the second time I have had to use it to restore order, the first being the result of a rather tense discussion over the nature of matter and the transmutability of lead into gold." His eyes swept the room again. "Now, what have we learned?" he pointed at a student in the fifth row. "You! What did you learn?"

"Umm... that the ancients did not see women as intellectual inferiors?"

"How about that girls are disruptive to learning?" suggested Keith.

Professor Dodds blew on the instrument again, making everyone groan and cover their ears. "You were not asked!" He pointed to a second student. "You!"

"Uh... that... uh... that the philosophy of the Ancients regarding women does not align with the teachings of the Church of the High Father?"

He pointed to Thomas, "You!"

"Not to walk into your class unannounced?"

"Remember that for next time, young man. You!" he pointed to Eileen, "Come here!"

Eileen shot a look of fear to Thomas, but got up and walked to the podium.

"Stand there," said Professor Dodds, pointing to a spot beside him. "Remove your robe."

Eileen's eyes went wide. "What?"

"You are wearing clothes underneath are you not?"

"Yes!" Eileen started turning red. Several of the boys snickered.

A glance from Professor Dodds silenced them. "Take off the robe. And be quick about it!"

Eileen looked furious but said nothing and unbuttoned the robe, pulling it off with angry motions and folding it over her arms. The brown skirt and sweater she wore made her look like a small mouse in a room full of black cats. Professor Dodds pointed at Eileen, "Now, what do you know about this person standing beside me? Anyone?"

After a moment, someone called out, "She's short!"

The laughter that followed that broke some of the tension.

"She's a red-head!"

"She looks better with her hair down!"

"Her boots are dirty!"

"She has ink on her cheek!"

"She's punches really hard!" called Henry, bringing more laughter and a glare from the professor. "Well, she does."

"I will forebear asking how you know," said the professor. "Try again, lads. This time go for something more obvious."

"She's a girl," shouted out a student from the back.

"Very good!" said Professor Dodds. "She is a girl! Excellently done. There may be hope for some of you! And was there anyone in this room who was not aware she was a girl at the beginning of this class?" When the room filled with silence, he pointed to Keith. "Did you, sir, fail to notice she was a girl?"

"No, sir," said Keith.

"Then would you say that your words were meant as a deliberate attack on this young lady?"

"Not on her, sir, but on—"

"On her!" the professor thundered. "Now, I understand that there is disagreement about whether or not young ladies should attend the Academy. And I know there are many arguments one way and another and I know that feelings run high, *but I will not tolerate personal attacks on anyone in this classroom! IS THAT UNDERSTOOD?"*

Heads nodded around the room. The professor blew on the instrument again. A hundred hands went over ears. *"IS THAT UNDERSTOOD?"*

"Yes, professor!" the students chorused.

"And as for you," said Professor Dodds to Eileen, "your emotional, hyperbolic reaction, not to Mr. Ralston's question about the inferiority of women, but to his use of a relatively modern text to answer a question about ancient beliefs can only mean one thing." He let the words hang in the air a bit. "You're one of us."

Half the class cheered. The other half grumbled. Keith Ralston steamed in his seat.

"Now put your robe back on, Eileen," said Professor Dodds. "You and your friends who dashed in may be excused. The rest of you can clean up this mess. Master Rolston and I will discuss the new assignment he has due by the end of the week once you are all finished."

Eileen, Thomas at her side, led the company out of the room. Brian, Ronald and Mark took the moment to sneak out with them. Eileen's hands shook as she buttoned up her robe. She looked more dazed than happy, and more tired than either.

"I do believe we won that one," said Henry. "Not surprising, mind you, with Dodds, but good."

"Very" said Thomas. "Are you all right?"

"I'm fine," said Eileen, though her tone said the opposite. She managed a small tight smile at Thomas. "I just can't believe they're being so..."

"Obdurate?" suggested Wilson.

"Annoying?" Bill said.

"Stupid?" said Henry.

"Stupid," said Eileen. "Definitely stupid. Why are they being so stupid?"

"And what was that crack about witchcraft?" said Wilson. "I thought it was Thomas—"

"I never used witchcraft," said Thomas, glaring at Wilson.

"I know, I know," said Wilson, holding up his hands to block any more protests. "I just mean, yours is the name that everyone is bandying around. Why pick on Eileen?"

"Because imbeciles grab whatever weapon they can get," said Henry. "Too bad you held Eileen back. I would have loved to see her punch Keith in the nose."

"Thomas should have thrown lightning," said Bill. "That would have shown him."

"Will you shut up about it?" hissed Thomas.

"Oops. Sorry."

Thomas sighed. *Somewhere, sometime, someone is going to say the wrong thing, and then...*

They reached the gymnasium before Thomas had time to worry brood on it further.

"I'm for Case Law," said Henry. "Then lunch at the Green Griffon, if you want to join us."

Henry and most of the rest of the company walked off through the drizzle, leaving Mark and Wilson behind with Thomas and Eileen.

"And what are you wearing for fencing, Eileen?" asked Wilson wiggling his eyebrows and dodging Thomas's swat.

"Don't get too excited," said Eileen as the four went inside the gymnasium. "I've re-sewn one of George's shirts, so you won't be seeing anything."

Wilson looked disappointed just to irritate Thomas as the four stripped off their cloaks and coats, and hung them with the other dripping clothes in the front hall. Eileen also stripped off her sweater and skirt, much to Mark and Wilson's interest. Thomas slapped them both on the back of the head, but neither paid attention.

George's shirt reached down to her knees, with a thin belt around the middle to hold it in place and breeches underneath. Eileen had tacked the sleeves back, so her arms were bare to the elbow. She hung her skirt with the rest and led the others into the fencing hall. The other boys were all lined up in shirtsleeves and breeches, practice blades in their hands, waiting for the fencing master. All of them stared when Eileen stepped into the room. She shook her head. "I've been training with you for months. You've all seen my legs."

"We didn't know you were a girl, then," said one of the students. "Now it's... different."

"Yes," said Eileen. "Because my legs have changed so much since you found that out."

"Well," said another, blushing. "We didn't know your legs were worth looking at before."

Eileen rolled her eyes. "I suggest to you that I've beaten half of you. And since none of you want to be beaten by a girl *again*, I suggest you stop looking and start practising."

Thomas chuckled and then had to smother it when Eileen raised an eyebrow at him. She took her place in line with the others.

"Say," said John, one of the fencers, looking at her chest. "Did you get bigger?"

Thomas's eyebrows went up at that. Eileen smiled. "They're not tied down, John, and if you don't raise your eyes, I'll run you through."

"If you can."

"Did the last two times. Want to try for three when the master comes?"

"The master is here," said Master Parres Brennan. "Eileen Gobhann, step out of line."

Eileen stepped forward and the master met her before she could reach the fencing floor. His bald head was red with anger. "You lied to me," he said. Eileen opened her mouth to protest, and he stopped her with a raised finger. "I don't care your reasons. I do not teach women to fight. It's an obscenity. Leave my class."

"Please, Master..."

"I am not your master!" The words came out harsh and clipped. "You think this is a game, silly girl? It is a horrible thing to kill a man."

"I know," said Eileen.

"You know?" the Fencing Master's voice rose in volume. "You think you know, but until you sink a blade into a man's flesh, you know nothing!"

"Five."

"What?"

"I've killed five men," said Eileen, her voice flat. "Four with my rapier. One..." she swallowed convulsively,. "One with fire. There was another one I nearly killed, but he lived."

The Fencing Master's expression grew harder. "Then you, Miss Gobhann, are an obscenity as well. Now leave." When she hesitated, the Fencing Master pointed to the door. "Out!"

Eileen tensed, sucked in a breath, and Thomas half-expected her to explode. Instead, she only said, "I thank you for the lessons, Master," and raised her blade to salute.

The Fencing Master caught the dulled blade in his hand. "Women do not salute. Get out."

Eileen's face tightened, but she let the sword go, and walked out.

Thomas, furious, stepped out of the line. "You should have let her salute!"

"What?!"

"You don't want to teach her, that's your right," said Thomas. "But you should have let her walk out of here with some dignity."

"I do not train girls to be killers, and I will not have them give themselves false airs when they come in my gymnasium!"

"False airs?" Thomas did explode. "Eileen saved my life and helped stop a war! And when she tries to thank you for helping her learn, you say she's taking false airs? Apologize to her!"

The Fencing Master's bald head was growing brighter red. "I will not."

Thomas stared, unbelieving, at the man. For the last five years Thomas had studied with Master Brennan. Thomas had gone from knowing nothing to being one of the best fencers at the Academy. He'd loved every minute of it. *But he shouldn't do that to Eileen.* "Please, Eileen's as good as half the students here, and she wants to be better. She needs you to teach her."

"No. Now get back in line."

"No," said Thomas. "If you won't teach Eileen, I don't want to learn from you." Thomas turned his back on the Fencing Master without saluting and walked away, tossing his sword to one of the other students.

Thomas half-expected the Fencing Master to challenge him or try to call him back, but the man said nothing. Thomas grabbed his robe and cloak and ran out of the door without putting them on. He spotted Eileen, struggling into her clothes and cloak as she walked across the grounds. "Eileen, wait!"

Eileen spun around, horrified. "What are you doing, you idiot? Get back to class!"

Thomas pulled up to a halt in front of her. "Too late." He threw on his coat and started on the robe.

"What do you mean, too late?" Eileen demanded, doing up her own robe.

Thomas started on his buttons. "I told him to apologize for not letting you salute. He wouldn't apologize and he wouldn't teach you, so I walked out."

"That is stupid!" Eileen said, stomping her foot. "You love fencing! You're great at it! You can't just leave the class!"

"Already did," said Thomas. His heart sunk at the idea. *I really liked that class, too.* "He should have let you salute."

"It's not that important!"

"It *is* that important! We knew not every professor was going to accept you into his class when you became a girl. I hoped he'd do better but..."

"Professor Dodds."

"What?" Thomas was confused.

Eileen looked at the ground. "Professor Dodds was the only one to let me into class," said Eileen. "The mathematics professor stopped me at the door and told me I could not come in. The history professor..." Eileen looked away, crossing her wet arms in front of her. "He waited until the room was full then announced that he would not begin class until I left."

Thomas took her cloak from her and wrapped it around her shoulders. "I'm sorry."

Eileen shrugged. "Professor Dodds said my opinion was as informed as anyone else's so why shouldn't I participate? And the class was fine until Keith started making his stupid remarks. Then everyone started shouting and it all got out of hand."

Thomas squeezed her shoulder. "Fencing was my last one for today. Let's go someplace warm and get lunch."

"Your place," said Eileen. "I don't want to be out around people and I can't face George right now."

"My place it is," said Thomas. "We'll get some food on the way."

They left the Academy and went into the city. The rain was still coming down, bringing with it a sneaking chill that crept under their clothes and left them shivering.

"Is this what it's going to be like, Thomas?" Eileen asked. "Am I going to have to put up with this all the time?"

"I don't know," said Thomas. "I hope not."

"Even if they let me in there'll be professors who don't want to teach me, won't there?"

"Probably," said Thomas. "But they'll have no choice."

Eileen sighed again. "Oh, Thomas, what have I gotten myself into?"

Thomas didn't have a good answer, so he wrapped an arm around her shoulder and kissed the top of her head. Eileen leaned into him and let him lead her through the streets.

There was a market square just past Thomas's apartment. It was small compared to the one near Eileen's house, but there was a baker there and a wine-seller, and that would do well enough for lunch. They'd nearly reached the apartment when Thomas realized that the man in the blue cloak was following again. After the third time Thomas glanced behind them, Eileen asked, "What are you looking for?"

"There's a man following us," said Thomas. "Same one we saw last night."

"You didn't tell me you'd been followed last night!"

"I didn't told you anything about last night," said Thomas.

"You should have!"

"I haven't really had the time," said Thomas, with some annoyance.

Eileen looked back. "Where is he?"

After another quick glance, Thomas said, "Half a block back. Blue cloak, green coat. Just passing the green door. On the far side of the street."

Eileen looked back again. "I see him." She shook her head. "He doesn't look that dangerous."

"He doesn't need to be dangerous," said Thomas. "He needs to be inconspicuous."

"Well, he's good at that," said Eileen. "Who do you think he is?"

"I think he works for the Church," Thomas said. "Henry said it was that or the king, keeping tabs on me. Either way we should just leave him alone."

Eileen grimaced. "I don't like the idea of being followed."

"Me, either," said Thomas. 'But there's nothing we can do, so..."

The man stayed behind them while they shopped their way through the square. One shop yielded a basket, another a bottle of wine. From a third they bought meat pies and fruit tarts. All went into the basket and under Eileen's robe to keep dry as they walked the slick, cobbled streets to Thomas and Henry's apartment.

"This is the first time you've been here without George," Thomas said as he unlocked and opened the apartment door. "I just realized."

"Not worried about my reputation right now," said Eileen, stepping inside. "And no one around here will tell anyone anyway. Is he still there?"

Thomas looked back one more time. He nearly missed the man standing in a doorway across the street, so still that he seemed to fade into the shadows. "He is. And he can stay there for all I care. Hope he catches cold."

"Me, too."

A horse whinnied from nearby, and hooves clopped on the cobbled streets. A moment later a team of four matched brown horses pulled a long, green carriage into the square. It had the emblem of the High Father embossed on the door. Two men sat on the front bench—one carrying a carrying a crossbow and sword, the other driving. Two more guards were on the back, swords at their sides.

Thomas swore under his breath.

"What is it?" Eileen asked, looking out. She saw the carriage and let out a pair of choice words of her own. Together they watched the carriage pull to a halt directly in front of Thomas's apartment. The guards at the rear stepped down, opened the door, and brought out a step for whoever was inside.

"Are they here to arrest you?" asked Eileen.

"I don't think so," said Thomas. "They would have sent guards, not whoever..."

The guard held out a hand and assisted Father Alphonse to step down. Thomas's breath stopped. He tried to take another, but it didn't want to come. His stomach roiled, and he had to will himself to stay still instead of running inside and locking the door.

"Ah, Thomas," said Father Alphonse, smiling. "So glad you are home. There's someone who wishes to speak with you."

Thomas could only stare as the Inquisitor stepped aside. Archbishop Culverton stepped down from the carriage, patted Father Alphonse on the shoulder and headed up Thomas's stairs.

7

The two guards followed the Archbishop up the stairs and stood behind him. Archbishop Culverton smiled at Thomas. "Thomas Flarety. I hope this time is not inconvenient?"

"Uhhh... No, your Grace," said Thomas, stepping back from the door. "How did you...? I'm not usually home."

"We had a man watching the Academy," said the Archbishop. Thomas's eyes went to the man in the blue cloak, still standing in the doorway across the street. The Archbishop chuckled. "Oh, he didn't follow you. The king made it quite clear he wouldn't want that."

"Of course," said Thomas. *Then who is he working for?*

After a moment's wait, the Archbishop said gently, "Will you be inviting me in? It would be much more pleasant than talking in the streets."

"We could invite Thomas to join us in your carriage," said Father Alphonse, "if that would be more comfortable."

"I think not," said the Archbishop. "It may be mistaken for us taking Thomas into custody, and the king has made his opinion on that matter quite clear as well."

Thomas finally gathered enough wits to say, "My apologies, your Grace. Please, come in." Thomas stepped back and held the door wide. "And forgive the poor surroundings."

"Hardly poor," said Archbishop Culverton. "Most students don't have nearly so lavish accommodations."

"Most students don't share their homes with the heir of the Duchy of Frostmire," said Father Alphonse, following the Archbishop. Thomas dearly wished to slam the door on the man's face, Instead he held it open and waited for Father Alphonse to limp inside. The two guards took up positions on either side of the door as Thomas closed it.

"We..." Eileen's voice came out as a squeak. She swallowed, curtsied and tried again. "We have only just arrived. If your Grace will excuse me, I will make up the fire and prepare some tea."

"Of course, my dear," said the Archbishop. He removed his cloak—made of very expensive wool, lined with silk, and embroidered with gold trim—and handed it to Thomas who hung it very carefully on a hook. The cloak was easily worth as much as their month's rent.

"I will keep mine on, if that is all right," said Father Alphonse. "I find that, since my visit to Frostmire, I do not deal with the cold so well as before."

"Please have a seat, your Grace," said Thomas, indicating his chair. The Archbishop nodded his thanks and sat.

"I will have the fire in a moment," said Eileen. It took longer than it should have from her hands shaking, but she managed to pile the tinder and logs in the fireplace and coax small, bright sparks out of the flint and steel. Some of the tinder caught, an Eileen breathed gently on it and slowly added more until a blaze flickered in the fireplace. She positioned a log where it would catch without smothering the fire and rose to her feet. "I'll get water for the tea."

"Thank you," said Thomas. "Let me take your cloak."

She handed it over and practically fled the room. Thomas hung it on the hook, then hung his own beside it and sat down in the middle of the couch. Father Alphonse took the other chair, and again the room fell into silence. The Archbishop looked serene, Father Alphonse was smiling, and Thomas fought to calm his heart and keep his hands from clenching into white-knuckled fists.

No one spoke until Eileen returned from the kitchen. "The fire is made and the kettle on," she said. "We will have tea shortly."

"Thank you, my dear," said the Archbishop. "Please join us."

Thomas made room on the couch and Eileen sat beside him. The Archbishop smiled at the fire and held out his hands. "A good fire is wonderful thing," he said. "Especially on days such as these, when older bones ache." He leaned back in the chair and looked into Thomas's eyes. "Now tell me, Thomas Flarety, why did Henry Antonius call you north?"

"The Duchy of Frostmire was under attack," said Thomas.

"By raiders throwing fog and fire," said the Archbishop. "Hardly a fitting place for a student."

"Unless the student has experience, your Grace," said Father Alphonse. "What experience do you have with such things, Thomas?"

Thomas's eyes narrowed. He had no idea how to talk to the Archbishop, but the Inquisitor was another matter. "Malloy."

"Bishop Malloy." The Archbishop sighed and leaned back in his chair. "Malloy was misguided. He believed that he could cure those who possessed witchcraft. I witnessed it for myself, and it did work, but the cost was rather high."

Thomas remembered the burning pain in his chest when Malloy had sought to steal his magic. "Bishop Malloy tore people's souls apart so he could gain more magic for himself."

"He removed the witchcraft from people," said the Archbishop. "If doing so destroyed part of their souls, then that is the price they have to pay for trafficking with the Banished."

None of them trafficked with the Banished. "And the little boy Malloy murdered? What was he paying for?"

"Bishop Malloy had no witchcraft," said Father Alphonse. "He merely had a way of curing those who used it. And in doing so, he fell prey to the Banished, which led to the most unfortunate death of the child." He turned to Eileen. "And how about you, my dear? Why did you go north?"

"Because you threatened to arrest me for being Thomas's friend," said Eileen.

Alphonse smiled slightly. "A threat that would not have been necessary, had Thomas spoken the truth under question."

"I spoke the truth," Thomas snapped. *Temper is weakness,* he could hear the Master of Laws intone in his head. *Keep your head and you won't be stupid.* He forced himself to sound as calm as possible. "And it was illegal for you to question me in the first place."

"We answer to a higher law," said the Inquisitor.

"I don't," said Thomas.

"All men do."

"Enough." The Archbishop's tone was mild, but Father Alphonse fell silent. "You must forgive our Chief Inquisitor," said the Archbishop. "He is zealous in his beliefs."

Chief Inquisitor? Thomas looked over the little man in surprise. Father Alphonse smiled back at him. *No wonder the Church got him back from Sir John.*

The Archbishop leaned forward again. "You went north, and you faced raiders, and you used witchcraft to defeat them."

"No," said Thomas.

The Archbishop's eyebrow went up. "You went north?"

"Yes."

"You fought the raiders?"

"Yes."

"You used witchcraft?"

"No."

"You threw lightning at them," said Father Alphonse. "Just as you did at Bishop Malloy's house to kill his guards." Thomas felt his mouth go dry. Father Alphonse's smiled at his shock. "Bishop Malloy's chapel and house were burned," the Archbishop continued, "as were many of his guards. Once we heard what you did in Frostmire, it was the obvious conclusion."

"Did you throw lightning, Thomas?" asked the Archbishop.

Thomas fell silent.

"Do you not have an answer?"

Thomas's mind raced, searching for some way out.

"I want you to understand what is at stake here, Thomas," said the Archbishop. "I want you to understand why I've come to you, rather than just sending Father Alphonse, or having you arrested. The Banished are powerful and wicked, and they can tempt a man beyond all reason. Look what happened to Bishop Malloy. Look what is happening in the south. For a young man such as yourself, these things may seem as games, but..."

"Games?" Thomas grabbed onto the word and let his anger pour out. "Bishop Malloy killed three of my friends. The raiders killed eight students. *I've* killed a score or more men. Eileen..." Suddenly he was in Frostmire, holding Eileen as she wept herself dry in his arms after the battle in the streets. Then he was in the caverns seeing the terrified, terrifying look on her face after she had burned the magician alive. Thomas's throat sealed itself with grief and horror. He closed his eyes and shook his head until it cleared. It was a long moment before he could say, "This last year has made us all into killers, your Grace. So kindly don't speak of *games*."

"My apologies," said the Archbishop, and his tone made Thomas believe he was sincere. "It has been a very difficult time for you," his eyes went to Eileen, "all of you—this last year. But you must understand that this is a very grave matter, and so I must ask you again: Did you throw lightning at the raiders?"

Thomas forced his anger and pain down; forced himself to *think*. "Your Grace knows I can't answer that question."

"Not answering proclaims your guilt as loudly as any answer you could give," said Father Alphonse.

"It does not," said Thomas, keeping his voice firm. "Any conclusions you make from my silence are based on your own suppositions, not evidence, and are therefore not a proclamation of my guilt."

The Archbishop smiled again. "You are studying law, indeed, Thomas Flarety."

"Yes, your Grace."

"Why did our men die in Frostmire?"

The change of topic caught Thomas off-guard and it took him a moment to gather wit enough to answer. "They were going for help. Lord Richard made a deal with your envoy, and asked him to go south for reinforcements. On their way, Richard had his knights and the raiders ambush them and slaughter them all." This time it was Thomas's turn to be sincere. "For what it is worth, I am sorry, your Grace. No one deserves to die like that."

"I thank you," said the Archbishop. "Can I prevail on you to give me more details on your part in the events in Frostmire, Thomas?"

Thomas shook his head. "Any words I say will be turned against me by Father Alphonse."

"Then let me speak plainly, Thomas Flarety." Archbishop Culverton paused, weighing his words. "There are things that are outside of those gifts which the High Father has bestowed upon his creations; things that are linked to the Banished and to those who have opposed the Church in the past. The stories that are going around of a hero who fought fire and fog with lightning and steel; who healed the heir to Frostmire with the power of his touch alone; we cannot allow them to continue."

Thomas's mouth went dry. The Archbishop's words left a sick feeling in his stomach, like he was slipping over the edge of a pit.

"Your actions have left a mark of suspicion on you, Thomas Flarety," continued the Archbishop. "They have brought the eyes of the Church upon you, upon the Academy, and upon the king. It is the belief of Father Alphonse that you are practising witchcraft, and that you are directly engaged in activities that would undermine the authority of the High Father, and cast doubt into the minds of his followers."

The Archbishop put on a sad smile, like a loving parent gently chastising his child for errant behaviour. "I wish to believe that you are a good son of the Church," he raised a hand, as if to stop an expected interruption, though Thomas did not give it. "I know you are not a devout member, Thomas. I know that your life and mind is filled with the Academy and learning, and that you do not go regularly to chapel. But that does not mean that you have your heart set on destroying the High Father's Church. Only now, for the sake of the Church—and for the sake of the Academy—I must ask that you do more."

The Archbishop stopped. Thomas waited for him to finish, but the man stayed silent. Across the room, Father Alphonse was smiling again. At last Thomas asked, "What more?"

"We need you to publicly refute the Banished," said the Archbishop. "We need you to forsake their working and swear your loyalty to the High Father and his Church. In the Cathedral. And we need you to undertake such penance as we will give you, to show the strength of your loyalty."

Thomas felt his anger growing again, and heard it come out in his own voice despite his resolve to stay calm. "Why?"

It was Father Alphonse that answered. "Because, Thomas, if one who has witchcraft does good work, it does not mean that that one has not compromised his soul, or that that one will not spend an eternity being tortured at the hands of the Banished. We must show the people that the ways of witchcraft are the ways of the Banished, and the ways of damnation."

Thomas nodded slowly, while his mind raced. At last, he said, "Your Grace is very kind to come see me personally."

"This is important," said the Archbishop. "More important than you can realize."

Why? Thomas practically screamed, though the words never left his head. *Why am I so important? Why can't you just leave me alone?* "Does your Grace expect me to make a decision today?"

"It would be best if you did," said Father Alphonse. "The longer you wait, the greater grows the suspicion, and the more intently the Church must scrutinize you." His gaze shifted to Eileen for a long moment. "And all those around you."

"You would be able to return to your studies, once your penance is done," said the Archbishop. "And you would be able to do so with a clear conscience, knowing you have helped prevent other souls from straying as you have."

But I haven't strayed anywhere, Thomas thought. The magic was a part of him, and no amount of public penance would change that. He took a deep breath, and forced himself to sit up as straight as possible and look the Archbishop in the eye. "I am sorry, your Grace. I am afraid that I cannot."

"Cannot?" repeated the Archbishop, his eyebrows rising.

"I answer to the king," said Thomas. "Not to the High Father's Church."

"You risk your soul for your king?" demanded Father Alphonse.

Thomas ignored him. "I have never consorted with the Banished. I have not compromised my soul, and I will not do so now by lying." He forced a breath in, then another. "I believe the tea should be ready, if you would like a cup."

The Archbishop shook his head, and pulled himself slowly to his feet. "I am afraid not, Thomas Flarety. I have other appointments today, and I cannot stay. I do thank you for the warmth of your fire and for your time."

Thomas rose and fetched the Archbishop's cloak, and held it while the man put it on. When it was secure, the Archbishop held out his ring. Thomas bowed low and kissed it.

"There is time to change your mind," said Archbishop Culverton. "Not much time, but some. If you do, please come to me. Or even if you just wish to speak with me about this. I shall receive you at any hour, and I guarantee your safe entry and exit."

"I thank you," said Thomas, straightening. *But it's not going to happen.*

The Archbishop leaned on one of the guard's arms as he went down to the carriage. Father Alphonse took his time standing and walking to the door. He stopped in the doorway and watched the Archbishop descend.

"You're hiding, Thomas," Father Alphonse said. "You're hiding behind your king's robe while you consort with the Banished and accept their gifts of power."

Thomas had to actively restrain himself from throwing the man down the stairs. "The Archbishop awaits you, Father Alphonse."

"If I were you, I would come out of hiding quickly," the Chief Inquisitor said. "The kings of Criethe are not to be trusted in times like these. When the Archbishop's patience runs out, the king will not protect you." He looked back at Eileen. "Nor those you care about..."

If you hurt any of them, I will kill you, Thomas swore to himself, knowing anything he said out loud would come back to haunt him. He watched in silence as the Father Alphonse carefully limped down the stairs and got into the carriage. Thomas waited until the guards mounted and the carriage drove off before he closed the door. As soon as it was shut, Eileen ran to him and wrapped her arms around him. For a time they just stood there, gasping as if they'd both just run a race.

"You're shaking," said Eileen said.

"I know." Thomas gently pushed Eileen away and looked down at his hands. Rage rose up in him and he fought the urge to destroy something, anything, just to drive it out. "What in the name of the Four was that about? Why would the Archbishop come here? Why?" He pushed his fists hard against the sides of his head and squeezed his eyes shut. He made himself breathe slow and steady until he felt something close to normal. He let his hands drop to his sides and opened his eyes. Eileen was watching him, her own eyes wide.

"I'm all right, now," Thomas said.

"No, you're not," said Eileen. "You're... frightening. You look ready to commit murder."

"Well, that's true," said Thomas. His hands were still shaking. He tried putting on a smile, though he suspected it looked ghastly. "Today was supposed to be about you," he said. "We were supposed to have a nice, relaxing lunch and I was going to try to make you feel better." His laugh came out brittle and false. "So that didn't work out, did it?"

Eileen shook her head. "No." She tried a smile. "But we still haven't eaten yet."

"No," said Thomas. "No, we haven't. I'll get the food onto the stove."

They were curled up on the couch, staring into the fire when Henry came home two hours later. They'd manage to eat, but neither had much to say.

"Well, aren't you two cozy?" said Henry, stepping in the door and letting in a gust of cold, wet air. He saw the looks on their faces and frowned. "What's this about Eileen insulting the Fencing Master and walking out of the class?"

"I didn't insult him," said Eileen. "Thomas did."

"He insulted Eileen said Thomas. "He threw Eileen out and didn't let her salute, so I left without saluting him."

"Which is an insult."

"Not going to argue about it, Henry."

"All right," said Henry. "How were the rest of your classes?"

"No one except Professor Dodds let me into their classes," said Eileen. "You saw how that turned out."

Henry's eyes narrowed. "What else happened?"

"We had a visit," said Thomas, "from the Archbishop."

Henry hung up his cloak and sat down in his chair. He managed to sound almost calm when he said. "And what did the Archbishop want?"

"Me to confess my sins, renounce witchcraft and give my life over to the Church of the High Father," said Thomas. "Apparently, having someone using magic for good is bad for the Church."

"Interesting," said Henry. "Why didn't he arrest you?"

"Appearances," said Thomas. "I need to show that I'm a true son of the Church." He shook his head, trying to clear his mind. It didn't work at all. "I haven't the slightest idea what to do about this. The Archbishop. Here! Trying to convince me to change sides! Why would he do that?"

"No idea," said Henry. "What are you wearing to the party?"

Thomas's memory jolted. He groaned. "Oh, by the Four, I'd forgotten."

"Party?" said Eileen. "Whose party?"

"Malcolm Bright's," said Thomas. "The merchant on the beach. He's having a Festival of the Rains party tonight."

"And you're going?" Eileen sounded horrified "What about Cormac? And Anthony and Ethan? What if they're there?"

"They won't be," said Thomas. "Malcolm was appalled by them."

"Are you sure about that?" demanded Eileen. "What if he's on their side?"

"Then I'll find out when I get there," said Thomas. "Malcolm said it was a place I could meet people with 'similar interests.' He might have meant people who do magic. And that means I have to go."

Eileen frowned. "That's a pretty big might."

"I know," said Thomas. "But the king told me to find magicians, so I've got to keep looking."

"When does it start?"

Thomas pushed himself off the couch and went to his coat. He pulled the invitation out of the inside pocket. "It starts at the first bell of night," he said, reading it. "Four hours from now."

"Four hours?" Eileen jumped to her feet, appalled. "Why didn't you tell me sooner? I need to get dressed!"

"You?" Thomas shook his head. "It's dangerous. You shouldn't be..."

"Thomas, I have had a whole day of people saying 'shouldn't' to me," Eileen warned. "I am going to the party and I'm going to help you, so don't argue about it!" She ran to the door to grab her cloak. "I need to have a bath and get cleaned up before I can even think of changing. And so do the two of you! Get moving!"

8

In the next four hours, Thomas and Henry managed to escort Eileen home, get baths at a nearby bathhouse, get dry, and get dressed for the party. At Henry's suggestion, Thomas wore the black formal uniform Henry had commissioned for him in Frostmire. Henry, in contrast, was dressed in crimson from his cloak to his boots. Both wore their rapiers.

They arrived back at the forge with time to spare and stepped right into the middle of an argument.

"If you're so worried, why don't you come with us?" Eileen was demanding

"Because you're not going!" said George. "It's a stupid risk and I forbid it!"

"It's not!" Eileen shouted. "It's a *party.* What do you think is going to happen?"

"If it's just a party, why are you bringing the rapier?"

"Because I'm walking through the city at night, George, why do you think?"

"Well, it looks stupid with the dress!"

"Actually, I think it's rather dashing," said Henry. "How about you, Thomas?"

"It's..." Thomas swallowed, caught between Eileen's glare and George's glower. Eileen was wearing her fiery orange dress, and with the rapier in her hand looked at once dangerous, beautiful, exotic and strong. Thomas felt a warm flush crawling up his neck to his cheeks. He managed, "You look wonderful."

"She looks ridiculous," said George, "and she wouldn't have to wear it if you weren't dragging her into trouble again!"

"He's not *dragging* me!"

"No, he just leads the way and you come running after!"

Eileen turned her back on her brother. "George thinks it's stupid for me to go."

"It is stupid!" thundered George. He rounded on Thomas. "It's stupid to go looking for magicians with the Archbishop after you and it's even stupider to take Eileen with you!"

"Say it louder, George," snapped Thomas. "I don't think they heard you in Frostmire."

"Don't give me that!" George snarled back. "Eileen told me what happened this afternoon!"

"Then you know the Archbishop isn't going to do anything right away! He said I have time."

George rolled his eyes in exasperation. "And we've never known the Church to lie before, have we? What if they see you doing magic?"

"I won't be doing any magic!"

"Then how are you going to defend yourself?"

"The same way I am!" snapped Eileen. She pulled her coat on over her orange gown and started strapping her sword-belt over top of it. "Come with us, George. You have your clothes from Frostmire. You can get changed in no time and you can *come with us!*"

"I'll not!" said George, his jaw setting. "I'll not be doing this again!" He pointed a grease-stained finger at Eileen. "And you're not going either!"

"If you children are quite done," said Henry, "We have to go meet the others who 'know what it is to be blessed.'"

George's eyebrows went up. "What?"

Thomas sighed. "That's what Malcolm Bright said."

"And you're still going to his party?"

"Yes."

"Well, Eileen isn't!"

"Eileen is already gone," said Eileen as she stomped toward the door. "And if you want to make a scene in the street you try and stop me!"

George stood, bright red and fuming beside his anvil.

"I'll take care of her, George," said Thomas, going after her. "I promise."

"And a lot of good your promises do," George growled. Thomas bit the inside of his cheek and kept walking. Henry was on his heels a moment later. It was a good half-block before any of them dared look back. When Thomas finally did he saw George standing in his doorway, watching them until they turned a corner out of sight.

"By the Four, he's a brick sometimes," growled Eileen.

"He wants you safe," said Thomas. "He's just worried."

"Well, I'd be a sight safer with him here, wouldn't I?"

Eileen stewed about it for the rest of the walk.

The streets were filled with people coming home for the night, and none paid them much attention to the three save to glance at their swords and keep out of their way. Thomas, Eileen and Henry walked around the city walls and to a neighbourhood with clean cobblestone streets and large, comfortable houses near the western gates. It had close access to the warehouses and docks that probably brought most of the men's wealth to them.

When they reached Malcolm's house, Thomas stopped in the street, staring at it. He pulled out the invitation and double-checked it. "This is it."

Eileen stared. "*This?*"

"That's what the invitation says."

"The invitation lies," said Henry. "This isn't a house. It's a palace."

Thomas couldn't argue with that. The house took up most of the block. Every window—and it had many—was large, glassed, and elegantly shaped. Instead of wood-framed stucco, the walls were made of precisely cut and mortared stone. The front door was deeply inset into the wall half a block away, with a torch and a man in bright green livery on either side of it. High above the door, the roof sloped sharply upward to a single tower. *No doubt for Merchant Bright to watch his ships coming into the harbour.*

They walked to the door and one of the men stepped forward. "This is a private party," he said, looking with distaste at their rapiers. He stopped when he reached Eileen, stared hard a moment, and then looked scandalized. "Not for troublemakers."

"We're guests," said Thomas, holding out his invitation. The man took it and squinted closely as if hoping to find some proof of forgery. The expression of distaste stayed on his face, but he said, "You'll find a cloakroom on the right, then the banquet hall further down."

"Thank you."

The hallway was bright with candles whose friendly, warm yellow glow helped fight off the cool of the evening. At the cloakroom they gave a serving girl their cloaks and coats. Her eyes went wide at the sight of their swords.

"I take it no one else came armed, then?" asked Henry.

"No, sir," said the girl.

Which is good, thought Thomas. *Unless she's lying, which she might be.*

"Then we might as well leave the rapiers as well," said Henry, taking his off. "Will that be all right?"

"Yes, sir," squeaked the girl. She took the sword-belt, then Thomas's and Eileen's, and hung them on hooks. "They'll be safe here."

"Thank you," said Henry. "Is there supper?"

"A... a cold buffet, sir," said the girl.

"Good," said Eileen. "I'm starving.

At the banquet hall's ornate double doors, a middle-aged man in bright green livery stepped in front of the three of them. "Good evening," he said politely. "May I have your names and titles, so I may announce you?"

Henry stepped forward and rattled off a list that made Eileen's eyebrows go up and Thomas splutter in protest. The man bowed. "Very good, sir. I'll ask that you line up, in order of rank, if you please."

"Of course," said Thomas, stepping behind the other two. "Thought I don't think that last was necessary," he muttered to Henry.

Henry waved off his concerns. "You want to get attention, you enter with a splash. Now, everyone look impressive."

"Ladies and Gentlemen!" the servant's voice rose above the rumble of the crowd, and eyes around the room turned in his direction. "May I announce to you Lord Henry Antonius, brother and heir to Duke John Antonius, Captain of the Knights of the White Wolf, and protector of the city of Frostmire!"

Henry stepped through the doors and bowed low. There was polite applause and an excited buzz of conversation. He straightened up and smiled before stepping to the side. The buzz grew louder.

Well, he is the handsome one, thought Thomas.

"Miss Eileen Gobhann," called the servant, "sister to Sir George Gobhann of the Order of the White Wolf, and in her own right, Lieutenant of the Royal Academy's Expeditionary Company!"

The buzz in the room grew louder at that last bit. Eileen walked through the door and did a deep curtsey that would have made Lady Prellham, Eileen's guardian in Frostmire, very proud. She stepped off to the opposite side of Henry, waiting.

"Thomas Flarety, Captain of the Royal Academy's Expeditionary Company, and hero of the battle of Frostmire castle!"

Henry had to put in that last bit. Thomas stepped through the doors and nearly froze in surprise. The banquet hall was huge, with gold-gilt pillars rising up to a magnificently painted ceiling showing a beautiful girl dancing amid flowers and blooming plants, with artists, musicians, dancers and cheering crowds surrounded her on all sides. The walls of the room were painted with more murals, each with its own archway, as if the viewer were looking through a door to another world.

The room was filled with gaily-dressed men and women of every age, from younger than Eileen to old men and dowagers. In one corner a dozen musicians were playing a dance tune. There were easily a hundred people present, and all of them had stopped dancing, eating, talking and laughing to look at him.

Thomas, in his black uniform, felt like a crow among peacocks. He managed to keep walking forward, and bowed as low as Henry had.

The room broke into applause.

Thomas froze. Everyone in the room was smiling at him. He managed to bow again, and stepped to Eileen to offer her his arm. "Well, that's surprising," he muttered.

"Not at all," said Henry. "Everyone loves a hero."

"What about Eileen?" Thomas said. "Or you? You were there, too."

"Yes, but we're not the ones trying to find magic," said Henry.

Thomas looked over the crowd and sighed.

"At least we'll get to dance," said Eileen, squeezing his arm.

Thomas smiled at her. "And without a hundred students treading on our toes."

"Is that our host, coming this way?" asked Henry.

"Yes," said Thomas. "Malcolm Bright."

"Who is the woman on his arm?" asked Eileen.

"I don't know her," said Thomas. "But I'm guessing his wife, which would make the young lady beside them his daughter."

Malcolm was dressed in sumptuous green, with gold lace trim along the sides of his knee-length jacket. The woman beside him had black hair, worn high, and a brown dress cunningly crafted of a dozen different shades, with gold woven through the fabric to make it shimmer as she walked. The girl with them was nearly as tall as Thomas. She was sturdy and buxom with a mass of black curls on her head. She was wearing a dark lime-green gown with a plunging neckline. The dress clung to her curves, and the high waist emphasized the length of her legs. Her curly hair was interlaced with a gold chain and her brown eyes sparkled as she walked towards them.

"Wow," said Eileen. "That girl is... wow."

"She's not as beautiful as you," said Thomas.

"Oh, yes, she is," Eileen said. "And then some."

Malcolm arrived in front of them and held out a hand to Thomas. "So good of you to come. And to bring your fair lady with you!" He took Eileen's hand and bent over it. "You are as beautiful as your description."

"My what?" said Eileen, startled.

"The three young men who came south with my ship," Malcolm said, almost apologetically. "They spoke of you as a fiery beauty, I believe. And now I can see why. Though they did not mention you were with the Academy's Expeditionary Company."

"Eileen fought beside Thomas in the battle for Frostmire," said Henry.

"Really?" said the girl, breathlessly. "Wonderful!"

"And led the rescue when I was taken prisoner," said Thomas. "Without her I wouldn't be here."

"Henry led the rescue," said Eileen. "I was just first into the caverns."

"And we could not have succeeded without you," said Henry.

"Yes, well..." Eileen shook her head and forced a smile. "I thank you for the kind words, Merchant Bright."

"Please, call me Malcolm," he said. "And let me introduce my own beautiful lady, Delores Bright." Thomas bowed low over her hand. Henry bowed lower and smiled at her. Delores laughed at him and turned to Thomas. "Hero of the battle of Frostmire castle?"

Thomas shook his head. "I believe Henry put him up to that."

"Of course I did," said Henry. He smiled at the girl. "And who is this charming young lady?"

The young lady in question blushed. Malcolm smiled. "This is my daughter, Claudine Bright. Claudine, may I introduce Lord Henry Antonius, Miss Eileen Gobhann, and Thomas Flarety."

Claudine curtsied, revealing some rather impressive cleavage. "I love your dress," Claudine said to Eileen. "How did you manage to fight the raiders in Frostmire? Didn't people try to stop you?"

"I was dressed as a boy," said Eileen. "Most people thought I was part of the Student Company."

Claudine's mouth dropped opened in surprise. "I haven't been able to pass for a boy since I was twelve! And you rescued Thomas?"

"I was part of the rescue," said Eileen, her voice catching just a little. The smile on her face faded a bit. "I didn't do it all by myself."

Claudine frowned and looked concerned. "Was it so bad?"

"Yes."

"Oh." Claudine bit her lip a moment, then put on a fresh smile. "Then let's talk about better things," she said. "Is it true you danced with Thomas at the Duke's ball? And that Thomas was challenged to duels because of you?"

"Claudine!" Delores sounded at once appalled and amused.

"Please accept my apologies," said Claudine. "I talk too much sometimes."

"So does Eileen," said Henry. "In fact, I have heard her speak for five minutes straight without taking a breath."

"You have not," protested Eileen.

"I was there when you argued Beudlean philosophy with James."

"He was wrong!"

"You study philosophy?" said Claudine, her eyes lighting up, "Then you must come up and see my books. Who is your favourite philosopher?"

"Later, Claudine," said her father, laughing. "Let our guests have some refreshments and dance before you drag poor Miss Gobhann off to look at old books."

"I like old books," said Eileen. She smiled at Claudine. "Call me Eileen, all right?"

"All right," said Claudine. "Father, may I introduce Eileen to my friends?"

"In a few minutes," said Malcolm. "Leave our guests alone until they have eaten."

"Oh, but she can't," protested Henry. "I have no one on my arm and I would hate to be the odd man out. Claudine, would you lead us to the buffet and give your recommendations?"

"Of course," said Claudine. She took Henry's offered arm and led them forward. "Most of the fruit is in preserves this time of year, of course, but our chef has done a wonderful job with his tarts."

For the next few hours it was a party much like any other. Thomas danced with Eileen, then with Claudine and several other girls. Henry danced with Claudine first. Both young men and Eileen were drawn into a variety of discussions, from their adventures in the north to how the war would affect the price of fur or steel, to the doings of the young men of the town and the Academy. Henry flowed smoothly from one conversation to the other. Thomas, who had been attending his father's parties since he was a child, knew enough about the ways of merchants to keep up his end of the conversation. Claudine stayed close by Eileen most of the evening, and several times took her away to introduce her to the other girls in the room.

"I trust you are having a good time, gentlemen, lady?" asked Malcolm after the second bell of the night. They had just finished a circle dance, amid much merriment and missteps, and now fresh glasses of wine were being handed out.

"A very good time," said Thomas. "You throw an excellent party."

"I thank you," said Malcolm, practically beaming with pride. "I have good friends and business associates, and the Festival gives me an excuse to entertain them. But now, do you think I could take you three away from the festivities for a short time? I promise we will return."

"Of course," said Thomas.

Malcolm led them to a parlour just off the main hall. It, too, was sumptuous, though on a smaller scale. It ran the width of the building and while it had only three thin, high windows on the street side of it, the other side was almost entirely made up of one large window that gave view onto a pretty courtyard with a garden in the middle of it. The walls were painted in elegant murals depicting men and women dancing and laughing and sharing food. The high ceiling boasted an image of the same beautiful young woman from the banquet hall. Here she spread rose petals over a host of smiling men and women. The furniture matched the walls; green and red and gold fabrics with embroidered flowers decorated the overstuffed chairs and footstools. Everything was done in the most modern fashion possible, and at an expense that made Thomas almost fearful to touch anything.

"Please, sit," said Malcolm, when Claudine burst into the room. Malcolm's eyebrows went up. "I don't recall inviting you, my dear."

Claudine blushed. "Apologies, father." She curtsied to Thomas and Henry. "And apologies to you, too." She stayed low in the curtsey, giving Thomas and Henry an excellent view, and looked up at them through long brown eyelashes. "Would you permit me to stay for your conversation?"

"Of course," said Henry before Malcolm could open his mouth. Henry held out a hand and helped Claudine to rise. "Your presence will brighten up the room."

"Oh, thank you," said Claudine. "Miss Eileen, may I sit beside you?"

"Please," said Eileen, whose eyes were on Henry. "It's probably the best place."

Eileen and Claudine took one couch, with Henry and Thomas flanking them in chairs on either end. Malcolm took the other couch and beamed at them all.

"Let me once more apologize for those three young men yesterday morning." Malcolm said. "Had I known they were going to behave that way I would have never led them to the beach."

"My father told me about their manners," said Claudine. "I cannot believe they would spoil the Festival like that. Do you not have the same rules for it in the north?"

"The Festival of Rains isn't celebrated in Frostmire," said Henry to Claudine. "At this point there are still two months of winter. Calling for rain is viewed as wishful thinking."

Claudine smiled at him. "Too bad. It works."

Henry smiled back. "Now, do you really believe that?"

"It does seem to work," said Malcolm, gesturing out the windows. "For we certainly are getting the rain, despite yesterday's sun."

"We are in a port town," said Henry. "Rain is its natural state."

Malcolm smiled. "But still, one must think that the will of all those people must account for something."

"Not really, no."

"I take it you do think that," said Thomas, resisting the urge to kick Henry.

Malcolm smiled. "It is clear that the will of man may cause change in the natural order of things. Look at your experiences in Frostmire. Surely what you saw there was not what one could call a natural occurrence."

"A son killing his father for his money and power?" said Henry, his voice neutral. "Happens all the time."

"The magic, Lord Henry," said Malcolm. "Surely you must admit that was not of nature as we know it."

"We did see things we have never seen before," Thomas said. "That doesn't mean they're not natural."

"Was there really magic?" Claudine asked Eileen. "Did you see it?"

Eileen looked uncertain of how to answer. Thomas spoke up instead. "There was magic there and yes, Eileen saw it."

Claudine's eyes widened. "Are you sure?"

"We saw men using stone rods that threw fire, and wood rods that made fog," said Thomas. "And a man who drained the energy from my body to fuel their magic."

"Oh, no!" Claudine looked shocked. "Did it hurt?"

"It just made me feel weak," said Thomas, "as if I'd been struck ill."

"Amazing." Malcolm leaned back in his chair. "And what of the lightning?"

"What of the lightning?" Thomas repeated.

Malcolm's eyes narrowed. "The lords said that the captain of the Student Company fought the fire of the raiders by shooting lightning from his fingers."

"The lords were not present at any of the battles," said Thomas. "So their accounts are suspect."

"Even so," Malcolm leaned closer, "they said that in the street battles, the Church's troops and the students were ambushed by raiders who threw fire. And that the students killed both magicians with lightning."

"Actually, one of them was thrown out a window," said Henry. "By Eileen's brother, Sir George, in fact."

"Really?" Claudine was practically breathless with the thought of it.

"Really," said Eileen. She shuddered. "Thomas had to go in and get George out."

"What of the other magician?" asked Malcolm. "What happened to him?"

"He died," said Thomas.

Malcolm leaned back in his chair. "You are afraid to speak plainly," he said. "I understand. There are certainly forces working against magic in the world. But there all also forces working for it." He looked up at the ceiling. "I'm sure you know who she is?"

Thomas looked up at the ceiling. "It looks like the Blessed Daughter," Thomas said. "Giver of music, dance, and love."

"And magic."

Now Thomas was the one to lean forward with interest. "I have heard that before."

"Of course you have," Malcolm's eyes lit up. "It's uncommon knowledge, but some of us know the truth."

"And which some would those be?" asked Thomas.

"Those who know that there are things beyond what is taught at the Academy or in the churches of the High Father. Those who see things as they truly are."

"You're talking in riddles," said Henry.

"One tends to do that, when one talks of magic," said Malcolm, smiling. "Tonight, after the party, there is a special ceremony to the Blessed Daughter. Will you stay?"

"Of course," said Thomas.

"Then let's return to the party." Malcolm smiled. "I, for one, am not done dancing."

9

They had two more hours of dancing and conversation before the midnight bell sounded and guests began to leave. Malcolm and his wife saw them out, thanking them for coming. Thomas and Henry had their hands shaken by many young men, and Eileen was hugged and had her cheek kissed by many of the girls. The merchants and their wives and families headed out into the night, leaving only fifteen people in the room. Most were older, though there was a pair of young men—twins by the look of them—that stayed behind. Those two were watching Henry, who had Claudine on his arm, with a fair amount of suspicion.

"It is time," said Malcolm. "Let us take ourselves to the chamber."

There was a murmured agreement. Malcolm took the small group out the courtyard door, past the kitchen which still had wonderful smells wafting out of it and into the building on the other side. He led them upstairs to a smaller, sparsely furnished chamber. There were benches here, and a small, covered table in the front. The walls were decorated with murals of the forest, and against the far wall, an image of the Daughter smiled down at them. The guests took the benches and Malcolm went to the front to stand beside the table. Claudine sat herself down beside Eileen in the back, and Thomas and Henry took places on either side of the girls.

Malcolm smiled at the group and said, "Let me begin by thanking our guests. I hope that the party was pleasant, and I am deeply grateful that they joined us for this, our true purpose tonight."

The small group applauded lightly. Malcolm let it die down and continued, "Tonight, we mark the true end of the Festival of the Rains. For tonight is the night when the Blessed Daughter began to weep.

"It is said that the Great Mother was angered at how badly the people were using her creations. They would kill when there was no need, they would waste what they did not use immediately. For in those times there was always plenty and never hunger.

"And so the Mother called down the first snowfall. It blanketed the earth. The animals hid and the plants slept and food became scarce. Man, who was not ready for the winter, tried as best he could to survive, but he began starving, and many died.

"It was then that the Blessed Daughter came down to visit. She saw how unhappy man was. How miserable, bitterly cold, and how close to ruin he was. The sight of it made her weep. For a month she cried, and her tears washed away the snow, and the Mother relented and the summer returned. But, so man would not forget, every year the Mother makes winter return, and every spring, the Daughter weeps for us all.

"This winter, for the first time in two hundred years, we have proof that she has not wept in vain."

Malcolm Bright smiled at Thomas. "For the first time in nearly two hundred years, we have heard of Great Magic coming back into the world. We have heard of invaders that throw fog and fire, and of a friend whose lightning defended a northern duchy and drove off the invaders."

He held out his hand to Thomas. "Please, step forward, Thomas Flarety, Captain of the Student Company, and tell us what you saw and what you did in Frostmire."

"Now what?" asked Henry, his voice quiet.

"Now, I talk," muttered Thomas, rising from the bench.

"Better talk really fast."

Malcolm Bright took a spot on the front bench, and with the others, waited in what Thomas was sure was near-breathless anticipation.

Thomas reached the front and took a deep breath, unsure of where to start. He turned and looked over the small crowd. Claudine's eyes were wide, and the entire congregation seemed to be holding its breath in hope.

The king said I couldn't tell anyone about my magic. He didn't say anything about magic in general. "There is magic in this world. True magic." The small party practically bubbled with excitement. Whispers of "I knew it!" and "I told you!" went through the little room. Thomas waited until it quieted. "I have seen it. My friends have seen it. We have seen Great Magic, as Merchant Bright called it. It was created by stealing the magic of others, and used to cause harm and destruction." Several people in the room looked dismayed at that. Others looked downright angry.

"We have seen small magics as well," Thomas continued. "A person whose touch can heal; another who could make a ball of light appear. These small magics were not evil. They were not used to hurt or destroy. Rather, they were gifts."

"Gifts of the Daughter," said Malcolm, smiling now.

"Gifts," repeated Thomas, hoping Malcolm thought he was agreeing. "Gifts that should be nourished and cherished. Not falsely called witchcraft or declared evil by those who have no understanding of them. Nor stolen by those who want them for no other purpose than to gain power."

"Gifts should be shared," said Malcolm, rising to his feet. "Especially the gifts of the Daughter. Thomas, will you share your gifts with us?"

What? "I... I don't know what you mean."

"Your magic. Can you share your magic as the Blessed Daughter intended?"

"Uhhh..." Thomas looked back to Eileen and Henry. Eileen looked as confused as Thomas felt and Henry was looking speculative. "How does one do that?" Thomas asked. "How do you share magic?"

"It is in the Daughter's teachings," said Malcolm.

"Is it?" Thomas's ears perked up.

"It is," said Malcolm, his always-ready smile growing wide on his face. "All can partake of the Daughter's gifts, though the sharing. So I ask you again: will you share your gift with us?"

Thomas looked at the fifteen eager faces in the room. Claudine was practically bouncing in her chair. The others were looking on expectantly.

And I have to disappoint them. "I don't know you," said Thomas, trying to make his voice as gentle as he could. "I don't know any of you by name, save Malcolm and his family, and they I know only from tonight. I don't know who any of you are, what you do, or whom you serve. I don't even know if you are all true believers in the Daughter, or if one or two or all of you are working for the Bishop of the High Father." He paused for a moment, watching the accusation sink in. Everyone in the room looked outraged.

Of course, an agent of the Church would be perfectly capable of looking outraged, too.

Malcolm's smile almost masked his disappointment. He spread his hands. "Then we have a problem," he said. "Is it an insurmountable one?"

He really wants this. "I don't know," said Thomas. "It requires some thinking."

"Then let us call an end of discussions for now," said Malcolm. He turned to his congregation. "I will ask all of you to respect Thomas's wishes, and not enquire further tonight. Let us instead complete our rituals, in which all are welcome to partake," he nodded toward Henry and Eileen, then to Thomas. "Please, be seated."

Thomas went to the back and sat with his friends and Malcolm took the front. Malcolm led the group in a prayer to the Daughter, asking for her to bring in the coming spring. He sprinkled water on each person's head, as a reminder of the daughter's tears, shed for them all. Then he led the small congregation in a song whose lyrics Thomas had never heard before, but whose rhythm and tune was the same as one of the High Father's hymns. All the while Thomas could see the many glances shot his direction. None of them were friendly, though only one or two seemed outright hostile.

At last, Malcolm drew the service to a close with, "May the Daughter's blessings be upon us, her eyes watch over us, her arms protect us, and her heart guide us. Let us rejoice and leave this place."

He led them out and back down to the banquet hall, where the buffet had been refreshed.

"Please," he said. "Eat, relax, and enjoy. I shall return momentarily."

The members of the congregation nodded and thanked Malcolm. Then they went to the buffet without a word to Thomas, Henry or Eileen.

"Now what?" asked Eileen.

"Watch and wait," said Thomas. "See if anyone else reveals something."

Claudine turned back from the line to the buffet and swept over to Eileen. "I wanted to say that I *really* have enjoyed talking to you this evening."

Eileen blinked in surprise. "Thank you."

"Would it be all right for me to call on you sometime? I think we could be friends, and it would be wonderful to have someone to share books with."

"Yes," said Eileen, smiling. "I think I'd like that."

"May I borrow Thomas for just a moment?" Claudine asked. "I want to speak to him privately. And we'll only be over there," she pointed at a pillar on the far side of the room. "Do you mind?"

Eileen shot a look to Thomas then nodded. "Of course not."

"If you would be a gentleman, sir?" Claudine held out her hand to Thomas. Thomas took her hand in the crook of his arm and walked her across the room.

Claudine led him around the far side of the pillar. She was wearing the scent of lavender and some other flower that Thomas couldn't identify. She stepped very close to him and dropped her voice low "I wanted to tell you," she said, laying her hand on the lapel of his jacket, "that what you did was completely inexcusable." Thomas tried to step back, but her hand became a fist, trapping the fabric of his jacket inside. "Completely! You made a fool of him in front of everyone!"

"I didn't intend..."

"It doesn't matter what you intended!" Claudine hissed. "They were there to see magic! They were there to have some hope that maybe the Daughter is looking after us! That maybe the long persecution by the Church will end and we'll be able to meet in public again, and you ruined it!"

"I didn't do anything," Thomas protested.

"Exactly! You could have done something! You could have shown us something, and you did nothing!"

"And if did I show you something," said Thomas, "what would you show me?"

Claudine blinked in surprise. Her mouth opened, and just as Thomas realized what his words had sounded like, she reached up and slapped Thomas's face, the noise of it ringing through the ballroom. "You! You... you... If my father knew what you just asked, he'd have you thrown out of here by the ears! If you were lucky! He'd—"

"Not what he was asking," said Henry, right behind them. Claudine jumped and squealed as she spun around. "In fact, if he had asked for that, you would only need tell Eileen, and she would cut his ears off for you."

"True," said Eileen. She shook her head at Thomas. "For someone so good at flattery, you did that really badly."

"I had noticed," said Thomas, shaking his head to clear the spots from his eyes. "My apologies, Claudine. I was not referring to..."

"Your charms," finished Henry. "Though they are lovely."

"Oh," said Claudine, blushing at Henry. "I thought..."

"Thomas is far too much of a gentleman to do such a thing," said Henry, taking her hand and kissing it.

"Unlike Henry," said Eileen, taking Claudine's hand away. "Him, you have to watch out for."

"Here comes your father," said Henry. "Shall we pretend this never happened?"

Claudine raised her nose and turned her back on Thomas. "I'm still angry at you." But she put a smile on her face and took Henry's arm. Malcolm strode across the floor with his wife at his side and a book in his hands. His congregation saw him and gathered around until they were surrounding Thomas and his friends.

"Here, Thomas," said Malcolm. "Look."

He held out the book. It was plain, with a faded green leather cover. There might have been letters painted on the front of it once, but they had long since faded or rubbed off, leaving only a few traces. Thomas took it, feeling how brittle the leather had become. He opened it slowly, listening to the binding crackle. On the first page inside, the title read: "The Teachings of the Daughter."

"Interesting," said Thomas. He turned the page, then more pages. The first section described the Daughter's cult and their rituals, all of which, on a quick skim, seemed benign enough.

"Go to the middle of the book," said Delores. Thomas did, and found page after page of poetry and spells.

"Anything?" said Eileen, which made Claudine look sharply at her, then at Thomas.

"It is the first book I have found that contains the spells the Daughter's priests used to strengthen their followers," said Malcolm. "It was what gave the Daughter's church the strength to resist so long against the Church of the High Father."

Thomas flipped through the pages. Not a single one of the spells in the book glowed. He sighed and handed them back. "These aren't magic."

"They are," said Delores, putting a hand on Thomas's arm. "All you have to do is read it aloud."

"And believe," said Malcolm. "It is belief in the Daughter that brings magic."

"Please," said Claudine, her voice eager, though Thomas could see her anger in the tightness around her eyes. "Please read it?"

Thomas looked for a way to say *this won't work* without further upsetting Claudine. He held the book out to Malcolm. "You believe in the Daughter. How many of these have you managed to make work?"

The silence in the room spoke volumes.

Thomas nodded. "So belief in the Daughter isn't the only thing that's necessary."

"I..." Malcolm looked worried. "I know those young lords were not to be trusted. But I heard the words of the Archbishop. What he calls witchcraft, we know is magic. What I don't know is why you won't share it with us."

"Maybe he doesn't have any," suggested one of the acolytes.

"Maybe he's a coward," said Claudine. Her eyes widened with a sudden thought and she turned quickly to Eileen. "Please don't let anything I say about Thomas get in the way of our being friends. You seem very nice and I *would* like to exchange books with you, if I could."

Eileen did a fairly decent job of keeping a straight face and said, "Of course."

"Have any of you done magic?" asked Thomas. "Ever?"

The silence was deeper this time, and no one in the congregation would meet his eye.

"No," said Malcolm. "No one here has ever done magic."

Well, now I know. "Thank you, Merchant Bright," said Thomas. "We should probably take our leave now. Classes begin early."

A look of terrible upset passed over Malcolm's face so quickly that Thomas thought he might have imagined it. "Of course," said Malcolm, taking his arm and walking him to the buffet. "But do help yourselves to the food before you go. I know students are always hungry, and the pastries will make an excellent breakfast." His voice lowered. "And, if you don't mind, I would like to speak to you more about this."

What more is there to say? Thomas wondered. "I am at the Academy most days, and can always be reached through there."

They helped themselves to the pastries, with Claudine making suggestions to Henry and Eileen and pointedly ignoring Thomas. When they each had a handkerchief full, Malcolm escorted them from the hall and helped them into their cloaks and coats. His eyes widened when all three strapped on the belts with the rapiers and daggers.

"I am sorry we could not find common ground," said Malcolm, still wearing his smile. "But I have faith that we will soon enough."

"I am sorry as well," said Thomas.

"Thank you, Eileen," said Claudine, "for a delightful evening. May I hug you?" Even before Eileen could say yes, Claudine had pulled her into an embrace. "And you, Lord Henry. I hope I may see both of you again, soon." She held up her hand and Henry bent over it, giving it a gentle, lingering kiss. Claudine went quite red but managed a deep curtsey for him. "And Thomas?" She held out her hand. Thomas took it and Claudine pulled him in closer to whisper. "I should have hit you harder."

She stepped back. "Good night, all. See you soon."

Thomas, Henry and Eileen stepped out into the street. The big doors closed behind them, shutting out the warmth and light of the hallway. Thomas sighed. "So, that was a waste of time, then."

"Oh, I don't know," said Henry. "The pastries are lovely."

"We got to dance," said Eileen. "And Claudine seemed nice."

"She said she should have hit me harder," grumbled Thomas.

"And so she should have," said Eileen. "I would have clubbed you senseless. But she does want to drop by and it would be nice to see another girl once in a while."

"And Malcolm Bright wants to talk to you again," said Henry. "Maybe he knows something more."

"Maybe," agreed Thomas, *but probably not*. The wind had picked up, blowing cold wet air from the sea directly into the neck of Thomas's cloak. He sighed and pulled his hood up over his head. "Let's get home."

The walk was cold and damp and by the time it was done, Thomas was stumbling tired. He tripped once over a cobblestone and only having Eileen on his arm kept him from falling. He muttered an embarrassed apology and forced himself to pay better attention for the rest of the walk. When they reached Eileen's house, they saw a candle burning in the kitchen window above the forge.

"George is awake," said Eileen.

"Not surprising," said Thomas. "Hope he's not pacing the floor, waiting."

"Knowing him, probably," said Eileen. She looked at the window and sighed. Thomas put his arm around her and pulled her close. She leaned against him.

"I'm sorry things didn't work out like you wanted," said Eileen.

"It was too much to hope for," said Thomas. "I should have known it wasn't going to be that easy."

Eileen managed a smile. "At least we got to go dancing."

Thomas found himself smiling back. "Aye, we did."

"And we got breakfast out of it," said Henry. He patted Eileen on the shoulder. "And now, I'm going to go look at that very fascinating patch of wall over there. I can't tell in the dark, but I think there are posters on it."

"We should both go," said Thomas. "We've all got class and..."

"Don't be stupid, Thomas," said Henry. "Kiss her. And hurry up about it. It's cold."

"You're actually a nice person, Henry Antonius," said Eileen. "When you want to be."

"I know," said Henry, over his shoulder. "Don't take too long!"

They didn't, though what time they did take was exceedingly pleasant. When their lips parted Eileen sighed and leaned her head against Thomas's chest. "We really need to spend some time together," she said. "Though the Four knows when."

"Not tonight, apparently," said Henry, right beside them.

"You were supposed to be by the wall!" said Eileen, reaching out to smack him.

Henry caught her hand. "I was. And now you need to be there, too. Thomas, we need some light."

Mystified, Thomas and Eileen followed Henry to a pair of posters on the wall. Eileen looked close. "What does that say?"

Thomas scanned the street. There was no sign of anyone. With a thought he brought a ball of light to life in his hands. He made it small, and the same colour as a candle, in case anyone saw it. He held it up and for the first time all three got a good look at the posters.

The first showed a priest standing on the crushed, broken backs of two of the Banished. He held out his hand as though it were a shield, blocking fire thrown from the hands of a wart-covered, ugly woman wearing rags. Beneath them, the caption read, "The High Father will destroy those who work the will of the Banished!"

The second one showed the same wart-covered, ugly woman dragging a crying girl in torn, dishevelled clothing by the hair toward one of the Banished. Both the woman and the Banished were leering in delight. It read, "Save your daughters from witches!"

It was a long time before anyone could say anything. At last Thomas managed, "Lousy drawing."

"It's printed," said Henry. "Not drawn. Which means they're probably doing hundreds of them."

"You think they're putting them up over the city?" asked Thomas.

"I would."

"They?" said Eileen. She looked at the priest in the picture. "The Church."

"Who else?" asked Thomas.

"But the Archbishop said we had time," Eileen protested. "He said so."

"He said *I* have time," Thomas replied. "This is more of what he was saying at the beach. It probably doesn't have anything to do with me."

"Except it's outside my brother's forge and he's going to be furious when he sees it!" Eileen dug at the paper with her fingernails, tearing a strip of it away from the wall. "George can't see these. Not first thing in the morning. He's already worried about his reputation."

"You're right." Thomas started on the second poster. "Let's hope they don't come back tonight."

Together Eileen and Thomas tore until there was nothing left but strips of paper pasted to the wall. Henry stood back, watching the streets as if he expected Church soldiers to ride up on them at any moment.

Afterward Eileen gave Thomas a long, hard hug. "You two be careful going home," she said as she went into the forge. "I don't want to lose you."

"I'm rather partial to not losing me also," said Henry, as Eileen shut the door. They listened until they heard her footsteps going up the stairs, and then headed for their apartment. "It's going to be a fun day tomorrow."

"Aye," said Thomas. *By the Four I'm tired.* "We should go armed, and tell the rest of the company to do the same. In case the Archbishop doesn't keep his promise."

"Good thought," said Henry. "What are you going to say to George?"

"I don't know, Henry," said Thomas, wearily. "Let's get some sleep and hopefully I'll think of something in the morning."

10

Someone banged hard on the apartment door, dragging Thomas out of sleep. The sky outside the window was dark, though not black, as if the sun was trying to shine but the clouds were refusing to let it through. Thomas sat up and pulled on his breeches as the banging continued. He grabbed his rapier and stumbled to the door. "Who is it?"

"King's messenger! Open in the name of the king!"

Thomas blinked a few times hoping to get his brain going. Henry came out of his room, looking annoyingly well rested and also holding his rapier. Thomas spared a moment to hate him and opened the front door. It was the same messenger who had escorted them to the palace, only this time he wore no livery. Instead, he held up a ring emblazoned with the king's seal. "Good morning, gentlemen," he said. "Thomas Flarety is to accompany me."

"Ugh," was Thomas's reply. "Give me time to get dressed."

"Quickly please," said the man. "And bring your rapier, if you would."

"I was planning on that last bit," muttered Thomas.

If the weather was anything to go by, Malcolm's prayers to the Daughter for rain were most emphatically being ignored. The temperature had dropped in the night and snowflakes were swirling in the air. The cobbles were slippery with ice and the footing treacherous. To Thomas's surprise, the messenger was on foot, and led Thomas *away* from the palace. Thomas, munching on leftover pastry as he walked, kept his cloak open at first, hoping the cold air would wake him up. Instead, he started shivering. He wrapped the cloak around himself and tried hard not complain.

The messenger stopped beside a small cluster of warehouses. "There," he said. "Up those stairs."

"Really?" said Thomas, not at all certain of what was happening. "I'm meeting his Majesty here?"

"You are," said the messenger. "In the hall above."

Hall? "All right, then." Thomas went up and knocked at the door. It was opened at once.

"Thomas!" said Sir Walter with a smile. "Excellent to see you. Come in."

On the other side of the door was a long, narrow fencing hall, with a high ceiling and windows dotting the length of it. Four braziers lined the space, and a fireplace was crackling in one wall. Practice blades, fencing jackets and masks lined one wall. Two men in livery were standing to one side while Sir Walter watched the king drilling by himself on the fencing floor. Guards were placed around the room. Thomas stared at it all, open-mouthed.

"Ah, Thomas," said the king. "Excellent. Come join me for a warm up, will you?"

Thomas took several moments before he gathered the wherewithal to say, "Of course, your Majesty."

One of the guards stepped between them and held out his hand. Thomas gave the man his weapons and hung his robe and cloak on a hook near the door. Another guard presented him with a fencing jacket and practice rapier. Thomas took them and shrugged into the jacket. "Whenever you are ready, your Majesty."

They ran through the parries and cuts and footwork, blades flashing the air and feet moving across the fencing floor, slowly at first, then faster and faster. "Excellent work," said the king after a quarter of an hour. He was sweating and breathing heavily. He stood up out of his fencing position. "They told me that you practised this way every day in Frostmire."

"Most every day."

"Fencing every morning is a good habit," said the king. "It used to be my habit, in fact, but that was many years ago. I'd given it up as I got busy with being king." He smiled at Thomas. "It is a very busy job, Thomas."

"I can only imagine, your Majesty," said Thomas, wondering where all this was leading.

"Fortunately, being king, one can also declare some time for oneself. How was Eileen's first day as a girl?"

"Rough," said Thomas. "Only one professor let her into class and a brawl broke out in it."

"Unfortunate. Do you think they'll change their minds?"

"They'll have to if we can get her accepted into the Academy," said Thomas.

"And do you think you can do that?"

"We're doing our best."

The king nodded. "And you walked out of fencing class yesterday."

"Your Majesty's knowledge is impressive," said Thomas, wondering who told on him.

"Insulting a fencing master is not wise, Thomas," said the king.

"Wisdom has been escaping me lately, your Majesty."

"That does happen to the young," said the king. "Gentlemen, if you would?"

The servants and guards bowed and left the room. When they were gone, the king asked, "How goes the search for magic, Thomas?"

"Not well, your Majesty," said Thomas. "We had no luck two nights ago at the docks, though we did stop a man from being beaten up. Last night I went to a merchant's party. He's a follower of the Daughter."

"There are several," said Sir Walter. "Which one did you speak with?"

"Malcolm Bright," said Thomas. "He invited me to attend his party so I could meet 'others who were similarly blessed.' Turns out he wanted me to share my magic with his congregation."

"And did you?" asked the king.

"I didn't show him any magic, your Majesty. But I don't think that's what he meant. He meant 'share,' as if I could give part of my magic to them."

The king's eyebrows rose. "Can you?"

Thomas shook his head. "I don't think so. Anyway, he told me none of his followers have magic."

"No luck at all, then," said the king. "What will you do, now?"

"I don't know, your Majesty," said Thomas. "Keep looking."

The king nodded. "Find them quickly, Thomas," he said. "I should like to know who the magicians are in my city sooner, rather than later."

"Yes, your Majesty." *And where am I supposed to look?*

"And how was your visit with the Archbishop?" asked Sir Walter.

Do they know everything that I do? "Nerve-wracking. He brought Father Alphonse with him."

"Interesting," said the king. "What did Culverton want to talk about?"

"My renouncing all witchcraft in the Cathedral on the High Father's day and accepting the penance the Church gives me so that others might not follow my bad example."

"I see." The king smiled. "I take it you did not?"

"No, your Majesty," said Thomas. "I told him I was under your command, not his."

"I assume he didn't like that."

"I think not," said Thomas. "Though he did invite me to speak with him at any time, and promised me safe return home if I did."

"Very interesting," said the king. "If he should come to see you again, do send me a message at once." He gestured to the hall around them. "Since you are no longer fencing at school, this is now your fencing hall. Sir Walter will be your instructor, and you come here every morning after the first bell. Do not be late."

"Uhhh... Yes, your Majesty."

"And now, if you will excuse me," the king went to the door. "Find me the magicians, Thomas. Quickly."

"Yes, your Majesty," said Thomas, bowing low. Once the king was gone, Thomas straightened and turned to Sir Walter. "I don't suppose you have an idea of where I could find some magicians?"

"None at all," said Sir Walter. "Now, let's see what you can do."

For the next hour, Thomas fenced, fought with daggers, and wrestled with Sir Walter. The man had a very different style than Thomas. Sir Walter moved soundlessly across the fencing floor, despite his heavy boots, and made Thomas practice to do the same. He showed Thomas how to kill a man from behind with a dagger and several ways to end an unarmed fight quickly whether one's opponent was armed or not. By the time Sir Walter called a stop, Thomas was both impressed and horrified.

"Time for you to be on your way," said Sir Walter, at last. "Keep an eye out in the streets. We'd like to know what the preachers are up to, as well."

"Yes, sir."

"If you have an urgent need to contact me, there is a stable near the Green Griffon. Ask for the stable-boy Percy and tell him you have a message for Merchant Gwilliam. I will meet you here as soon as possible."

"Yes, sir."

Thomas spent the walk home huddling in his cloak and wondering what he was going to do next. He had barely stepped through the door of the apartment when Henry pounced on him, demanding to know what had happened. Thomas grabbed his book bag and promised to answer when they got to Eileen's house.

George was actually wearing a shirt in deference to the cold and damp when they arrived at the smithy. He raised an eyebrow at them. "You lot came home late last night, didn't you?"

"But we did come home," said Henry. "I'd have thought you'd be pleased."

"You didn't have to wake Eileen," George pulled a long piece of steel—a wheel-iron—from the forge and began shaping it on the anvil.

"It wasn't that hard," Eileen said, coming down the stairs. She was dressed to go, and had her rapier at her side. She also had dark circles under her eyes, and her face was red and blotchy, like she'd been crying.

"I take it you told him about the posters," said Henry.

"Yes," said Eileen, glaring at her brother.

George kept pounding on the wheel-iron, his face bright red with heat and anger.

Thomas stepped closer to George, ignoring the heat from the forge. "I'm sorry. I didn't know the Church was going to do that."

George's hammer came down wrong and with such force that it bent the steel in the wrong direction. In disgust, George shoved the wheel-iron back into the coals.

"If it was up to me, I'd take her home to Elmvale," said George, "where she'd be safe instead of sending her out with you lot."

"It's not up to you," snapped Eileen. "It's up to me!"

"Not that she'd listen," said George, as if Eileen had not spoken at all. "She never listens. Not to me, not to Mother and Father back home, never!"

"Mother and Father have nothing to do with this!" shouted Eileen, "And don't you dare tell them!"

"I'm not going to tell them!" George tossed his hammer onto his workbench and glared down at his sister. "I'll not have them worried to death like when you ran away! But I'll not have anything happen to you, either!"

"Nothing will happen to me!" Eileen stomped her foot in frustration. "I'm not stopping just because of a stupid poster."

"It's not just the posters! Those stupid lords were here as well!"

"What?" Thomas, Eileen and Henry chorused.

"They came marching down the street as cool as you please, right up to my forge!"

"By the Four," said Eileen. "Why didn't you say something?"

"When have I had the chance?" George picked up the wheel-iron in his tongs, looked it over and shoved it back into the forge. "They stood outside the doorway, talking loud enough for the whole street to hear. Said how nice the place was, and how well I must have made out by helping kill Lord Richard. And what a wonderful, charming, friendly girl my sister was. And how much they had enjoyed her company in Frostmire!"

Eileen went white. "I'll kill them."

"Well, you can't," said George. "Because when I told them to go away or I would break all their heads, they showed me a little scroll with the king's seal on it, forbidding them to fight, or anyone to fight with them!" He rounded on Thomas. "And you know as well as I do that they'll break that rule the first chance they get. And that's why I want Eileen out of here!"

"George," Eileen's words were slow, and anger flickered like flame behind each one. "I did not run away from them in Frostmire and I am surely not going to run away from them here!"

"Of course not," said George. "You don't run away from anything. Even when anyone with brains would!"

Eileen breathed in deep and looked ready to explode. Instead, she grabbed her book-bag and stomped out the door.

"Aye, go on with you!" George yelled after her. "You won't listen to me, so go!" He poked angrily at the fire then growled at Thomas and Henry. "And you get out of here, too!"

George picked his hammer up and turned his back on them. Thomas tried to think of something to say, but George's eyes were on the steel and his body was hunched with anger. Thomas knew anything he said would be ignored or start a fight. He turned and followed Eileen, Henry on his heels.

They caught up to her a block away from the forge. Eileen was still stomping. Thomas walked beside her, but didn't reach out to take her hand. "I'm sorry."

"Don't be," said Eileen. "None of this is your fault."

All of it is my fault, thought Thomas, but left it alone. Instead, he told them both about his meeting with the king that morning.

Henry whistled, impressed. "The king has you training with his chief spy? That's interesting"

"They want me spying on people," said Thomas. "It makes sense."

"No, it doesn't," said Henry. "You're not training with just any spy. You're training with his chief spy. That means it's important."

"Hm." Thomas thought about that. "Why? Why is it so important?"

"No idea, just yet," said Henry. "I'll let you know when I've figured it out."

In the market square, the preacher was standing on his crate again.

"And who are these witches?" he was demanding as the three went by. The man had a small crowd around him. A few were mocking him, but most were listening. "Who are these horrors whose unnatural, depraved acts so threaten our Church? They are women! Women and the men who are their slaves! Beware your neighbours! Beware your wives and daughters! Yes, even the innocent among you may have been seduced by the Banished, and exchanged their purity for the power to control men's minds and make them their slaves!"

His words sent a shiver through Thomas. *All we need is a witch-hunt to make things perfect.*

Eileen, on the other hand, was seething. "How dare he say that!" She glared at the preacher. "Bet I can hit him with a rock from here."

"He'd just call you out as a witch," said Henry. "And then he'd follow us all the way to the Academy."

"Not if I hit him hard enough."

"And how, you ask?" continued the preacher. "How is it that these women grew to be so depraved that they would willingly give their bodies to the Banished? Look no further than at yourselves, my friends. We as a city—we as a *nation*—have fallen. We who were once pure in our desire to serve the High Father have turned our eyes from him and onto worldly matters. It is our greed, our desire, our thirst for knowledge beyond that which men should know that has led us to this point." He pointed directly at Thomas, Henry and Eileen. "And if you need proof of this, look no further than the king's own Academy!"

Thomas, Eileen and Henry didn't stop moving.

"Look at the boys who go there! Look at the men they become! Drinkers! Debauchers! Deceivers! For who can name a more drunken, lying, depraved group than the king's students?"

There were more mutters of agreement.

"Bet you want to throw a rock at him, now," said Eileen.

"Well, yes," said Henry, grabbing an arm on each of them and leading them out of the square at a faster pace. "The problem is, that's our reputation."

"And it's not like we haven't earned it," said Thomas. "There have been brawls between students and townsfolk before, and there is usually a girl or two with child by students every year."

"That's terrible!" said Eileen. "What happens to the girls?"

"Marriage, mostly," said Henry. "Or the student's family has to pay a hefty fine to cover the cost of raising the child."

"And if the girl was raped?" demanded Eileen. "What then?"

"There hasn't been a claim of rape against a student for fifty years," said Thomas.

"By order of the king," said Henry, quoting the Academy laws, "convicted rapists are to be hung at the gate by their fellow students. They are to suffer slow death by strangulation, not by breaking of the neck, with their boots no more than three inches from the ground. All students in the Academy will witness the death. The rapist's body is to be left there until his corpse rots enough to fall off by itself." Henry smiled his wolf's smile. "Serve them right, too. We may be a depraved, debauched lot, but we have standards."

The preacher's voice faded as they slipped and slid their way through the icy streets to the Academy.

A double line of students, with Keith in the middle of them, blocked the Academy gates.

"Oh, by the Four," said Eileen. "What is this?"

"There she is!" shouted Keith. "Link arms! No hurting anyone! She doesn't come in!"

"What are you doing, Keith?" demanded Henry. "We have to get to class."

"You and Thomas can go right on in," said Keith. "But she's not coming in."

"Who's 'she'? The cat's mother?" demanded Eileen, stepping forward. "I'm right here."

Keith ignored her. "We can keep the gate blocked all day, if we have to," said Keith. "She's not coming in!"

"The Headmaster said Eileen could attend classes," said Thomas.

"He didn't say anything about us having to let her onto the grounds," countered Keith. "So she can stay outside."

Eileen, furious, turned her back on the gate. "Anything we can do? Aside from running him through?"

"Run him through was my thought," said Henry. "Unfortunately it would get us expelled."

"Maybe we can wait for more of the company and force our way in," suggested Thomas.

"I'm not sure that would be enough," said Henry, "And they might already be inside."

Thomas growled in frustration and wished he were as big as George. *The gates might as well be closed...*

"Side entrance," said Eileen. "The one under the vines where we snuck in the first time."

Henry smiled. "Very good. Thomas, you distract them."

"Me?"

Henry ignored him and taking Eileen's arm in his own, led her down the wall away from the gates. The boys at the gates cheered.

"Right," Thomas muttered. He walked straight toward the students. "Why are you being so stupid about this?"

"Stupid?" said Keith, as an angry rumble went through the gathered boys and young men. "You're ready to throw away two hundred years of tradition and you're calling *us* stupid?"

"Just you, actually," said Thomas. "But what about the rest of you? Why are you doing this?"

"Girls don't belong here!" yelled one.

"They're distracting!" said another.

"They're not allowed!"

"They're not smart enough!"

"They're getting in!"

The last was a shout of dismay. Thomas tried to put himself between Eileen and the charging boys but was shoved aside at once. The boys ran for the small gate but were too late. Henry had already slipped open the latch and pushed Eileen inside. He stood in front of the little gate while the boys around him grumped and grumbled.

"She has a rapier!" said Keith. "She can't go armed on the Academy grounds!"

"'Had' is the word you're looking for," said Henry, holding up Eileen's sword belt. "Now if you will excuse me, I do need to get to class." He walked back to Thomas. "A lot of good you were."

"You try stopping twenty of them by yourself next time."

"There won't be a next time," said Henry. "We need to ask the Headmaster for free access to the grounds for her."

"It won't work," said Keith. "We'll keep her out!"

"Why?" asked Thomas. "Seriously. Why does it matter so much to you?"

"Because it's our Academy, not hers," said Keith, following them in. "And we won't let her in!"

"You already did," said Henry. "And now, if you will excuse us?"

They handed in their rapiers at the gatehouse and found Eileen waiting on the other side with Michael, Evan, Wilson and Philip from the Student Company. The boys had sheaves of papers clutched in their hands. "We're ready!" said Michael. "Petitions written out and ready to spread throughout the Academy!"

"Excellent!" said Thomas.

"Petitions?" sneered Keith from behind them. "What good do you think those will do?"

Thomas ignored him. "Remember the rules: no petitioning in class, no forced signatures, no false signatures. If they aren't willing to sign their own names, we don't want them. Where's everyone else?"

"Already collecting," said Wilson. "James and Marcus are at the dormitories, collecting names as they come out from breakfast. The others are at the apartments, doing the same thing."

"Good."

"You can't think the Headmaster will accept a petition to bring that little liar into the Academy?" demanded Keith.

Eileen turned, her hands in fists. "What did you call me?"

"A liar. You lied to get in here, and you lied to stay. You probably lied about fighting in Frostmire!"

In the silence that followed that remark, Eileen stepped forward until she and Keith were toe to toe. "I fought," she said, her voice cold and hard and furious. "And don't you *ever* say I didn't."

"Or what," sheered Keith. "You'll kill me?"

Henry caught Eileen's arm as her punch flew and pulled her away. Thomas stepped into her place and the members of the company formed a line behind him. Keith's supporters outnumbered them three to one.

"What are you going to do?" Keith sneered at Thomas. "Challenge me?"

"I don't duel," said Thomas.

"Because you're a coward?"

"Because I've already killed twenty people," said Thomas, his voice quiet. "Go away."

Keith paled, but tried to cover it with a sneer. "You think you can scare me?"

"What are you standing about for?" demanded the gatekeeper. "Get to class!" When no one moved, he added, "Now! Or I'll have the whole lot of you up before the Headmaster! You hear me? Move it!"

"This isn't over," said Keith, stomping off.

"Let. Me. Go," said Eileen, fury still in her voice.

"Of course," said Henry, loosening his grip. "Thank you for not kicking."

Eileen pulled free of his hands and glared after Keith, "Give me some petition sheets." Wilson held some out and Eileen practically snatched them from his hand. "I'm getting more signatures than anyone today."

"Bets?" said Henry. "The one with the most gets a free pint at the Quill."

"Bets," said Eileen. "Now let's get to class before those idiots try something else."

11

Eileen's class was in the Languages Building, on the other side of the Academy's grounds. It took half the walk for Eileen to stop stomping. Henry and Thomas walked beside her. Thomas couldn't think of anything to say to make her feel better, and so kept quiet.

They were three quarters of the way there when Eileen sighed. "I shouldn't have done that. I shouldn't have let him get to me like that."

"I don't blame you," said Henry. "I wanted to hit him, too."

"But you didn't." Eileen growled in frustration. "I just… I'm not a liar. I fought in Frostmire. I…"

"We know," said Thomas. "We were there. You saved my life, remember?"

"I remember." She shuddered, wrapping her arms around her body. "God, it was awful."

"Try to remember you saved lives," said Henry. "It helps."

"There she is! Block the door!"

"Oh, by the Four," Eileen said. "Again?"

A dozen students stood in front of the Language Building door.

"Henry, your turn," said Thomas. "Let's go to the other door."

Eileen looked ready to argue about it, but let Thomas lead her away. Henry's voice, calling something about sheep, faded away as they walked around the building. Eileen growled. "Is the whole day going to be like this?"

"No," said Thomas. "We'll talk to the Headmaster. He said you could attend class. Those idiots don't have the right to stop you." He stopped. Eight more students stood in front of the side door. "Apparently, they learned from the gate."

Eileen swore and began walking forward. The boys jumped up and stood shoulder to shoulder to block the entrance. Eileen stopped directly in front of them. "Let me in. Now."

"No girls," said one of the ones in front. "You're not coming in."

"And what will you do if I push my way through?" Eileen demanded.

"You won't get through," said the big one. "Not without throwing some punches. And the moment you do that, we'll have you thrown out for brawling."

"Pretty cowardly," said Thomas. "Picking a fight with someone half your size."

"I'm not picking a fight," said the big student. "I'm just not moving."

"Aren't you?" said Eileen. "We'll see."

Eileen walked back to Thomas, took his hand, and led him back twenty paces. Other students were gathering around to watch. "What do you want to do?" asked Thomas. "We can go to the Headmaster."

"Later," said Eileen. "I'm not letting him get the best of me." She put on a polite smile to conceal her fury and stopped one of the other students coming up. "Hello. How are you? Could you stay here a moment?"

Four stayed with her. Others shook their heads and went past. One of the ones who stayed said, "We're all going to be late for class."

"No, we're not," said Eileen. "We'll be going to class in just a moment. Meanwhile, we have a petition to allow girls into the Academy. Would you like to sign it?"

Three signed it at once, using Thomas's back as their table. One said he wasn't sure if it was a good idea, but would think about it.

The bells rang.

"Now!" Eileen shouted. "Quick! Run!"

She led the charge, hard and fast down the path to the side door, the other four hard on her heels. The line at the door wavered, and Eileen charged the space between two of them, bursting through. They tried to grab her, but the other students were only paces behind and crashed through behind her. It was chaos for a moment, and when it was cleared, Eileen was dashing for her class. Thomas grinned and took off at a run for his own.

By the time they finished lunch, which was bread and cheese eaten in the Assembly Hall to keep out of the cold, Thomas had ten signatures on his petition and Eileen had twelve. Both got a dozen refusals and a few very nasty suggestions about where to put it.

"Now what?" Eileen asked. "We should be fencing, but..."

"Library," said Thomas. "I've got assignments, you need to study."

"That, I do," agreed Eileen. "Bets they block the door again?"

Some students did try to block Eileen's way, but the librarians shooed them off, declaring that, if they didn't have a good reason to be there, they could go away.

The library was cold, despite the fireplaces, and the students there kept their coats and cloaks on. Thomas and Eileen sat at one of the tables on the first floor where students copied notes from library books—no one was allowed to take them out.

The air was filled with the smell of paper and leather. Tall shelves filled with volumes lined the walls, and stairs at each corner led up to four more floors of books. The grey light coming through the large windows left the place gloomy. Students hunched over the tables, making the most of what light there was to scribble down quotes and arguments from their books.

For the first hour, Thomas and Eileen sat side by side. Eileen worked on memorizing trigonometric identities and Thomas tried to work on his assignments. He couldn't keep focused on them, though. Between the Archbishop and the king Thomas felt like he had enough to worry about without adding schoolwork to the mix.

At least no one's trying to drive me out, Thomas thought, watching Eileen angrily flipping pages. He sighed and straightened up, stretching his back. *Where am I going to find people with magic? It's not like they post bills. And what will the king do if I can't find any?*

Alphonse said 'We all know what Kings of Criethe do in times like these.'

Thomas closed his schoolwork and went to the wall of history books. *When was the last time there were times like these?*

The church histories on the first floor talked of "The War of the Righteous" two hundred years ago, where the Church of the High Father defeated the Churches of the Mother, Daughter and Son. There were mentions of "foul witchcraft" used against Church soldiers, but no mention of what type. The war ended when King Darren III declared the Church of the High Father to be the religion of the state and banned worship of the others, though he kept the convents of the Mother open, and did not forbid the Smiths to have their traditional altars to the Son in their smithies.

King Darren III? Thomas put the Church books back and went to find a history of the kingdom. He paged through until he found the reign of Darren III, then read closely. When he finished, he put it back and found a second history. Then a third.

All three spoke of the war for the Church, but only in passing terms, declaring that King Darren had, after ten years of war inside his kingdom, declared the other churches outlawed and so returned peace to the kingdom. The years that followed were called "A flowering of the High Father's Church."

And that's all? Thomas wondered. *A ten-year war and it only merits a passing reference?*

He put the book back on the shelf and went back to the table. Eileen looked up from her trigonometry. "Looking for something?"

"Aye."

"Find it?"

"No," said Thomas. "And that's very odd." *There has to be more here somewhere.*

The bells rang, and the two packed up their books and headed to the Law building. The wind had turned blustery and threatened to yank the cloaks from their shoulders. Thomas pulled his tight as he brooded his way across the Academy grounds. *There should have been far more about the Church War. So why wasn't there?*

"Oh by the four," said Eileen. "They're blocking the Law Building." She shifted her book bag to her back. "Ready to charge?"

"Keith's there," said Thomas. "Whoever knocks him flat gets a pint?"

"Too cold for a pint," said Eileen, picking up speed. "Hot whiskey. Go!"

Surprisingly, the Law classes themselves went well. Eileen was allowed in, and no one commented during class. From that, the fourteen signatures Eileen collected—Thomas got eight—and from the expression on Keith's face when Eileen had knocked him flat, Thomas and Eileen were in fairly good moods when they stepped out of the building.

The sun was already well on its way down, though it was still far from the horizon. Eileen looked toward the Academy gates and sighed. "I should go home and get supper for George but, by the Four, I don't want to."

"Can't blame you," said Thomas.

"What is wrong with him?" Eileen looked to the sky as though it might have an answer. "It's not just worry about me. It's like... like something's broken in him."

"Broken?" Thomas stopped walking. "Broken how?"

"I don't know. He... shouts in his sleep. He swears at things that aren't there. One night I found him in the kitchen, stomping back and forth and swinging his sword."

Thomas frowned, trying to imaging George doing those things. "That's... frightening."

"It is. And every time I try to talk to him about it he says nothing's wrong. And since the problems with the Church started, it seems like everything sets him off."

"Thomas! Thomas!"

Thomas looked across the green. "James! What's up?"

James dashed toward them and skidded to a stop, gasping. "They're going to duel!"

"*What?* Who?"

"Wilson and Mark," said James. "They're heading for Bricker's fields."

Thomas swore. Bricker's fields were where masons and others gathered clay for bricks. It was also a preferred duelling ground. The fields were a half-mile outside the city and hidden from view by a low rising hill– far enough to keep the city guards from looking but close enough to summon a doctor if needed. "They're going to fight each other?"

"No," said James. "Wilson came home, grabbed his sword, said he and Mark were going to Bricker's to defend Eileen's honour, and ran out again."

"I can defend my own honour!" Eileen snapped. "What were they thinking?"

"That they were helping," said Henry from behind them, making both Eileen and Thomas jump. "Half of them see you as their little sister and the other half have a crush on you."

"Idiots," declared Eileen, dashing across the green. "When I get my hands on them..."

The three grabbed their rapiers from the gatehouse and charged across the city in the fading light of the evening. They made it to the field in under an hour with James on their heels, and found eleven of the Student Company together, waiting.

"Thomas," shouted Wilson. "Thank the Four!"

"What are you doing here?" demanded Eileen, descending on them in full dudgeon. "What were you thinking?"

"We were insulted," said Mark, backing up a pair of steps.

"How?" demanded Eileen. "Who could have insulted you enough for this stupidity?"

"Hanley Smythe and Wilbur Carmichael," said Wilson. "After fencing class yesterday, Mark and I both told the master we thought he owed you and Thomas an apology. He told us we could leave and we did."

"Wilson!" Eileen was appalled. "You need fencing class!"

"We were sitting in the library today when Hanley Smythe and Wilbur Carmichael came up to us," said Mark. "They said we're a pair of liars and fools, a disgrace to the fencing floor and that we don't deserve to be in the Academy."

"Tell me," said Eileen, horrified, "that you didn't start a fight in the library."

"We didn't!" said Wilson, indignant. "We called them cowards and idiots, and *they* challenged *us* to a duel. We agreed to meet here just before dusk."

Thomas looked at the others. "And what are you doing here?"

"Making sure they didn't bring friends," said Kevin. "I heard them talking to some others, and figured they wouldn't be coming alone."

"There they are," said Mark. Thomas looked and saw Hanley and Wilbur coming down the rise, leading a dozen other students. All of them were armed.

"Oh, this is not going to be good," said Henry. "Tell your troop to spread out."

"You heard him. Spread out, but no drawing weapons until they do."

Thomas stood beside Henry, his hand on the hilt of his sword.

Hanley and the others stopped twenty feet away. "Are you going to fight for them, then?"

"No," said Thomas. "We're going to ask you to stop this stupidity."

Hanley sneered. "Afraid I'll kill your man?"

Thomas cocked his head. "How many men have you killed Hanley? Any?" Hanley looked away and didn't give an answer. "Mark and Wilson have killed half a dozen men between them on the field of battle. I suggest that you should not be fighting them."

"*They* accepted the challenge," said Hanley. "If they don't want to fight, they can admit to being cowards and apologize to the Fencing Master."

"Or you can drop the entire matter and they'll forget that you insulted them."

"They didn't have to respond," said Wilbur, drawing his blade. "Now let's get on with it before the light is gone."

"They're fools," declared Henry. "There's no arguing with them."

Thomas sighed and shook his head in disgust. "Fine. Which of you is taking which?"

"I'm for Wilbur," said Mark. "We're nearly of a height."

"Which means Wilson for me," said Hanley, drawing his blade.

"Clear some space!" shouted Henry. "The duel goes to first blood, no further!" Hanley started to protest, but Henry over-rode him. "No further! Anyone who tries for more gets to duel me, understood?"

The four combatants glared at each other, but nodded.

"Watch your step, all of you," warned Henry. "The ground is wet and we don't need anyone dying from slipping on the grass. Now, step to your positions."

"There!" called the Fencing Master. "I knew they would be there!"

The Fencing Master came down the rise at a trot, his own rapier on his hip and a squad of watchmen with lanterns jogging behind him. His bald head was dark crimson with anger and his expression promised mayhem. He stopped in front of Thomas. "First you insult me, and now *this*?"

"I was trying to stop it," protested Thomas.

"Not very hard." The Fencing Master looked over at Eileen. "And here is the source of the trouble."

"*Me?*" Eileen's face went nearly the same colour as the Fencing Master's head. "You're blaming me?"

"Actually," said Henry, stepping between the Fencing Master and Eileen. "*You* would be the source of the trouble."

Master Brennan stepped nose to nose with Henry. "You watch your tongue, Henry Antonius."

"*Lord* Henry Antonius," said Henry, not moving at all.

The Fencing Master stayed eye-to-eye with Henry, glaring. Henry was unmoved. Master Brennan growled in disgust and turned to face the four combatants. "Blades away. Everyone. Now! And everyone back to the Academy!" He turned back to Henry, who hadn't moved. "Including you, *Lord* Henry Antonius. Move!"

The six watchmen escorted the students back the Academy and waited outside until the gatekeeper had taken all their weapons. Unarmed, the group marched to the Headmaster's house and stood on the grass while the Fencing Master went inside. Not a few of them were looking nervous by the time the Headmaster stepped onto the porch. The Fencing Master stepped around him and stomped down the porch to stand beside Wilbur and Hanley.

"And what," said the Headmaster, his tone suggesting very dire consequences indeed, "is going on?"

"A personal matter," said Mark.

"You don't need two dozen men to solve a personal matter," said the Headmaster. "Try again."

"A duel," said Master Brennan. "Two from each group with the rest there to watch and cheer."

"And what was the cause of the duel?"

"She was," said Master Brennan, pointing at Eileen.

"I was not!"

"Hanley and Wilbur challenged us!" protested Mark. "It had nothing to do with Eileen!"

"You insulted us!" protested Wilbur.

"You deserved it!" said Wilson. He turned to the Headmaster. "Master Brennan refused to teach Eileen, then he refused to let her salute him when she left. Thomas walked out of the class in protest and so did we!"

"Without saluting!" snapped Wilbur. "Thomas should have saluted!"

"And Master Brennan should have let Eileen salute!" yelled Mark.

"Now see here..." the Fencing Master started.

"No, you see here!" shouted Wilson. "Eileen's one of us and you insulted every member of the Student Company who fought beside her in Frostmire when you didn't let her salute you!"

The Fencing Master's head started going red again. "It is an abomination for a woman to fence!"

"By the Four!" Eileen shoved Wilson aside. The master was easily half a foot taller than her, and Eileen didn't care in the slightest. "What, then? We should be left helpless? We should be raped and murdered in the streets? Is that what you would like to see?"

"I did not say that! True men defend women..."

"True men don't stop women from defending themselves!" Eileen yelled. "They don't leave them helpless, and they don't try and stop them from helping their friends!" She turned to the Headmaster. "I did not start this duel. I am not the cause of this duel, and I will not be blamed for this duel by *him*," she jabbed a finger in the Fencing Master's direction, "or by anyone else!"

The Fencing Master grabbed her arm and spun her back towards him. "Don't you take that tone with me, girl!"

Eileen kicked the man in the shins and shoved him backwards. "Get *OFF* me!"

The Fencing Master raised his hand and stepped forward to hit her. Without thinking, Thomas caught Master Brennan's arm, yanked him off balance, and kicked out the man's leg. Master Brennan hit the ground hard enough for everyone to hear.

Well, thought Thomas, who'd learned the move from Sir Walter the day before, *that works.*

All the students were frozen in place. Even Eileen, who had her own fists up, ready to attack, stared in shock at Thomas.

"That is quite enough," The Headmaster's voice cut through the air like a razor.

The Fencing Master pushed himself to his feet, his hand going to the rapier on his hip.

"I said, enough." The Headmaster's voice was quieter this time, but no less sharp.

The Fencing Master let go of his weapon and turned to the Headmaster. "You see?" he said. "You see what happens with this girl around the Academy?"

"On the contrary," said the Headmaster. "Eileen has been nothing but unfailingly polite and has caused no trouble of her own accord." He surveyed the crowd. "I know what has been going on today. I know of the attempts to block Miss Gobhann from class. I know of the insults and threats that have been driving wedges through the fraternity of our institution. And now, we have this." The Headmaster's gaze swept over them. Most had the decency to look embarrassed. "This is unacceptable. You are students and I expect you to behave as such. I expect you to argue as such and when there is a matter that you feel strongly about, I expect you to support that matter as *students*, no matter which side of it you happen to be on.

"Therefore, there will be no more brawling, there will be no more duelling, and there will be no more attempts to block Miss Gobhann from attending her classes. She is a guest of the Academy and will remain so until I say otherwise. Is that understood?"

Two dozen heads nodded.

"You will disperse home tonight, and tomorrow morning each one of you will hand in to me three hundred words on the subject of honour and fraternity. And if there is another incident the participants will be writing a thousand words on the salutary effects of the flogging they received. And Thomas?"

"Yes, sir?"

"In the future, do not knock down the faculty. Now all of you, go. Master Brennan, a word please?"

Hanley and Wilbur and their supporters dispersed and grumbled their way towards the Academy gates. Master Brennan stepped in front of Thomas. "You don't come near my classes, *boy*," he said. "You do not speak to me. And be thankful you are forbidden from duelling, or I would demand satisfaction."

"Five gold on Thomas," said Henry.

"Shut up, *Lord* Henry." The Fencing Master spat on the ground, turned on his heel and stalked toward the Headmaster's porch.

Eileen grabbed Thomas's hand and dragged him away from the Headmaster's house. "Are you trying to get kicked out of school?"

"No!"

"Then what were you thinking?" She glared at them other students. "What are any of you thinking? I don't need my honour defended and I don't need you getting in trouble! Got it?"

Heads nodded, and Mark and Wilson had the good sense to look embarrassed. Eileen shook her head. "You are all idiots," she said. She turned her glare back on Thomas. "Especially you."

She didn't, Thomas noticed, let go of his hand. He decided to keep quiet.

"Agreed," said Henry. "Let's go to the Quill."

"We have three hundred words to write," Michael reminded him.

"And we can do it in the tavern as well as in the apartment," said Henry.

"Here, here," said Wilson. "We fight together, we write together! Come on!"

Eileen shook her head in disgust but headed for the gate, her hand still tight in Thomas's.

They were halfway across the campus when Thomas realized who was missing. "Where's Charles? And Liam and Jonathan?"

"I haven't seen Charles since Festival," said Michael. "And I haven't seen Liam and Jonathan since yesterday."

The Archbishop said they were waiting. They can't have gone after them yet. Thomas frowned at the thought. "Has anyone seen Charles since Festival?"

No one had.

"I'll look in on Charles," said Mark. "I left my paper at home when I got my rapier, and he's on the way to my place. I'll meet you in the Quill after."

Halfway to the Quill, Thomas spotted the man with the green coat under the blue cloak following them. Thomas swore and told Eileen.

Eileen glanced back. "Where?"

"The doorway half-way up the block," said Thomas, keeping his voice low so the other students wouldn't hear. "Standing in the shadows. Don't tell the rest of them."

"I only see shadows," said Henry. "Nothing else."

"Me, too," said Eileen.

Thomas looked over his shoulder and saw the man clearly in the shadows of the doorway. "He's fifty feet away. Stone arch doorway, slight recess, blue door. See him now?"

"No."

"No."

"How can you miss...?" Thomas stopped dead in the street, his mouth dropping open. *No. That would be too simple.* He glanced over his shoulder again and saw the man, plain as day, walking behind them.

"Thomas," said Eileen. "What is it?"

Thomas picked up Eileen, and spun her around, landing her facing back the way they had come. "Kiss me."

"Here? Now?!"

"Here and now," said Thomas, smiling. He leaned in close to her. "Tell me if you see him."

He leaned in and kissed her. Eileen resisted a moment then kissed him back. When they parted, she said. "He's not there."

Thomas picked her up, spun her again, ending with him facing backwards, and kissed her soundly on the mouth once more.

"What are you doing?" Eileen demanded as soon as he lifted his lips away from hers. Her face was flushed, and not only with confusion.

I am an idiot, thought Thomas. *A complete idiot.* "He's right there."

"Where?" said Henry.

"Doesn't matter," said Thomas. "I know who he is."

"Who?" asked Henry and Eileen simultaneously.

For the first time in several days, Thomas actually felt happy. "I'll tell you later, I promise."

An hour later they were drinking and writing with the rest of the company. Thomas did his best to write the essay, but his mind was on the man in the blue cloak. He found himself pausing on every second sentence to wonder, *how do I get to talk to him?*

"Not bad at all," said Henry, looking over Thomas's shoulder. "I may just copy that."

"I wouldn't," said James. "The Headmaster tends to be put out by such things."

"The Headmaster tends to be put out by nearly everything," said Henry.

"He could have done much worse to us," said Wilson. "Last time two students were caught duelling, they each had to spend a day in the stocks."

"Which is no less than they deserved," said Eileen. "Idiots. All of you."

"They were fighting on the grounds of the Academy," grumbled Wilson. "We were outside the city, minding our own business."

"We still shouldn't be doing it," said Eileen. "We can't afford to lose anyone to something as stupid as that duel."

"So we should have let them insult us?" demanded Wilson. "Let them ridicule us?"

"Better than letting them kill you," retorted Eileen.

"Remember what the Headmaster said," said Thomas. "We need to fight like students. We need to use our heads, not our swords."

Wilson muttered something about swords being far easier, but turned back to his work.

"Finished!" shouted James. "Slowpokes!"

"Says you," said Eileen, blowing gently to dry the ink on her own essay.

Thomas shook his head and went back to work. He was nearly finished when Mark came in. "I can't find him!"

"Who?" said Wilson. "And where have you been?"

"Charles," snapped Mark. "Where do you think I've been?"

"No need to get snippy."

"Where have you looked?" asked Thomas.

"His apartment first. Neither of his roommates has seen him since the Festival. Then I went to William Traverse's place. He said Charles stumbled out after the second bell of the night. He hasn't seen him since."

"That's an impressive bender," said James. "Even for Charles."

"That's impressive even for Henry," said Wilson, earning himself a glare.

Unless something is wrong. Thomas looked down at his essay. "Mark, you stay here and write your essay. I'm finished in ten words then Eileen and I can check the hospitals nearby. Kevin, can you and Wilson go to the City Watch, see if anyone has seen him?"

"You mean arrested him for doing something drunk and stupid?" said Kevin. "Sure thing."

"The rest of you, divide up into pairs and hit his favourite spots. We'll meet back here in three hours." Thomas looked over the concerned faces of the rest of the company and lied, "I'm sure he's fine. He's probably just with some girl or other."

"He usually is," said James. "For a guy with one hand, he certainly gets around."

"Proof that girls like personality," said Wilson.

"You just say that in the hope that there's one who doesn't notice your face."

"Finished," said Thomas, blowing on the ink to dry it. "Eileen?"

It was full night when they stepped out into the street. The air was damp and chill, and the wind carried the smell of the harbour. The man in the blue cloak was nowhere to be seen. *Of course not. He's probably gone home.*

"There are two hospitals close to the student quarter," said Thomas. "There's a bunch of surgeons and physics around, but they either treat patients in the patient's home or send them to the hospital."

"You think he's in the hospital?"

"I hope he is," said Thomas. *I doubt it.*

Three hours later they came back to the tavern. Kevin and Wilson were already back. "Any sign of him?" asked Thomas.

"None," said Kevin.

"He wasn't at either of the hospitals."

"I'm worried," said Mark. "Something must have happened to him."

"Something *might* have," corrected Thomas. "We'll wait until the others come back before we say 'must'."

The others came back in dribs and drabs. Charles hadn't been seen in the bath-houses in the last three days. He hadn't been to any of his preferred taverns since Festival. The girls that he knew hadn't seen him either. "And their parents weren't too happy to see us at this hour," said James. "One girl's father threatened to beat me with a stick."

Henry and Marcus came back last. Both looked grim.

"Let me guess," said Mark. "You haven't seen him either."

"No," said Henry. "And we couldn't find Liam or Jonathan, either."

By the Four... Thomas felt his heart sinking. "What's chance that they're all hiding and drinking somewhere?"

"Slim?" suggested Henry.

"They wouldn't have run away from the Academy," said Marcus. "They were all doing well in their classes, and I know Charles was messed up about his hand, but he was doing all right."

"He was sulking a lot," said James. "Feeling sorry for himself and all that. But he wouldn't just run off."

"Would he have thrown himself in the sea?" asked Henry.

"No!" James thought about it. "I mean... I don't think so."

"And even if he did, it's not like Liam and Jonathan would go with him," said Wilson.

"We haven't done a full search," said Marcus. "I mean, it's a big city and they could be anywhere in it."

"If Charles was in the city, he wouldn't be missing class," said James.

"What if he's dead in an alley?" said Mark.

"Him and Liam and Jonathan?"

"It's possible."

"It's not likely!"

"Well, then where are they?"

"The Church," said Thomas.

There was silence until Marcus said, "They've gone to church?"

Thomas looked around the tavern. If things were got loud they were certain to be overheard, and Thomas was pretty sure things were going to get loud, "Let's get a private room."

Once they were all in, Thomas told them about the Archbishop's visit, and the offer that came with it. He watched their faces grow hard and angry.

"So, what?" asked Marcus. "Churchmen just grabbed them off the street?"

"It's what they did to Thomas," said Eileen. "Remember?"

"I don't understand," said Evan. "You just said he was going to give you time. Why would they come after us?" Evan's eyes went wide. "What if they hang them for witchcraft?"

"They won't," said Thomas, trying to sound as certain as possible. "They'll use them as witnesses against me."

"If the Church wants you, why don't they just take you?"

Because the king told them not to. Thomas didn't say the words out loud because it didn't make sense. *They didn't care before. Why would they care now?*

"Will you take the Archbishop's offer if it means they don't kill Charles?" asked Philip. "Or Liam or Jonathan?"

The room fell silent. Thomas looked down at his drink and didn't say anything.

"They're your friends!" Evan stood up, furious. "By the Four, Thomas, you need to help them!"

"I know!" said Thomas. "We need proof."

"What? You just said...!"

"I know what I said!" Thomas shoved himself to his feet. "We have no *proof!* If the Church took them, it means they're acting against the instructions of the king, which means they'll deny everything."

"So what do we do?" demanded Evan. "Leave them there to rot?"

"We have to go to the Headmaster," said Philip. "We have to tell him what happened."

"What we *think* happened," said Thomas. He thought fast. "All right. Check all their apartments in the morning. If they're not there, I'll go to the Headmaster and I'll tell him that they're missing and what I suspect." *And I'll tell Sir Walter first.* "At the very least the Headmaster can ask around, and he's more likely to get answers than us."

"And if he doesn't?" demanded Evan. "Then what do we do?"

"We think of something else," said Thomas.

"Like what?" demanded Evan.

"I don't know!" snapped Thomas. "Give me some time. And until we find them, stick together. Don't go anywhere alone or unarmed. And don't take any risks."

"You think they'll come after more of us?" Marcus said.

"I didn't think they'd come after anyone," said Thomas. *Not after the king's warning; not after what the Archbishop said.* "But if they went after Charles and Liam and Jonathan, then there's nothing to stop them coming after all of us."

"They should have just come after you, if they wanted you," muttered Evan.

"Yes," agreed Thomas, "they should have."

12

Thomas never slept well when he was worried. He spent most of the remaining night trying to study and then lay in the bed, staring up at the ceiling until the early hours of the morning. When his eyes finally shut, he was haunted by dreams of battle, blood and fire. And through them all the Archbishop loomed in the background, frowning at Thomas like the entire thing was his fault.

But it isn't, was Thomas's first thought as he woke up. *I didn't start it.*

He dragged himself out of bed on the first bell of the morning and stumbled to the fencing hall with his eyes half-open. Even the chill, wet weather did little to help wake him. He found Sir Walter already on the floor with a practice blade in his hand.

"You look much the worse for wear," said Sir Walter. "Had too much fun after yesterday's almost-duels?"

Of course he knows about that. "Three of the Student Company are missing."

Sir Walter's eyebrows went up. "Really? Since when?"

"Charles has been missing since Festival. Liam and Jonathan vanished yesterday."

"And?"

"And I think the Church has them."

Sir Walter frowned. "I thought the Archbishop was giving you time to think about it."

"He said he was," said Thomas. "But I don't know who else would want them."

"If the Church has them, he's going directly against the king's orders," said Sir Walter. "Do you have proof?"

Thomas shook his head. "No, sir."

Sir Walter rubbed his chin as he thought about it. "I'll look into it," he said at last. "Any luck finding the magicians?"

"I might have something, but I'm not sure."

"I see. When will you be sure?"

"Hopefully in the next two days," said Thomas.

"Be more than hopeful," said Sir Walter. "Be sure. What did the preachers say yesterday?"

"Uhh... I don't recall."

"Tomorrow, recall," said Sir Walter. "I want a full report. Now, shall we fence?"

They did. And wrestled, boxed, fought with knives and practiced moving silently. By the end, Thomas had learned several new tricks and had a host of new bruises from them. Sir Walter ended the class with a lecture on how to follow someone without being seen, then made Thomas try it as they left the fencing school. Two blocks later he told Thomas he needed practice and left.

Thomas stood in the street, watching the man go. He didn't want to go to class at all. He just wanted to crawl back into his bed. Instead, he scrubbed his face with his hands to force back his exhaustion and went to get Henry and Eileen.

The forge was blazing when Thomas and Henry got there. George was hammering out nails from the end of a flat piece of iron.

"You're late," said George as he knocked another nail off of the iron. "Eileen!"

"Right down!"

"She has company," said George, glowering.

"Company?" repeated Thomas. "Who would..."

"I'm sure you'll like it," said Eileen over her shoulder as she came down the stairs. She pointed a finger at Henry and Thomas. "Why are you late?"

"Fencing," Thomas began. "I..." He stopped, mouth hanging open, as Claudine came down the stairs behind Eileen, cradling a book.

"I can't thank you enough," said Claudine. "I haven't read this one before."

"You're quite welcome," said Eileen. She smiled at Thomas and Henry. "Claudine loaned me Rouldy's treatise on the Forvishi philosophers."

"That's..." Thomas forced his brain to work, "very generous of you."

"Not at all," said Claudine. "Eileen and I share a love of books, and that should not be affected by how little you respect my father's wishes. And speaking of that, my father would like to talk to you."

"Oh." Thomas looked around for some answer to that. "All right."

"He's in the Hammer and Steel," said George. "They serve a good breakfast."

"We realized yesterday that we didn't have an address for you," said Claudine. "And since I wanted to meet with Eileen again, and knew that her brother was a smith, I suggested we come here early and see if we could find the smithy which we did. And now, Master Flarety," Claudine said the name with a fair bit of distaste, "would you be so kind as to follow me?"

They found Malcolm Bright sitting in the tavern, sipping tea and talking with a pair of older smiths. As soon as he spotted the four of them, he rose to his feet. "And here is my reason for coming here today, gentlemen," said Malcolm. "Thank you both for your time, and I promise I will return to further discuss our business."

The men rose, shook Malcolm's hand and left. Malcolm followed them to the door so he could greet Thomas. "Good morning, gentlemen. And lady," he said, with a short bow at Eileen. "My apologies for accosting your brother, Miss Gobhann." His smile widened. "I may have managed to secure two new smiths to do work on my wagons and horses, so it has been a very profitable morning for me. Daughter, did you and Eileen have a chance to chat?"

"We did," said Claudine. "And she had a book to loan me in exchange for mine!"

"Excellent! Now, why don't we all have a seat. Can I offer you some tea?"

"No, thanks," said Thomas. "We're already running late, I'm afraid."

"We won't be long, I promise," said Malcolm. He took them to a large table in the back, ordered breakfast for himself and his daughter, then extra pastries, "For you three to take to school."

The five of them sat in silence after that. Malcolm did his best to look like he was enjoying his tea. Claudine refused to look at Thomas. Eileen looked impatient to be on her way, and Henry looked sublimely unconcerned.

Finally, Malcolm put down his cup and smiled at the three of them. "Thomas, I was hoping we could continue our discussion from two nights ago."

"All right," said Thomas, warily. "Continue it."

Malcolm leaned close and dropped his voice. "Have you ever wondered what would happen if magic became common?"

"I don't think it can," said Thomas.

"The teachings of the Daughter are quite clear," said Malcolm. "Magic is to be shared among all, for the betterment of all. Just think what could be achieved if we all had magic in us."

"But we all don't."

"But we could."

"How?"

Malcolm glanced around. The tavern was empty save for them, and the woman who took his order was nowhere in sight. When he spoke his voice was so low it was hard to hear. "Those are some of the most secret teachings of the Daughter."

"Then why are you telling *me*?" asked Thomas. "I'm not a believer."

"But you have magic!" interrupted Claudine. She clapped her hand over her mouth and her eyes darted back and forth. It would have been funny if they'd been talking about anything else. Claudine's next words were whispers. "You do. Why won't you help us?"

Malcolm put his hand on his daughter's arm, and she fell silent. "Thomas, your magic could be the key to releasing the Daughter's power and turning the tide against those who would destroy magic everywhere."

Thomas frowned. "I don't understand."

"It's in the writings of the Daughter," said Malcolm. "'A magician will come, with great power, and open the doors of magic to the world. And all shall possess magic and none shall be without.'" Malcolm's eyes became brighter, his voice fervent and passionate. "Once you've read them, then you will understand. Will you at least do that? Will you read the writings?"

"I will look at them," said Thomas. "I can't promise anything else, and I don't think it will change anything." *Unless there really is magic in the writings...* "But I will read the writings. Will that do?"

Malcolm nodded. "That will do."

"We are at our apartment most evenings." Thomas gave Malcolm the directions. "And now, we really have to be on our way."

"Of course," said Malcolm. "I am only sorry the pastries didn't come in time."

"We can wait for those," said Henry, earning a glare from Thomas.

"It was very good talking to you today," said Claudine to Eileen. "And may I call on you again? In two days, perhaps?"

"I would like that," said Eileen. "I'll try to have a good start on the Rouldy."

"Excellent," said Claudine. "And here are the pastries! Do have a wonderful day at the Academy, Eileen. And you Lord Henry." She gave Thomas a glare. "Master Flarety."

The pastries were warm and fresh and tasted especially good as the three walked through the cold streets toward the Academy.

"What do you think?" asked Henry.

"No idea," said Thomas. "I've never seen any magic associated with the Daughter. Just bad poetry made to look like spells. But if there is something..."

"It would make the king very happy," said Henry. "Speaking of which, are we going looking again tonight?"

"In a way," said Thomas. "If you'll both help me."

"Of course," said Eileen. "Where are we going?"

"I'll explain this afternoon," promised Thomas. "I'm glad you and Claudine get along."

"Can I tell you how good it is to talk with another girl?" asked Eileen. "It's a relief from all you boys." She took Thomas's hand. "Pity she doesn't like you."

"I'll survive," said Thomas. "Did she say anything about me? Or what her father wants?"

"No," said Eileen. "In fact, she made a point of telling me that she wouldn't discuss her father's business because it might lead to strife between you and I, and she wasn't going to be responsible for that."

"That's..." *Surprising.* Thomas's opinion of Claudine went up a notch. "That's very good of her."

"I think so, yes," said Eileen. "If she sticks to it, we might be friends."

Thomas nodded. "What do you two think of Malcolm?"

"I hadn't figured him for a religious fanatic," said Henry. "He is quite desperate to have magic be real."

"'To turn the tide against those who would destroy magic everywhere,'" quoted Eileen. "The Church?"

"The Church destroyed the Daughter's temples last time," said Thomas. "Maybe they're hoping for enough power to return the favour?"

"Probably," said Henry. "There's nothing like the possibility of revenge to keep the followers in line."

Thomas sighed. "I was hoping he'd have some clue about the magicians and instead..."

"He has religion," said Henry.

"Speaking of which," said Thomas. "It's time to go listen to some other fanatics."

Eileen looked puzzled. "What?"

Thomas explained what Sir Walter had asked as they made their way to the market square. The preacher was there again, and the crowd around him was bigger than the day before. Thomas, Henry and Eileen stood to one side and listened.

"Now, I ask you," the preacher ranted, "who is it that is going to take control of the wild elements in our city? Who is it that will bring back decency, faith, and virtue? Do you think it is the king?"

To Thomas's surprise, he saw some people shaking their heads and heard a few calls of "no!"

"Of course not!" said the preacher. "The king is immersed in worldly matters! He thrives on trade and politics and law!" He jabbed a finger out as he spoke, as if he could stab his points home. "Which means that he is up to his neck in the heart of all that is wrong with our city! He is immersed in corruption! Immersed in gluttony! Immersed in depravity! Look at his students! Look at the ones that the king so prides himself on! The ones who debauch our young girls and despoil our streets!"

Thomas and his friends backed further away, hoping the preacher wouldn't point at them again.

"These are the ones whom the king holds up as examples to us all! These are the ones who the king says are the finest of our youth! And I say he is wrong!" The preacher took a breath and leaned forward, dropping his voice so the people had to strain to hear him. "Do you know what the students are doing now? Do you?

"It isn't enough to seduce our girls in the streets of our city," his voice grew steadily louder. "It isn't enough to come after your daughters in plain sight, where you can try to stop them, no! Now they are trying to bring girls into the Academy! They are trying to get your daughters behind the Academy walls where they can carry on without your watchful eyes on them! And is the king stopping them?"

"No!" someone called.

"Is he restraining them, to keep them away from your daughters?"

"Not likely!" said someone else.

"NO!" shouted the preacher. "He encourages them! He supports them. He writes his laws so that these students may do whatsoever they wish, and no one may censure them for it! He lets them run wild when they should be under the rule of someone with true moral authority! He is letting his *students* destroy the good name of our city, destroy the reputations of our daughters, and destroy our businesses!

"Well, I say enough!" The preacher was hitting the climax of his speech. "I say it's time to get the students back where they belong! Back under the control of the High Father!"

"We were never under the High Father's control," muttered Thomas.

"I know," said Henry. "Tell them."

"No, thanks," said Thomas.

"Heard enough?" asked Eileen, her voice taut.

"Yes," said Thomas. "Let's get out of here. We're nearly late now."

They half-jogged their way to the Academy, only to pull up short at the gates.

"Oh, by the Four!" said Eileen, her mouth staying open in surprise. "What is this?"

The wall around the Academy gate was covered in new posters that said, "NO girls!" and "Keep them out!" and "Say NO."

Just inside the gates a student was handing handbills out to everyone who walked in the door. He shoved one into Thomas's hand and then ran off, calling, "She's here!"

"Women: the Bane of Learning," the handbill was titled. Thomas read through it, and then handed it to Eileen. She took it and read it, her eyes growing wider with every moment. "Really?" she sputtered. "Really? *'With their preoccupation on matters of the body, with the uncleanness that comes upon them every month, and with their weaker intellect, there can be no doubt that women cannot measure up to the standards of the Academy.'* Who wrote this garbage?"

"The Headmaster said fight like students," Thomas said, taking back the handbill. "Apparently Keith's side has taken up arms." He pointed to the bottom of the sheet. "'Traditionalists,' they're calling themselves."

"We'll have to make up a name for our side," said Henry.

"This is fighting?" said Eileen, incredulous.

"A war of words," said Henry. He winced. "There won't be songs again, will there? Last time there were some truly execrable songs."

Thomas shuddered. "I hope not."

They were barely ten feet further in when two more students accosted them. "Sign the petition!" one said. "No girls in the... Oh!" The pair skidded to a stop. "Sorry!"

"Get out of here," growled Henry and the two ran off, laughing. Henry turned to Thomas. "I'll rally the troops at lunch. We need to have an answer to all this before the end of the day."

"How do we answer this?" demanded Eileen. "There's so many of them!"

Thomas looked over the Academy grounds. There were students running all over with petitions, others putting posters up on walls, and a couple standing on crates making speeches. "Maybe thirty at most," said Thomas, taking her hand and squeezing it. "We can get just as many."

"There, father!" said Keith from the gates behind them. "There she is!"

Keith led a trio of men, all wearing thick fur robes and gold chains, through the gates. He stopped at the gatehouse and spoke to the keeper. The men, meanwhile, walked right up to Eileen.

"Well, if I had not seen it I would not have credited it," said the first man, who was thin with a wispy beard and a brow wrinkled from much frowning. "A girl in Academy robes."

"Eileen Gobhann, at your service," said Eileen, with a curtsey only barely deep enough to be respectable. "And you are?"

"Hardly seems like a creature capable of destroying three hundred fifty years of tradition," said the second man, whose face was a perfect match for Keith's save that he was bald as an egg.

"Two hundred," corrected Eileen.

"And this is your boy, I suppose," said Keith's father, looking over Thomas as if inspecting a horse. "The one who won a war single-handed, to hear the stories they tell."

"The stories are much exaggerated," said Thomas, bowing no lower than Eileen had curtsied. "You would be Keith's father. And your companions are?"

"Very, very concerned," pronounced the thin one.

"Why?" asked Eileen. "Are you worried I'll do better than your sons?"

The third merchant, who was fat and wore a thick fur hat and squinted when he looked at people, laughed. "Hardly that! We're afraid you'll distract them from their studies. No boy can concentrate when girls are around."

"I've found that they work harder," said Eileen, her voice falsely bright. "Especially once they know that I'm smarter than they are."

"Impudent, too!" said the wispy one. "Why, if my daughter talked to me in that tone, I'd take the back of my hand to her."

"Then it's a good thing you aren't my father," said Eileen, all false cheer gone from her voice. Her hands curled into fists at her sides. "Because then I'd have to explain to my mother how you lost a hand."

The wispy man's mouth dropped open, and he turned bright red. The fur-hatted merchant stepped in front of him "My apologies," he said. "My friend is letting his emotions get the better of him, which does no one any good at all." He squinted at Eileen and held out his hand in greeting. "I am Merchant Danson. And a graduate of the Academy myself, I might add, which was not easy with eyes like mine. Eileen was it?"

"Miss Gobhann, actually." said Henry.

"Her brother is Sir George Gobhann," added Thomas. "Knight of the Order of the White Wolves."

"I see. Well, Miss Gobhann, you must surely notice that young men are not... shall we say... the wisest of creatures?" He realized Eileen wasn't going to take his hand, and withdrew it. "Young men are so easily led astray, especially by such a pretty young woman as yourself."

"Especially if the boy thinks the girl is interested in them," said Keith's father. "Then it's nearly impossible for them to manage any concentration at all."

"I hadn't realized your son was so pathetic," said Eileen.

"And now we must go see the Headmaster," said Henry as all three merchants opened their mouths in protest. "Eileen, if you please?"

"Of course. "Eileen took Thomas's hand. "Shall we?"

"We shall," said Thomas, and led them off to the Headmaster's house at a brisk pace. He waited until they were out of the merchant's hearing to say, "Well said back there."

"Thanks," said Eileen, sounding at once pleased and irritated. "I thought so."

"As did I," said Henry. "They're following us, by the way."

"What? Why?"

"Because they're probably on the way to see the Headmaster," said Thomas. "Part of the Traditionalist's campaign, you think?"

"It's what I'd do," said Henry. "When in doubt, bring in the parents. Especially if they're wealthy, sit on the city council, and have the ear of the king."

"Will it work?" Eileen asked.

"No," said Henry. "The king is on your side. At least as long as Thomas makes him happy."

Which I will hopefully do today, thought Thomas, as they trooped across the grass to the Headmaster's house. *If the man in the green cloak comes.*

"Thomas!" Evan and the rest of the Student Company were already at the house. "Where have you been? You're supposed talk to the Headmaster! Quickly!"

"I take it none of them came home," said Thomas. "Everyone give me your essays from last night."

They all handed them over and Thomas went up the steps, and knocked at the door. Matron Marshall opened it and looked suspiciously at Thomas and the crowd behind him. "What do you lot want, then?"

"*I* want to speak to the Headmaster," said Thomas. "*They* want to make sure I've delivered their essays."

"I'll take the essays in," said the Matron, "but the Headmaster has no time for you today."

"It's important," said Thomas. "Three students have gone missing."

The Matron sniffed. "Still recovering from whatever party they were at, you mean."

"No, I mean they haven't been seen for three days," said Thomas.

"Three days?" The Matron frowned. "You wait here."

She took the essays and shut the door in Thomas's face. Thomas sighed, expecting to be kept waiting. He looked back over the grounds and saw Keith the merchants slowly making their way across the grounds.

And wouldn't that be just what we need. "Henry!" When Henry looked, Thomas pointed to the four coming. Henry saw, and a moment later had the rest of the company surrounding Eileen. Thomas heard Eileen's indignant voice and winced. *I'm going to be in trouble for that.*

The Headmaster's door opened and the Matron said, "This way, Thomas."

Thomas followed her to the Headmaster's study. It was a very comfortable room, with bookshelves along the walls and a large desk with a very large chair behind it and two smaller ones in front. The Headmaster was sitting behind the desk. He, too, wore a frown. "Who is missing?"

Thomas told the Headmaster everything he knew, as well as what they had done so far to look for them. The Headmaster listened, nodded and sat back in his chair. "And you say these three were the ones who were badly injured?"

"Yes, sir. Charles lost his hand, and Jonathan and Liam both have permanent limps and other damage."

"There's no chance they just left? They could have gone home."

"They didn't."

"Are you sure?"

"They had no reason to go, sir. They were doing all right." Thomas took a deep breath. "I think the Church of the High Father has them."

The Headmaster's eyebrows went up. "The Church?"

"Yes, sir."

"Why would the Church want them?"

"They were in the north with me, sir," said Thomas. "They saw everything I saw and... I think the Church wants to question them about it."

"About it?" repeated the Headmaster. "Or about you?"

Thomas sighed. "About me, sir."

"To prove that you have witchcraft?"

Thomas nodded.

"Why wouldn't they arrest you?" asked the Headmaster.

"I don't know, Headmaster."

The Headmaster sighed. "Can you prove any of this?"

Thomas shook his head.

"Of course not," The Headmaster bit his lip and chewed it for a while. "I will have this looked into at once. Meanwhile, get to class."

Thomas slipped out just in time to pass Keith and the merchants coming up the wide porch stair. Thomas nodded politely but didn't stop moving. On the grass in front of the house, the company was still in a line with Eileen behind them. On a word from Henry, they let Thomas through and then closed ranks again, blocking Eileen from the merchants' sight.

Eileen was fuming.

"This way," said Henry, leading them back toward the common.

"I don't need to be herded!" snapped Eileen.

"And we don't need a fight in front of the Headmaster's house," said Henry. "Yet."

Eileen stomped away from the house. "I don't understand why all this is so important! I want to study! So what?"

"I don't know," said Thomas. "It's just a rule. We'll get them to change it soon enough."

"Not if those men have their way!"

"Well?" demanded William. "What happened inside?"

"I told the Headmaster," said Thomas. "He said he'd look into it."

"Which is something, at least," said Henry.

"Not much," grumbled Evan. "And who are those men with Keith?"

"The 'Traditionalists' organized themselves last night," said Thomas. "And apparently they've brought their parents into it."

"That is..." William was turning red. "That's..."

Mark suggested a word, and John and James had others. William shook his head. "Those things, too, but I was thinking, 'unfair.' It's not right!"

"It's all unfair," said Eileen. "How do we stop it?"

"Same tactics," said Michael. "We need handbills printed up. And posters. We need to get more people on our side than against."

"How?" asked Eileen. "And when?"

"Lunch," said Henry. "We'll meet at lunch and come up with a plan. Can someone write a handbill before then?"

"I can," said Mark. "I have spare time this morning."

"Do it, then. The Law Building has a printing press," said Henry. "They'll let us use it if we give them paper and ink. I'll buy some this morning."

"I'll write another petition for the parents," said William. "We'll ask everyone who's signed to have their parents send letters."

"What if the parents don't want to?" asked Philip. "What if they don't like the idea of girls at the Academy?"

"We have three hundred signatures on the petitions so far," said William. "If we can get that many students, we can get some of their parents as well."

"Three... hundred?" Eileen looked flabbergast. "So soon?"

James was practically beaming. "We were going to tell you later."

"We'll get more, too," said William. "Just you watch. See you in the Law Building at noon!"

13

Thomas spent the morning barely able to concentrate. He kept thinking about what was happening to Charles, Liam and Jonathan. Jonathan and Charles probably weren't in a bad way yet, but Charles had been there for days now.

I'll think of something later, Thomas promised himself. *I just need to get through today, first.*

The air was still chill and the wind high enough to drive the wet under Thomas's clothes and make him shiver the moment he stepped outside at noon. Students were moving briskly across the compound, looking for shelter and a place to eat whatever lunches they had brought. Thomas spotted Eileen walking with Michael and being followed by a half-dozen others. Thomas met them on the commons.

"Really an embarrassment to herself," were the first words Thomas caught as he came closer, followed by. "She ought to go home and save herself the shame."

"What's going on?" he asked Eileen, though he was looking at the crowd behind her.

"They're following Eileen," said Michael. "They've been doing it since this morning."

"Ah." Thomas looked the group over. "Why?"

"They're jerks," said Eileen. "They think—"

"WHY IS IT THAT A GIRL THINKS SHE SHOULD BE IN THE ACADEMY?" bellowed one of the students. The others joined in, yelling over one another and drowning Eileen's voice.

"SHE'S AN EMBARRASSMENT!"

"SHE'S DISTRACTING THE STUDENTS!"

"HER MOTHER MUST BE SO ASHAMED!"

"WHAT MUST HER FAMILY THINK?"

"Wow," said Thomas. "That must be really, really irritating."

"Oh, yes..."

"SHE LIED TO GET IN, YOU KNOW."

"SHE SHOULDN'T EVEN BE HERE!"

"SHE'LL NEVER PASS THE EXAMS!"

"That's enough!" said Thomas.

"We're just giving our opinions," said one of the larger students.

Eileen glared at him, "You're being a bunch of—"

"THE KING BANNED ALL THE GIRLS, WHY IS THERE ONE HERE?"

"SHE LOOKS RIDICULOUS IN THAT ROBE."

"HOW CAN HER FAMILY EVEN FACE HER?"

"SHE'S A DISGRACE TO ALL WOMEN!"

Eileen threw up her hands. "Idiots!"

"SHE INSULTS US ALL!"

"HER PRESENCE HERE IS OBSCENE!"

"SHE'S TOO FORWARD TO BE A STUDENT!"

"Oh, by the Four," said Thomas, taking Eileen's hand and leading her away. The Traditionalists followed them to the Law Building and waved as Eileen went inside. "See you when you get back!" called the big one.

Eileen kept her mouth closed until they were out of sight, then let loose with a long string of curses, ending with, "Immature, stupid, BOYS!"

"All morning?" asked Thomas.

"Every moment I wasn't in class, they were there! Talking constantly about how disgraceful it was for me to be there, and how I should go home, and how I have no hope of getting in! And every time I opened my mouth they'd start yelling so I couldn't talk to anyone!"

Thomas was impressed, despite himself. He was also smart enough not to say so. "I wonder if Keith came up with that one?"

"Well if he did, he can go sit in George's forge and stay there!"

The printing room was in the basement of the Law Building, and as soon as they went down the stairs they heard voices—many voices. Eileen looked in the door and froze in place. There were easily fifty students in the room.

James, standing at the press, spotted Eileen and waved. "I spread the word and asked who wanted to help!"

Eileen stood, mouth open, staring at them all.

"I think she's overwhelmed," said Henry. "Now, where's that handbill?"

"Here," said Mark.

"And here's a tract on the advantages of having girls in the Academy," said Michael. "Did it in Languages this morning."

The rest of their lunch they spent prepping the printing press for posters and reviewing the Mark's handbill. Michael's tract was too long to go on a single sheet, but James cut it down and Evan re-wrote it neatly enough that the printer could read it.

"We'll have it printed up tonight and distribute it tomorrow," said Marcus. "Same with the posters."

Several students volunteered to heckle any of the Traditionalists that were speaking publicly. Others promised to recruit more students to their cause. Petition sheets were spread around the room for everyone to take.

"Wait!" called Henry. "What do we call ourselves?"

The room went silent. Students looked at one another, puzzled. Then the names started flying fast and furious.

"Eileen's Army?"

"That's stupid. Girl-lovers?"

"And you called mine stupid?"

"The Best Cause Ever!"

"True-Edge!"

"No sword metaphors," said Thomas. "We're not supposed to be the violent ones, remember?"

"They're the Traditionalists," said Wilson. "That makes us what?"

"A pain in their neck?"

"Radicals!"

"Revolutionaries!"

"Forward-thinkers!"

"I like that," said Eileen.

"Too long," said Henry. "One word!"

"Forwardists!"

"That's not a word.

"Developers."

"Progressives!"

"Idealists!"

"That one," said Henry. "Eileen?"

"I like it," said Eileen, who was starting to look a bit dazed at it all.

"Right. Idealists! All in favour!"

"AYE!" The shout filled the room, followed by laughter.

"Idealists it is," said Henry. "Back to work!"

"You are all..." Eileen surveyed the room full of excited, arguing students. "Hey!"

The talking stopped. Everybody turned to look at her. Eileen smiled at them. "You are all amazing," said Eileen. "Thank you."

Eileen's good spirits didn't make it through the afternoon. The Traditionalists followed Eileen everywhere, talking at the top of their voices every time she opened her mouth. Thomas and other members of the company tried to stop it, but every time they did, more of boys would join in. It was completely ridiculous and very effective. At the end of the day, Eileen stomped her way out the gates, fuming. Thomas wished with all his heart he could let her go home. Instead, he led Eileen and Henry down the street that ran parallel to the Academy wall.

"And why this way?" asked Henry. "Is there a new tavern to try?"

"Yes," said Thomas. "Wilson said they have a great stew and a really good brandy for a decent price."

"I don't want to go to a tavern," said Eileen. "George is waiting for me."

"Just come with," said Thomas. "It's important."

Thomas turned down the first street they came to, then he went a different way down another street, then a third. When he came to the next intersection, he stopped. "Oh, by the Four."

"Lost?" Eileen asked, her tone and posture making it clear what she thought about that.

"I'm not lost!" Thomas stared down each street a moment, then pointed to a narrow street with a sharp curve in it. "That way. It's down that street."

"I hope so," said Eileen. "I'd rather not spend the night wandering."

Thomas glared at her and led Eileen and Henry down the street. As soon as they rounded the corner, Thomas pulled Henry and Eileen against the wall and flattened himself there, drawing his dagger but leaving his rapier in his belt. He whispered, "Wait!"

Henry and Eileen looked mystified, but drew their own daggers and waited. A few moments later the stout man in the blue cloak and the green coat came around the corner. He saw them and jolted to a stop. Thomas launched himself off the wall and caught the man's cloak. "Got you!"

"Please, sir!" the stout man cried out. "Please don't hurt me!"

"Shut up," hissed Thomas. Several people turned on the street to see what was going on, but no one came near. Thomas put his dagger into the man's armpit and pushed up, just enough so the man could feel the point. "Come with me!"

The man stumbled the first two steps but caught his balance and walked beside Thomas. Henry and Eileen put their daggers away and fell in on either side of them. They kept their hands on their rapier grips and glared at anyone who thought to come near. Thomas led the man to the nearest alley. It was a dead end, which suited Thomas fine. He pushed the man into it. "Keep people out," he said over his shoulder.

He took the man another dozen steps into the alley and let him go. The man pressed himself against the back wall, his breathing rapid and his eyes wide with fear. Thomas sheathed his dagger. "Given that you've been following me since Festival, I thought I should introduce myself," Thomas said. "I am Thomas Flarety, Captain of the Academy's Expeditionary Company, fifth year student at the Royal Academy of Learning and son of John Flarety, a cloth merchant of Elmvale." He bowed deeply, and when he straightened up, looked the other man in the eye. "And you have magic."

The man swallowed loudly, but said nothing.

"We thought you were an agent of the Church at first," said Thomas. "But you weren't following us around all the time. And then there was the fact that I was the only one who could see you." Thomas shook his head. "You think I would have been able to figure it out faster. But then, I've been tired a lot, lately. And I think I was expecting something obvious. Healing or fire or something. Care to tell me your name?"

The man didn't move or say anything. Thomas sighed, and stepped closer. "You have magic. You have the ability to be unseen when you want. Not invisible, just unnoticed. That's very impressive. So I have to ask, why are you following me?"

The man bit his lips. Thomas waited. Witnesses, the Master of Laws had said, would often talk just to fill the silence, if it went on long enough. Thomas hoped he was right. The man swallowed and bit his lip again. Then he fidgeted where he stood. Thomas felt his insides roiling with excitement and worry. *Please, give me something!*

"I'm Robert," said the man. "Robert Smithson. I'm a baker."

Thank the Four. "Pleased to meet you, Robert. Why you are following me?"

"I… I heard them talking about you on the beach. They said you could throw lightning. And do other things. And I never met anyone that could do more than one thing. So I wanted to learn how, but I didn't know what to say or when to talk to you so… So I…"

He's met others! "So you followed me."

"From the beach," said Robert. "Until I saw you go with the king's messenger. And everyone said you were a student so I went to the Academy. My wife isn't happy about me being gone from the bakery, but…" Robert trailed off and looked at his feet. "Sorry."

"You said you never met anyone who could do more than one," said Thomas, forcing himself not to speak too fast or eagerly. "Who have you met that could do one?"

Robert opened his mouth, shut it, and looked at the ground.

"I'm sorry," said Thomas. "I don't mean to ask for names. But you do know other magicians, yes?"

Robert kept looking at the ground. Thomas thought about it. "If I asked to meet the other magicians, would you be able to arrange that?"

Robert bit his lip again. Thomas forced himself not to shout *'Tell me!'* Instead he lowered his voice and stepped closer. "Let me tell you about magic. It's like having a secret that no one else has. It's wonderful and exciting, and sometimes it is very, very lonely. More than anything, you want to tell people, but you can't because if they don't have it, they won't understand."

Robert raised his eyes to meet Thomas's.

That's a start, Thomas thought. "I imagine that when you found the others, it was a great relief for you. To know you're not alone. And that's all I want," said Thomas. "I don't want you to tell me their names or where they are. I just want you to tell *them* who *I* am and see if they'll talk to me. All right?"

Thomas waited. Robert bit his lip some more. Thomas fought the urge to shake him. *Think, idiot,* he told himself. *Robert followed me. Why? What does he want?*

Magic. He wants more magic.

"Take an unlit candle," Thomas said. "Sit in front of it and close your eyes. Imagine the candle as lit. And when you have a clear picture of it in your mind, open your eyes, and put that image from your head to the candle, and the candle will light."

"What?" Robert blurted. "Is that possible? I mean… I've heard of such tricks, but…"

"The hard part is taking the vision in your head and making it real," said Thomas. "It takes a few tries, so don't be worried if it doesn't work the first time. And once you've done it, tell the others about me. If they're willing to meet me, I'd love to meet them. Will you do that for me, Robert?"

It was a long moment before Robert nodded.

"Thank you," said Thomas. "Have a good evening."

Thomas stepped out of the alley, took Eileen's hand and gestured Henry to walk back the way they had come. The people on the street looked suspiciously at them. Thomas didn't care. He'd found a magician, and he might find others. Thomas was half-ready to break out into song.

"Well?" demanded Eileen, once they were well away from the street. "Is he, really?"

"Yes," said Thomas. "I'll tell you all about it when we're someplace warm, all right?"

The walk to Eileen's place had rarely gone so fast. Thomas was practically dancing and Eileen and Henry, eager to hear what happened, walked faster and faster.

When they reached the smithy, George looked up from the anvil and saw their expressions. "What's happened?" He asked, suspicious. "You all look happy."

"We are," said Thomas. "I am, anyway."

"Well hurry up and get upstairs," said Eileen. "I want to hear. George, come with! I'll get the stew warmed up while we listen."

"It's important, George," said Thomas. "Come up and listen, please."

"And hurry," said Eileen, leading Thomas and Henry upstairs. Thomas used his magic to light the stove and Eileen put the stew pot on.

Below, George's hammer rang on iron another hundred times, then clattered onto his workbench. He stomped his way up the stairs and sat down on the bench. "All right, by the Four, what happened that's so important?"

Thomas told the story from the start, and gave all the details. By the time he was done, Henry was looking impressed and Eileen was beaming with excitement. "This is wonderful!"

"Wonderful?" echoed George, who looked like a storm cloud ready to burst. "You taught him how to do magic? Are you insane? You gave him enough to have you charged with witchcraft!"

Thomas shook his head. "I only *told* him how to light a candle. I didn't *do* anything."

"You told him to try it!"

"No, I didn't," said Thomas. "There's no crime there."

"Trust him," said Henry. "He's studying to be a lawyer."

The thunderclouds in George's expression grew darker. "You shouldn't have taken Eileen."

"Like he could leave me behind," said Eileen.

"You don't know he's really a magician!"

"Yes, I do!" said Thomas. "I see magic, remember?"

"So because someone was able to follow you, you think it was magic?"

"No, because Henry and Eileen couldn't see him fifty feet away without me pointing him out, I *know* it's magic."

"So what?" snapped George. "Bishop Malloy had magic! What if this one works for the Church? What if he was just trying to get you to confess?"

Thomas took a deep breath, then another. "If he works for the Church, I haven't given him anything to arrest me on. And maybe he can help me find other magicians so I can stay on the king's good side!"

"If he doesn't just lead you to the dungeons and the Inquisitor again!"

"By the Four, George!" Thomas was furious. "I'm trying to do what the king wants me to do. Do you have a better suggestion?"

"Aye, stay out of it!"

"I can't stay out of it! I'm it! I'm what everyone is fighting about!"

"Then keep us out of it!"

"You're already in it!"

"Enough!" said Henry, his voice cutting off George even as he opened his mouth. "You can be heard in the street. Now stop it before you say something you don't mean."

"We should never have come with you," said George, glaring at Thomas. "When you were running from Elmvale, we should have stayed behind."

Henry sighed. "Like that, for example."

Thomas shoved his anger down inside. He rose to his feet, said, "Good night, Eileen," and walked out.

It took Henry a while to come down. By the time he did, Thomas was leaning on the wall outside the smithy, glaring at a puddle in the road in front of him. Henry smiled. "Well, that went..."

"Shut up, Henry," said Thomas. He pushed himself off the wall with his shoulders and started walking away from the street.

Henry followed him. "Don't take it out on me."

"I'm not taking it out on anyone, I just..." Thomas looked for something to kick. "I just don't want to talk about it, all right?"

"Fine."

"Fine."

14

Sir Walter was impressed the next morning, when Thomas told him what had happened. He was less so when he learned Thomas didn't know where the man lived.

"Do you know how many bakeries there are in this city?" Sir Walter said.

"Many?" ventured Thomas.

"Too many," said Sir Walter "You should have followed him home."

"Oh," Thomas felt very foolish. "I didn't think of that."

"I didn't think you had," said Sir Walter, shaking his head and picking up a rapier. "Do better next time."

That afternoon, between classes, Thomas went back to the library. He'd had no time the day before to search for more information on the last Church War. This day, though, he was determined to find something, or to find out why there wasn't anything there.

He started with the Church histories, looking for any mention of the king or Hawksmouth during the Church War. There were several mentions in the various books of "Noblemen who did not support the Church's cause," but nothing more specific. Thomas put the books back and went to find Albert Bootman, the librarian. "Excuse me?"

"Yes?" Albert Bootman squinted to see who it was. He was a short, stout man and near-sighted. His robe was always neat and he was known for getting very grumpy when books were misfiled. He was also an expert on every single book in the library, and several thousand outside of it. "Thomas Flarety. Yes, Thomas, how, may I help you?"

"I'm looking for histories of the Church War," said Thomas.

"Which Church War?" asked Albert. "There must be a hundred, if you include skirmishes."

"The one in Criethe," said Thomas. "Against the Mother, the Daughter and the Son."

"The official versions are in the Church histories," said Albert. "The Royal histories only mention it in passing, which is strange. And there's an unofficial version by Harald Grifson that tells a bit more about it."

"Do we have that version?"

"Unfortunately not," said Albert. "It was removed from the collection ten years ago."

"Really," said Thomas, his ears perking up. "By whom?"

"Me. Silverfish had eaten through most of it."

"Oh."

"The only way to get access to the records of the war would be through the Theology department. Ask the Head of Theology and he can petition the High Father's Church to let you see their records."

And won't that go over well. "Thank you. I'll think about that."

That evening, Thomas and Henry went out once more in search of magicians.

Eileen begged off, saying she needed to study, and that a night with her home would improve George's mood. They wished her the best and headed into the cold night.

"Bookstores, tonight," said Thomas.

"Bookstores?"

"I found a dozen spells in books," said Thomas. "If we can find a book with spells, maybe we can find the owner."

"You'll probably have to bribe the shopkeeper to get the name," said Henry.

Thomas smiled and pulled his cloak tighter against the wind. "That's why I have you."

By the time the stores closed Thomas owned a used book of poetry and another of astronomy, but had not found a single spell. They spent the rest of the night watching entertainers in taverns and had no luck there, either.

The next morning, Sir Walter took Thomas's report with a disappointed frown. Then he taught Thomas how to pick a lock, and made him practice for the rest of the hour. At the end of the class, Sir Walter gave Thomas a small set of tools.

At least there are some advantages to being taught by a spy, Thomas thought on his way back to his apartment. *If I ever get locked out I can break into my own house.*

In the streets, the preachers were getting more strident and drawing larger audiences. Thomas, Henry and Eileen, their robes hidden under their cloaks, listened, but the themes didn't change. More posters against witches, witchcraft, the king and his students had appeared. Graffiti started being scrawled on doors and walls of houses, declaring the occupants to be witches. Students talked of being refused entrance into some taverns or shops, and being booed by the crowds around the preachers.

At the Academy, the rhetoric had reached new heights. Over lunch hour, students debated, argued and made speeches in the commons to impress on each other how important it was for girls to be let in or kept out. Petitioners accosted both sides continuously, hoping to wring out more signatures. A dozen different handbills made the rounds, with points ranging from how distracting and inferior women were to how important women were as a civilizing and quieting influence. The majority of the Academy was divided into the Idealist and Traditionalist camps. More posters for both sides appeared on the Academy walls, as well as one that declared, "Who Cares? Go STUDY!"

And at the end of the day, when Thomas, Eileen and Henry stepped out through the Academy gates, Lords Cormac, Anthony and Ethan were standing across the street.

"By the Four, what do they want?" Eileen hissed, her hand going to her rapier.

Across the street, Lord Cormac saw them, smiled, and waved.

Eileen's hand squeezed so tight around her rapier grip that the leather in her glove squeaked.

"We should go," said Thomas.

"*They* should go," said Eileen. "This is our place and *they* don't belong here!"

"No, they don't," agreed Thomas. "But anyone can walk the street and trying to make them to clear off will just make things worse."

Eileen stayed where she was, her eyes locked on the three men. Cormac said something to Anthony, who laughed. Eileen's face tightened and went red.

"Eileen," Thomas said, "We have to go."

"If you kill them the king will hang you," said Henry. "And then you will never be a student."

Eileen stayed where she was a moment longer, then turned on her heel and started walking the other direction. A block later she turned on Henry. "How did you know I wanted to kill them?"

"What else would you want to do?" asked Henry. "Given the way they treated you?"

"But I was actually going to," said Eileen. "I was going to cross the street and..." Eileen started shaking. She put her hand on the wall beside them and stood there, head down and breath coming in short, hard bursts.

"It happens," said Henry. "The way to not do it is to remind yourself of what's important."

Eileen looked up. "Is this what's happening to George?"

"Maybe," said Henry. "Thomas gets nightmares, George..." Henry shrugged.

"Does... does this happen to you?"

"Sometimes."

"What do you do?"

"Concentrate on keeping you two alive long enough to get married." Henry smiled as Eileen and Thomas both blushed bright red. "Now let's get out of here. You need to study and Thomas and I need to spend another wonderful night searching the taverns."

"And bookstores," said Thomas.

"Well, we can't forget those..."

By the time the midnight bell rang, Thomas was stumbling tired.

"I begin to think this is a waste of time," said Henry.

"Maybe we should try surgeons next," said Thomas. He shivered, as much from exhaustion as cold. "We can ask around and see if there's anyone with a special gift for healing. Then I can ask to see them work."

"Good idea," said Henry. "Because these late nights are making it difficult to study."

The next morning began too early, and was mostly a blur. Sir Walter gave another disappointed frown and then took Thomas outside and showed him how to climb a building. He made Thomas practice for the rest of the hour, coming in through each of the windows in the studio. It was wet, slippery, dangerous and exhausting. Thomas went home with a dozen new scrapes.

When Thomas, Henry and Eileen reached the Academy, there were new posters plastered on either side of the gates, covering all the others. Thomas whistled with surprise. "That's nasty."

"And impressive," said Henry.

Two of the posters showed students dragging girls into the Academy. One had a pair of students, drinks in hand, throwing rocks at children. A fourth had a student threatening a merchant at sword-point. Two more had rather graphic depictions of students engaged in activities that had nothing to do with studying.

"Wow," said Eileen. She pointed at one of them. "What are they doing?"

"Exactly what it looks like," said Henry.

Eileen looked closer, then her eyes widened and she blushed. She looked away from the wall, to Henry and Thomas. "Do... do boys really do that?"

"Some have been known to," said Henry, "Though I think they may be overstating some things for effect."

I thought they were riled up before, thought Thomas, staring at the posters. *This is like kicking a hornet's nest.*

The students inside, Traditionalists and Idealists alike, talked about nothing else between classes. Halfway through the morning, new posters went up on the Academy grounds: "All students, professors and masters are invited to the Assembly Hall at lunch, to discuss the grievous accusations levied against our most noble Academy and to hear the remedy for them."

By the time Thomas, Henry and Eileen arrived at the Assembly Hall it was already half-filled. A dozen of the masters were there, including Theology, Rhetoric and Law. The students in the room were divided into Traditionalist and Idealist camps, and Keith was standing in the middle of the stage.

"Wonderful," muttered Eileen. "And the solution will be, 'let's throw Eileen out of the Academy.' Bets?"

"No bet," said Thomas.

"Brothers! Look here!" Keith raised a hand with a copy of each of the posters in it. He displayed them one after the other. "Brothers! Look at this, the latest round of insults directed at our Academy!" Each poster received the expected boos and shouts of derision, plus some speculation on the ones with two students engaged together.

"Since the Festival of Rains, we have been being taunted!" continued Keith. "We have been insulted in the streets and we have been the object of scorn and derision!"

"So what else is new?" yelled someone from the Idealist side.

Keith ignored him. "Two days ago, students were booed in the streets! Yesterday, others were refused service in the Black Bull tavern. And today, another was attacked by mud-throwing children while their parents looked on and did nothing to stop them!" He threw the posters to the ground. "We are being mocked and ridiculed for one reason and one reason only!" He pointed to Eileen. "This is because that *girl* has been allowed to enter our Academy!"

The Traditionalists let up a resounding cheer of agreement.

"Liar!" yelled Graham Silvers. Thomas blinked in surprise as the young man leapt onto the stage. "The posters have nothing to do with Eileen. Is there a single one that shows a girl going to the Academy of her own free will? No!"

"The preachers are shouting about it in the streets!" Keith pointed a finger at Graham. "You just don't want to admit that that chit is causing all this trouble!"

"Chit?" Eileen spoke the word through clenched teeth. To her credit, she didn't move.

"They are slandering our Academy! They're slandering us! And they're doing it because of her!"

"They're doing it because of the king!" said Graham. "And if you'd bothered to look at *all* the posters and listen to everything the preachers are saying, you'd know that. This whole thing is about the king! The Academy is just a tool they're using. And you know what?" He turned to his audience. "No matter what the preachers are saying, no matter what the people in town are doing, what goes on in the Academy is not the town's business. It's our business! And whether or not you agree with Eileen joining the Academy, the town can keep their noses out of it!"

The arguing rose to new heights. Thomas tapped Eileen and Henry, and led them out of the building. "Nothing they say in there is going to change anything. Let's get lunch."

They collected their rapiers and stepped out of the grounds into the street. Eileen touched Thomas's shoulder and pointed.

Robert, with his blue cloak and the green coat, was leaning against a wall across the street, waiting.

15

Thomas put on his friendliest smile and went over. "I'm glad to see you again, Robert. How are you?"

The man looked around them, saw no one else near, and leaned in close to Thomas. In a tight, awed, whisper he said, "It worked!"

"Excellent!"

Robert smiled, wide and shy. "I can't believe it worked. Where did you learn it?"

"It was in a book."

Robert shook his head. "Spells in books don't work."

"Most don't," said Thomas, remembering the many books he'd had to go through to find real magic. "But some do."

"We never found any," said Robert. "We figured they didn't work, from the books."

"We?" said Thomas. "Who is we?"

"That's why I came today," said Robert, "After what you told me, well... there's some others who'd like to be told some things, too. They'd like to meet with you. Tonight."

Oh, thank the Four. "When tonight?"

"After the first night bell," said Robert.

"Where?"

"They don't want you to know that," said Robert, he dipped his head, looking embarrassed. "They don't know you."

Thomas remembered what he had said to Malcolm Bright. "Fair enough. But I can't meet them if I don't know where to go."

"I'll guide you there," said Robert. "Where will you be after the first bell?"

"The Broken Quill," said Thomas. "Student pub. Do you know where it is?"

Robert nodded. "I'll see you there." He shook Thomas's hand and walked off.

"Good news?" asked Eileen, coming up behind him.

"Very," said Thomas, feeling elated. "Dinner at the Broken Quill. I'm buying."

"Magic words," said Henry.

"Which means you're buying lunch," said Thomas. "Green Griffon, everyone?"

The Academy continued to buzz for the rest of the day, and feelings ran ever higher. Henry rallied the Idealist and had them working hard to collect the last signatures before the end of the day. The traditionalists argued and pointed to the posters around the school as reason to not sign.

At the end of the day, Michael and the others from the company declared they were going to spend the night putting together the petitions and making certain everything was order. "We'll get a room at the Quill and do it there."

"Sounds good," said Thomas. "I'll have to step out for a bit, though."

"Sure," said Wilson. "Shirk the work."

They all ate a very good pork stew and drank hot, mulled wine at the Broken Quill. The petitions were ordered and counted, though Michael refused to tell Eileen how many signatures they had, which sent her mad with curiosity.

At the first bell of the night, Thomas, Henry and Eileen stepped outside. Robert was waiting for him.

"Well, he's prompt, I'll give him that," said Henry.

Thomas shook Robert's hand. "Robert, may I present Eileen Gobhann and Henry Antonius."

"I was told you were to come alone," said Robert. He looked at his feet. "I can't take you if you don't come alone."

"Of course," said Thomas.

Eileen frowned. "I don't like it."

"I'll be safe enough," said Thomas. He hugged Eileen. "Not to worry."

Eileen glared at Robert, but said, "Fine."

"Not quite," said Henry. He stepped very close to Robert. "If Thomas does not come back to us by morning—Robert Smithson, Baker—we will be very, very upset. And there will be no place in this city where you can hide from us." He pointed a finger at Eileen. "Ask Thomas what Eileen did to the last person who kidnapped him."

Robert looked ready to bolt.

"Enough, Henry," said Thomas. "I'll be back before morning, I am sure." He gave Eileen a kiss. "Henry will walk you home."

"Be careful," said Eileen, kissing him back

Robert led Thomas away from the Broken Quill. After a few blocks, he asked, "What did Eileen do? When you were kidnapped?"

"You really don't want to know," said Thomas. The stench and screams of the magician burning alive leapt up into Thomas's mind. He shuddered. "How far do we have to go?"

"A fair way," said Robert. "But I promise, you'll be home before the midnight bell."

They made their way across town, skirting the old city wall and the fashionable districts to the more comfortable and worn areas where tradesmen and their families lived. They ended up near the shipyards, on the other side of the city from the merchant docks. The streets were dotted with signs for shipwrights and carpenters, rope-makers, sail-makers, brass-workers and a dozen other professions besides. It was a working area and mostly quiet this time of night, save for the odd tavern with light and laughter coming out of it. Robert avoided those, crossing to the other side of the street to stay out of the light from the tavern's torches.

They stopped outside a large, shuttered building. The sign marked it as "O. G. Redcappers, Sail-makers." Robert looked to make sure no one was in the street. When he was satisfied, he produced a key and opened a side door. "This way."

He led Thomas up a flight of narrow stairs to and down a hallway to an equally narrow door. Robert knocked three times, then three more, then took out another key. He unlocked the door, knocked four times and pushed it open.

The room beyond was dark, and lit by a single candle. Six figures in dark cloaks sat around a large table. No one's face was visible in the dim light. Robert gestured for Thomas to go in first and closed the door behind them. Thomas heard the lock click shut.

"Who is this one who wishes to join our company?" rumbled the black-cloaked figure at the head of the table, in a voice too deep to be that of a woman.

"A seeker," answered Robert. "One who would learn the mysteries."

"And what mystery does he bring us in exchange?"

"He taught me how to light a candle using my talent," said Robert.

"That's not possible," said another of the cloaked ones, his voice sounding much younger. "Magi... the mysteries can't be taught!"

"Silence," said the deep-voiced one.

"It's true," said Robert. "I'll show you."

"Whether or not it is true," said deep-voice, "if he cannot show his mystery, he cannot be a true seeker."

"Are you going to speak like this the whole time?" Thomas asked. "Because I do have to get back soon, and if you're going to talk about me like I'm not here, this is going to take a while."

"The seeker does not speak," said the cloaked man. "The seeker shows."

"And what is it that the seeker shows?" asked Thomas. *Because there's no way I'm going to show you my magic.*

"Silence! Show!"

"No," said Thomas. "Not to six figures in the dark who can see my face when I can't see theirs."

"If you wish to learn the mysteries..." began the figure.

"I'm not here about mysteries," said Thomas. "I'm here about magic. And I'll wager I know a fair amount more about it than you do."

The room was completely silent. Thomas looked at Robert. "Did I say something wrong?"

Robert looked embarrassed. "We don't speak of magic here."

"The seeker must be silent! The seeker must show his talent!"

"You're asking me to put my life in your hands," said Thomas. "You already know who I am. I'd rather see your faces first."

"If the seeker has nothing to show," said the deep-voiced man at the head of the table, rising. "This meeting is at an end."

By the Four... "I am Thomas Flarety, son of John Flarety, merchant of Elmvale, Student of the Royal Academy of Learning and Captain of the Academy's Expeditionary Company. I trust my reputation precedes me?"

"Rumour proceeds you. But rumour is not mystery."

"Neither is wearing a hood and sitting in a dark room," snapped Thomas. "I haven't seen anything that shows me *you* have 'talent.'"

"You are the seeker, not us."

"I've introduced myself," said Thomas. "And you are?"

"We do not give names upon first meeting," said the deep-voiced one. "We ask to be shown the mystery, then decide if the seeker is worthy of our company."

"What makes one worthy of the company?" said Thomas.

"You have to be able to contribute," said Robert. "That's why I brought you." He turned to the group. "He has already contributed. I can show you!"

"Contribute what?" said Thomas.

"To the breadth of our knowledge," said another one in a cloak and hood—a woman, judging by the voice. "We are a learning group."

"Learning what?" asked Thomas. "How to do more?"

"This is not proper!" said the man at the head of the table. "We should not be saying so much!"

"But since you are, you might as well keep going," said Thomas, putting on a smile.

"We will not! You have not proven worthy!"

"Oh, by the Four, what more do you want?"

"Proof."

I can't give you proof. "Why don't you let Robert show you what I taught him and then decide from there?"

"The mysteries cannot be taught!" exclaimed the deep-voiced one, slapping his hand on the table. "Man is born with his gift from the High Father. To do more is to give one's soul to the Banished."

"No it isn't," said Thomas. "To call on the Banished for power, to strike a bargain with them, *that* is giving one's soul to the Banished. Not that I think it's possible," he added. "In fact, as near as I can tell, outside of the records of the Church there has been no evidence of anyone giving their soul to the Banished or performing a successful ritual to summon them." He stopped, suddenly remembering something he'd read in the church records. It was something about the word *witchcraft*...

"The mysteries can be taught," said Robert. "Thomas taught me how to light a candle. I did it, too!"

The other man's voice became more irritated. "It goes against everything this order believes!"

"I thought you were a learning order?" asked Thomas. "How can you learn more if you don't try new things?"

"About the mysteries!" exclaimed the man. "Not about congress with the Banished!"

"There is no congress with anyone!" said Thomas, exasperated.

"I can show you," said Robert. He reached into his jacket and pulled out a candle. "Watch!"

"Not with him here!"

"I want to see," said a woman.

"And I," said another.

"I think we all should," said the woman. "In fact, I think we should have a vote on it."

"It is against our principles!" insisted the man at the head of the table.

"But it's a chance to learn more," said the young one. "Please, Father?"

Father? Well, now I know something, anyway.

"I still say we should vote on it," said the woman.

"Whether we do or not," said the deep-voiced one, "we should not be discussing it with one present who is not a member. Please remove him."

"Shall I wait outside the door?" asked Thomas.

"Let him wait," said the tall woman. "If we decide that we do want to learn more, I should like to begin tonight."

"And me," said the young one.

Thomas bowed slightly. "I'll leave you to it," he said. "Perhaps Robert can light another candle for you," Thomas suggested as Robert opened the door. "It's rather dark in here."

Thomas stepped out the door and heard Robert close and lock it behind him. Thomas pressed his ear against it, but the wood was too thick and the people inside speaking too quietly for Thomas to make out more than the occasional bark of "We do not do such things!" and "Why not?" and "Then let us vote on it!"

Thomas gave up on listening and leaned against the far wall, arms crossed, waiting. It was a quarter of an hour later when the door opened and Robert stepped out. He wasn't smiling.

"I'm sorry," Robert said. "Unless you show magic, they can't let you join."

Oh, by the Four... "That's problematic." *Henry would have handled this so much better.*

"Do you not... I mean," Robert blushed. "I thought you could do magic. The stories said you threw lightning."

"Yes, well..."

"So why not show us?"

Because one of you may work for the Church. Because the king said not to do magic. Because I don't want to be interrogated again. Because you might not be the only one watching me. "Did you show them the candle?"

Robert shook his head. "Not yet."

"Show them," said Thomas. "And then maybe they'll listen."

"Show them yourself," insisted Robert. "Right now."

Thomas shook his head. "I can't. I'll talk to you later."

Robert walked him down the stairs and out the door, and Thomas heard the click of the lock after Robert closed it behind him.

Thomas walked a half-block until he found a place where he could stand in the shadows and still keep an eye on the other door. It was cold, but at least the rain had stopped. He wrapped his cloak tight around himself and tried to keep warm as he waited.

It was another hour before the door opened again. One at a time the people from the meeting slipped out into the night. It was too dark for Thomas to see anyone's faces, and even though he could see the inner light of each person, it was nothing that would help him know who was who. Finally, one person stepped out who was the approximate shape and size of Robert. Thomas followed him.

Remembering his lessons from Sir Walter, Thomas tried to move as quietly as possible and kept far enough back that his footsteps would not be easily heard. Robert—if it was Robert—didn't notice him. The man moved quickly through the streets, intent on getting home as soon as possible. Thomas had trouble keeping him in sight and still keeping his distance.

It took them an hour to cross the city, from the warehouse district to one of the more affluent merchant areas. Robert—Thomas had seen his face in the torchlight from a tavern—picked up his pace. The man finally stopped in front of a bakery, pulled out a key, and let himself in. Thomas waited in the shadows for a good while before he walked up to the bakery.

The Pie and Tart, the sign announced. Robert Smithson, Proprietor.

It's not much, Thomas thought, *but at least I know where one of them lives.*

16

Thomas forced himself out of bed at the first bell of the morning and stumbled blearily through the streets to his fencing class. It was the day they were going to present the petitions. *And given how things are going, that will probably fail as well.*

He tried to shake his bad mood, but didn't manage it by the time he reached the fencing hall. Sir Walter was already inside, running through sword exercises by himself. He stopped and smiled when Thomas came in. "And how did yesterday go?"

"Badly," said Thomas. "I attended a meeting of magicians where I failed to see any magic."

Sir Walter frowned. "Then how do you know that they were magicians?"

"Robert took me there," said Thomas. "He owns the Pie and Tart in the northeast section of the outer city, by the way. I followed him home last night."

"That was well done, at least," said Sir Walter. "Why didn't they show you their magic?"

"Because I can't show them mine," said Thomas. "Because the king told me not to in case any agents of the Church see it!" Thomas rubbed his face. "Apologies, Sir Walter. It was not a good day yesterday. And today is the day we deliver the petitions. I am somewhat worried."

"We can find the others through him if we have need." Sir Walker picked up a pair of wooden knives. "I find knife work the best for settling one's mind."

An hour and a fresh set of bruises later, Thomas walked with Henry to George's smithy. Eileen was pacing back and forth, muttering to herself. George was half working, half watching his sister, and doing his best to not look amused. "About time you got here," said George. "She's about to explode."

"Thomas!" Eileen ran to him and hugged him. "It's petition day! What did the magicians say?"

"Magicians?" George looked at his sister. "What's this about magicians?"

"Thomas met with the magicians of Hawksmouth last night," said Eileen.

"And you didn't tell me?"

"I didn't feel like getting yelled at," said Eileen, tartly. "Were they really magicians? Did you learn anything new? Did you tell Sir Walter?"

"I don't know. No. Yes," said Thomas. "And how are you?"

"I'm a wreck," said Eileen. Her eyes were wide, and there was a slightly frantic look about her. "It's petition day!"

"I know," said Thomas, trying to sound calming without sounding condescending. He hugged her. "It will all be all right, I'm sure."

"What's this about the magicians?" demanded George.

"You don't want to know," said Thomas. "Remember?"

George drew himself up, hurt clear on his face. Thomas ignored it. "We have to get to the Academy," said Thomas. "It's not a day we want to be late."

"I know," Eileen squeaked. She immediately covered her mouth. Around her hand she mumbled, “Sorry. I’m nervous.”

“Nothing to be nervous about,” said Henry. “We come together, we deliver the petition, it goes to council, and everything goes quiet until we present our arguments at the council meeting.”

“What if it doesn’t go to council?” asked Eileen. “What if they reject our arguments?”

“They are required by Academy tradition to consider at council any petition which has the required number of signatures,” said Thomas. “King’s rules.”

“What if we don’t have the signatures?” Eileen asked.

“We do,” said Thomas. “I’m sure of it.”

“What if...”

“Enough!” said George. “There’s no sense worrying about what hasn’t happened. Get yourself to the Academy, and deliver your petitions. You’ll be all right.”

“You sure?” demanded Eileen.

“No,” said George. “I’m not. I don’t know what’s going on there and I don’t know what they will say. But I do know that they’d be damn fools not to take you, and that these two wouldn’t steer you wrong about the Academy.”

Henry looked at Thomas. “That’s the nicest thing he’s said about us in a while.”

“Don’t get used to it,” growled George. He looked at his sister. “It will be all right, you’ll see.”

Eileen hugged her brother. “Thanks, George.”

They went on their way. The crowd around the preacher was larger this morning, and his ranting louder and more raucous. There were new posters up and some new graffiti as well.

Not what we need to worry about today, thought Thomas as they left the square.

“There you are!” said Mark, pouncing on the three of them as soon as they got through the gate. “Dump your blades and come on! Today’s the big day!”

“We know,” said Henry. “Eileen’s been obsessing on it all morning.”

“And most of last night,” said Eileen. “I couldn’t sleep at all. Then I couldn’t wake up. Then I couldn’t get out of bed.”

“Well, now you’re here and everything is ready!” said Mark. “Today we deliver your petition to the Headmaster. We’ve got six hundred signatures!”

Eileen’s mouth fell open, and for a few moments all she could do was stare. At last she managed to repeat, “Six hundred?”

“And three masters and a dozen professors as well!” said Mark. “You are really well-liked!”

Eileen stared at him. “I... I...”

“She is stunned,” supplied Henry. “Overwhelmed and full of heart. She does not know what to say. She may have to kiss you.”

Eileen hit Henry without even looking. Henry grinned. "Oh, good. She's back."

"We're meeting after class in the commons," said Mark. "We're getting as many students as we can to march with us to the Headmaster's house to present the petition. The whole company will be there!"

Except the ones we're missing, thought Thomas. "Thank you, Mark. You did great."

Mark smiled. "It's the most fun I've had in months. Now off we go, and see you after class!"

By noon, the Academy had been transformed. The grey buildings were festooned with banners. "Let Eileen in!" "We Want Girls!" and "Yes! For Eileen!" vied with "Keep Tradition!" and "Girls are a Distraction!" and "Women OUTSIDE the walls!" Students were running around with sheets of paper, cajoling last-minute signatures on petitions and exhorting others to march at the Headmaster's house at the end of the day.

"Remember!" Thomas heard a dozen times from both sides, "No missing classes! No violence! Let them know what we think!"

By the afternoon, the level of rambunctiousness in class was growing ever higher and the masters were giving stern warnings about proper behaviour.

Thomas finished his last class and stepped out into the late afternoon sun. Water was in the air again and the wind was just strong enough to rob warmth from flesh. Despite that, no one was heading for shelter. Some students were chanting, others were arguing, others were trying to gather everyone together. Thomas dodged through them all to the law building, where Eileen had been sitting in on a class with Henry. A dozen Traditionalists were standing outside.

"Oh, look," said one, pointing at Thomas. "It's the one who wants his girlfriend to destroy the Academy!"

"WRECKER!!" shouted the Traditionalists. "WRECKER! WRECKER! WRECKER!"

"Really?" said Thomas. "That's the best you could come up with today?"

"They are incredibly unimaginative," said Henry, coming out of the building with Eileen right behind him. "I think they ran out of anything interesting to say about noon two days ago."

Eileen nodded, "I agr..."

"HOUSEWRECKER! SCHOOLWRECKER! SHAME SHAME SHAME!"

Thomas held out his hand to Eileen. "Ready?"

Eileen took Thomas's hand and kissed his cheek. Henry stepped up beside them, and Eileen reached out and grabbed his hand as well. "Together," she said, putting on her bravest smile.

"HOUSEWRECKER! SCHOOLWRECKER! SHAME SHAME SHAME!"

"Oh, shut up."

Outside of the library, the twelve remaining members of the Student Company joined them, forcing the Traditionalists back. They shook Eileen's hand and followed her to the commons. All over the grounds, students saw her and fell in behind. They had banners and flags, made of strips of cloth or sheets of paper glued together. The conversations around them grew into a steady, excited buzz. "What do we do?" asked Eileen when they reached the commons.

"Speeches first," said Mark, pointing to a pile of crates stacked to make a podium, "Then we march to the Headmaster's house to present the petition."

"Who has the petition sheets?" asked Henry.

"I do," said William, holding up a very thick sheaf of papers.

"Will..." Eileen wallowed convulsively. "Will the Headmaster see us?"

"Oh yes," said Henry. "We have an appointment."

Thomas nearly tripped over his own feet in surprise. "We do?"

"Aye," said Henry. "I made it before the debate. Didn't want to give him any excuses."

"Very clever," said Thomas.

"Thank you."

The common was now a sea of black robes, signs, banners and flags. There were flags for Law, Philosophy, Physicians and the Engineers. Even the Theology school had a small contingent, much to Thomas's surprise. And in front of all of them, Evan raised the flag of the Academy's Expeditionary Company—a black square with the coat of arms in red, and crossed swords underneath.

"Right," said Henry. "Thomas gets their attention, then Eileen speaks. Then we march. Ready?"

"Oh, no," said Eileen.

"You'll be fine," said Thomas, wishing he'd had time to make up a speech. He took a deep breath to force his stomach out of his throat and stepped onto a pile of crates. There were two hundred of them at least, and there were masters interspersed with the students.

Another deep breath. Then Thomas called out, "Fellow students!"

The crowd fell silent.

"A week ago, we debated the simple idea that young women are as capable of learning as anyone else." Thomas found himself smiling. "And I must say, after the debate, we weren't sure if we would still be students!" A chuckle rolled through his audience. "Four days ago we began a petition that any girl who passes the entrance exams should be admitted to the Academy! And today, in keeping with our traditions, we will formally present our petition, along with our request to change the laws of the Academy, to the Headmaster!"

The cheering was louder than Thomas thought the speech deserved. He raised his arms, and shouted over it, "Students of the Royal Academy of Learning, I present to you the young woman we hope will be the first to attend the Academy in two hundred years! The Academy's honoured guest, a Lieutenant of the Student Company, and as brave a person as any I have known, Miss Eileen Gobhann!"

The audience clapped and yelled their approval as Thomas stepped down and Eileen stepped up. She had to call "Students!" three times before they were quiet enough to hear her. "Five years ago, when I learned that Thomas was going to the Academy, all I could think was, 'Why not me?' And when I asked, I was told it was because I was a girl." Eileen's finger stabbed at her chest. "And I am here to tell you, that is not answer enough!

"She's better at this than you," Henry said to Thomas as the students cheered. Thomas elbowed him but didn't disagree.

"I study hard!" Eileen yelled. "I work hard! And those of you who faced me on the fencing floor know I fight hard!" A round of laughs went up. Eileen smiled back at them. "You don't have to be a boy to learn! All you have to do is be willing to work hard and I am here to prove it!" The students applauded again. Eileen let it die down before she spoke again. "I am not asking for a free place at the Academy, I am asking to be forced to study harder than I ever have, to learn more than I ever have, and to sit the exams. And when I have passed those exams, when I have earned my place here, I am asking for the right to come back and say to you not, 'students', but 'my fellow students!'"

Eileen bowed and stepped down from the podium. The audience clapped and shouted their approval. Thomas called out, "Student Company! Fall in!" He and Henry took places beside Eileen at the front. Eileen grabbed both their hands and began marching towards the Headmaster's house. A sea of students followed. Someone started singing the school song, and two hundred voices joined in.

"Look there!" said Mark, pointing. Another group was marching in from the front gate, in nearly the same numbers as they had. Less than half of them wore black robes. The rest were older, and wore the clothes of merchants and craftsmen. All of them were marching behind a large banner that declared "UPHOLD TRADITION!"

Lords Cormac, Anthony and Ethan were marching at the front.

"They can't be serious!" Eileen fumed. "They have nothing to do with this! With any of this!"

"Now we know why they were here yesterday," said Henry. "Don't kill them on school grounds."

"No promises," Eileen said through clenched teeth.

Thomas gauged the distance to the Headmaster's house. "At least we'll get there first."

"We'd better," said Eileen. "I'll not have Keith stealing our thunder, and certainly not those three idiots!"

"Master Brennan is marching with them as well," said Mark.

"Of course." Thomas sighed. *I used to admire him.* "Sing louder!"

They raised their voices higher, and marched a little faster. The Headmaster was standing on the porch, watching with eyebrows raised, as the two groups grew closer. Some words were tossed back and forth between the groups, and a scuffle nearly broke out as one student marching in the Idealist group was grabbed by the scruff of his neck and given a thorough tongue lashing by his father, who was marching with the Traditionalists. A dozen others from the Idealists managed to pull the young man back into the crowd where his father couldn't reach him.

"Shame!" shouted the Traditionalists.

"Change is good!" shouted the Idealists.

"Tradition!"

"Girls!"

"No Girls!"

"Yes, Girls!

"TRADITION!"

"CHANGE!"

"SILENCE!"

That last word came from the Master of Rhetoric who, with the Master of Laws, was standing on the porch beside the Headmaster. He had to repeat it a dozen times before both groups quieted down enough to hear.

"We are very glad to see such a healthy spirit of debate," said the Master of Rhetoric. "And we are even more pleased to see it occur in an atmosphere of benign fraternity, instead of acrimonious conflict."

The glares from either side suggested otherwise, but both groups held their peace.

"And now, since both sides have come to meet with the Headmaster, and since both sides are equally weighed in members, I think it best that both sides should be able to speak their piece to all those assembled. Does that not seem reasonable?"

"It does not," said one of the burghers in front of the Traditionalists. "Though our numbers may be equal, make no doubt our importance is not. I stand before you as a representative of the merchants of our city, whose children attend your Academy, and as a member of the city council and advisor to the Lord Mayor. And I have with me here a dozen other men of standing. We are not to be treated on the same level as these boys."

Henry stepped forward. "I am the brother and heir of the Duke of Frostmire, and by his leave, ambassador to the king. And behind me are the sons of a dozen nobles whose importance, according to custom, is a great deal higher than yours."

"The young lord does have a point," said the Master of Rhetoric.

"We have spent our lives working for the betterment of this city and all those who are in it!" snapped the burgher, who was growing rather red.

"We represent the majority of students in this Academy and therefore have a vested interest in this matter," said Henry.

"We are the parents of the students of this Academy!"

"We are acting in accordance with Academy tradition and law!" said Thomas.

"We pay the tuition that allows your Academy to exist!"

"We have an appointment," said Henry. "You don't. So in accordance with the rules of courtesy, business, nobility and the Academy, we take precedent."

"Headmaster!" appealed the burgher, "Please! This farce of letting girls into the Academy has gone on quite far enough!"

"Farce?" repeated Eileen, but before she could say another word, the Headmaster raised his hand.

"I am afraid that Lord Henry is right," said the Headmaster. "He does have an appointment."

The Headmaster waited until the laughter from the Idealists died down before continuing. "And while I will most certainly hear your views," he said to the Traditionalists, "nonetheless, Lord Henry's appointment does take precedence in this matter." He looked down his nose at Henry. "Step up, young man, and speak."

"Oh, I'm not our speaker. I just made the appointment." He pushed Thomas and Eileen forward. "Have fun."

"Always," muttered Thomas. "William, with us, please."

The three mounted the stairs and stood before the Headmaster.

"Headmaster," said Thomas, making his voice loud enough to carry over the crowd. "On behalf of the majority of the students of the Academy, and in accordance with the traditions and laws that govern our beloved school, we are pleased to present you with the following petition." He turned to William. "If you please?"

William held up the sheaf of papers. "Whereas it was once the case that women were a part of our Academy, whereas, through trial of battle, through power of intellect, and through strength of will, Miss Eileen Gobhann has shown herself to be as worthy as any man; and whereas, though she would be a most worthy addition to the ranks of students, she is prevented from doing so because of her sex, we hereby petition that the Academy change its laws so that Miss Eileen Gobhann, and any other girl or woman who has the necessary skills and recommendations, may sit for the Academy entrance exams and, upon achieving the marks necessary to pass those exams, be granted entrance to the Academy!"

The Idealists cheered, while equally loud boos and catcalls came from the Traditionalists. Thomas let them go on for a bit, then said, "In accordance with the Academy rules, laws, and traditions, will you, Headmaster, bring our petition to the ruling council of the Academy, that it may be properly debated and, if accepted, brought into Academy law?"

William handed the sheaf of papers to Eileen, who held it out to the Headmaster. He smiled at her, though there was something sad in it and took the papers. He passed them to the Master of Laws. "Master Greyfields," said the Headmaster. "Is the petition in good order?"

The Master of Laws peered closely at the pages a while, then nodded. "It is."

"The Master of Laws has reviewed the petition," said the Headmaster. "He has found it to be in good order—as we would expect—and in accordance with the laws and traditions of the Academy. We therefore decree that on the next meeting of the Council of Rules, the petition will be given serious consideration, witnesses will be called, and both sides shall be able to present their cases."

"We did it!" yelled Mark. "We won!"

A cheer went up from the Idealists, followed immediately by boos and protests from the Traditionalists. One of the burghers yelled, "This decision cannot be allowed!"

"There has been no decision," the Master of Rhetoric's voice carried clearly over the noise. He stepped up beside the Headmaster. "These young men and this young woman have only won the right to have their petition duly considered by the Council of Rules. Nothing more."

"It is a matter for the Council to decide," said Headmaster, "which it will do at the end of the month!"

"And since that's what we came to do," said Henry, "we're declaring victory!"

The Idealists went insane. The Traditionalists grumbled and snarled.

"This is not over!" yelled Keith from the front of the Traditionalists' ranks.

"Indeed it is not," said the Headmaster. "But it was properly presented, well said, and well argued." He looked over the crowd. "No matter what comes of this, let it be noted that you all have behaved properly, and fought this matter as all matters at the Academy should be fought: with words and brains! The committee will meet at the end of the month, and both sides will be afforded the right to have their say."

"We will attend the committee to present our case," declared the burgher. "Girls will not come into the Academy!"

"Good luck with that!" called Henry. "Today, victory is ours!"

Shouts of victory came from two hundred throats. The Idealists jumped up and down and hugged each other in glee.

"Now disperse," said the Headmaster. "And in the spirit of fraternity, let there be no recriminations among you for the events of today!"

"To the Broken Quill!" shouted Henry. "Let the celebrations begin!"

The Traditionalists grumbled and mumbled and rallied around four or five of the burghers and Keith. Thomas and Eileen, hand in hand, practically leapt from the porch and led the cheering Idealists across the grounds. Thomas kept an eye out for Cormac, Anthony and Ethan, but they seemed to have vanished.

"We have to tell George!" Eileen shouted over the din.

"You'll never escape!" said Henry. "I'll send someone!"

They flowed out the gate and down the street. Henry went into a stable on their way and hired one of the boys to run the news to George. As the students went down the streets some dropped out and came back pulling girls behind them. The whole group, still singing and laughing, descended on the Broken Quill. Soon, the pub was even louder than it had been during Festival. Eileen, with Thomas at her side, did the rounds of the room, taking in congratulations and thanking everyone.

George came in, bringing Linda Gatron with him. Eileen spotted her brother and pushed and pleaded her way across the room to throw herself into his arms. George spun her around and squeezed her until she squeaked. "You won!"

"We won!" said Eileen. "Everyone was wonderful!"

Henry brought drinks for George and Linda before dashing back into the crowd. The Master Smith's daughter looked shocked at the happy mayhem in the room but waded into the throng beside George. Soon, she was being chatted up by a small group of students while George loomed behind her. Tables were pushed out of the way and a dozen of the students pulled out instruments. Music struck up and everyone who had a partner went out on the floor. Eileen danced with Thomas and every boy in the Student Company. Linda danced with George, then Thomas and Henry. Students and their girls were moving constantly on and off the dance floor, while the musicians did their best to be heard above the joyous racket.

When the midnight bell rang everyone spilled into the streets. Some went home, some went to friends' houses to continue the celebration. George and Linda said their goodnights and went back to the Street of Smiths, arm-in-arm. Thomas offered him an escort home, but George refused.

"Not tonight," said George, smiling at his sister. "It's Eileen's night. Let her celebrate it."

"But..."

George held up his stick. "I'll be fine, Thomas. We'll stay on the main streets. You take care of my sister."

"We'll try to have her home before dawn," said Henry.

"Before dawn?" Linda looked at once thrilled and appalled. "Eileen! What would your parents say?"

"They're not here," said George. "And I trust that Thomas will bring her back home safe and sound."

"Always," said Thomas. He smiled at Eileen. "Seems only fair, since she did the same for me."

Eileen smiled back and leaned against him.

"Then good night," said George. "I will see you in the morning."

Thomas watched George and Linda go until they were out of sight.

"Don't worry about them," said Henry. "They couldn't get George with a block and tackle. Now come. The party is at Mark's house."

For another two hours, they celebrated. Mark played mandolin, and Nicholas was a fair guitarist. At the end of the second hour, Thomas and Eileen excused themselves. Henry, who was in the midst of arguing philosophy with Nicholas, offered to go with them.

"No need," said Thomas. "I'll stay at the smithy tonight. I'm sure George won't mind if I sleep in the kitchen."

"Just be sure it's in the kitchen," teased Mark.

"It will be," declared William. "Otherwise George will feed him to the forge!"

"George wouldn't leave enough of him to feed to the forge," said Evan.

Eileen made a rude gesture and led Thomas out into the night. As soon as they were out of sight of the building, she stopped him and leaned in close for a long, deep kiss. When they finally broke apart, she took his hand. "I don't think I can remember the last time I felt this happy."

"Me either," said Thomas. "Everything is feeling right, for a change."

"I don't want to go home," said Eileen.

"All right," said Thomas. "Did you want to go back to the party?"

"No."

"Then where?"

Eileen looked down at her boots When she looked back into Thomas's eyes, she was smiling. "Your apartment?"

It took Thomas's slightly drunk brain a while to comprehend that. "If you like. Yes." His own smile grew wider and wider, no matter how he tried to control it. "Definitely, yes."

The walk to his apartment took nearly twice as long as it should have, as they stopped to kiss a dozen times on the way. When they finally slipped inside the door Eileen kissed him hard on the mouth and led him to the couch before the fireplace.

"Let me get the fire started," said Thomas. He stacked the tinder and set the logs in on top. He stepped back and stared until the fire leapt into life all at once.

Eileen's eyebrows went up. "Show off."

"Aye." Thomas laughed. "Tonight, everything is right."

"It is," said Eileen. "Come here."

It was the last bell of the night when they untangled themselves from the blankets on the couch. Eileen, wearing only her drawers, stretched and yawned. "That was very, very nice," she said, smiling over her shoulder at Thomas.

Thomas smiled back, as he watched her slim body move in the yellow light of the fire. "It was indeed." Thomas picked her shift off the floor and wrapped his arms around her. "I'm just surprised Henry didn't walk in on us."

"Knowing Henry, he's probably sleeping on Mark's floor," said Eileen. She kissed his bare chest and took the shift, pulling it on over her head. She found her skirt on the floor. "My shirt and bodice?"

"Behind the couch," said Thomas, looking for his breeches. He found them and pulled them on over his braies, then looked around for his shirt. "We'll get you home before dawn," he said. "But not by much."

"By just enough," said Eileen, kissing him again.

It was late enough that even the footpads that lurked in the alleys had mostly sought out their beds. The walk was cold, but not as bad as it had been the night before. Thomas wondered if the weather was finally going to get warmer, or if it just meant they'd have rain instead of snow the next day.

The Street of Smiths was completely dark when they arrived.

"Not even a candle in the window," said Thomas.

"We are very late," whispered Eileen. "He's probably in bed fast asleep."

Thomas yawned. "I can't blame him."

Hand in hand, they walked to the doors of the forge.

"What's that?" Eileen asked, pointing to a piece of paper, nailed up on the door.

"I don't know," said Thomas. He squinted at it.

"Can you read it?"

"Too dark," said Thomas taking the piece of paper from the door. "Let's get inside."

Eileen fumbled with her key and opened the door. The two slipped inside, and Eileen closed the door behind them. Thomas waited until the door was shut tight, then raised a hand and willed a little ball of light into existence. Together they looked at the paper.

"Oh, by the Four," Eileen breathed.

It was in Henry's handwriting:

Attack. Michael's apartment. Come at once.

-H.

17

Nicholas, John, Robert, and Wilson were standing in the street outside Michael's apartment. They carried torches and rapiers in their hands and were pacing back and forth, anger radiating from them like heat from a stove. Thomas and Eileen, who had run all the way from the forge, skidded to a stop on the wet, icy cobbles, gasping for air.

"What happened?" Thomas demanded, between breaths. "Where's Henry? Where's George?"

"Inside!" said John. "Hurry!"

Thomas tried to swallow the fear that threatened to block his throat. He mounted the stairs to Michael's place two at a time. Philip, William and Mark were on the balcony, swords in hand and ready to use them.

"About time!" snapped Philip. "James is dying!"

Thomas pushed past him without a word. Marcus stood on the other side of the door, his sword in hand. The room stank of blood and sweat. James was sitting on the floor in a pool of dark red. His legs, wrapped in bandages and splinted, were splayed out in front of him. His chest and stomach were bandaged as well, but the cloth was already wet and red through in three different places. George was sitting behind him, holding him upright. Henry knelt at his side, speaking softly. Kevin held a pair of bloodied cloths against James' stomach and Bruce held another one against his chest.

"The healer's been and gone," said Henry, the words coming out fast and angry. "He wasn't going to bother straightening James' legs, until I told him I'd kill him if he didn't." James body convulsed in pain, and he gasped in air. "He's dying, Thomas. Hurry up."

He's lucky he's not dead already. Thomas knelt in front of James, and pulled the bandage off his chest. Blood spurted out. Thomas pressed his hands to the wound and began chanting. It took a long moment before the magic started flowing. Then bright white light, invisible to everyone but Thomas, flowed from Thomas's hand into other man's body. James cried out in pain as his body began knitting itself back together. The blood that was pouring from James' body slowed. Thomas could feel himself getting light-headed, and the room began to swim in and out of focus.

Henry pushed Thomas away, breaking his connection with James. The magic died at once, and Thomas collapsed back onto the bloody floor.

"Don't you pass out!" said Henry. "We may need you!"

Thomas struggled to sit up. "Is he all right?"

"No, he's not," growled James between gritted teeth. "Gods, it hurts!"

Thomas forced himself to concentrate until the room came into focus. James was still bleeding, but his injuries were now only cut skin and muscle, not gaping holes in his body. "Bandage him back up," said Thomas. "What happened?"

"Where have you been?" demanded Henry. "We needed you an hour ago."

"At the apartment," said Thomas. "What happened?"

"The apartment?" George rumbled. "What were you two doing at the..."

"WHAT HAPPENED?" yelled Thomas. The room went black on him for a moment and he nearly fell over. Eileen grabbed him and pulled him back upright.

"Ambush," said James, his breath hitching in pain. "Hit Michael on the head when we walked through the door. I managed to draw and stab one, but others came after me. I ran down the stairs and screamed for help."

"Most of us were still at Mark's place next door," said Henry. "We came charging out. They'd already stabbed James pretty bad by the time we got here."

"They had horses," said Bruce. "They rode us down. That's how James got the broken legs. He was already on the ground." He shook his head, his face pale and grim. "Lucky the beasts didn't step on his head."

"They threw Michael over one of the horses," said Kevin. "Rode off with him."

"And of course they weren't wearing colours," said Thomas. Rage began building inside him, now that the fear was gone. *I will hunt them down, this time.*

"They didn't need to be," spat Henry. "I recognized them."

"What?!"

"Not all of them," said Henry. "Just three."

Eileen paled. "No."

"Cormac, Anthony and Ethan," said Henry. "King's peace or not, they're *mine*."

"Do we know where they went?

"Evan ran after them," said Kevin. "We dragged James in here, then I sent Marcus to get the healer and Mark to get the ones that had left, and John to George's place, which you weren't at."

Thomas swore. "I'm sorry."

"Can't blame you," said James, managing a smile through gritted teeth. "I'd take Eileen back to my place, too, given the chance." He groaned in pain. "Can't you do any more?"

Thomas shook his head, trying to clear it. "Not tonight. I'll just pass out and be useless."

"So what do we do?" demanded Kevin. "We can't just let them get away with it!"

"We won't," said Thomas. He tried to think but his head was muzzy and the room was slowly trying to spin. "We have to..."

The darkness that hovered on the edge of Thomas's vision closed in again. He could feel Eileen clinging to his coat, but couldn't focus his eyes to see.

"We have to stay safe," Henry was saying. "And we have to clean this place up before the blood drips on the neighbours below. James looks too healthy now to have lost so much."

"What about the Watch?" asked Eileen. "I'm surprised they haven't shown up yet."

"They only show up at night in the rich neighbourhoods," said Bruce. "Here they don't come until morning, unless the screaming doesn't stop or there's a fire."

"Then let's get this place cleaned up before they come in the morning," said Henry.

"That's what, an hour from now?" asked George. He shook his head. "I have to get back to the smithy If I'm not open people will wonder what happened." He stood up and looked down at his blood-soaked shirt. "I'll need to change as well."

"What about Thomas?" said Bruce. "He's looking worse than James, right now."

"Just what I need to hear," said Thomas. The darkness faded to grey, then to light, and he could see again. "I need to sleep. Then I'll be all right."

"Put him in Michael's room," said Henry. "We'll wake you when Evan comes back."

Thomas let Eileen drag him to Michael's room, and gave into the darkness.

"Get up, Thomas. Evan is back."

Thomas opened his eyes and blinked until they focused. A faint, dull light was coming in through the window. "What?"

"Evan is back," said Henry again. "How are you?"

Thomas sat up and waited to see if he would pass out. He didn't. "Better. How long have I been sleeping?"

"Just over an hour. First morning bell has already rung."

"Right." Thomas pushed himself to his feet. "Did Evan manage to follow them?"

"All the way," said Henry. "Want to hear it from him?"

"Oh, yes," said Thomas.

He followed Henry into the main room. All of the Student Company were there. James was sitting in one of the chairs with Bruce helping him stay upright. Evan was in another chair. He looked pale, tired and incredibly angry. When he saw Thomas, his face twisted even further.

"Churchmen," Evan spat the word out. "Dragged him right to their buildings behind the cathedral and hustled him inside."

Proof, thought Thomas. "We'll get them out of there."

"How?" demanded Evan. "Offer you instead?"

"We'll think of something," said Henry.

"This is all about Thomas!" snapped Evan. "The Church wants to convict him and they're taking all of us to do it!"

"We don't know that," said Mark.

"We do," said Thomas before Mark could protest further. "Evan is right."

Evan rounded on Thomas. "You could have stopped all this!"

"No, I couldn't."

"They have our friends!"

"I know!" snapped Thomas. "But screaming at me won't help!"

"Will handing you over?" demanded Evan. "Because I'm about ready for that!"

"Evan," Henry's voice was low and deadly. "That's enough."

"Then give me another idea!" Evan turned his glare on Henry. "What do we do?"

"Get sleep," said Thomas. "And food. Everyone."

"How will that help?"

"And when you've done that," continued Thomas, "write your statements. All of you. Write out exactly what you saw and heard, in as much detail as you can remember."

"We need to get them back!"

"We can't do that today!" Thomas felt ready to collapse again, but knew that he couldn't. "Today is the High Father's Day. There's no way we'll get near the church buildings. So today we prepare and tomorrow we go to the Headmaster and tell him everything that has happened."

And tonight, I'll get them back. All of them.

18

Thomas led Eileen and Henry away from the student quarter to Sir Walter's fencing salon. Eileen looked as haggard as Thomas felt. Even Henry, usually unaffected by lack of sleep, looked pale and exhausted.

The rest of the company had stayed together at Michael's place. They were angry, scared and ready to lash out, but Thomas had convinced them to wait until the next day before they acted. He also ignored their questions about where, exactly, he was going. There was much grumbling, and Evan glared at Thomas as he went.

It's all my fault, Thomas thought as they climbed the stairs to the warehouse. *Why shouldn't they be angry?*

Sir Walter was already at the warehouse, running through drills with a short stick. He frowned when he saw Henry and Eileen come in behind Thomas. "What are they doing here?"

"Looking for a place to fence," said Henry. "You come highly recommended."

"I pick my students," said Sir Walter, looking daggers at Thomas.

"You have no students," said Henry. "You're the king's chief spy and we don't have time for this."

"You know Lord Henry," said Thomas. "This is Miss Eileen Gobhann."

"I know," said Sir Walter. He tapped the tip of his stick against his other palm. "Why are they here, Thomas?"

"Michael was kidnapped last night."

"Went missing, you mean," said Sir Walter.

"Kidnapped," repeated Thomas. "By the High Father's men and Lords Cormac, Anthony and Ethan. The entire company will bear witness."

Sir Walter tucked his stick under his arm. "And you know the kidnappers are churchmen how?"

"Because Evan followed them back to the High Father's building behind the cathedral."

"This is a direct violation of the rights of students and the authority of the king," said Henry. "It's also a direct violation of the King's Peace as sworn by Lords Cormac, Anthony and Ethan. The students are preparing their statements now, and will take them to the Headmaster and Master of Laws tomorrow morning."

"Will the king demand their release?" asked Thomas.

Sir Walter wouldn't meet Thomas's eyes. "That is for him to say. Not me."

"Our friends are being tortured!" protested Eileen. "You know they are!"

Sir Walter shrugged. "What do you want me to say?"

"That you'll take it to the king. That he'll sign a writ, and that you'll get them out of there!"

"What makes you think a writ will get them out?" asked Sir Walter, his tone a bit more gentle than before.

"It got Thomas out!"

"A writ and two hundred armed students at the Church's door is what got Thomas out," said Sir Walter.

"I can get two hundred armed students in an hour," said Henry. "By noon I can get a thousand."

"The Church didn't want a riot last time," said Sir Walter. "This time, they don't care and they have more cavalry in town."

"So they're hoping we'll try something?" Thomas couldn't believe it. "The Archbishop said he would wait!"

"They aren't hoping *you* try something, but it won't hurt them if you do," said Sir Walter. "They'll just ride you down and claim they were helping curb a riot."

"Then the king has to intervene!"

"No, he doesn't," said Sir Walter. "In fact, it's better if he doesn't."

"Not for our friends!" cried Eileen.

Thomas was seething. "So the king will not even try?"

"I will talk to the king, and I'm sure he will compose a writ," said Sir Walter. "And given the pride he takes in his Academy, I have no doubt he will engage in dialogue with the Archbishop's representatives."

"Why not the Archbishop himself?" asked Henry. "Or does the Archbishop no longer come when the king summons him?"

"The Archbishop claims to be answering to a higher power at the moment," said Sir Walter.

"What about the lords?" asked Henry. "They're not protected by the Church."

"They'll be brought before the king," said Sir Walter. "If we can find them."

"They'll be brought before *me*," said Henry, his tone grim. "You tell the king that the Ambassador of the Duke of Frostmire has been gravely insulted and is demanding satisfaction."

"But what about our friends?" Eileen was nearly crying. "We can't leave them to be tortured!"

"It would be the wisest course." Said Sir Walter.

Thomas looked out the window. It was drizzling now and showed no signs of letting up. The long night and the magic had taken a great deal of Thomas's strength, and the walk over had sapped most of what was left. It was going to be a cold, miserable night to be out in the dark.

By the Four, I'm tired.

"We're students," Thomas said, bringing his eyes back to meet Sir Walter's. "What possibly makes you think we'll take the wisest course?"

Sir Walter didn't say anything for a long time. At last, he nodded. "Do you even know where the dungeons are?"

"No," said Thomas. "Do you?"

"Yes." said Sir Walter. "Anything you do is without the king's knowledge or consent."

"I know."

"Where can I reach you?"

"Our apartment," said Thomas. "We need sleep if we're going out tonight."

"You certainly will."

***

"Are you insane?" was George's rather predictable response. "You can't possibly raid the Church!"

"It's not like we haven't done it before," said Henry. "We burned down Bishop Malloy's house, last year."

"And fought his troops," said Eileen.

"And Thomas ran him through."

"That's different!" George protested.

"How?"

"There's hundreds of them at the cathedral!"

"Not at night," said Thomas. "The soldiers are in their barracks and they won't have that many guards in the cells."

"How do you know?"

"He doesn't," said Henry. "But it's a reasonable assumption. You don't put a lot of guards out, if you're trying to keep your prisoners secret."

"A reasonable..." George began turning purple. "You can't do it!"

"Yes," said Thomas. "We can."

"Not you!" said George. "Eileen! You are absolutely forbidden to go!"

"What?!"

"I'll not have you raiding the..."

"SHUT UP!" yelled Thomas, surprising them all. Before George could recover and start arguing, Thomas hissed. "The world does not need to hear our business, so keep it quiet!"

George was definitely purple, now, but he kept his words to a very heated whisper. "You are not taking..."

"I am taking who I please, George," said Thomas. "I need Eileen and I need Henry with me. And I need you here and awake. You're closer to the cathedral than any of us, so this is where we're bringing them when we get them out."

"You don't get to give me orders, Thomas," George's voice had an ugly undertone in it.

"We're bringing them here, George," said Eileen. "And that's that. They're our friends."

"After last night how can you even *think* you'll get to stay out of it, George?" demanded Thomas.

"It's not me I'm worried about!"

"It *is* you you're worried about!" Thomas snapped, barely remembering to keep his voice down. "Since this whole mess started it's been you and your reputation you've been worried about!"

"I don't want to kill anyone else!" George bellowed, shaking the room. Then his whole body began trembling. George looked down at his hands in horror, then collapsed onto one of the benches. "Oh, by the Four. Not again. Not now." The trembles became shakes, and George clutched at the table.

"George?" Eileen's voice was filled with alarm. She put her hand on her brother's shoulder.

"DON'T TOUCH ME!" George shoved her away hard and jumped to his feet, both hands in fists. Eileen flew back, slammed into the cupboard and hit the floor. Thomas and Henry jumped to their feet.

George stared at his sister, his face pale and tears in his eyes. Then he turned and slammed his fists against the table, making it jump. Eileen's hand went over her mouth. Thomas, unsure what to do, moved toward George.

"Don't!" said Henry. "Stay back!"

George's fists crashed down on the table again and again until the long boards of it cracked. His jaws gritted tight together and tears streamed down his face. Then his legs gave out and he collapsed on the floor, burying his face in his hands.

Long, racking sobs shook George's body. Henry circled around him and sat down on the floor out of reach. Thomas helped Eileen to her feet. She clung to him, her own face white with shock.

"How long?" asked Henry. "Did they start right after we got back, or just recently?" George didn't answer. "You should have told me, George."

"Told you what?" George's voice came, broken and hollow, from behind his hands. "That I lie in bed crying like a baby every night? That half the time I sit in the back of the forge with the door shut, shaking in the dark? That sometimes I go to the tavern in the middle of the morning because the smell of the fire reminds me of the caves? That it's turned me from a man into a wreck?"

"Yes," said Henry. "All of it."

"What good would that have done?"

"You wouldn't have been alone," said Henry. "Eileen, go get Linda."

"No!" George tried to grab Henry, but couldn't reach. "She can't see me like this!"

"She can if she actually loves you," said Henry. "Does she?"

George didn't answer.

"Henry," said Eileen. "What's going on?"

"It happens," said Henry. "Sometimes after a man's first battle, sometimes after a war. I knew one knight who was fine for years before it happened to him."

"What is it?"

"Horror," said Henry. "It catches a man and holds him, rather than going away. Then this happens. George. George!"

The last one snapped out as a command. George's head came up. "It will be all right," said Henry. "It takes time, but it will be all right. Eileen needs to get Linda because we need to go and you shouldn't be alone right now. Do you trust Linda?"

George hesitated. Then he nodded.

"Good. Eileen, go get her. Tell her your brother is ill and that we need her help. Go now before she goes to service."

Eileen went, her feet clattering on the stairs as she ran out.

"I didn't know," said Thomas. "George I'm so sorry. I didn't know."

George looked wretched and didn't say anything.

"We'll find another place to go," said Thomas. "We can take them back to our apartment."

"No," said George. He didn't raise his eyes, but he shook his head. "No. You bring them here."

"Are you sure?"

"I won't have them hurt," said George. "I don't want anyone else hurt."

Thomas nodded. "Thank you, George."

***

Thomas and Henry managed to get George off the floor and upstairs to his bed before Linda came over. Linda took one look at him and promised to sit with George for the day.

"I didn't even think about it," said Henry on the way back to their apartment. "I just thought he was tired of being involved. The more fool me."

"Will he be all right?" asked Eileen.

Henry hesitated. "I've seen men who had it worse pull out of it."

Thomas frowned. "And?"

Henry sighed. "And I've seen some not get better." He took Eileen's hand. "Your brother is very strong. He'll pull through this."

"What... what do I do?"

"Wait," said Henry. "Listen to him. Make him take time with Linda, and get out of the house and around people. It seems to help."

They were silent for the rest of the walk back to the apartment. The last of Thomas's energy was rapidly fading, and he wanted nothing more than to collapse. Eileen was stumbling as she walked, and Henry was looking glassy-eyed with exhaustion.

"We sleep until dinner," said Henry. "Then we get organized."

Eileen and Thomas curled up together in Thomas's bed, holding one another until they both fell asleep. Thomas drifted in and out of sleep, dreams of blood and violence chasing him through the day.

At dinner time a messenger delivered a small sealed envelope. Inside was a map of the Church of the High Father's main administrative building with the note: *Back door. Go left. Third corridor, all the way through, then right, fourth door. Keys on peg at bottom of stairs. Burn this map before you go.* The three stared at the map until they'd memorized it and threw it on the fire.

Thomas and Eileen went out to buy dinner and came back to find Henry cutting up one of his robes to make black scarves for their heads and faces.

As they ate Henry taught Thomas and Eileen simple hand signs so they could work without speaking, and touch signs to use in the dark.

After the second bell of the night, they left.

Just after the midnight bell, Thomas stood in the alley behind the High Father's administrative building, his rapier and dagger in his hands. Eileen and Henry were right behind him.

"Anything?" whispered Eileen.

Thomas once more scanned the dark alley between him and the door, as well as the windows of the building in front of them. There were some lights flickering from the higher windows—lamps from those working late, Thomas guessed—but he couldn't see the inner light of anyone, or anything, alive. "Nothing. Wait until I get the door open, then follow."

Thomas forced a deep breath into his lungs, then a second. When he was fairly sure his heart wasn't beating hard enough to be heard outside his body, he stepped across the alley. He turned in a circle, checking the rooftops and windows of the buildings behind him. No one was there, either. He sank down to his haunches in front of the door. It was old-fashioned, with a large keyhole. Praying he was remembering Sir Walter's lessons correctly, Thomas pulled out his lock-picks and began working.

It took longer than he wanted, and Thomas felt like he was going to be caught at any moment. Finally, he heard a click and when he turned the handle, the door opened. Thomas let out a breath he'd been holding far longer than he should and pushed the door the rest of the way. It swung silently open.

Thomas stepped inside and was surprised to see candles in sconces lighting the corridor. He listened as hard as he could. There was nothing. Thomas leaned back outside and waved. Eileen and Henry slipped across the alley and inside. Thomas pointed at himself and circled his hand once—Henry's signal for scouting.

He slipped ahead to the end of the short corridor and looked out.

The halls were wide, with polished marble floors and high ceilings. Five-headed sconces filled with candles dotted the walls, making the hallways light enough to easily see anyone in them, if not actually bright. There was no one. *Really wish Sir Walter had mentioned that they leave candles burning all night.*

Thomas waved again. Henry and Eileen joined him. Thomas stepped out into the corridor and walked casually down the middle of it. *Act as if you belong,* had been Henry's suggestion. *As long they don't see us, they'll assume the footsteps belong to someone who is supposed to be there.* Thomas reached the first of the cross-hallways and peeked around the corner. The next corridor was empty. Thomas waved and waited.

Eileen came after Thomas, moving at the same casual pace. She passed him and kept going to the next corridor. A flip of her hand showed the coast was clear. Thomas signalled and Henry followed a moment later.

"If they hear a bunch of footsteps at once, they'll come looking," Henry had said. *"If they just hear one set, they probably won't even look up from their work."*

Thomas watched Henry stroll down the corridor as if he hadn't a care in the world, past Eileen to the next corridor. Thomas gritted his teeth and waited, watching the hallway. All it would take was for one door to open at the wrong moment and they would all be lost.

They're empty, Thomas reminded himself. *They were all dark and there's no one in them.*

Of course, that's only this hallway.

Henry flipped his hand, and Eileen walked up to join him. Thomas gripped his weapons tight and walked to where the other two leaned against the wall. Thomas stepped around them and looked down the other corridor.

Right, same again.

They covered the ground between the back hall and the front in casual steps that belied how tense they were. They saw no one and heard nothing except their own harsh breathing and beating hearts until they reached the end of the corridor.

The sconces in the walls were closer together here, and candelabras decorated the ceiling. The hallway was higher and wider, and they could see the main doors from where they stood. Thomas looked around the corner, then pulled his head back fast.

Two men were walking together down the hallway, directly towards them.

Thomas flattened himself against the corridor wall and shoved Eileen back as well. Henry faded back into the wall behind them. The men's footsteps and voices grew louder with every passing moment. Thomas waited, wondering if they could manage to subdue the men before they raised a cry. He didn't think he could bring himself to kill them out of hand, even though it was the fastest way to make sure they weren't caught.

"So how should we handle it?" asked the one of the men.

"Carefully," was the reply. "First, spread the word of the blasphemy that has been committed beyond our borders, and of the necessary sacrifice that has to be made to end it." The men were just about at the corridor. "Then talk of how the merchants' financial support may allow us to bring in mercenaries to fight the war, rather than their sons..."

The men walked past, neither of them noticing the black-clad figures pressed hard against the corridor wall. The conversation and the men's footsteps slowly faded into the distance, until Thomas heard a door open and shut. He managed to keep his sigh of relief quiet and looked out into the corridor again.

One of the men was coming back.

Thomas ducked his head back in and slipped across the corridor to press his back against the other wall. Eileen and Henry came beside him in a flurry of black fabric. *Please don't let him come this way. Please don't let him come this way. Please...*

The man kept going right past them without stopping or looking.

Thomas didn't let his breath out until the man's footsteps faded in the distance.

The hallway was clear when Thomas looked out again. With the same forced, casual pace, he walked to the door that led to the cellar and pulled on it. It opened. Eileen, then Henry slipped down onto the staircase below. Thomas stepped in, closing the door behind them. There were no candles to light their way down the steps. Thomas sheathed his dagger and cupped his hand, making a ball of light that was just bright enough for them to see the steps in front of them.

The steps went down father than Thomas remembered. *Of course, I was being dragged by a pair of guards that time.* The hallways below were as black as the stairs, but not as silent. In the darkness Thomas could hear someone crying, and someone else swearing. And further away, muffled by distance and the walls around them, someone crying out in pain.

Thomas let the light grow brighter. The hallway was long, with stone walls and floor, and an arched stone roof above. Four other hallways branched out from the one they stood in.

"Well," said Henry, breaking his own rule about speaking. "This should take a while."

"Not too long," said Thomas, keeping his voice low. "The hallway they dragged me through had a locked door at the end of it. My cell had a barred window in the door. If the rest do, too, we should see who is in them quick enough."

"Then get moving," said Henry. Somewhere in the darkness someone screamed in pain, making them all jump. Henry shuddered "Before whoever is causing *that* decides it's time to take a walk."

The corridor in front of them was storage. The next one led to cells. The keys were hanging on a peg outside the corridor. *Makes sense, I suppose,* thought Thomas. *If you assume no one is stupid enough to break in.*

Thomas unlocked the door and led them inside. The corridor had ten identical doors with small barred windows. Thomas peered in the first one and saw the steel ring in the middle of the floor. He shuddered. He'd spent two days chained to the floor of a cell just like that one, while the Inquisitor had droned questions at him. He could still remember the moment when he thought they were going to beat him and realized he was completely helpless to do anything about it.

"Pull it together, Thomas," hissed Henry, forcing him back to the present. Thomas shook his head and went to the next cell, and the next. Each was identical. Each was empty.

The cries of pain were louder at the next corridor. Thomas opened the hall door. "Keep your eyes out," he whispered. "If anyone comes..."

"If anyone comes," said Henry, "we kill them or we die."

Please don't let it come to that.

The first two cells were empty. The third held an old man who shied away from the light and cried out in fear, startling Thomas so badly his light nearly faded. The man in the cell huddled against the wall, crying, and Thomas felt sick leaving him there. *It can't be helped,* he told himself. *I can't take everyone.*

Liam was asleep in the next cell. His feet were shackled to the cell floor.

Thomas whistled softly to get Eileen's attention. "Here."

"You found one?" Eileen asked.

"Liam," said Thomas, as he struggled with the lock on the door. "Chained."

The lock clicked open and Thomas pushed at the door. It creaked. Liam started awake and pushed himself as far back as he could with his hands behind his back. He had bruises on his face, and gasped in pain as he moved.

"It's all right," said Eileen. She pulled a hammer and a short pry-bar out of her coat, then a thick length of fabric. "We've come to get you out!"

"Eileen?" Liam blinked in surprise and confusion, then his eyes widened. "Is that you?"

"It is," she said. "And Thomas and Henry."

"Thomas?" Liam looked horrified. "You can't be here! Are you insane?"

"Yes," said Thomas. "Now stand up and hold still."

Eileen pulled on Liam's arm and helped him struggle to his feet, while Thomas knelt before him. Liam smelled of sweat and fear and filth, and it was all Thomas could do to be near him. The shackles on his ankles were held in place by bent iron pins, just as Thomas's had been. Thomas took the pry-bar from Eileen, braced it against the steel bracelet around Liam's ankle, and then slid it under the pin. "Ready."

Eileen wrapped the head of the hammer in the cloth and knelt beside Thomas. With a series of short, hard blows, muffled by the cloth, Eileen straightened the pin. Thomas pulled it out and then braced the bar against the other ankle. In a moment, that pin was straight and out, too.

"Can you get my hands?" asked Liam.

"I think so," said Thomas. "Just hold still."

"Can you make any more noise in there?" complained Henry in a hiss from the hallway. "You'll have the whole building in to see what's going on."

"You want to do this?" asked Thomas, not expecting an answer. Eileen went to work on Liam's wrists, and soon had the shackles undone.

"Now what?" asked Liam.

"We get Jonathan and Charles and Michael and we get out of here."

"Jonathan *and* Charles *and* Michael?" repeated Liam. "How many of us have they got?"

"That's all so far," said Henry from the door. "And if you don't want it to be more, hurry up!"

Seven cells later they found Jonathan. He wore the same bruises as Liam, and stayed curled in a ball until Thomas helped him to his feet. He shook as Eileen hammered out the pins on his shackles. He nearly collapsed, weeping, when they led him out of the cell. "Thank the Four," he said. "Thank the Four, I thought I was a dead man. Thank the Four."

"Here!" called Michael from the end of the hall. "Jonathan, Liam, is that you?"

"Yes!" Jonathan hobbled to the cell. "Thomas! Eileen! Bring the light and the hammer! Hurry!"

In short order Michael was free as well, and all six stood in the narrow corridor.

"Can we get out of here, now?" asked Jonathan.

"Not without Charles," said Thomas.

"Well, he's not in here," said Henry. "That leaves one more place to look."

"I know," said Thomas, handing his dagger to Liam. "Eileen, give the hammer and bar to Michael and Jonathan. It's all we've got for extra weapons."

"It'll do," said Jonathan, taking the pry-bar. "In fact, I wouldn't mind shoving this down someone's throat right now."

Thomas led them out of the hallway and to the last door in the corridor. Unlike the others, this one had no lock on it at all. Thomas was about to push it open someone on the other side cried out in pain. This time he recognized the voice.

"Charles," he whispered to Henry.

Thomas let the light in his hand die, and drew his blades. He gently pushed on the door, opening it just a crack. Now, under the cries of pain, he could hear someone speaking in a gentle, quiet tone of voice.

"All this can end," the man was saying. "All you have to do is tell the truth."

"I told the truth!" sobbed Charles. "I told you!"

"More," said the man.

This time, Charles howled in agony.

Thomas kicked the door open the rest of the way. The room was large, lit by the red light of a pair of coal-filled braziers. There were a dozen devices Thomas didn't recognize scattered throughout the room. Charles was strapped to a chair, his single hand locked in a device that isolated each finger and had a dozen screws on it. A large man stood beside him, tightening the screws. An Inquisitor sat at a desk in front of Charles, watching.

Thomas charged across the room, the others right behind him. The big man jumped back in surprise, and the Inquisitor knocked over his stool. Thomas's blade went to the torturer's throat. "No one moves or we'll kill you both."

"I am an officer of the Church," squeaked the Inquisitor. "You have no right to be in here! You have no right to do..."

Henry punched the man in the face, sending him sprawling. "Thomas, see to Charles."

Charles' face was a mass of bruises, his lips were split and bleeding, and one of his eyes was swollen shut. He was still howling. Thomas felt his stomach roil, but forced it down. He began loosening the screws on the device.

"Not all the way off," said Henry. "We can use it as a splint until we get him to the doctors."

Charles' howling turned to moans as Thomas loosened the last of the screws.

"What do we do with these two?" asked Liam.

"Strap them down in the other chairs," said Thomas. "With luck, no one will look until morning."

"Which isn't that far away," Henry said. "We need to get out of here. Now."

The Inquisitor and the torturer didn't resist. "Can you walk?" Thomas asked as he undid the strap around Charles' body. Charles sagged forward. Thomas caught him and held the battered man's face in his hands. "Charles! Can you walk?"

"Thomas?" the word was slurred, and Charles squinted his good eye.

"Yes. It's Thomas. Can you walk?"

"I didn't tell them anything," said Charles. "They kept asking but I didn't tell them anything."

"You did well," said Thomas, "Better than any of us would have. Now, can you walk?"

"I... I don't know."

"Jonathan, Michael. Carry him."

They went as fast as they could back up the stairs with Jonathan and Michael carrying Charles between them and Liam leaning on Eileen. The front door was less than twenty feet away, and Thomas desperately wished they could go out it. There were guards outside, though, and there was no way to get past them without raising an alarm.

There's too many of us to be quiet. "Back the way we came," he said. "As quickly as possible. Henry, take up the rear."

They walked fast. Liam began muttering under his breath, praying to the Four that they wouldn't be taken again. Their sounds of their boots echoed through the hallways. Charles moaned with every step. Thomas prayed the noise didn't travel out the door to the guards, and that no one in the rooms above would come to see what the ruckus was. They reached the back door in less than a quarter of the time it had taken them going in.

The alley behind the building was empty and silent. Thomas breathed a sigh of relief and led them out into the night.

19

The temperature had dropped since they'd gone inside, and their breath came out in white clouds. Charles cried out every time Michael and Jonathan jostled him. Thomas kept them all moving as fast as he could, praying no one would sound an alarm and send the Church cavalry to ride them down.

"Where are we going?" asked Michael through chattering teeth. All four of the prisoners were in shirtsleeves.

"My house," said Eileen. "George is waiting."

"He will," said Thomas. "He said he would."

"We stink," said Jonathan. "At least, Liam and Charles and I do. They wouldn't let us..." he glanced at Eileen. "You know."

"I do," said Thomas, who'd had the same treatment. "We'll get you some clean clothes after we get off the streets."

The walk took forever, but they reached the Street of Smiths without anyone stopping them. George was standing in the door of his smithy his thick walking stick in his hand. He pushed the door wide the moment he saw them. "Eileen! Are you all right?"

"I'm fine!" said Eileen. "We need to get inside! Now!"

Thomas led the others in, the heat of the smithy a shock after the cold of the night. George hadn't banked the forge for the night, and the warmth from it was a welcome relief from the freezing air outside. George pulled the door shut the moment the last of them were inside.

"We need a healer," said Thomas. "Charles is hurt. Badly."

"They tortured him," Eileen, her voice shaky with relief and horror and pent-up fear. "They broke all the bones in his fingers."

"And a few in his face, from the look of it," said Henry.

"We need to get his fingers straightened," said Thomas. "Otherwise they'll heal crooked and he won't even be able to hold a pen." *He already lost a hand because of me. I'm not letting him lose his fingers, too.*

"At least I'll get out of exams," said Charles through gritted teeth. They were the first words he'd spoken since they'd left the dungeon.

"No one gets out of exams," said Henry, helping Charles to lie down. "They'll make you write with your nose dipped in ink. Better we get your hand fixed."

"The healer that helped James," said Thomas. "Get him."

"There's one closer," said George. "The smiths use him." George looked down at Charles' hand. His face contorted a moment, and he swallowed hard, as if keeping something from coming up. "He specializes in broken bones and burns."

"Then get him," said Thomas. "Please. Henry, go with him."

They went.

"What about us?" asked Jonathan. "We're filthy and we stink." He looked at Liam, who had collapsed in a corner and was curled up in a ball again. "And Liam..."

"I just got you back," said Thomas. "I'll not risk having you get taken again. Especially after what we just did." He looked over the bruises on Jonathan and Liam. "Anything broken on any of you?"

"No," said Jonathan. "They just beat us."

"And made us watch the other getting it," said Liam, from his place on the floor. He pulled his legs closer to his chest and wrapped his arms tighter around them. His whole body shook. "Bastards."

"Aye," said Thomas. "That they are."

"Can we wash up?" asked Jonathan, "And get our clothes?"

"Not yet," said Thomas, taking up a position at the door and looking out. "Wait until George gets back. Then we'll go."

"I'll get you blankets," said Eileen. "And water from the fountain. I'll get some food, as well."

"I'm going to keep watch outside," said Thomas. "Keep warm by the forge. I'll let you know as soon as George and Henry get back."

Thomas stepped out into the night and the door. *They'll all be messed up,* Thomas thought. *Maybe not Michael, too badly, but the others...*

And there's nothing I can do about it.

Time dragged. From inside Thomas could hear occasional moans of pain from Charles, and soothing words from Eileen. There was no other conversation.

George and Henry came out of the dark, leading a rumpled, tired looking man with little hair and a large bag. He saw Thomas's rapier and blanched. George put a hand on his shoulder, saying, "It's all right," and guided him forward. Thomas opened the door and got out of the way.

The healer stepped past him, starting to say, "Who is my..." then stopping with a gasp of horror.

"What happened to this man?" the healer demanded. "Who did this?"

"He's been tortured," said Thomas, stepping in and closing the door behind him. With nine of them in the forge, there was barely room to stand, let alone walk. The room stank of filth and steel.

"I can see that," snapped the healer. "Who did it?"

"Not important," said Thomas. "Can you straighten his fingers?"

The healer looked down at the wooden device wrapped over Charles' hand. "I don't know. It depends how badly the fingers are broken."

"They broke each finger in two places," said Charles, his voice weak. "The bones. That way I'd still be able to sign my confession. He was going to start on the joints next."

The healer's expression became much more gentle. "Then I'll be able to straighten the bones," he said to Charles. "But it's going to hurt a great deal."

"He'd be best unconscious for it," said Henry. "The neighbours don't need to hear him scream."

"He will be," promised the healer.

"Michael, Liam and Jonathan can come with us," said Thomas. "Henry and I will take them to the all-night and get them clothes."

"This one stinks, too," said the healer, looking down at Charles.

"We'll clean him up once you've fixed his fingers," said Henry.

"Can... Can Eileen sit with me?" Charles said. "While he works on me?"

"Always trying to steal my girl," said Thomas, shaking his head and smiling. "Just mind your manners."

Charles managed a smile back, though doing it hurt him. Eileen sat down beside him. "I'll sit with you," she said. "As long as it takes."

"We'll be back as fast as we can," said Thomas. He picked up his rapier and headed for the door. He stopped in front of George. "George, thank you."

George nodded. "Just get back fast, Thomas."

"We will," said Thomas. "And we're not coming back alone."

20

Thomas and Henry roused the entire company on their way to the baths. None of them were happy until they heard why they'd been woken. Thomas told them to get armed, armoured, in uniform, and to get the statements they had written about Michael's kidnapping. Then Thomas ran to their own apartment to get their uniforms and armour while Henry guarded Liam, Jonathan and Michael at the baths.

When they left the baths Thomas and the others wore the black of the Student Company. Henry wore the white of the Order of the White Wolf. Jonathan, Liam and Michael stayed close to Thomas on the way back to the forge and spooked at every sound, as if expecting Church soldiers to come out of the alleys after them.

By the time they returned to the forge, the whole company was there. Even James, whom the others had carried over, was sitting on the floor beside Charles. Every man of them was furious, horrified and ready to kill. The healer had left. Eileen stood watch with Thomas outside the forge while Michael and the others stripped Charles, cleaned him up, and put him into clean clothes.

When they were done, George brought down a big iron plate and laid it over the coals. Eileen cooked bacon and cut bread and brewed tea for them all.

It was nearly time for the first bell of the morning when they heard the horses.

"Fan out in front of the smithy," ordered Henry. "Jonathan, Michael and Liam stay inside with Charles. Go!"

They did. George stood still, indecision and pain in his face. Then he pulled his sword down from the wall and drew it. He stood in the doorway to his smithy, his face grim, tired and angry.

The riders came around the corner and straight for the forge. There were nine of them. None were wearing uniforms, and eight of them had long battle swords at their sides. Though he couldn't see it, Thomas would bet they had chain mail under their coats. They looked tired and angry as they reined up in front of the forge.

"I would have thought we had longer," said Henry. "More the fool, me."

"Interesting that they knew to come here," said Thomas.

"They didn't," said Henry. "See how their horses are lathered? They went to our apartment first, I bet." He frowned. "They'd better not have wrecked the place."

The horses parted and Father Alphonse, dressed in plain brown clothes, rode forward. "I should have guessed you'd come here. It's closer than the Academy."

"Come here for what?" asked Henry. "We're having breakfast with friends."

"Give them back," said Father Alphonse.

"Everyone here is a student, save George," said Thomas. "The Church is not legally allowed to hold students, and George was here to start with."

Father Alphonse looked down at him. "I have eight men on horseback."

"We have fifteen who hate *you*," said Thomas, stepping forward. "And we have me."

"You?" Father Alphonse sneered. "You will do nothing in front of witnesses. We both know it."

"Do we?" asked Thomas. "Because this morning, I don't."

"Anything we do would wake the entire street," said Henry. "And the wrath of the Academy. Remember what happened last time."

To Thomas's surprise, Father Alphonse dismounted and handed the reins of his horse to one of the guards. "A private word, Thomas," said Father Alphonse. "If you would."

Thomas didn't move.

Father Alphonse sighed. "You can bring your sword with you if you like, Thomas. Now, please, walk with me."

Thomas looked to Henry. Henry shrugged but said nothing. The other riders stayed where they were and their swords stayed sheathed.

"If he does anything," said Thomas, "kill them all."

"Don't worry," said Henry. "We will."

Thomas sheathed his swords and walked beside Father Alphonse until they were half a block from the others. There were sounds of life in some of the houses, now. Thomas saw a few of the shutters slightly open, and eyes peeking out at them. *This is going to do nothing for George's reputation.*

"You must think you're very clever," said Father Alphonse.

"I think I'm very tired," said Thomas. "And I think you being here is making me very angry."

"Your existence is an affront to the High Father," Father Alphonse hissed. For the first time since Thomas had met him the man's composure was gone. "Your witchcraft endangers your soul and the souls of everyone you know. You corrupt everything around you with your very presence."

"And you couldn't say that over there?" asked Thomas. "Because they've all heard it before."

"*Despite this,*" continued Father Alphonse, "the Archbishop still wishes to extend to you the hand of friendship. He is still willing to take your confession and forgive you your sins if you will recant."

"Why does it matter?" asked Thomas. "Why does he need me to confess?"

"Have you considered the Archbishop's offer?"

"The Archbishop kidnapped my friends. Forgive me if I don't trust his word."

"*I* kidnapped your friends, Thomas. He knew nothing about it." He smiled at Thomas's expression. "The Archbishop is not ready go against the king. Not yet."

"Why am I so important?"

"You?" Father Alphonse's smile became condescending, though there was a bitter twist to it. "You're not important, Thomas."

Thomas nearly laughed. "You've kidnapped my friends. You have preachers and posters in the streets attacking the Academy and the king, just to get at me. Apparently I am."

"To get to you?" Father Alphonse laughed a short, sharp bark that echoed off the buildings around them. "Foolish boy. You're just a symptom," he said, "like your young lady."

"Eileen?" Thomas's brows came together. "What does she have to do with it?"

Father Alphonse looked east, where the sky was growing lighter. "Morning is here, Thomas, and it has been very long, this night." He started back towards the horses. "Will you come with me? Come to the Archbishop, confess your sins and end all this nonsense?"

Thomas shook his head in disbelief. "You're actually asking me that? After all this?"

"You will come to him in the end," said the Inquisitor. "One way or another." Thomas followed and watched him mount. "We will leave you to your morning," said Father Alphonse. "Make the most of it."

With a tug at the reins and a kick of his heels, he turned his horse and led the Churchmen away. Henry waited until they were out of sight before he called, "Weapons down."

"I thought that was going to be the end of us," said Marcus, sheathing his blades. "I've never fought anyone on horseback before."

There was murmured agreement from the others. The first bell of the morning rang, and around them, the smiths began opening up shops. Many of them stared in surprise at the crowd of students in armour in front of George's forge.

The Academy gates will be opening soon, Thomas thought. He looked up at the sky. For the first time in days he could see patches of sunlight and blue sky through the clouds. The cold wind still bit into his skin, but not as badly as it had before.

"Get them organized," he told Eileen. "I'm going to heal Charles and then it's time to go."

"Shouldn't you go to fencing?" asked Eileen.

"Not this morning," said Thomas. "This morning we get everyone safe. Tomorrow I'll report to Sir Walter."

Charles was lying on a pile of blankets on the floor of the smithy. He looked awful. His face was still swollen and bruised, and Thomas suspected Charles' nose would never look the same again. He was awake, though, and his fingers were straight under their splints and bandages.

Thomas knelt down beside him. "Time for me to heal you."

"No," said Charles.

Thomas rocked back on his heels in surprise. "What?"

"You can't heal me."

"I can," Thomas protested. "I know I couldn't help you when you lost your hand but this..."

"No, idiot," said Charles, rolling his blood-red, swollen eyes. "I don't mean you can't heal me ever, I mean you can't heal me now!"

"But –"

"If you make it go away, no one sees what they did to me, and they get away with it."

"Charles," Thomas spoke slowly, gently. "I can't imagine the pain you're in."

"That's right. But I can, and I can handle it," said Charles. "I want everyone to see, and I want to tell everyone!"

"If you're sure..."

"I'm sure," said Charles. He smiled, which made him wince in pain. "But as soon as you can, after, that would be good."

"Deal," said Thomas.

"Forgive me for not shaking on it."

Thomas tousled Charles' hair and stood up. "We're moving out! Now."

They left together, with Charles and James cradled and protected in the middle of the group. They kept the pace slow and steady, but Charles groaned every second step and James swore with every jolt.

In the market the preacher was already up on his crate, cursing against witchcraft and calling for the king to drive the witches out of hiding and into the streets where justice could be done.

"And what must we do with them?" the preacher demanded. "What will we do with these foul men and women who so abuse the love the High Father by daring to traffic with the Banished? Hanging is not good enough for them! Beheading is not good enough for them! They must be purified with fire! They must learn what torments the Banished face, that they may be purified before they pass from this world! It is the only way to cleanse them of their sin! To cleanse them of the vile witchcraft that they have allowed to possess their bodies!"

Cheers rose up from the crowd.

"There must be a reckoning!" the preacher continued. "There must be a cleansing of all those who would defy the high father's will!"

Thomas shook his head in disgust and kept walking.

"There!" The preacher was practically jumping up and down on his box. "Look there to see the defilers of innocence! The profaners of Church law!" The preacher pointed directly at Thomas and his friends. "Too long has the Academy been a shelter for impure thoughts and irresponsible behaviours. And now, now they harbour witches in their midst!"

His audience booed and hissed.

"And look!" called the preacher. "That one is a girl! A girl dressed up as a student! Worse, armed and armoured! Oh, people of Hawksmouth! Oh, children of the High Father! Will you tolerate this? It is not enough that the rich send their sons to be debauched and tainted by the Academy, but now they prey on your daughters as well? It must be stopped!"

"Draw!" said Thomas, his voice loud enough to be heard through the square. A dozen rapiers left their sheaths. The crowd went silent at once, and Thomas could see fear in their faces. The preacher himself stopped speaking and stared.

"If we were as debauched and depraved as you think," said Thomas, his voice loud enough to carry through the entire square, "we would cut you down where you stand." He looked over his shoulder at the company, and saw the fury in their faces. All it would take was one wrong move...

"Be thankful we are better than that," said Thomas. "Company, keep walking."

They kept going, not bothering to sheath their blades. People in the streets cleared out of their way, muttering and whispering to one another as the group went past. Thomas was beyond caring. He was exhausted and furious and wanted nothing more than to get to the Academy and tell everyone what had happened.

The troop reached the Academy as the second bell of the morning rang. A black river of students was flowing through the gates. One of them saw the company coming and shouted. The river stopped and turned back on itself, the students swirling around them.

"What's happening?"

"Why are you armed?"

"Who did you fight?"

"By the Four, look at Charles!"

"Look at James!"

"Jonathan, Liam, what happened to you?"

"Keep moving," said Thomas to the company. He raised his voice loud. "We'll answer questions after we speak to the Headmaster! Move out of the way! Please!"

The gatekeeper saw them coming and ran out of his little house. "Hold on! You can't come in here like that!"

"Weapons away," called Thomas, sheathing his own as he stepped through the gate. The men marching behind him did the same in a hiss of steel on leather.

"You lot stop and you hand in your weapons!" said the gatekeeper.

"No," said Thomas. "Not today."

"You can't come in here like this! I'll have to report you!"

"Keep going," said Thomas to the company, and walked around the man.

The Gatekeeper grabbed him. "You think you can flout the rules, boy? I'll have you up in front of the Headmaster!"

"Then follow us," said Thomas, pulling his arm free, "because that's where we're going."

As the company walked across the grounds, word spread like fire through the Academy. By the time they reached the Headmaster's house, they had several hundred students behind them.

"Evan, gather the statements," said Thomas. Evan slipped through the ranks gathering papers from everyone. Thomas walked up the porch stairs and hammered on the door with his fist, loud enough to echo off the buildings around them.

Thomas was about to pound on the door a second time when Matron Marshall opened it and glared. "What is all this racket?! If you think that's the proper way to get the Headmaster's attention, I can tell you it is not!" She looked beyond Thomas. "And you lot! Clear out and get to class where you belong!"

"Get the Headmaster," said Thomas. "We have injured—"

"And who are you today that you think you can order me about?" demanded Matron Marshall. "You just watch your tone and be on your way-"

"THEY'VE BEEN TORTURED!" Thomas's shout echoed off the walls to those behind him, and through the Headmaster's house. A buzz went through the crowd. "Get the Headmaster, *please,* or I will go in and get him myself!"

"What... what are you...?"

Thomas stepped aside and pointed to James and Charles. Matron Marshall opened her mouth, closed it, and opened it again. "You wait here. I'll get him."

She left faster than Thomas had ever seen her move. Thomas turned from the door and found all the gathered students staring at him.

"Tortured!" yelled Thomas. "Seven days ago the first member of the Student Company disappeared. Five days ago, two others vanished. Two days ago, they took another student and attacked a fifth!

"Last night, we broke into the High Father's dungeon and we got all of them back!"

The buzz grew even louder. Thomas turned his back on it and waited. The Headmaster appeared at the door moments later. His face was pale. "The Matron said students have been tortured?"

Thomas pointed to Charles and the others. "Evan! Statements!"

Evan stepped up and handed the Headmaster the sheaf of papers. "Sworn statements on what happened," said Evan. "From everyone who was there, including James, who was attacked."

"We didn't have time to get a statement from Liam, Jonathan, Michael or Charles," said Thomas. "But you can see what happened to them."

The Headmaster took the sheaf of papers. "I heard what you said about raiding the dungeons. Is there a statement in here about how you took them from the Church's custody?"

"Not yet," said Thomas. "Do you want it now or later?"

The Headmaster's eyes narrowed. "Be very careful, Thomas." He looked at the crowd. "All of you! LISTEN TO ME!"

The students fell silent. "Yes, the High Father's Church was wrong to take our students," said the Headmaster, "and yes, you have every right to be angry, but you must not let your anger dictate your actions!" His expression was fierce. "Tell everyone; no one is to leave the Academy grounds before this afternoon's assembly. And in the meantime, there are to be no arguments about this, no fights, and no blame-throwing. Is that understood?"

There were nods and a few muttered replies.

"*IS THAT UNDERSTOOD?*" the Headmaster barked.

"Yes, Headmaster!" chorused back two hundred students.

The Headmaster turned to Thomas. "Is it?"

"Yes, Headmaster," said Thomas. "Now what do we do about Liam, Jonathan, Michael and Charles? Especially Charles. They broke all his fingers. We can't let them go home. The Church will take them again."

"They'll stay in the infirmary in the dormitory," said the Headmaster. "They'll be safe there."

"And if the Archbishop decides to come in like Bishop Malloy did last summer?"

"He will not," said the Headmaster. "I will issue an edict this afternoon."

"We need to warn everyone," said Thomas.

"I know." The Headmaster's voice became steely. "I will warn them, but I will not have you panicking them. Do you understand?"

"Yes, sir."

"Take your friends to the infirmary. Then I'll ask you and your company to turn in your rapiers at the gate and get to class."

"Yes, sir."

Thomas led the company to the infirmary. The other students surrounded them, asking question after question, and growing angrier with every answer.

The Headmaster called the Assembly at noon, and the entire student body and faculty jammed into the Assembly Hall. All the masters were on stage, and all looked grim. The Headmaster's lips were pushed tight together, and his cheeks pinched with anger. In clipped tones he relayed what had happened. A wave of fury rumbled through the room.

"It is my belief," said the Headmaster, raising his voice above the others, "that this unseemly incident is a direct result of the rumours and lies being spread by the preachers who have taken up residence in our streets. It is a situation I was willing to tolerate, so far as no attacks were made on our students.

"I will tolerate it no longer.

"Beginning today we will launch our own campaign, aimed at the people of this city. We will remind them that we are their neighbours, their friends, and in many cases, their children. We will remind the people that we, like they, are servants of the king, and that we will not allow him or our Academy to be insulted—or attacked—without answer.

"We will develop our own posters to replace the obscenities that they have posted on our walls," continued the Headmaster. "We will publish our own pamphlets and treatises to counter the foul words of the preachers who malign our school. Where the preachers speak, we will speak, and we will speak better than they!

"Those who wish to be on the poster committee, report to Professor Givins in the Astronomy building. The Master of Laws will assign senior laws students to prepare for court action the Church of the High Father and its officers, and to petition the king. Those who wish to help write treatises may see Professor Dodds. Those who wish to speak, see me. By tomorrow, we will have our first responses to these cowardly attacks!"

The students and faculty cheered.

"The gates of the Academy will be guarded from this time forward," said the Headmaster. "The Master of Fencing will see to the physical defences of the Academy and will assign all students where appropriate. You are all expected to arm yourselves when possible, and are permitted to wear those arms on the grounds." The Headmaster's brows came down and he skewered Keith, Mark and several others with his eyes. "Do not use this as an excuse for stupidity. We have had quite enough of that already.

"The Master of Theology will speak to all of you who are Theology students after this assembly, so that you may understand the position of the Academy and its relation to the position of the Church. Please be assured that the actions of a few reckless individuals in the High Father's Church or the streets do not invalidate your faith, or your service. Those who are not Theology students will treat those who are with respect. Anything less will not be tolerated.

"Now, go. Maintain your honour, your dignity and your strength. You are the king's students!"

Thomas stayed in his seat as the others filed out. Whatever energy had carried him through the raid and the morning were gone, and all he wanted was to shut his eyes and keep them that way.

"That was interesting," said Henry.

"What do you mean?" asked Thomas.

"He's putting students in harm's way," said Henry. "He never does that."

Thomas tried to wrap his mind around it and couldn't. Instead, he dropped his head into his hands, enjoying the darkness there. *By the Four, I could sleep for a week.*

"I think we should skip the rest of our classes today," said Henry. "Judging from Thomas being asleep on the bench, there."

"I'm not," said Thomas, pushing himself upright. The room tilted slighted, and he waited for it to right itself. "I agree, though."

"What about the Church?" asked Eileen. "Will they be coming after us?"

Thomas shook his head, as much to clear it as by way of reply. "Father

Alphonse said the Archbishop had nothing to do with the kidnappings. We should be fine."

"Do you think he's telling the truth?"

"Why would he lie?" Thomas grabbed the bench in front of him and used it to pull himself to his feet. "Henry and I will walk you home."

George had a wet broom in his hand, and was scrubbing at the floor of the smithy. The place smelled of soap and hot water. There was no sign that three beaten, filthy young men had been lying on it hours before.

"George," Eileen called. "We're home."

George set aside the broom and wrapped his sister in his arms, holding her tight. Eileen tensed for a moment in surprise. Then she wrapped her own arms as far around her brother as she could and clung to him. Thomas and Henry waited, but neither seemed inclined to let go.

"We need to get some sleep," said Thomas. "We'll see you tomorrow, all right?"

George raised his chin off Eileen's head. He had dark circles under his eyes, and looked like a man haunted. "Do you want to stay here? You can sleep in the kitchen."

It was the nicest thing George had said to them in a week. And while the floor of George and Eileen's kitchen was close, Thomas really wanted his bed. "No, thanks. We'll just go home."

"All right," said George. "Thanks for bringing Eileen back. And Henry?"

"Yes?"

"Thanks."

Henry smiled. "Don't thank me yet. You've a long way to go before things get better."

"I know. But thanks anyway."

Thomas and Henry both were shivering with cold and exhaustion by the time they reached the apartment. Thomas was halfway up the stairs when he realized the front door was open. "Oh, no."

"What?" said Henry just before he saw. "Oh. Of course."

"Alphonse said they were here." Thomas drew his rapier. He didn't hear anyone inside, but that didn't mean they weren't there. He pushed the door open and looked. "I don't think they did more than kick in the door."

"They probably didn't have time," said Henry.

"Good." Thomas went in first. The furniture hadn't been overturned and there was no obvious sign of damage. He checked the kitchen and bedrooms. None looked any the worse for wear.

"The bolt still works," said Henry, pushing the door shut and throwing the bolt into place. "We'll need to replace the lock."

"Tomorrow," said Thomas. "Or maybe the day after."

"We should block the door in case they come back."

Henry was right, and Thomas knew it. It was still all Thomas could do not to stomp in exhaustion. They shoved the couch against the door, and Henry went to the kitchen. He came back with the kettle and a pair of pots that he balanced on the edge of the couch.

"That should make enough noise to wake the dead," Henry said. "It might even be enough to wake us."

"By the Four, I hope it doesn't," said Thomas. He thought about what he said. "I mean, I hope it doesn't make any noise... Or that no one moves it so it doesn't make..."

"I know what you mean," said Henry. "Go to bed, Thomas. I'll see you tomorrow morning."

Thomas stumbled into his room. He struggled to pull his chain mail shirt over his head then fumbled with his clothes. Even without the armour, he felt heavy, as if his body weighed more than it should. He could barely keep his eyes open and his head up. He stared at the bed, knowing he should get into it and sleep until the next morning.

Instead, he picked up his dagger from his belt, knelt by the wall and very carefully pried at a section of the baseboard. It scraped a bit, but slid easily away from the wall.

Thomas reached into the hole in the wall and pulled out the four packages he'd placed there when Henry had first rented the apartment. He had not touched them since.

The more fool me. Inside the packages were the three large books he'd taken from Bishop Malloy and the small one he'd stolen from the Academy's Theology library. He put Bishop Malloy's books back and pushed the baseboard back into place.

Thomas crawled into bed and unwrapped the small book. It was filled with magic—real magic that worked. Every page glowed with it, though only Thomas could see. He leafed through it, wondering which spells he could cast easily and quickly if he were attacked. *I should never have stopped studying*, Thomas thought. *I should have been ready for them. I should have stopped them.*

The part of his brain that was slightly more awake reminded him that he hadn't been anywhere near his friends at the time of the kidnapping and wouldn't have been able to help anyway.

And what did Father Alphonse mean that Eileen and I are symptoms of the problem?

The thought strayed in and out of his head, as he read until he fell asleep with the book on his chest.

21

"You missed class yesterday," said Sir Walter as soon as Thomas entered the fencing hall the next morning.

"I apologize, Sir Walter," said Thomas as he hung up his coat and cloak. "After the raid we had to get the students to safety and by that time—"

"*Never* miss class," said Sir Walter. "Not without sending word. Not even if your activities have kept you up all night. How many did you kill?"

"None," said Thomas.

"Fortunate. Did you wear masks?"

"Yes."

"Good. Tell me everything, from the moment you left here to this moment now."

Thomas recounted the midnight raid, the early morning confrontation with the Inquisitor, the return to the Academy and the fallout from it.

"Very good report," said Sir Walter. "And when does the Academy's campaign against the preachers begin?"

"Today," said Thomas. "The complaint against the Church should be lodged tomorrow."

"Not sure what good it will do," said Sir Walter.

Thomas hesitated. "The speech the Headmaster gave. It didn't have anything to do with what happened to Charles or the others. It was as if he'd already written it."

"He had," said Sir Walter. "The king gave him orders to rouse the Academy two days ago. He wants to counteract the preachers without actually running them off the streets. How long before the first incidents, do you think?"

By the Four, I hadn't thought of that. "I don't know. The Headmaster has control right now but..."

"And the magicians? How soon can you find out who they are?"

Thomas shook his head. "I don't know. I haven't seen Robert since the meeting. The other magicians won't trust me without seeing my magic first. Can I show them?"

"No."

By the Four... "Can I tell Robert it's for the king? Maybe that will work."

"You can't mention the king," said Sir Walter. "Not yet."

"Then what?" asked Thomas, exasperated. "If I can't tell them I'm a magician, and I can't tell them the king wants them, how am I supposed to get their trust?"

"You aren't," said Sir Walter. "You're supposed to find out who they are."

Thomas sighed. "All right. I'll..." He thought about it, and then thought about it some more. "I'll give Robert another spell to learn. If I do that he might tell the others and then I can follow them and find out who they are."

"Do that," said Sir Walter. "And now, let's see how well you can use your fists."

Thomas groaned and stepped forward.

An hour and a half later, Thomas, Henry and Eileen walked through the market square on their way to the Academy. The preacher was nowhere to be seen. Instead, Graham was standing on the box, his low, impressive voice rolling out over his audience. Six armed students stood around him.

"We are not mythical creatures," he was saying. "Though it may certainly be said that we are strange!" The small crowd—much smaller than the one that usually gathered around the preacher, chuckled. "And we have a reputation that we have, sadly, earned. We drink, sometimes to excess. We eat as well as we can whenever we can, and yes, we have been known to engage in the pursuit of lovely young women." He smiled at a pair of maids in the audience and got a tongue stuck out at him for his efforts. "To that I can only say that we are young men, and have the foibles of young men! But we are also something more.

"We are scholars! And we are the king's men!

"It is with great dismay that we have listened to the words of these men who stand in the squares and claim to speak for the High Father's Church. We have heard them again and again, insulting our king, insulting our Academy, and insulting you! And why?

"I have lived in this city all my life. I know the people who live here and I say you are good people! I say that our king is a good king! I say that no one in this city practices witchcraft and I defy those preachers to prove otherwise!"

"He's doing well," said Henry.

"He is," agreed Thomas. He went up to one of the students standing guard. "Where's the preacher?"

"Delayed," was the answer. "We had a bunch of Theology students surround him and demand to know under what basis he is making his claims against the king, the Academy and the women of the city. We told them to take about an hour."

"Clever," said Thomas. "Good luck."

The student smiled. "So far, so good."

When they reached the Academy, they found new posters covering the walls around the gate. One showed students buying food and drink, and read "We spend our money in Hawksmouth." Another showed two students kneeling before the king with "We serve the king" written in large letters above it. Thomas's favourite was the one that read, "We help!" and showed two students protecting an old woman from a robber—something which had actually happened, if Thomas remembered correctly. There were twenty students going down the length of the wall, putting up their posters. Thomas figured the Church posters would be covered by the end of the morning.

Everyone in sight was armed. Those who could afford them wore swords. The others carried staves or daggers. Four students with staves guarded the gate.

"Nice start," said Henry. "Hope it makes a difference."

"It should," said Thomas. "At least it should get some attention."

It was strange to be in classes with everybody armed. There were some difficulties at first finding the right way to keep one's weapons in place while sitting at a table or in a desk. By noon most had figured it out, and the Academy had settled into something only slightly off its normal rhythms.

"It's been odd," Eileen was saying. "The boys didn't heckle me every time I talked, and even the professor of Mathematics let me sit in his class."

"That is impressive," said Henry. "Now that the petition is in, there's nothing they can do but wait, so I imagine they're saving their energy."

"It was so quiet," said Eileen. "It was wonderful."

"That must have been a relief," said Henry. "What about you, Thomas?"

"I've been thinking," said Thomas. "Father Alphonse called us—Eileen and me— symptoms."

"Symptoms of what?" asked Eileen.

"He didn't say. But remember at my apartment when he said that abandoning me was what kings of Criethe do in times like these?"

"He was trying to rattle you," said Henry.

"I know," said Thomas. "But what times like these?"

"I assume he meant the last war," said Henry.

"I did too, and I've been looking, but there's nothing in the histories."

Henry looked thoughtful. "The last major conflict *was* between the churches, not between Church and State."

"I've already looked at that," said Thomas. "King Darren III is supposedly responsible for a flowering of the High Father's Church."

"King Darren III?" asked Eileen. "The one who kicked women out of the Academy?"

"Yes," said Thomas. *And the preachers are preaching against women.* "But the histories only say that he declared the other churches banned and brought peace to the kingdom again. They didn't say anything about him being involved."

"They wouldn't if he lost," said Eileen. "I mean, if I was king and I'd lost, I'd change the histories."

"Very good," said Henry. "We'll make a scheming noble out of you yet."

Eileen shuddered. "Don't even joke."

"So how do we find out what's going on?" asked Thomas.

Henry thought about it. "Decrees."

"What?"

"The academy keeps a record of all royal decrees, separate from the histories. Those won't have been rewritten. East end of the fourth floor."

Thomas frowned at Henry. "You never study. How do you know this?"

"You never see me study," Henry corrected. "The Royal laws shelves have complete copies of all declarations, decrees and laws since the Academy started. Shall we look?"

The library was mostly empty and quiet when they arrived. Henry led them up the winding stone staircases to the fourth floor. There were few windows on the higher levels of the library, and they did not let in much light. The fourth floor was grey and empty and quiet. Henry pointed to the shelves.

That, thought Thomas, *is a lot of decrees.*

There were shelves and shelves of them, dating back 350 years. Thomas could *smell* the age of the books—dust and old leather and mould filling his nose. The books themselves were in relatively good condition. *Probably because almost no one reads them.*

He walked down the shelf, fingers running over the spines until he found "King Darren III" etched into one of the books. He nearly smiled until he saw the other nine sitting beside it. He sighed and started passing books to Eileen and Henry.

"How many decrees did the man write?" Eileen complained as they hauled the volumes off of the shelves and took them to the tables in the centre of the hall.

"Too many," said Thomas. "Three each and whoever gets done first gets to look through the fourth."

"Could be worse," said Henry. "Could be precedent cases. Those are awful."

"Why exactly are you becoming a lawyer?"

"Because it beats being a captain in my father's army," said Henry. "Brother's army, now, I suppose. Right, let's see what Darren III actually did."

They skimmed through the volumes. The man had passed laws on everything from clothing one was allowed to wear, to the cost of wheat. More than anything, though, Thomas saw proclamations calling for soldiers, and raising taxes for arms, and calling for the strengthening of defences of the kingdom. By the end of a half-hour, he was certain. "He *was* in the war. By the time he got to the..." he flipped to the front of the volume, "sixth year of his reign, he's constantly calling for soldiers, money, and demanding the nobles strengthen their fortifications. Which book are you looking at?"

Eileen looked. "Eleventh year of his reign. Henry, what do you have?"

"First year," said Henry. "Lots of the usual beginning of reign silliness, and an incident of stripping away Church lands for the crown."

"Interesting," said Thomas. "High Father's lands?"

"Aye. Seems they owned a small patch on the coast that Darren wanted for himself." He looked closer. "Looks like the place where Bishop Malloy had his summer house."

"The ones here are about women," said Eileen. "He seems to have been far too interested in how they lived their lives."

Thomas thought about it. "Go back. Let me know when he first started doing that."

Eileen put down the book she was reading and picked up an earlier one and skimmed through it. "Here! Look at this. Tenth year of his reign. King Darren

III proclaims the supremacy of the Church of the High Father and declares that all other gods are but subjects of the High Father."

"Very interesting," said Henry. "Because in year three and he issued a proclamation outlawing the High Father's services and declaring the supremacy of the Mother."

"He was a Mother worshipper?" Thomas put down his book and skimmed back through the fourth-year volume. "The first call for troops happened midway through the fourth year."

"To fight against the High Father, you think?"

"He was at war for nearly seven years, then," said Eileen.

"And it's never mentioned," said Henry. "Very odd."

"Here!" said Eileen. "End of the tenth year. Look."

The three leaned over the book and read the proclamation.

By the Grace of the High Father, I, Darren, third of that name, king of the realm of Criethe, defender of the Faith, and true son of the High Father, do give greetings to all my subjects.

Let it be known to all subjects of the kingdom, all true sons and daughters of the High Father, that, in accordance with the High Father's will and with the guidance of his most noble Archbishop Fallon, who brought me, your king, out of darkness and into the Light of the High Father, that the false priestesses of the Consort and of the Daughter, who to this day still resist the rule of the true Church, are using the guilds, the Academies, and the soldiery to spread their heresy to true daughters of the Church, tempting them into immodest and unwomanly actions such as would disgrace them in the eyes of the High Father.

Therefore, it is declared that no girl or woman shall be admitted to any School of Learning, nor to any of the guilds, nor to serve as warriors, nor to any other business save those suited to a woman's station, as weaving, cloth-making, dress-making, healing and inn-keeping. Let it be known that those who now hold position in guilds must now lose their position, and submit themselves to the wills of their husbands. And let it be known that this must be accomplished by the end of the Festival of the Rains, and that any girl or woman still found engaged in these trades or professions will suffer the extreme displeasure of the king, which shall be first flogging, then parading through the streets naked, then branding, then turning out naked from the city or town or village in which she has lived and being declared unprotected by law or Church, to receive succour from none.

"Wow," said Thomas. "That is..."

"Awful!" said Eileen, her face pale. "Horrible! He turned women out of the cities just for working!"

"No," said Henry. "They were turned out because having women in positions of power would encourage the Mother worshippers."

"So he threw them all out?"

"Much easier to punish them all than search out the guilty."

"That... that... He was..." Eileen shoved her chair back from the table and began pacing in her anger. "They could have been killed! They could have been made slaves or worse!" She stamped her foot hard against the floor. "Gods! There are no words!"

"Try 'defeated king,'" said Henry. "And now we know why girls aren't allowed into the Academy."

"Because they aren't allowed to do anything," snapped Eileen. A moment later, her mouth fell open, and a look of horror dropped over her face. "By the Four. Thomas, does this mean I can't attend the Academy. No matter what?"

"I don't..." *By the Four, it could. No matter what the committee says, they wouldn't be able to go against a royal proclamation. Not without the consent of...* "The king," Thomas said. "He must have known why Eileen couldn't go to the Academy. And that he can't change the rules for her without nullifying the proclamation of Darren III."

"And he can't do that without disobeying the laws of the Church," said Henry.

"Then why am I allowed to attend at all?" demanded Eileen. "Why even bother?"

"Because the king doesn't want to be subordinate to the Church anymore," said Thomas.

Henry nodded. "That's why you're still here, Eileen. And that's why Thomas hasn't been handed over."

"By the Four," Thomas breathed. "He's starting a war."

The three fell silent, staring at one another. Eileen was still pale, and Thomas guessed he looked no better himself. Henry's face was tight and angry. For a long time no one spoke.

"Now you know why he wants the magicians on his side," Henry said at last. "He needs all the help he can get."

"What do we do?" asked Eileen.

"What can we do?" returned Henry. "Act normal, know that it's coming, and get ready for it."

"I'll talk to Sir Walter in the morning," said Thomas. "Let him know that I know. Tonight, we'll go to the Pie and Tart and see if we can get to the other magicians. If not..." Thomas shook his head. "I'll find another way. Tomorrow." He rose to his feet. "Let's go back downstairs. There's one more thing I need to look up."

22

They saw the first clash on their way home that evening.

The preacher was back up on his box, exhorting the townsfolk. Most were listening avidly. To Thomas's surprise, there were four Church soldiers standing around his box, armed with clubs. *And what happened to bring them here?*

The preacher was demanding that the Academy be turned over to the Church of the High Father when a voice piped up, "Why give them to the Church? What's the Church know about anything?"

"They don't know anything about the law," called someone else. "Otherwise they'd know the Academy belongs to the king!"

"The Academy should not belong to the king!" thundered the preacher. "The Academy should be put in the charge of those capable of keeping the students properly in line!"

"You don't think the king's capable?" someone else yelled. "What are you, a traitor?"

"He's a seditionist!" called a fourth voice.

"He wants to overthrow the king!"

"Down with the traitor!" More voices picked up the chant. "Down with the traitor! Down with the traitor!"

"Silence!" shouted the preacher. The chanters ignored him. The Church guards waded into the crowd, looking for the offenders. There was shoving and shouting and seven students, not in their robes but wearing their rapiers, broke free.

"Long live the king!" yelled David, who had been whispering annoying questions at Thomas in their law class only the week before.

"Long live the king!" the others echoed. The Church guards formed a line between them and the preacher. "Clear off, you lot!" said one of the guards. "No one wants to hear from you!"

"No one wants to hear 'long live the king?'" David sounded almost shocked. "What sort of people are you? Without the king we'd not have peace! Without the king we'd not have law and order! I say, long live the king!"

"And I said, get out!" The guards pulled their clubs. "Clear off."

Almost as one, the students drew their swords. "And I said, long live the king," said David, pleasantly. "And I will happily leave, as soon as you say it as well."

"You lot think you can beat us?" the guards advanced forward.

"Draw," said Henry, putting deed to word. Thomas and Eileen did the same, and the three walked forward.

"Hi David," said Thomas. "What is this?"

"A minor disagreement," said David. "Now, who wants to shout it with me?" he demanded. "Who loves their king and their country? Who will say it? *Long live the king!*"

There were rumbles from the audience, and many people looked confused.

"Again!" said David, *"Long live the king!"*

All the students joined in, and a few voices from the crowd. "Long live the king!"

"More!" called David. *"Long live the king!"*

"Long live the king!" came from a dozen or more spots.

"Long live the king!"

"Long live the king!" Half the people in the square said.

"Excellent!" said David. He stepped forward and raised his blade to point in the eyes of the leader of the Church guards. "Long live the king."

The guard stared at the sword point. He spat in disgust, and sneered at David. "Long live the king."

"There," said David. "Not so hard, was it? *Long live the king!*" he turned to Thomas. "May we escort you out?"

"Yes," said Thomas. "Quickly." He waited until the guards were out of earshot before saying "This isn't part of the Headmaster's plan."

"Not at all," said David. "James is a friend of mine."

"Just be careful," said Thomas. "The last thing we need is for it all to end up in street brawls."

"Don't worry," said David, waving. "It will."

Thomas shook his head in disgust as the seven went off, carefully checking behind them to be sure they weren't being followed. Henry and Thomas went to Eileen's place to drop her off, and found the Master Smith and his daughter Linda both there. The Master Smith was looking very serious. Linda was holding George's hand. As they got closer, Thomas could see George was shaking and his face was pale and sweating.

"It is a serious matter," the Master Smith was saying. "After all we cannot have our customers frightened by such things. Nor our children, for that matter."

"I am hardly a child, father," protested Linda.

"Pardon me," said Thomas. "What happened?"

"You did, young man," said Master Gatron, frowning and sounding very stern. "You and your companions, with swords and armour, facing down men on horseback and carrying injured men out of George's smithy in the early hours of yesterday morning. It raises questions."

"As well it should," said Thomas. "But I hope it doesn't raise questions about George. Without his help, one of our companions may well have been crippled for life."

The Master Smith blinked in surprise.

"Unfortunately we can't share the details of what happened," continued Thomas, "because the Royal Academy of Learning is preparing to bring those responsible for our friends' injuries before the king's court to answer charges of kidnapping, assault and torture."

"Torture?" repeated Master Gatron. "They were tortured?"

"Yes, Master Gatron," said Thomas. "And were it not for George and Eileen lending us their smithy and bringing a healer to help our wounded, things could have gone much, much worse."

"I... I see."

Linda smiled radiantly at George and squeezed his hand tight. "You are a good man, George Gobhann. I knew you were."

"One of the best," said Henry. "And Eileen makes an excellent breakfast."

"Which reminds me, I need to start dinner," said Eileen, smiling at Linda. "I'll get to it, if you'll excuse me."

"No need," said Claudine from the foot of the stairs up to the kitchen. "It's all taken care of! How are you, Eileen?"

"Claudine!" Eileen ran forward and gave Claudine a hug. "How are you?"

"Who is this?" asked Linda, trying to keep her inflections polite, even as her tone cooled considerably.

"Claudine!" exclaimed Henry, stepping forward and sweeping up her hand to kiss. "So good to see you again. And what brings you here?"

"Why, Eileen, of course! I brought another book she doesn't have. And I do hope she has the time to talk for a while."

"But where are my manners?" said Henry, tucking Claudine's hand into her arm and walking her forward. "Linda Gatron, Master Smith Gatron, this is Claudine Bright, a new friend of Eileen's. Claudine, this is Linda Gatron and her father Master Smith Roland Gatron, head of the Smiths' Guild of Hawksmouth.

"My pleasure," said Claudine, dropping into a deep curtsey. "My father, Malcolm Bright, speaks highly of your smiths, Master Gatron, and says that without them his work would not be nearly so well done."

"My thanks," said Master Gatron. He cast an amused glance at his daughter, who was still looking unsure.

"And now, we must go to dinner," said Claudine. "My mother brought it and is waiting upstairs for us." Her eyes went to Thomas. "Unfortunately, we were not expecting so many. I am sure we would have room for Linda, but I don't think we can feed you all."

"I was just leaving," said Thomas.

"Unfortunate," said Claudine, sounding not at all sincere.

"And I have business to attend, I'm afraid," said the Master Smith. "But my daughter would be delighted to stay, I am sure."

"Perhaps Lord Henry could stay, too?" Claudine asked, leaning against him and looking up at him with her wide brown eyes.

"Unfortunately not," said Henry, gently taking her hand from his arm and kissing it. "Another time, my dear."

Claudine pouted prettily. "You promise?"

"I do," said Henry. "And now, if you will excuse us?"

They said their good-byes and headed out. Henry waited until they were out of sight of the forge. "And now, where to for dinner?"

"The Pie and Tart," said Thomas. "I need to talk to Robert."

***

The Pie and Tart was doing a very brisk business, with a line that went out the door and into the street. Thomas and Henry, their robes left at home, joined the queue and waited their turn. The smell from the place was delicious; mixing a dozen different spices with warm, fresh meat and baking apples and berries. Thomas's mouth was watering by the time they got inside. The room was small, with two doors for customers and a counter that ran the length of it. Behind the counter an entire wall of shelves contained enough breads, pies and pastries to satisfy even George if he were to come. There was no sign of Robert, but there was a stair leading to the basement. As Thomas watched, more pastries came up the steps. *Bet he's down there. The baker would be baking, not serving the customers.*

They bought themselves small meat pies and fruit tarts, and stepped back out into the night. "Now all we need is a bottle of wine and some warm weather and everything will be wonderful," said Henry. "I don't suppose you brought either?"

"Sorry," said Thomas. "There's a spot."

They found an alleyway that sheltered them from the worst of the wind. The meat pies were delicious and warmed them up for a time. The fruit pastries were exceptionally good. As they watched, the line at the store grew smaller and eventually petered out to nothing.

"What exactly are we doing here?" asked Henry.

"Waiting for everyone who doesn't live there to go home," said Thomas. "The fewer people who see us with Robert, the better for him."

Another hour passed, and the bakery disgorged its workers. Thomas counted eight men and women saying good-bye and heading on their way. Through the window, Thomas could see another woman walking through the bakery, sweeping the floor and wiping counters.

"Now, I think," said Thomas, and led the way back to the bakery. The door was still unlocked. Thomas knocked and stepped inside.

"I'm sorry, gentlemen," said the woman, eying their weapons. "We're closed for the day."

"We're here to speak with Robert Smithson," said Thomas. "Is he in?"

"He's cleaning up downstairs," said the woman. "What would you be wanting him for?"

"Business," said Henry. "I am Lord Henry Antonius, Ambassador of the Duke of Frostmire, and I am looking to bespeak pastries for a party. Robert comes highly recommended and, having just tasted your wares, I have found the recommendations to be true. Would he be willing to speak with us?"

"Of course," said the woman. "I'm Hazel Smithson, his wife."

"A pleasure, Hazel," said Henry. "Now, if you would be so good as to send him up?"

The woman curtsied and went down the steps. A moment later Robert came, wiping his hands and trying to look impressive. His face fell when he saw Thomas. Robert glanced behind him to see that his wife had not followed, then hissed at Thomas, "What do you want here?"

"I wanted to give you something," said Thomas.

Robert frowned and huffed out his cheeks. "You should not be here!"

Thomas ignored him. "Close your eyes. Envision a small ball of light. Whatever colour you like. Imagine it floating just above your hand. When you can see it clearly, hold out your hand, call it there, and open your eyes."

Robert frowned even more, but Thomas could see his curiosity rising. "Why..." Robert looked over his shoulder again. "Why are you telling me this?"

"Did you show the others the candle?" asked Thomas.

"I can't tell you that!" Robert looked furious. "They said I can't. You're not one of us. You can't know what happens at our meetings."

I bet that means yes. "Try this one, and once you have it working, share it with the others."

"Why... why are you telling me this?"

Thomas smiled. "I have to tell someone. Might as well tell someone who can make it work."

Robert shook his head. "They still won't trust you."

"I'm not asking them to," said Thomas. "Good-night, Robert."

Thomas led Henry out of the bakery and back to the alley. They wrapped their cloaks tight around them and waited. The hours crept. One by one the lights from the windows of the bakery went down, until the place was completely dark.

Henry sighed. "Next time, I'm bringing my flask."

"We watch until midnight," said Thomas. "And I promise to make the tea when we get home."

"Only if there's whiskey in it," said Henry.

"There will be," promised Thomas. "And I'll build up the fire to drink it by."

They waited, shivering, until the midnight bell rang, but Robert didn't leave the house.

***

The next morning was slightly warmer, as if spring was trying to peek out from behind winter's gloom. The sun was out and some of the water in the streets was beginning to dry up when Thomas reached the fencing studio.

"Good morning, Thomas," said Sir Walter. "How are you?"

"Worried," said Thomas. "Is the king planning a war with the Church?"

Sir Walter blinked once, but showed no other reaction. "What makes you think that?"

"The preachers," said Thomas. "The Academy suddenly out in the streets. Eileen being allowed to attend the Academy even though King Darren III forbade it. The king wanting magicians. Me not being in jail."

Sir Walter nodded. "Very good, Thomas."

"Why?" Thomas demanded. "Why is he going to war? Is the magic that important?"

"No," said Sir Walter. "The Church is trying to bully him into sending half his troops and most of his treasury to Tali and Beudlea to help the Church put down the tribes there who are resisting the High Father's Church."

"Oh." Thomas thought about this. "So this is about money?"

"Not just," said Sir Walter. "The kings of Criethe have chafed under the rule of the Church since King Darren III. With you around, this seemed like the ideal time to break free."

"Please tell me he doesn't think I have enough power to stop the war."

Sir Walter laughed. "Not in the slightest. You and all the magicians in Hawksmouth couldn't stop the Church's cavalry for more than a moment. No, the king is using you to test the Church's resolve, and to buy time to get his men into place."

"Oh," said Thomas. "Then why does he want the magicians?"

"Because they're his citizens," said Sir Walter. "Because the Church wants to claim control over them and the king doesn't want to let that happen. And in case of a war, they're better where we can keep them safe."

Sir Walter's expression hadn't changed at all as he'd said the words, nor had his tone. *So why don't I believe him?* Thomas wondered. *What does he really want them for?*

"Now," said Sir Walter. "Swords today."

Thomas told Henry and Eileen what Sir Walter had said, and the three were very sombre by the time they reached the market square. Graham and the preacher were both on crates today, trading barbs. There were six armed students around Graham, glaring at the four Church guards in front of the preacher. The preacher had more people on his side, but Graham was a very good speaker and much louder.

"Servants of the Banished!" the priest was saying. "You have given your souls to the Banished and you will suffer horribly for it!"

"Another lie!" Graham's voice cut through the other man's words. "We serve the king!"

"You serve a corrupt king, who favours the opinions of those who worship evil to those who spent their lives serving The High Father!"

"And here we have the lie again!" said Graham. "You say there are Banished worshippers and witches, but you will not say who they are! You will not name names, because you have none!"

"I'm beginning to think he could have won the debate," said Henry.

"Me, too," said Thomas. *So why didn't he?*

"Classes," reminded Eileen.

The morning was half-done and Thomas was walking between classes when he heard cheers from the main gate. He looked and saw a mob of students charging in. Four of them were being carried, and others were leaning on each other. Thomas ran toward them. "What's going on?"

"We sent them running!" one student yelled. He was so excited he was practically dancing. "The preachers, the guards, everyone!"

"What? Where?"

"The dockworkers district! And near the Carpenters' Guild! We sent them running!"

Thomas spotted Graham being carried in, blood running from his forehead, and livid bruises on his face. "What happened?" Thomas demanded. "How did you get hurt?"

"We forced them away," groaned Graham. "We were at the docks. The preacher was telling lies about us and we managed to convince the dockworkers he was insulting them, too. They started throwing things at him and chanting and we managed to drive him out of the square. Then we marched together to the square near the Carpenters' Guild." The students holding him headed for the infirmary. Thomas kept pace. "We marched in chanting 'King's men!' We were met by two dozen of the Church's guards on foot and another half-dozen on horseback, plus one of the preachers and about two dozen of the carpenters' apprentices." Graham smiled, and the blood flowing down his forehead threatened to overflow his lips and go into his mouth "I think the apprentices were there for the fight, more than anything else."

"A riot," said Thomas. "You started a riot."

"*We* didn't start it," protested Graham. "We managed to get the square cleared of the preacher and his supporters, but a bunch of us got hurt. We were on our way out when the city watch was on its way in. I'm guessing some folks got arrested."

If not killed, thought Thomas as Graham was carried to the infirmary.

Thomas spent the day worrying about what would happen if war did break out. He didn't pay much attention to his classes and got scolded for it. By the time he met Henry and Eileen at the gates he was more than ready to go home.

"How did it go?" Henry asked. "Anything exciting?"

"Graham and the others got in a riot," said Thomas.

"I'd heard," said Henry. "In fact, the entire Academy heard."

"That's not good," said Eileen.

"It is and it isn't," said Henry. "It means people care."

"It means people are siding with the Church against the king," said Thomas. "That's bad."

"But they're also siding with the king against the Church," Henry pointed out. "And that's good."

"Be better if they didn't have to take sides," said Thomas.

"But since that's not happening, isn't it good to know that some are on our side?"

"Can we avoid the market square tonight?" Eileen asked. "I don't feel like being called names."

"Your wish is our command," said Henry. "In fact, if we were to take the street just south there is an excellent wine shop where we could stop. Just the thing to go with dinner."

"Whose dinner?" asked Eileen. "Or do you think I'm cooking for you?"

"One had hopes."

"One is going to be disappointed," said Eileen. She shook her head. "I have enough trouble keeping George fed. I'm not going to feed you as well without notice."

"What if we fed George?" said Thomas. "Buy some bread and a chicken or something. It's been a while since we all sat down for a meal."

"I think he'd like that," said Eileen. "I know I'd like it."

"And me," said Henry. "But how do we do that without going through the market?"

"There's a baker south of the Street of Smiths," said Eileen. "And a cook-shop. They always have a decent bird or two ready."

"Then follow me," said Henry. He led them south a pair of streets and across the city. The wine shop in question yielded two bottles at a price that made Thomas raise his eyebrows, but which Henry paid without blinking. They were following Eileen towards the cook-shop and baker when they heard someone yelling, "Stupid witch!"

"Do some tricks, witch!"

There came a clatter of something being thrown, then another.

"Help! Oh, help," came a new, female voice, drowned out at once by other, younger voices jeering at her.

"This way," said Thomas, drawing his rapier. Henry and Eileen followed, drawing their own blades as they went. Thomas followed the sound to an alley and found six boys surrounding an older woman, blocking her from leaving. None of them came close to her. All were yelling. As Thomas watched, one threw a rock that connected with the woman's arm. She cried out in pain.

"You stop that," she scolded. "You stop or I'll get the Watch!"

"The Watch won't come here," said one of the boys. "Not for the likes of you, witch!"

The other boys jeered and made mock-charges at the woman. The woman tried to slap at them, but they danced out of her reach. Several threw pieces of rotted vegetables at her. The boy with the rocks raised his arm to throw another.

"Hey!" shouted Thomas. "Enough!"

One of the boys turned to say something and saw the rapiers. He yelped in surprise and stumbled back. The other boys turned to look and immediately fell silent.

"That's enough of that," said Thomas. "Get lost."

"She's a witch!" said the boy with the rocks. "Witches don't deserve to walk the streets."

"She's not a witch," said Thomas. "There's no such thing."

"She is!" protested another boy. "Everyone knows it."

Thomas advanced, his blade in front of him. The boys fell back.

"If you would like to come with us?" said Thomas to the woman.

"Thank you, young man," she said, still glaring at the boys.

"She makes babies sick!" called another boy. "She kills cats!"

"Doesn't make her a witch," said Henry.

"You should know better," scolded Eileen. "Who are your parents? Do they know you're out here?"

"It was my dad said she's a witch!" said the boy with the rocks. He raised his arm to throw.

Henry crossed the distance in three fast steps, stopping with the tip of his blade in front of the boy's face. "Get lost. All of you."

The boy scrambled away, his friends on his heels.

"We need to get out of here," said Thomas. "Before they come back with their parents."

Eileen glared after the boys. She offered the woman her arm. "Are you all right?"

"I think so," said the woman. "Thank you so much. They... they just surrounded me. And wouldn't leave me alone. I don't know why they called me a witch. I don't... I don't go near children or herbs or anything like that. I don't even have a garden. I'm.... I'm a weaver."

"They called you a witch because they're stupid," said Eileen. "Because they think they can get away with it. We'll help get you home."

They were late getting to the forge, and George looked ready to grumble about it until he saw the chicken, bread, wine and pastries—Thomas had insisted on the pastries. His frown came back as soon as they told him what they'd seen.

"Foolishness," he declared.

"Well, what were we supposed to do?" demanded Eileen.

"Not you three," said George, waving away her protest. "At least the preachers are gone."

"Gone? They were in the square this morning."

"Linda went to the square just an hour ago," said George. "She told me that the students were there but there wasn't any sign of the preacher."

"Well, that's something," said Thomas.

"Maybe the riot did some good," said Henry.

"Riot?" exclaimed George. "What riot?" He rounded on his sister. "When did you get in a riot?"

"I didn't," said Eileen, rolling her eyes. "I'd have said that first, if I had."

"It was Graham," said Thomas. "And a bunch of the others. They got in a riot with the preachers and their followers."

George swore. "That's bad, Thomas. Really bad. Did anyone die?"

"None of the students," said Thomas. "I'm not sure about anyone else."

George shook his head. "What's going to happen next?"

"Nothing I'd like to talk about in the streets," said Thomas. "Let's go inside."

Over dinner Thomas told George all they'd figured out the day before, and how Sir Walter confirmed it. George's expression went bleak as he listened, and he started shaking. "This is bad," he said. "Very, very bad."

"I know."

"I don't want to be in another war."

"Neither do I," said Thomas. "But maybe it won't come to that. Maybe the Church will back down."

"Or the king," said Henry. "What are you going to do if that happens?"

"No idea," said Thomas. "Run away, probably."

George put his head in his hands. "Stupidity, all of it."

"Aye, it is that," said Henry. "But it's no reason to waste all this lovely food, is it?"

A chuckle rippled through George and he brought his face up again. "No. It certainly is not."

They talked mostly of inconsequential things through dinner; of Eileen's classes and Thomas and Henry's law studies. Eileen talked of the dinner they'd had with Claudine the night before, and how the girl was thinking of trying for the Academy. Henry teased George about Linda and was growled at for it.

"Enough of this," said George as the last of the wine was finished. "Eileen needs to study and you lot need to get home and get some sleep."

"Can't," said Thomas. "We've got to keep an eye on our baker friend, and see if he goes out tonight."

"I can come," said Eileen.

"No you can't," said George. Eileen opened her mouth to protest, but George spoke first, "You've done all this work to get into the Academy and it won't matter a bit if you don't pass your exams. You need to study. Especially trigonometry. Thomas and Henry can stand outside in the cold all by themselves."

"Sadly true," said Henry.

"He's right," agreed Thomas. "I doubt anything will happen tonight, so you might as well stay home. We'll tell you if something happens tonight."

Eileen frowned at them. "You promise?"

"We promise," said Thomas. "We'll see you tomorrow."

Eileen walked them down to the smithy and gave Thomas a kiss before he and Henry went on their way. The evening was cool and damp, but there were spaces in the clouds above, showing the last light of the sun.

They dropped their books and robes at home and headed for The Pie and Tart. It was just closing down for the night. Through the windows they could see Robert's wife sweeping the floors, and Robert himself looking over the shelves and chatting with her. Thomas and Henry took themselves to the alley and resumed their places.

"Here," said Thomas, pulling a package out from under his cloak. "I brought the leftover pastries."

"Which ones?" asked Henry. "The apple or the blueberry?"

"Can't remember," said Thomas. "Can't see which is which, either, in this light, so pick one and I hope it isn't the blueberry because I want that."

They picked and munched and discovered both were blueberry. As they watched, the cooks went home for the night and the lights went out.

"Do you think George is getting better?" asked Thomas. "I mean, we talked about a war and he only shook a bit."

"He isn't better," said Henry. "He's just strong enough to keep from showing it when we're around."

They lapsed into silence until the midnight bell rang. Then they began the long walk home.

"Maybe they only meet once a month," said Henry, once they were well away from the bakery.

"I hope not," said Thomas. "I need to find out what's happening before then."

They heard the mob before they saw it; an ugly mixture of yelling and stomping and horse's hooves on cobbles. Two men were shouting louder than the others, struggling to be heard above the din. Thomas and Henry followed the sound to a square near the city walls. It was half-full of people gathered around the central fountain. A dozen cavalry stood in line on one side of it. Each rider had a torch in his hand. Twenty or more Church soldiers on foot stood in front of them, spears in their hands held sideways to hold back the angry crowd that surrounded them.

"See!" screamed a preacher, standing on his little box, his arms waving with excitement. "See how the wicked are to be punished! See how the evil cannot escape! See the witches, ready for hanging!"

Seven women stood, chained together at the neck, their hands in shackles, in the centre of the footmen. Most were in their night clothes. Several had bruises on their faces. All looked terrified.

Thomas swore and stepped back into the shadows. Henry followed without a word.

One of the cavalrymen kicked his horse's flanks and rode forward out of the line. "By order of Culverton, Archbishop of Criethe!" he declared, "let it be known that witchcraft, so long an abomination against man and the one true faith, has shown its most hideous face once more in the fair city of Hawksmouth!" He raised an arm, pointing it at the fearful, chained women. "Here stand seven women accused of that most terrible crime!"

"Anna hasn't done nothing!" called a man. "My wife is a good woman!"

"Claris would never practice witchcraft!"

"Delores did nothing!"

"Liars!" the preacher yelled. "Liars all of you! They're witches! They conjured the Banished! They gave themselves to the Banished to gain advantage over their neighbours! They bewitched men to their service!"

Someone threw a cobblestone at the preacher, narrowly missing his head. The cavalry leader shouted a command and the troop drew their swords.

"Hear me!" cried the soldier who spoke before. "Hear me! There will be no punishment without evidence! No sentence without a trial! Each of these women will face the question and the truth will come out!"

"No! Don't you torture my little girl!"

Another cobble flew, then a third. The cavalrymen raised their shields.

"What about the students?" demanded the preacher. "When will they be arrested? When will they face the High Father's judgement?"

"The students hide behind the king," said the cavalryman. "He keeps their wickedness from being punished, and protects them from the true law—the law of the Church!"

"No more!" screamed the preacher. "No more! Let the students pay! Make the students pay! Make the students pay!"

It became a chant, taken up by half the crowd. The other half yelled curses and tried to reach the women inside the circle. Men and women shoved and screamed, and fists flew. The cavalryman shouted an order, barely audible above the noise, and the cavalry began walking their horses forward in a line, forcing the people around them back and to the sides. The soldiers on foot followed. Half had their spears sideways as barriers; the others had their tips pointed toward the crowd, keeping them back.

Rage burned white hot inside Thomas. "We have to stop them."

"We can't," said Henry.

"I can."

Henry caught his arm before he could raise it. "Not against that many soldiers," he said. "You might get one or two, then the rest will ride down the crowd to get to you. Do you want that?"

"Bastards," Thomas forced his voice quiet and his anger down. He watched the cavalrymen make their slow way out of the square. "Why attack the women? This isn't like the last war. No women are fighting in the name of the Daughter or the Mother. Why not arrest their husbands or their brothers?"

By the Four, why not me?

"I don't know," said Henry. "We need to get off the street. Now."

Thomas swore at the soldiers' backs and followed Henry through the side streets and back to their apartment. Three more times they ran into mobs cheering or shouting at Church soldiers as they dragged women through the streets. One time Thomas caught a glimpse of the prisoners; three old women and two young ones, huddled together, ropes tied around their necks, their faces etched deep with shock, horror and despair.

And all the time he kept thinking, *The High Father's Church made the first move. It's war now. It's all going to be war.*

When they reached the square in front of their apartment, Thomas was spitting with rage and practically crying from helplessness. He half-prayed that the Church soldiers would be at his door so he could unleash his anger, magic and blades on them. Beside him, Henry was stone-faced, his hand gripping his rapier's hilt.

They both nearly tripped over the girl curled up against the base of the fountain, shivering and weeping silently. Thomas's eyes went wide. "Claudine?"

23

Claudine looked up, her face streaked with tears. "Oh thank the Daughter!" She staggered upright and stumbled forward, wincing as her bare, bloody feet touched the rough cobbles of the street. She wore nothing but a long shift, and shook with cold and fear. "Please, please, please, please..."

Henry caught her before she could fall and wrapped his cloak around her. "What happened?"

"My mother," sobbed Claudine. "My father. They've taken them both. Please help!"

"Inside," Thomas said. "Fast!"

Henry picked Claudine up and carried her. Thomas ran ahead and opened the door. Henry brought Claudine in and laid her on the couch. He put his cloak over her and headed for his room. "I'll get some blankets."

"I'll get the fire going," said Thomas, crouching before it. He laid in the kindling and logs then looked over his shoulder. Claudine was staring at the wall, her eyes barely focused. Thomas shifted so Claudine couldn't see the fireplace, and called flames into the kindling. It caught at once, and he fed it until it was crackling and the flames licked the logs.

By the time Thomas turned around, Henry had Claudine wrapped in a pair of blankets, and was holding his flask to her lips. Claudine swallowed some, then gasped and coughed. "Again," said Henry. "Don't try to breathe. Just swallow it."

Claudine made a face but swallowed the whiskey down.

"I'm going to make some tea," said Henry. "And then you can tell us what happened. Thomas, help me with the kitchen fire."

"Of course," said Thomas, following him into the kitchen.

"She can't stay here," whispered Henry as soon as the door closed. "Not if her parents have been arrested."

"She doesn't have any place else to go," said Thomas.

"I know *that*!" Henry grabbed the kettle and filled it from the bucket. "Light the fire."

Thomas tossed a pair of logs into the iron stove and stared at them until they burst into flames. He added a third log on top and closed the door.

Henry put the kettle on the stove. "They might be coming after us next and we don't want them getting her, too. We need to get her someplace safe. And find her some clothes."

"Maybe Eileen can loan her some."

"She'd pop Eileen's clothes at the seams," said Henry. He took another pot and poured the rest of the water into it. "She needs to be warmed up and cleaned up, and her feet bandaged."

"Do we have bandages?"

"I have a full kit under my bed," said Henry, putting the pot on the stove.

"Given our lives, I knew we were going to need them eventually. When the water in the pot is warm, bring it out."

The water in the pot took an inordinately long time to heat. Thomas spent the time pacing and cursing. When it was finally warm enough he brought the pot of water out to Henry and went back to the kitchen until the kettle whistled. Thomas made the tea and brought a tray with mugs and what was left of their bread out to the small parlour. Claudine was curled in a ball under the blankets, staring at the fire. Her feet, peeking out beneath the blankets, were clean and bandaged. Thomas served out, and Henry helped Claudine sit up.

Thomas waited until she'd taken the first sip of her drink before asking, "What happened?"

Claudine shuddered and huddled deeper in the blankets. "I don't know," she said. "I had just gone to bed. My father and mother were still up. I heard banging. Then my mother screamed and the cook burst into my room and grabbed me and told me I had to hide. That they were looking for me, too. He dragged me down the servant stairs and to the back door, and I ran out into the streets." She gasped for air and began sobbing. "I heard him yelling at someone and I think they might have hurt him, too. I hid and... Oh, by the Four..."

Henry plucked the mug out of her shaking hands before she could spill any of the tea. He put his arm around her shoulders. "You're safe here with us," Henry said. "No one is going to hurt you here."

"It's not me!" protested Claudine. "They took my mother! I saw them dragging her away with a rope around her neck. I saw my father trying to fight them, and the soldiers punching and kicking at him and..." Her words became wails. "I want my parents back!"

Henry set the tea aside and took her into his arms. "Shhh. We'll find out what happened in the morning. We will."

"We promise," said Thomas.

"No!" Claudine's hand came out from under the blanket and grabbed Thomas's wrist. "You could do it tonight, if you wanted to. You could find them and get them out."

"Claudine, I can't just..."

"You have magic! You can get them out with it. Please, Thomas!" Thomas tried to gently pull his arm away. Claudine squeezed harder. "You could! You know you could!"

"I can't help them with magic!" Thomas shook his head. "I can't get them out that way."

"Please!" said Claudine. "I know you have the power. Please, *please*, get him out!"

"It's not that simple." *Especially not now that we've already raided them once. The place will be crawling with guards.*

"Please!"

"I'm not saying no because I don't want to!" snapped Thomas, pulling his arm hard and breaking her grip. "I'm saying no because it won't work!"

"I hate you!" Claudine turned her face into Henry's chest and started crying again. Thomas sat back, feeling mean and useless.

But it won't work, he told himself. *We can't even get close to them.*

"I'll find another way," said Thomas. "I promise."

Claudine just cried, inconsolable, in Henry's arms. Henry held her until her wails dwindled down to weeping. "We should keep watch," Henry said. "Claudine can take my room."

Thomas nodded. "We'll switch at each bell of the night, one in my room, one here."

Henry wrapped the blanket tighter around Claudine then picked her up at once. "You rest. We'll make sure that no one hurts you."

Claudine, her head tight against Henry's chest, nodded, but didn't say anything else. Thomas stirred the fire in the parlour and waited until Henry came back out, shutting the door behind him.

"She's still awake," said Henry. He took a drink from his flask and passed it to Thomas. "I doubt she'll sleep any time soon."

Thomas drank, and let the whiskey burn its way down his throat and add its heat to rage in his belly. "I'll talk to Sir Walter in the morning. Maybe he'll know what to do."

"If he can do anything," said Henry. "The Church has obviously decided that the king can't. Or won't."

"Why?" said Thomas. "Why do they think they can get away with it?"

"Cavalry, for one thing," said Henry. "Soldiers. How many troops do you think they have in the city?"

"Enough to pull off raids all over," said Thomas. He thought hard. "Enough to make the king back down?"

"Maybe. The support of the people?"

"Some of them," said Thomas. "Not all."

"And they're not making many friends tonight," said Henry. "What do you think will happen tomorrow?"

"No idea," said Thomas. "After I see Sir Walter we'll take Claudine to George and Eileen's place."

"Think that will be safe?" said Henry.

"It's all I can think of, to be honest."

Henry took back the flask and took another drink. "Wake me at the next bell."

"I will," said Thomas. "Hey, why do you get to sleep first?"

"You can't sleep when you're worried," Henry said, smiling. "And right now you are very, very worried."

Thomas grimaced and nodded. "At least I can get some reading done."

For the next hour, Thomas tried to study, but the words all seemed to jumble together and he couldn't concentrate on them. In the end he put the books down and stared at the fire, trying to make sense of what was happening.

***

Henry roused Thomas as the first morning bell rang, and handed him another mug of tea. "You have to get to Sir Walter."

Thomas nodded and struggled upright. "I'll be back as soon as I can."

"I'll wait till then to get Claudine up."

"All right." Thomas struggled into his boots, coat and cloak then stumbled out into the city. He half expected to be accosted by cavalry on the way, but the streets were quiet and all the doors locked up tight. Thomas ran to the fencing hall and up the stairs.

The door was locked. Thomas knocked on it and waited. He put his ear against it. There was no sound on the other side.

Thomas checked to make sure no one was around, then knelt and used the set of lock-picks Sir Walter had given him. It took a bit of time, but he managed to get the lock open.

Inside, the fencing hall was dark. Thomas stood still and waited, wondering if this was a test. *If so, it's really bad timing on his part.* There weren't that many places to hide inside the room, and none where Thomas wouldn't be able to see a person's inner light glowing. He walked through the hall, checking the rafters and inside the fireplace, just in case. It was empty.

Unsure of what else to do, Thomas lit the fire in one of the braziers. The warmth of it was nice, and the yellow glow lit the room, casting shadows over the fencing equipment. In its light, Thomas could see a note, lying in the middle of the floor.

Events have made today's lesson impossible. Tomorrow.
- W

Thomas slipped out of the fencing salon and into the street. People were starting to come into the streets, now, talking with their neighbours. The conversations all sounded the same.

"They came after midnight. Broke down Merchant Biggan's door!"

"Did you see them leading away Widow Hildy?"

"What could Fred's daughter have possibly done? She's fifteen!"

"I've always thought Francine Henderson was up to no good. And now we know it!"

When Thomas got back to the apartment Claudine was in their kitchen, eating porridge. She glared at Thomas when he walked in.

She wants to hate me? Fine, Thomas thought. *Just let us get her out of here and someplace safe.* "Sir Walter wasn't there," said Thomas. "But the Church was in the area last night. Took at least four people from that neighbourhood from what I heard."

"Is there anywhere they weren't last night?" asked Henry

"Here," said Thomas. "Why not?"

"No idea." said Henry. He turned to Claudine. "As soon as you've finished breakfast, we'll get you someplace safer."

Thomas fetched his spare boots and cloak for Claudine. Henry helped her ease her bandaged feet into the boots, then bundled her in the robe, coat and cloak. Together they led her out into the city. Henry gave her his arm to lean on and she clung to it, limping and gritting her teeth.

The walk to Eileen's house had never seemed longer.

The big market square was buzzing with activity. The preacher was back, raging against the students and their wicked ways, and expounding loudly about the dangers of witchcraft. Many people were listening intently, while four Church guards stood watch. The other shoppers were looking down at their purchases or at the stalls, and spoke in hushed tones.

"Keep on walking," said Henry. "We don't have a care in the world, understand?"

"News!" called a crier. He was dressed in the Church's livery, and carried a small stool that he put down and stood on. "News! Come listen to the news!"

"News from the High Father!" shouted the preacher. "Listen to the news, everyone!"

The crier unrolled a scroll. "News! Listen to the news! Hear one; hear all! Hear the news!" He paused a moment, then raised the scroll. "By order of Culverton, by the Grace of the High Father, Archbishop of Criethe, defender of the faith, and keeper of the true words of High Father, let it be known that last night, this city was scourged of witches!"

The preacher's audience cheered. The crier let them for a moment before raising his voice again. "Too long has Hawksmouth been a haven for those who would do unholy deeds and follow the Banished in their wicked ways! Too long has the city been in their grip! Those who worship the Banished have inserted themselves into even the highest levels of society, perverting the leaders of this fine city and kingdom, so their crimes would go unnoticed!"

"All praise the High Father!" declared the preacher. The crowd around him repeated it, louder. Others in the square looked worried or downright scared.

"Let it be known!" continued the messenger, "That Hawksmouth will no longer be a haven for those who practice foul witchcraft. The Church of the High Father has risen! The Church has acted where the king would not, to clear this canker from our fair city! And let it be further known that the Church will not cease in its efforts to rid our city, our nation and our world of witchcraft! Therefore, I exhort all of you; where you suspect witchcraft, speak to your priest! Let those whose actions endanger their souls and the souls of their fellows be put to the question! Let this foulness be cleared from our land!"

The preacher's followers cheered again. The man stopped, rolled the scroll, and reached into his bag and pulled out another.

"Hear one, hear all!" The crier raised the second scroll. "By order of Culverton, by the grace of the High Father, Archbishop of Criethe, defender of the faith, and keeper of the true words of High Father, let it be known that the Royal Academy of Learning, long known as a breeding ground for ill-behaviours, and all manner of vices, is suspected of having fallen under the influence of those witches who would corrupt our city and nation! Let it be further known that the king, who has sole authority over the students of the Academy, and who is their final arbiter and judge, has refused to investigate these suspicions, but rather allows the students to continue unchecked and unrepentant in their wicked and vile ways."

And your point? Thomas wondered. They were two thirds of the way across the square, and so far, had been unnoticed.

"Therefore, the Church of the High Father calls on you all to shun these students wherever you may meet them! Let no man or woman of good conscience have any dealings with them! Offer them no credit! Do not serve them in your taverns! Do not sell them your goods! Do not speak to them, save to chastise them! Let them know that their wickedness is not welcome in our city! And at all turns, let your voices be heard by the king! Let him know that he must bring these students and their masters to heel! That the laws of the High Father must stand supreme! That all must bow to the will of the High Father!"

"Those are students right there!" The preacher yelled, pointing at them. "There!"

"Keep walking," said Henry. "And get ready to run."

"The High Father bless and protect you!" finished the crier. "Let your faith, your spirit, and your decency sweep away this plague of witchery and wickedness that threatens our lands!"

"You heard what the High Father has said!" screamed the preacher, pointing at Thomas, Henry and Claudine. "Show them the wickedness of their ways!"

The crowd around the preacher cheered. Several of the bigger men started to come forward, cheered by the others. Thomas and Henry put their bodies between them and Claudine, shielding her as they backed out of the square. Thomas looked over his shoulder. The street was only ten yards away. "Nearly there."

"Not close enough," said Henry. "Here they come."

"Take her out of here," said Thomas. "Carry her! Go!"

Henry picked up Claudine over his shoulder and jogged out of the square. Thomas kept walking backwards, letting the men come towards him. When they were twenty feet away, he drew his rapier and dagger. The men slowed.

"Typical!" sneered one. "Always has to go for his blades!"

"Let see you fight like a man!"

"Come on, boy! Put down the weapons and fight for real!"

Not a chance, thought Thomas, still backing away. The men followed him to the edge of the square, but stopped there. Thomas kept walking backwards for another twenty yards, then turned and ran, not sheathing his weapons until he caught up with Henry.

"That was bad," said Henry.

"And going to get worse," said Thomas. "We have to get to the Academy."

They reached the Street of Smiths and found it buzzing like a kicked hornet's nest. There were men and women in the streets, angrily talking to one another. It looked like more posters had been put up the night before, but there were only scraps of them remaining on the walls. Big men with hammers in their hands stood in groups arguing, while the women clustered together having arguments of their own.

One of the smiths spotted them. "You lot!" he raised his hammer and waved them off with it. "Clean out! We're closed! No business today."

"We're not here for business," said Thomas. "We're friends of George Gobhann. What happened?"

"Those Church bastards took Smith Franklin's wife, is what happened," said the smith. "And Smith Grayson's mother!"

Eileen. Thomas's heart leapt into his throat. "Did they take anyone else?"

"Thomas! Here!" George waved from the steps of the Guildhall. Thomas left Claudine with Henry and ran to the stairs. "It's all right," said George. "I mean, she's all right. They didn't take her. She's inside."

Thomas pushed past George and ran into the Guildhall. Eileen, rapier and dagger on her hips and robe on her arm, was talking to Linda.

"Eileen!" Thomas shouted. Eileen spun and ran towards him. They met in the middle of the floor, wrapping each other in their arms. Thomas squeezed her hard. A cold knot he didn't know was there loosed itself in his stomach. "I never thought," Thomas whispered. "I didn't think they'd come here." He squeezed her tighter.

"I'm all right," said Eileen. "I'm all right. They didn't come to our house. They rode in after the midnight bell. There were a bunch of them on horses. Thirty at least. They had swords out and no one could challenge them and..."

"She tried to go after them," said Linda. "By herself. George told me."

"You didn't," said Thomas, releasing Eileen enough that he could see her face.

"I did," admitted Eileen, blushing. "George stopped me. He said there wasn't anything to do except get killed. He held on to me and wouldn't let me go." Eileen shook her head. "I have some nasty bruises from that."

"So does he, I imagine," said Thomas.

"I can't believe they would do this to us!" cried Linda. "To claim that there is witchcraft here..."

"They did it all over the city," said Thomas. "And they took Malcolm Bright and his wife. We found Claudine hiding beside the fountain at our house and took her in for the night."

"Claudine?" Eileen's eyes went wide. "Is she all right?"

"Her feet are cut up and she's scared and angry," said Thomas. "But she's here."

"Eileen's friend?" said Linda. "She stayed with you?"

"There was no other place," said Thomas.

"She can't stay with two young men!" Linda looked appalled. "Her reputation..."

Not what I'm worried about, but reason enough. "That's what we thought."

"This meeting is for guild members and their families only," said Master Smith Gatron from behind them. "You need to be on your way now, Thomas."

"Father!" said Linda. "Thomas and Henry have Claudine Bright with them. Her parents were taken!"

"What? It's happened all over the city?"

"Yes, sir," said Thomas.

"Madness! This is totally against the rule of law!" The Master Smith shook his head. "It is completely wrong."

It certainly is, Thomas thought. *The law wouldn't even allow their arrest without...*

The idea flashed into his brain so fast he nearly staggered. He missed what Master Gatron was saying. It wasn't until there was silence that he realized the Master Smith was looking at him. "I beg your pardon?"

"I said is the girl all right?"

"No," said Thomas. "Her feet are cut up from running barefoot and her parents are missing."

"She has to stay with us," said Linda.

"Why were her parents taken?" asked the Master Smith.

"Why was Franklin's wife?" said George, coming in. "Or Grayson's mum?"

"Or anyone else, for that matter," said Henry, stepping into the Guildhall with Claudine on his arm. "Master Gatron, you remember Claudine Bright, daughter of the merchant, Malcolm Bright?"

Claudine's eyes were still red and swollen from crying, and she walked with a limp. Her hair was a tangled mess and the hem of her night-dress peeked out from beneath the robe.

"What have they done to you?" demanded Linda. "Father, she must stay with us. She must!"

The big man nodded. "Of course. Take her to our house."

"You promised," said Claudine, looking at Thomas. "You promised you would help them."

"I will," said Thomas *And now I think I know how!*

Thomas led Eileen and Henry away from the Street of Smiths at a jog. They circled around the square rather than going through it, and slipped onto side streets when crowds got in their way. When they reached the Academy they found eight students on guard at the gates, and hundreds more inside on the common. Angry words filled the air. Several students were bleeding. Others were bruised and battered. One sat with his back against one of the trees, shaking uncontrollably while his friends sat beside him, looking helpless.

"Thomas!" called Michael. "Here!" The Student Company was together. "We're thinking we should go get our armour. What do you think?"

"I agree," said Thomas. "But we need something else, first."

"What?"

"Lawyers," said Thomas. "Lots of them."

24

"Lawyers?" repeated the Master of Laws, leaning back in his chair. "Against the High Father's Church?"

"Yes, sir," said Thomas.

It had taken a half-hour of waiting and pleading before the Master of Laws agreed to see Thomas. Now he stood before the man's desk, hoping he could make the Master listen to reason. "They can't have evidence against all of them. In fact, I'd be surprised if they had evidence against anyone they arrested. We go out, take depositions, go to the Church's law courts and present a writ demanding proof of lawful incarceration for each person taken."

The Master of Laws frowned and thought about it. "We'll go see the Headmaster."

In short order Thomas was at the Headmaster's parlour, explaining his idea to the Headmaster as well as the masters of Theology, Law and Rhetoric.

"This does not seem like a wise course of action, Thomas," said the Master of Theology.

"I disagree," said Thomas, doing his best to sound sure of himself. "The law allows all accused a reasonable defence both against their arrest and against their trial. Even Church law."

"There must be evidence," said the Master of Theology. "Otherwise why arrest them?"

Because he wants to force the king's hand! Thomas made himself speak steadily, rather than giving the anger free rein. "If we really want to get the city on our side—on the king's side -what better way?"

The Headmaster nodded. "He does make a good point."

"Students have been assaulted this morning," said the Master of Laws. "We can't send them out alone."

"We'll protect them," said Thomas. "Group us into companies. Send us out."

"The older students," said Headmaster. "No one under sixteen. The young ones stay on the Academy grounds, with older ones guarding them, in case things get even more out of hand."

Not in case, thought Thomas. *When.*

The Headmaster called an assembly and for volunteers. As the third morning bell rang, two hundred fifty students marched out of the Academy. They split off into companies, each heading to a different part of the city. At his request, Thomas's company got the Street of Smiths. Henry led another group to the shipwrights' area. The senior law students—young lawyers, really—marched in the centre of each company, clutching leather briefs and papers as well as their weapons.

The streets were busy with people going about their day. Things could have passed for normal, were it not for the hushed voices people used when they spoke, and the houses where the doors had been smashed in.

The Street of Smiths was still busy and the smithies were open, but a group of men with sticks and hammers patrolled the length of it. They spotted Thomas and his troop immediately, and blocked the company's way.

"You can't come in here like that," said one of smiths. He was a wide man, with a sturdy, knobbed stick in his hand. "We'll not allow any more trouble here."

"We're not here for trouble," said Thomas. "The Academy heard of the raids last night. We're taking depositions, and creating a list of names of those taken. Then we will go to the Church courts to demand proof of lawful incarceration and, if no proof is offered, demand the freedom of the accused."

"We'll help anyone who has a family member taken by the Church," added one of their lawyers—a plump, short man who'd won every award in law the Academy offered, and most of his cases to date. "We just need to learn what happened and who in their family was abducted."

The smith frowned. "I never heard of such a thing."

"It's true," said Eileen, stepping forward. "You know me, Smith Jeremy. I'm Eileen Gobhann."

The smith looked close. "So you are. Didn't recognize you in all that get-up. Is the Academy taking girls now?"

"Not yet," said Eileen. "But I'm aiming to be first."

"Well, if that doesn't beat all," said the smith. "Still, you can't come here armed. We've decided we won't have it. And there's a curfew tonight, too, Miss Gobhann. We're blocking the streets after the first bell of the night, and no one is getting in or out."

"Fair enough," said Thomas. "Can you tell Master Smith Gatron that we are here, and let him know why?"

"Aye, I can do that," said Smith Jeremy. "But you lot wait here, all right?"

Master Gatron came quickly, with George beside him and Linda in tow. "Thomas Flarety," he said. "What is all this?"

Thomas explained and the Master Smith nodded his agreement. "Use the Guildhall."

"How is Claudine?" asked Eileen.

"Not well," said Linda. "She's been crying since this morning. She won't talk to anyone, and she won't eat."

"Can I go to her?" Eileen asked Thomas. "Maybe I can help."

"Go," said Thomas to Eileen. "But only for quick visit. If she won't come down, you have to let her be. We'll need every sword we can get if things go badly here."

Eileen followed Linda away, and Master Smith Gatron led the students to the Hall. The lawyers quickly set up on the tables, and the company, dividing into groups of four, went to the surrounding streets to spread the word. By mid-afternoon, they'd interviewed seven families whose wives, daughters, mothers or grandmothers had been taken. Claudine had been one of them. Thomas watched her come, leaning on Eileen's arm, and had stepped far enough back that she wouldn't have to talk to him. She was wearing a plain dress that mostly fit her, though the previous owner had obviously been a bit larger about the middle. She passed him without a look and mounted the stairs into the Guildhall.

"This is a good thing you are doing," said Master Smith Gatron to Thomas as the afternoon wore on. "A very good thing. To offer these people advice and hope."

"We had to," said Thomas. "We couldn't let the Church just take people away. Not after what they did to our friends."

"Your friends?" Master Gatron frowned at Thomas. "You mean those ones you brought to George's smithy three days ago? They were arrested by the Church?"

"Kidnapped," corrected Thomas. "Arrest without proper cause or warrant, and without legal jurisdiction is kidnapping."

"And you took them from the Church's custody?"

"Yes."

Master Gatron frowned some more. "Not with the Church's permission, I take it."

"Most certainly not," said Thomas.

"That is..." Master Gatron searched for the word. "Surprising."

Thomas found himself smiling. "It certainly was that."

The second bell of the afternoon rang before Claudine came out of the Guildhall, walking between Linda and Eileen. She walked slowly down the stairs and stopped in front of Thomas. "Have you done anything, yet?"

"This," said Thomas, opening his hand toward the law students in the Guildhall behind them. "We're going all over the city trying to help everyone, including your mother and father."

Claudine's hand flashed out, smacking Thomas in the face hard enough that lights flashed in his head. He blinked his eyes clear and saw Eileen pulling Claudine away in an arm lock George had taught her.

"You could do more!" Claudine yelled. "You know you could!"

Linda and several other women helped Eileen take Claudine away. George came out of his forge, his thick walking stick in his hand. He watched the women hauling Claudine to Master Gatron's house and looked at Thomas. "Went after you again, did she?"

"Aye," said Thomas, rubbing his face.

"What did she mean, you could do more?" asked Master Smith Gatron.

"He knows Claudine's mother and father," said George. "I think she hopes Thomas can get them out sooner."

"It seems to me you're doing a great deal." The Master Smith watched Claudine struggle and sighed. "The young lady is distraught. Otherwise she would appreciate what you are doing."

"Cavalry!" yelled one of the patrolling smiths. "There's cavalry coming!"

"Marcus, William," said Thomas, "get everyone together, fast!" William dashed inside the Guildhall. Marcus ran for the students standing guard at the other end of the street. Thomas sprinted toward the smiths. "Eileen! With me!"

Eileen was already running and met him as the cavalry came around the corner.

There were six of them in full Church colours, with swords on their belts and armour under their livery. They rode up to the group of smiths blocking the street and tried to ride through. The blacksmiths, not at all afraid of the horses, grabbed the bridles of the first two, making it near impossible for the others to pass.

"You let my horse go or I'll cut off your head, you hear me?" shouted the first cavalryman in a thick, guttural accent. He drew his sword. The smith holding the man's horse let go and jumped back. The soldier rode forward, kicking out at the man with his boot as he did. "Get back you Son-worshipping bastards! I'll gut you where you stand and send you to the Banished!"

Thomas and Eileen drew their rapiers. From behind, Thomas heard yelling and running feet. He glanced back and saw George and the entire Student Company coming. The three lawyers stood at the door of the Guildhall, weapons in their hands.

"Smiths and students." The soldier spat on the ground. "The Son worshippers and unbelievers together. Fine. Listen to what I have to say." He pulled a scroll from his cloak, unrolled it and read loudly. "Let it be known that, in order that Hawksmouth be cleansed of all false worship and witchcraft, the Church of the High Father calls upon the faithful of the city to come to church, or to the cathedral, this High Father's Day. There, they will kneel and swear their allegiance to the High Father in all things, and above all others!"

"We've sworn our allegiance to the king," said Thomas. "Not the Archbishop!"

"The king answers to the High Father," the soldier said, looking down at Thomas. "And he will come to heel, just like you Academy scum."

"The king will not come to heel!" William yelled. "Long live the king!"

"Shut up, boy!"

"Your message has been delivered," said Master Smith Gatron from behind them. "Now go."

Thomas looked back and saw that the street was filled with men carrying hammers and iron bars. All of them looked more than ready for a fight. The soldier sneered down at the Master Smith, but turned his horse and led his men away.

"This is bad," said Michael. "Very bad."

"Aye," said Thomas. "Master Gatron? I'm sorry for what happened here, both last night and today."

"Thank you, Thomas," said Gatron.

"You have friends at the Academy," said Thomas. "Hopefully we can get your people out soon."

A half-hour later, with no more dispositions to get, the company formed up and moved out, the lawyers once more in the middle.

"That was a bit worrisome," said Michael as they walked away from the Street of Smiths.

"More than worrisome," scolded Eileen. "I thought we were going to have to fight."

"Me, too," said Thomas. "We need to start wearing our armour, if we're going to keep doing this."

"Good idea," said Michael. "I'll spread the word."

Several blocks from the Academy, they began to hear chanting. It grew louder and louder the closer they came. Thomas ordered the company to halt before they reached the last corner. He went ahead, Eileen beside him, and looked.

The street in front of the Academy was filled with men and women—at least a hundred of them—throwing rotting vegetables over the Academy walls. The gates were shut and there was no sign of the guards. "Down with the scholars!" was the crowd's chant. "Down with the unbelievers!" In the midst of them, a preacher stood high on something, egging them on.

Thomas and Eileen went back to the troop and told them.

"Well, that's bad," said Michael. "Now what do we do?"

"Is there another gate?" asked Eileen.

"Only the small one, and they'll see us there, as well," said Thomas.

Someone whistled, loud and long, behind them. It was another student, waving them over. Thomas led the troop to him.

"Henry's got us together," the student said. "In the next square over."

Thomas and the company followed him to the square. All the students that had gone out were assembled. Henry saw Thomas and waved him over.

Thomas went to him. "What's the plan?"

"We push through them and get into the Academy," said Henry. "Not sure how we'll get out, after, but first we have to get the depositions in. How did you do?"

"Got eight," said Thomas. "Three from the Street of Smiths, four from outside, and Claudine's."

"Good." Henry raised his voice. "Company leaders, to me!"

Ten more students joined them, forming a loose circle.

"We need to get inside, we need to deliver our depositions, and we need to do it without killing anyone," said Henry. "We're going to march in. Eight wide, lawyers in the middle. No one is to draw any weapons. Period. The people out there are unarmed."

"Except for rotting vegetables," said one.

"Getting rot on you won't kill you," said Henry. "Draw a sword and that mob will come back with weapons. Then we'll have real troubles."

"We don't already?" asked another.

"No, we don't. Yet," said Henry. "We march until I give the word, then we charge, Fight with fists if you have to, but *no one* is to draw a blade. Tell everyone. Thomas, your company goes first."

Henry led them around the square and several blocks away to get them marching in time together. Then he led them to Academy gate. When they were in sight of the mob, he yelled, "Now!"

As one, the students stomped their left boots onto the cobblestone street, two hundred fifty feet hitting the ground in unison. The noise of it echoed through the streets. The people at the back of the crowd heard it first, saw what was coming and spread the word. The mob at the gates fell back.

Thomas, at the front with the Student Company, forced his breathing steady and his face to be expressionless. The distance between the two groups closed and Thomas could see fear and anger on the faces of people in the mob.

"Look at how they dare profane our streets!" shouted the preacher at his crowd. "The unbelievers dare walk through our city as if they are the ones who own it. As if their actions aren't the reason this city has fallen into disrepute! Show them our scorn! Show them what we think of them!" He seized a cabbage and hurled it. It fell short, splatting into the street with a burst of green and brown leaves and stench.

The mob let out a roar and vegetables started hurtling through the air.

"Charge!" screamed Henry. The students ran forward, driving into the mob and splitting it apart. Some of the crowd were shoved to the side. Others were knocked down and trampled. The initial rush, with the weight of the two hundred students behind them, carried them two-thirds of the way to the gate. From there it became a fight. Students and city-folk pushed and threw fists at one another. Several students were hauled out of the column and into the crowd. Others rushed out and fought the mob to get them back.

At the front of the column, a man twice Thomas's size tried to grab him. Thomas kicked the man's knee and punched him in the face. The man staggered back and another dove forward, hands stretched out in claws. Thomas caught one of the man's arms and twisted until he heard something snap. The man fell, screaming. Thomas stepped on him as he went forward. Someone punched Thomas in the nose. He lashed back, striking out near-blindly as his eyes watered.

By the time they broke through the crowd, Thomas was bruised and bloody and his robe was torn. Thomas pounded on the gates, screaming "Open up! It's us!"

The little viewport in the gate opened and a shocked gatekeeper peered out. A moment later the doors swung open and the students poured through. Some stumbled and fell. Others grabbed them and kept them from being trampled underfoot.

"Who's missing?" demanded Henry. "Company leaders shout out! Who's still outside?"

"Jimmy Talbot! He's not here!"

"Hubert's gone!"

"Frederick and Owen!"

Master Brennan's shout rose above the others. "Get out of the way!" The students threw themselves to the side as the Fencing Master led two dozen students armed with staves through the gate, swinging as they went.

"Hold the gate!" shouted Henry. Thomas and the company and dozens of others lined the gate, ready to drive off anyone that tried to break in.

The Master Brennan and his students fought their way to the clusters of men who were beating the students, and lashed out with their staves. Some of the townspeople tried to fight back and were battered unconscious. The students grabbed their comrades off the ground and retreated back to the gate, swinging their staves at anyone who came near. Henry ordered the others to back away as the Fencing Master came through. The mob, nursing their wounded, didn't follow, and the gatekeeper swung the gates shut and barred them.

"By the Four," said Eileen. "That was bad."

"Who isn't hurt?" demanded the Fencing Master. "Who's still walking? Line up and take a staff!"

Thomas and the others who hadn't taken too much damage lined up. Master Brennan and four students passed out staves until a hundred of them stood armed and ready.

"We clear the street," said Master Brennan. "We catch that damn preacher if we can. Anyone who fights gets brained. Anyone who runs we don't chase, except the preacher. Got it?"

There were nodded heads and calls of "Yes, sir."

"Open the gates!"

The gates swung in and the students swarmed out. Most of the crowd ran, some got blows to send them on their way. A few tried to fight and were battered to the ground. The preacher stayed on his box until it was clear the mob was breaking. He jumped down and tried to run, but a dozen students chased him down and beat him unconscious. They dragged him back face down through the blood and rotten vegetables that lay strewn on the street.

The Fencing Master sent groups of ten to each corner outside the Academy gates with orders to call for reinforcements if another mob came. He ordered the priest bound and then sent Thomas and the rest of his company to get the city guard. "And don't be afraid to draw, if someone tries to stop you."

They ran, and returned with a squad of the city guard. The guards were appalled at the mess in the streets in front of the Academy, and their leader looked more than a little upset at the condition of the preacher. The man had regained consciousness, but was bound and gagged and could do no more than whimper. He had a bloody gash in his forehead and bruises welling up all over his body.

"Was it necessary to beat him so badly?" asked the leader of the guard.

"Look around," said the Master Brennan. All over the common students sat on the cold, wet grass or leaned against walls. Most looked like they were in shock. Some were angry and paced back and forth, muttering under their breaths. Others were barely holding in tears. "He got what he deserved."

The Watch looked doubtful but dragged the man out.

Soon after, the Headmaster came out and declared classes over for the day. He urged them all to be careful going home. "Take off your student robes whenever you have to walk in groups of less than ten. And go nowhere unarmed. We want no more incidents if we can avoid them. All those who escorted our lawyers today will need to do likewise tomorrow. Nothing will come between the people of this city and the king's justice."

Thomas leaned over to Michael. "Armour and uniforms, tomorrow,"

"Yes, Captain," said Michael, and went to tell the others.

25

The first bell of the morning rang and Thomas once more stumbled out of bed. He'd slept in fits and starts, the night plagued by dreams of the violence and bloody battles mixed up with the riot. The sky outside his window was just changing from black to dark, dark blue. *Another sign spring is coming,* he thought as he splashed cold water from the jug on his face. He winced as it hit his bruised cheek and nose.

There was a fog that loitered in the streets, and enough light to see where he was going. Thomas opened his cloak to let the cool air wash over him. It didn't make him feel any more awake. *I really need to get some more sleep. At this rate...*

Thomas heard footsteps behind him.

He spun and drew his rapier. Two identical young men froze, staring at the blade. Neither was armed.

"Whoa, whoa! Wait!" said the first of them. "It's all right. We just want to talk is all."

"We were at Malcolm's party," said the second. "Remember?"

"Aye," said Thomas. "I remember. Why are you here?"

"Well, it's not just us," said one of them. "There's a lot of us here." He signalled and a three other men came out of the alley. They looked slightly shame-faced, as if none of them were there by choice. "And we need your help."

"I heard Malcolm was taken," said Thomas. "I'm sorry."

"Oh, he wasn't," said one of the other men—an older fellow with a thick red beard. He started stepping around Thomas. "In fact, he wants to see you." He looked down at the rapier. "Do you really need to have that out?"

"I don't know," said Thomas. "Do I?"

"No, you don't," said the first twin, moving to the other side. "No one here wants to hurt you. We just need your help."

"How did you know I'd be out in the street this time of day?"

"We didn't," said the man with the beard. "Malcolm gave us your address. We just saw you leaving and followed you."

"At this hour of the morning?" Thomas pulled his dagger and pointed it at the men trying to circle behind him. "Stop that," he said. "Stay where I can see you."

"Or what?" the man asked, still moving. "You'll kill me?'

"Yes," said Thomas.

"You need to come with us," said one of the twins.

"I have an appointment," said Thomas.

"It's important," said the man with the beard. "We're not going to hurt you."

"Why would you need to—"

The twins both jumped at once, tackling Thomas and driving him backward to the ground. Thomas tucked his chin and managed not to hit his head on the cobbles. Someone grabbed each arm, pinning them with their entire body weight and twisting at his weapons until he let them go. One of the men shoved a sack over his head, and others tied his hands and feet before dragging him up and carrying him.

Stupid, stupid, stupid, Thomas thought as they carried him through the street. *I should have killed them.*

But he couldn't have. They weren't armed, and didn't seem to want to hurt him. Even now none of them were actively trying to damage him as they carried him, face-down, through the streets. One of them even said, "It will be all right. Just wait."

The men lifted him up and manoeuvred him through a door, catching his shoulder then his hips on the side of it. They dropped Thomas onto a wooden floor that rocked slightly when he hit. The floor kept rocking while others moved around him, their boots hitting him in the head as they brushed past him.

Carriage, Thomas thought as he tried to squirm and struggle. He yelled for help and something sharp pressed against his neck.

"Shut up!" said one of them. "Or we'll cut your throat!"

No you won't, Thomas thought, *or you wouldn't have grabbed me alive in the first place.* He stopped shouting, though, and waited. The carriage started moving, and the men all put their boots on top of Thomas, holding him down against the floorboards. Thomas gritted his teeth and tried not to groan as the carriage jarred its way down the street, smacking the bruises on his face with every jolt. The ride was at least half an hour, and Thomas felt every ridge, bump and pothole on the way.

And now Sir Walter will be mad at me again, Thomas thought. *Or he'll come looking for me. Maybe.*

The carriage finally stopped and Thomas was bundled out. He felt the change in temperature as they carried him into a building, and heard a large door being swung shut. Then they put him down on a stone floor.

"You've got him?" said Malcolm from somewhere nearby. There was fear in his voice, and desperation.

"We do," said one of the men. "Didn't even have to go in the house. He left and we followed him."

"Put him in the chair," said Malcolm. "Then help us prepare the space."

They hauled Thomas to his feet and tied him to the chair but didn't remove the sack over his head. Around him he heard footsteps echoing, and brooms sweeping and something large and wood being pulled aside. Malcolm began chanting prayers to the Daughter, beseeching her help in his time of need, and asking her to consecrate the space. His voice echoed off the walls.

One of Malcolm's warehouses, Thomas guessed. *Not that that helps me at all.*

The bell of the morning sounded. "Everything is ready," said Malcolm. "Is he hurt?"

"No," said someone else. "We had to wrestle with him a bit, but we didn't hurt him."

"Then take that sack off his head. It's time"

One of the twins pulled the bag was pulled off Thomas's head. Malcolm gasped. "I thought you said he wasn't hurt!"

"Not by us," said the man with the beard. "He looked like that when we found him."

Definitely a warehouse, thought Thomas, taking in the large, dim room and the crates and barrels at the far end of it.

Malcolm was standing over an old book on a table, reading it carefully by the light of a lamp. His face was also bruised, and Thomas was pretty sure Malcolm's nose had changed shape. Under other circumstances, Thomas would have been more sympathetic. "You should probably get your nose straightened," he called. "It can really wreck your breathing."

Malcolm ignored him.

Thomas tried to free his hands. Whoever tied it was good at knots, and the ropes were tight enough that Thomas began to worry about his circulation. "Any chance we can loosen the ropes around my wrists?"

"No," said Malcolm, picking up the book. "Form a circle."

Malcolm's congregation joined hands in a circle, with one on each side holding one of Thomas's arms. Malcolm stood across from Thomas and raised the book so he could read it. Two of his followers wrapped their hands around his wrists.

"What are you doing, Malcolm?" asked Thomas.

"Saving Delores and Claudine. Now be quiet."

"And tying me to a chair helps, how?"

"Be quiet," repeated Malcolm. "You would not share your magic with us willingly, and so now you will share it whether you will or not."

Oh, by the Four. "It won't work, Malcolm."

Malcolm ignored him. *"Let that which is possessed be shared,"* he said. *"Let that which each holds be amplified, and let that which is in each of us be shared."*

Thomas remembered the feeling of having his magic drained from his body in the caverns below Frostmire. The thought made him shudder. *Malcolm has no magic,* he reminded himself. *You can't take magic without magic.*

I hope.

"Let the circle's magic be brought together," said Malcolm. *"Let it be guided through my body. Let it be directed where I will, and let it be bent to my purpose."*

Thomas closed his eyes and waited.

And waited.

And waited.

He opened one eye. Malcolm was still standing, looking up to the ceiling, as if the Daughter was going to appear before him. Thomas opened the other eye and said, "Told you."

"Shut up!" Malcolm yelled. "This is the Daughter's greatest secret! It is the core of her power!"

He raised the book and read through the incantation again. Again they waited and, again, nothing happened.

"Untie me," said Thomas. "Let me look at it."

"Be silent!" shouted Malcolm. "This is your fault! If you'd shared your magic in the first place this wouldn't be necessary!"

"Maybe it only works by holding hands," said one of the twins. "We can untie his hands but still leave him tied to the chair."

"Do that," said Malcolm.

They did. Blood rushed to Thomas's fingers, making them ache as the twins squeezed them. Malcolm ran through the incantation three more times with the book on the floor in front of him. Still nothing happened. Thomas, relieved to have feeling in his hands, didn't protest.

After the fourth time through, Malcolm screamed in frustration and rushed across the circle. He grabbed Thomas by the shirt, threatening to overbalance the chair. "Give us your magic!" he screamed. "Give it to us! Help us! *HELP ME!!!*"

"I can't!" said Thomas, trying to catch onto Malcolm to keep from falling over. "Magic doesn't work like that!"

"He's lying," said one of the twins. "He doesn't have any magic! He never did! That's why it doesn't work!"

Malcolm shoved Thomas hard, sending the chair over backwards. Thomas hit the ground hard and saw stars. When his vision cleared he saw Malcolm on his knees, weeping. The congregation was gathered around him, trying to comfort him. Thomas, thankful his hands were free, struggled with the knots on his ropes until he managed to untie them. Malcolm was still sobbing when Thomas rolled off the chair and to his feet.

"Hey!" said one of the twins. "He's free!"

The twins and two others left Malcolm and headed for Tomas, mayhem on their faces. Thomas looked for a place to run, but Malcolm and the others were between him and the door. In desperation, he picked up the chair. "I can't beat you all," he said, backing up, "but I will hurt some of you really, really badly."

"Why not use your magic?" sneered one of the twins. "Why not call lightning?"

"Because it would start a fire," said Thomas. *If I throw the chair at him, I can get to the door. Maybe.*

"Leave him!" shouted Malcolm, making everyone freeze. His voice dropped to a near whisper. "He's useless. Leave him."

The twins backed off.

"Where's my rapier?" asked Thomas. "And my dagger?"

"In the carriage," said the man with the big beard, his teeth gritted in anger. "Outside."

"Good." Thomas dropped the chair and walked past them. Malcolm's book was still open, and Thomas glanced down at it as he went by.

The words on the page glowed blue.

By the Four... Thomas stumbled, caught himself, and knelt beside the book, reading as fast as he could. A group of magicians working together, it said, could pool their power and multiply it. The longer the circle was held before the magic was released, the stronger the magic would become. Thomas looked closer, wondering if there were any warnings of what happened to the users.

"Get away from there!" snapped one of the men, shoving him over. "That's a holy book!"

But I need it. Thomas scrambled back. The twins advanced again, both looking more than ready to do him harm. *I have to have it.*

"Just get out of here!" said the man. "Now!"

Thomas looked past him. Malcolm was in a chair now, but still wept like a man destroyed. The rest of his congregation knelt near him. All laid their hands on him as if they could take the pain into themselves through the contact. The man who pushed Thomas over was standing over the book, now.

I could get my swords from the carriage. I could come back and...

And what, kill them?

"Malcolm!" Thomas called out. "Claudine is safe!"

Malcolm raised his head out of his hands. "What?"

"Claudine is safe," Thomas repeated. "She's staying with Master Smith Gatron's family."

Malcolm shook his head, squeezing his eyes tight and opening them wide, as if doing so would help him understand better. "Safe?"

"Safe," said Thomas. "And today the Academy is sending lawyers to the Church courts to demand proof of lawful incarceration. We might be able to get Delores out as well."

Malcolm began shaking. A woman jumped up and caught his arm to keep him from falling. "Oh, Blessed Daughter," he moaned. "Oh, thank you. Oh, my little girl."

Thomas stood up. "I need to borrow your book, Malcolm."

Malcolm, too overcome with emotions, didn't even look up. The man standing over the book shook his head. "It's a holy book," he said. "You can't have it."

"You should leave," said one of the twins. "Now."

"Please, Malcolm," Thomas pleaded. "You said you'd loan it to me. You said you'd let me read it. It's important!"

Both twins stepped forward. "We said get out!"

Thomas threw an arm into the air. *I hope the king forgives me.*

A ball of brilliant white light sprang into his hand, dazzling the men in front of him and filling the room.

The twins yelped in surprise and stumbled back with their eyes shut. The red-bearded man fell to his knees, covering his face. The congregation all gasped and clutched at one another. Thomas, a ball of glowing white light floating in the palm of his upraised arm, stood still.

Malcolm raised his face out of his hands, his eyes as wide like child seeing the full moon for the first time. “What... How?”

Thomas waited. Malcolm rose to his feet, his eyes still wide. He moved slowly, reverently toward Thomas. Thomas lowered the ball of light and dimmed it until it was small and blue.

“Our Blessed Daughter,” said Malcolm. “You *do* have magic.”

“Yes.”

“But... the ritual. Why didn’t it...?” Malcolm’s face twisted in confusion. “Why wouldn’t you share?”

“Magic only works if you have magic,” said Thomas. “I’m pretty sure that spell will work if cast by a magician, with other magicians. But it won’t work for you. I’m sorry.” Malcolm looked half-ready to argue. *Which is something I don’t have the time for.* “Please, Malcolm, I have friends who are in danger and I need to help them. Please loan me your book.”

Malcolm finally raised his eyes to Thomas’s. The merchant looked to have aged ten years in the past two days, but behind the worry in his face and the broken nose, there was hope in his eyes. “Claudine is safe?”

“She is.”

“And you’re trying to get Delores out?”

“We’re trying to get them all out.”

Malcolm nodded, then turned away. He picked up the book and handed it to Thomas. “Please be careful with it.”

“I promise.”

“Aiden, Aiken,” said Malcolm to the twins. “Please, give Thomas a ride anywhere he needs to go.”

A half hour later, Thomas jumped out of the carriage a block away from the fencing studio, sword and dagger at his waist and Malcolm’s book tucked under his arm.

“You sure this is where you want to be?” asked Aiden—at least, Thomas thought it was Aiden.

“It’s where I need to be,” said Thomas. “And home isn’t far.”

“We’re sorry,” said Aiken, “about... you know.”

“I do,” said Thomas.

“Can we ask you something?”

“I really have to go...”

“Your friend, Henry. Does he really like Claudine?”

It was not a question Thomas was expecting, at all. He stood in the street, his mouth open. “I... um...”

“Because she made us agree not to fight over her, but didn’t say anything about anyone else and we wanted to know... Well...”

"He's madly in love with her," lied Thomas. "He speaks of nothing else, and being as he is the current heir of the Duke of Frostmire, I can't imagine her father will have a hard time agreeing to the match." He started walking away, then stopped and called over his shoulder. "Henry's also one of the best swordsmen in the city, and my friend, so I wouldn't fight him if I were you."

Thomas turned away and started walking quickly, hoping they hadn't seen the smirk on his face. *Serves them right for kidnapping me. Though I'd better warn Henry. Eventually.*

The third bell of the morning rang as Thomas jogged up the stairs and pushed open the door to the fencing studio. He found himself face to face with three soldiers wearing the king's livery and pointing their swords at him. "Who are you?" they demanded. "In the king's name!"

"Thomas Flarety," said Thomas. "Here to meet Sir Walter Deehan."

"Thomas!" Sir Walter looked furious. "Where were you?"

"Kidnapped by Malcolm Bright," said Thomas. "Where were you yesterday?"

"Busy. You may have noticed that the Church arrested a large number of people."

"Aye. The Academy has lawyers trying to get them out."

"I know. Why did Malcolm Bright kidnap you?"

Thomas glanced at the soldiers.

"Get out," said Sir Walter, curtly. The men left. "Well?"

"He thought he could use my magic to break his wife and daughter out of jail."

"I take it that it didn't work?"

"*He* couldn't make it work," corrected Thomas. He opened the book to the page and handed it to Sir Walter. "Look. Magicians should be able to combine their power and increase it to make it as strong as they need."

"What?" Sir Walter studied the page. "How strong?"

"I doesn't say. It just says they can raise the strength they need. On a guess, the more magicians you have, the more powerful it is, but I won't know without testing it."

Sir Walter sat back and looked thoughtful. "That could make the magicians actually useful."

"It explains some of the spells in my book," said Thomas. "No one magician can do any of them with any great effect, but if a group got together..."

Sir Walter stroked his chin. "You'd be good for something more than just irritating the Church, Thomas. Good work."

"Luck is what it is," said Thomas. "Malcolm told me about the spell a while ago, but I never expected it would work. Of course, I doubt I'll be able to get the magicians to listen," Thomas added, "since I can't actually tell them anything."

"After this morning, you can tell them what you like."

"What?" Thomas's eyes narrowed. "Why? What happens this morning?"

Sir Walter smiled, but there was no joy in it at all. "Today, Thomas, the king will declare that, after much study and consideration, and in accordance with the opinions of scholars both in this country and others, there is no such thing as witchcraft, and therefore it is unlawful to arrest someone on suspicion of it."

Thomas felt a shiver go through him. "That puts him directly against the Church."

"It does. And even more so when his troops march to free the prisoners from the Church prison."

Thomas found himself feeling even more tired than he had before. "So this is war, then."

"Probably, yes."

"Does the Church know you're coming?"

"Yes," said Sir Walter. "They've been gathering their supporters all morning. And their cavalry."

Thomas swore quietly to himself. "I don't want to be in another war."

"You're in it," said Sir Walter. "You, your friends and the Academy."

"The Academy!" Thomas's stomach dropped. "They're delivering writs of proof of legal incarceration to the Church courts this morning. In Cathedral Square."

"I know."

"You know?! If the Church is gathering up their followers in Cathedral Square the students will be killed! We have to get them out of there!" Thomas started for the door.

Sir Walter caught his arm. "The magicians first, Thomas. If they can be of use to the king, we need them first."

Thomas swore. "Can you send someone to the Academy?"

"I have no one to spare."

"Dammit!" Thomas kicked the wall and did some fast thinking. "Right. First step, to my house to get my spell book," A second finger flicked up. "Second, we get Robert, we give him the spell book and Malcolm's book and get him to tell you where the rest of the magicians are. You do what you like with them." A third finger went up. "Third, I ride like a demon for the Academy, and try to warn the lawyers. Then fourth," the last finger rose, "I re-join you and direct the magicians. Is that acceptable?"

"Yes," said Sir Walter. "In fact, it's an order."

"Then tell me your men have horses here, because it's a long walk."

They did, and had a spare for Thomas. The group rode through the city at a canter with the guards in front shouting, "King's messengers! Get out of the way! Move!"

At Thomas's apartment, Sir Walter watched Thomas pull aside the section of the wall that hid his books and grab the book he had stolen from the School of Theology so many months before. Thomas tossed it to Sir Walter. "All the spells in it work when a magician casts them," Thomas said as he stripped off his cloak and coat and grabbed up his armour. Sir Walter tucked the book inside his coat. Two of his men helped Thomas put on his long mail shirt and the black uniform of the Student Company. Thomas grabbed up his weapons and cloak and the group went out into the streets once more.

They were cantering across one of the market squares when a trumpet sounded, followed quickly by a second, then a third.

"Halt," called Sir Walter, reining in his horse. The three trumpets wove a complex harmony that ran up and down the scale. "That's Kingsong."

The brassy notes cut through the chatter of the merchants and their customers. Everyone looked to see what was happening. Thomas reined in his own beast, desperately impatient but knowing they wouldn't be going anywhere until the Heralds had finished. He could hear other horns nearby, and guessed the Heralds were in every square in the city. *Including the one by the cathedral and the Church courts. The Four help the students if they're there.*

"Hear the word of the king!" shouted the Heralds. "All present, listen and hear the word of the king!" They repeated it until the people in the square went silent. "His Majesty, Harold Plastine, by the grace of the Four, ruler of Criethe, has heard of the many charges laid by the Church of the High Father against his subjects," called the Herald, his voice barely reaching Thomas. "He has listened to the cries of his people whose loved ones now lie in prison, awaiting torture.

"To understand the charges laid against his people, His Majesty has consulted with theologians, priests and scholars from this nation and from others. Having heard their opinions, and having thought long and deeply, it is his Majesty's belief that, while there may be matters beyond the experience of most men in this world, there is no such thing as witchcraft!"

The people buzzed in surprise. The Herald waited a moment to let his words sink in. "Therefore, let it be known that henceforth, in the Kingdom of Criethe, the charge of *witchcraft* is declared to be a baseless one, and that no individual may be arrested, held, questioned, or in any way harmed on the basis of such an accusation!"

Several hundred voices began talking at once.

"Go!" said Sir Walter. "Quickly. Now!"

The soldiers led the way again, trying to clear a path through streets now filled with people. Some were rushing to share the news with their neighbours. Others spoke of going to the Church Courts to demand their neighbours back. Some were already marching under the sign of the High Father. Twice they had to ride through crowds of men and women screaming and shoving each other as the king's supporter's clashed with supporters of the Church.

The Pie and Tart still had its usual line of customers, though they were talking non-stop about the king's announcement. Sir Walter left two men with the horses and pushed his way through the line to the counter. "King's business!" he declared. "This shop is closed for the next half-hour. Everyone out!"

"You can't do that!" protested Robert's wife. "We've done nothing wrong!"

"Quite the opposite, in fact," said Sir Walter. "Get your husband. Now. The king has need of him."

"Robert? He's a baker, nothing more."

"I didn't ask what he was, I told you to get him," said Sir Walter. He looked at the line of customers. "Everybody out! Now!"

Thomas and the soldier shepherded people out the door. When the last customer was gone the soldier stepped out as well, closing the door behind him. Robert's wife ran down the stairs, and came back with Robert and half his kitchen staff. "What can I do for you, Sir?" he began. He spotted Thomas. "Thomas, what's the meaning of this? Why have you closed my shop?"

"He hasn't," said Sir Walter. "I have. Everyone who isn't Robert go back downstairs. Now."

Several of the other bakers looked ready to protest, but Robert shooed them back down the stairs and closed the door behind them. His wife took a bit more convincing, but at last went down. Robert faced Sir Walter, fear in his eyes. "What's... what's going on?"

"We need your help," said Thomas. "You and all the rest of the magicians. And we need it now."

26

"I don't..." Robert looked at Sir Walter. "I don't know what you're talking about."

Thomas took the book from Sir Walter. "Sir Walter, could your men shutter the windows, please?"

Sir Walter relayed the order and the men pulled the shutters tight, sealing off the shop from prying eyes and most of the light. Then Sir Walter sent them outside.

"Please, Thomas," said Robert. "What's going on?"

"Your king needs the magicians of Hawksmouth," said Thomas. He put the book on the counter and lit a small ball of light. Robert gasped and his eyes went wide. He looked back and forth from the light to Thomas's face. "Read this," said Thomas, pointing at the spell. "Fast."

Robert put a trembling hand on the page and skimmed through the words, muttering as he did. When he finished, he looked up at Thomas in surprise. "This... this isn't possible."

"That's what we need you to help us find out," said Thomas. "Give me your hands."

"I..." Robert looked up from the page, confusion on his face. "Why didn't you show us your magic before?"

"The king forbade me," said Thomas. With a thought, Thomas made the light float up above his head. He held out his hands. "Please, Robert. For the king."

Robert read through the text once more and held out his hands to Thomas. "All right."

Thomas let the ball of light fade. "I want you to picture your magic flowing from your left hand into my right hand, just like it says. Can you do that?"

"I... I don't know if I can do that."

"Did you light the candle?" Thomas asked. "Did you make the ball of light?"

Robert nodded. "The light was fainter than yours and—"

"Then you can do this."

Thomas took Robert's hands. They were callused and strong and Robert clung to Thomas like a man in a flood clinging to a rope. Thomas took a deep breath, and another. He looked at Robert, and the third time he breathed deep, Robert breathed with him. "Close your eyes," said Thomas. "Picture it."

Robert closed his eyes. Thomas envisioned his own magic, flowing from his hand to Robert's, and began reading the incantation.

"Let the circle's magic be brought together. Let it be bent to our will, and guided through my body. Let it be directed where I will, and let it be bent to my purpose."

For a moment Thomas felt the magic moving; felt it flowing from his body and into Robert's even as he felt it flowing from Robert's into his. Then Robert gasped and yanked his hands away. His eyes were wide. "What... what did we just...?"

"It works," said Thomas. The wonder of it nearly drove everything else from his mind. He grinned at Sir Walter. "It worked! Robert, put your hands back!"

Robert looked scared, but did as he was told. Thomas repeated the incantation and once more the magic flowed between them. At first, Thomas could feel their separate magic, his own much more powerful than Robert's. Then the two blended together and the magic flowed smoothly between them.

And with each circle the magic grew stronger.

Thomas's body began to tingle like it had when he had accessed the Earth's own magic the summer before. He could feel the energy crackling through him. Thomas, unsure of what would happen if he didn't use the magic, said, "Hang on tight, Robert," and called the magic together.

Slowly, the two of them levitated into the air.

Robert gasped in surprise, but he didn't let go. The energy pulsed through Thomas, and he and Robert floated up until their heads were just below the ceiling. At length, the energy Thomas felt began to fade. Thomas let them drift to the floor and let go of Robert's hands.

Robert stumbled back, hit the wall, and sank to the ground. Wonder, shock and disbelief all warred for space on his face. "That...." the look of wonder was still on Robert's face. "That was... amazing."

Thomas stood where he was, feeling the magic dissipate. When it was gone, Thomas felt as he had before, but no worse. *And given that I'm already exhausted and in pain, I'm glad.*

"It was," agreed Sir Walter. His eyes were wide and not a little wild. "Amazing. Did it work the way you thought it would?"

"It did," said Thomas. He held out a hand to Robert. "You all right?"

Robert nodded. "I am. I'm just..."

"I know," said Thomas. "But right now we need to get the other magicians." He was going to say more, but the room began spinning gently. It wasn't nearly as bad as he had felt when he'd drained his energy before. *The spell must balance out the energy, and spare the caster from being too ill.* "We'll need food first, though," he said. "And water. Quickly."

Robert pulled the door open and stumbled down the stairs.

"What are you doing?" demanded Sir Walter. "We have to go!"

"We need food," said Thomas. "The magic takes away our strength. Not as bad as when I was doing it alone but we still need food and water."

Robert came back up the steps with a basket of pastries and pies. Two of his bakers followed with jugs of water and cups, and his wife was close behind them. Thomas grabbed eagerly for the pastries and shoved one into his mouth. It was blueberry and absolutely wonderful. "These are amazing!"

"I've brought extra for your soldiers," said Robert, taking one himself and holding out the basket to Sir Walter. "You can take these for your troops, if you like."

Thomas swallowed down a mouthful of pastry. "You need to go with Sir Walter, Robert. Now."

Robert blinked in surprise. "Now?"

"Now," repeated Thomas. "You need to go get the others and bring them together."

"What?" said Robert's wife. "What is he talking about?"

"He can't tell you," said Sir Walter, bowing to the woman. "Just know that your king needs your husband's service. Right now."

Robert wiped his hands on his apron, then pulled it off and tossed it at another baker. "Of course I'll go. Fetch my coat, Ashley."

Ashley, one of his bakers, ran downstairs.

"What?" said his wife. "In the middle of the day?" She turned to Sir Walter. "You can't take him now. There are customers waiting!"

"This takes precedence," said Sir Walter, taking the basket of pastries. "I'll pass these to my men and meet you outside."

"Are you coming, Thomas?" asked Robert.

"I have to go to the Academy first," said Thomas. "I'll join with you as soon as I can."

"Must you?" asked Robert. Ashley returned with the man's blue cloak and green coat and Robert struggled into them. "The others need to see what you've shown me, or they won't believe."

Thomas picked up the book and pressed it into Robert's hands. "*You'll* make them believe."

Robert kissed his wife and followed Thomas out of the bakery. Two of Sir Walter's men were already mounted. The third cupped his hands and helped Robert mount up behind one of the other soldiers.

"They'll take care of you," Thomas promised, mounting the horse Sir Walter had given him. "I'll be with you as soon as I can, I swear!"

"Take care of yourself, Thomas," said Sir Walter. "Things are going to get very bad, very soon."

And with those words he kicked his heels into his horse and sent the animal trotting down the street and towards the inner city.

Thomas turned his horse the other direction and headed for the Academy. Noise came at him from all directions. Cries of anger and the sounds of fighting came from side-streets and squares, as well as singing, drums, pipes and shouts for and against the king and the High Father's Church. Twice Thomas had to switch streets when a he saw a crowd marching toward him. He expected the road around the Academy to be blocked with protesters, but none were in sight. He rode up to the gates and banged on them as hard as he could. "It's Thomas Flarety! Open up! Now!"

As soon as the gate was pulled open, Thomas ducked down and rode through. "Have they gone yet?"

"Everyone but us!" said Michael, to Thomas's complete surprise.

"What in the name of the Four are you doing here?" Thomas demanded.

"Our Captain didn't show up so they made us stay here," said Kevin, "Where were you?"

"Kidnapped."

Kevin's eyes went wide. "The Church?"

"No. When did they leave?"

"An hour ago. Who kidnapped you?"

"Not important," said Thomas. "Get the company together and start heading for the Church courts. I'm going to ride out and see if I can catch them before they get there." He pulled on the reins and turned the horse. "Open the gates!"

The further from the Academy Thomas rode, the worse things got. He could hear fighting, and saw street riots breaking out. Several places, his horse skirted puddles of blood on the cobbles.

He rode the straightest route he could manage to the Cathedral, but the main thoroughfares were choked with people, and in several places wagons and crates had been pulled across, making barricades. Some people saw his uniform and started throwing cobblestones. Twice he was hit, leaving aching bruises on his chest and back. Some men tried to pull him off the horse. He managed to draw his rapier and cut at them until they backed off. From then on he rode with his rapier in one hand. It was tricky, and made controlling his already-skittish horse even harder.

There's no way I'm going to be able to fight mounted, Thomas realized. *I'll get killed if I come against real cavalry.*

As he approached Cathedral Square, Thomas sheathed the sword and used his hand to keep his cloak closed over his uniform instead. The main road was completely blocked with Church followers singing and cheering. Criers relayed messages from the Archbishop and preachers screamed to be heard above the mob.

Thomas turned his horse and manoeuvred back to the smaller streets. He had to yell at people to move and use his horse's weight to push through and get off the main road. The Church courts were near one of the side streets that emptied out onto the cathedral, and if he could find his way there, he'd be able see what was going on.

The back streets were thankfully much less crowded, and he managed to ride almost to the edge of the square, where the people were jeering and yelling and pushing to get at something. Thomas tapped a man on the shoulder. "What's going on?"

"The students!" said the man, whose face was red with excitement, and who was clutching a stick in his hand. "Those witch-lovers marched in like they own the place, and now they're trapped. They're stuck on the steps of the courthouse!"

Thomas turned his horse around, not waiting to hear the rest. There were too many people for his company to fight their way through, even if they were willing to kill everyone in the way.

Which I'd really, really like to avoid.

He stayed on the side streets until he was well away from the Cathedral Square then went back to the main thoroughfare. He found the company nearly halfway to the Cathedral, jogging steadily, staves in hand. Thomas pulled up the horse in front of them. "They're trapped on the courthouse steps," he said. "There's too many people around the square for us to get through. We need reinforcements."

"From where?" demanded Evan. "The entire city is in an uproar."

"We could go to the city watch," said Michael.

"If we can find them," said Jonathan. "If they'll come."

"Wait," said Thomas. "Where's Eileen? And Henry?"

"Eileen didn't come this morning," said Marcus, "Neither did Henry."

If something happened to Eileen...

"The smiths," said Thomas, turning the horse around. "Come on."

"You know, next time you could get one of those for all of us," called Marcus as the company jogged after him.

There were still men on patrol at the Street of Smiths. Thomas led the company straight toward them. "Thomas Flarety to see Sir George Gobhann and Master Gatron. Emergency."

The smiths sent off one of their number to fetch Master Gatron, calling in at George's smithy on the way past. Eileen, wearing her own armour and uniform, came sprinting out past the man before he finished talking, shouting, "Thomas!"

Thomas dismounted, dodged past the men and swept her into a hug. Eileen was crying and shaking with anger and relief. Even as she squeezed him hard, she demanded, "Where in the name of the Four have you *been*?"

"Malcolm Bright kidnapped me."

"What?" Eileen pushed him back, looking into his eyes. "You're joking. You're not joking. Oh, by the *Four!*"

"Thomas!"

Thomas turned just in time to be engulfed by George in a bone-crushing hug. "I thought you were dead, you idiot!"

Thomas felt a grin creeping across his face. "Not yet, but I will be if you don't let go!"

George did. "What's going on?"

"We need help," said Thomas. "Where's the Master Smith?"

"At his forge," said George, pointing. Thomas saw the messenger emerging from a large smithy with Master Gatron and his daughter following close behind. Thomas ran to him.

"Thomas Flarety," said Master Gatron. "What's going on?"

"We need your help," said Thomas. "Can you get everyone together?"

"I can," said Master Gatron, frowning. "What sort of help do you need?"

"The students went to deliver the writs to the Church courts this morning. Now they're trapped in Cathedral Square. We need to get them out before they're killed."

"I'll get my armour," said George.

"And your stick," said Thomas. "And staves for Eileen and me if there are any around."

The Master Smith's frown deepened. "I'm not sure I understand."

"I'll explain it all," said Thomas. "Just get everyone together."

It took surprisingly little time. George, who had put on his armour and the colours of the Order of the White Wolf, brought out a chair for Thomas to stand on.

"Talk well," muttered George.

Thomas nodded and stepped up onto the chair. The people looked anxious, worried and suspicious. Thomas, knowing that there was no easy way to deal with it, launched in. "This morning, the king declared that there was no such thing as witchcraft, and that any person being held on charges of it were to be released immediately," said Thomas. "The Church has responded by bringing together all their troops and supporters. The Archbishop will be making an announcement shortly, and when he does, there's going to be fighting in the streets."

"How do you know this?" someone demanded.

"I'm in the king's service," said Thomas, which was true and far shorter than the real explanation. "Right now, the students who were taking the writs demanding the release of your families are trapped inside Cathedral Square, and when the Archbishop declares war, they're going to be killed. I need to get them out and I need men to help me."

"Why us?" asked Master Gatron. "Why not the Watch?"

"The Watch is busy," said Thomas. "We need to go now, and I need help. Anyone who is willing to come. Please, I can't get through to them with only fifteen of us."

"Sixteen," said Eileen. "I'm coming."

"Seventeen," said George.

"It's not our fight," said one of the men.

"Yes it is," said George, before Thomas could speak. "The Church has already come here, taken away people, and told us that we have to swear allegiance to them instead of the king. The students have helped us, and we need to help them."

"If the crowd is as big as you say," said Master Gatron. "What are an extra ten men going to do?"

"Not men," said George. "Smiths. We're stronger than anyone else. Twenty of us could be enough to push through."

"We can't spare twenty," said Master Gatron.

"I'll go," said one of the older men with two younger versions of himself standing behind him. "Me and my lads. The Church took my wife."

"Smith Grayson," said George to Thomas.

"Thank you," said Thomas.

"And me and mine," said another man. "Smith Franklin. They got my mum." He stepped forward and four more stepped with him. "What do we do?"

"Get sticks or staves or something," said Thomas. "And thank you, too."

"Will that be enough?" asked Claudine.

"It's what we've got," said Thomas. "It will have to do. Can someone look after my horse?"

Master Gatron took the horse. Thomas assembled the company and told them his plan. "Who's leading the students?"

"The Fencing Master," said Michael. "Got them all organized like a proper army and had them march to the square."

"Think he'll listen to you?" asked Marcus. "Because he doesn't like you much anymore."

"I don't care," said Thomas. "We go in, we get them, we leave as fast as possible and preferably before the Archbishop makes his announcement."

"Any idea when that will be?" asked Eileen.

"None," said Thomas. I'm just hoping it's not soon."

"Look," said Jonathan.

Thomas looked. George, Smiths Franklin and Grayson were leading two dozen young men. All had long iron bars in their hands, and most had hammers at their belts. "The Master Smith said any apprentices who were over sixteen and wanted to come could join us," said George. "This is what we have."

"It will do," said Thomas. "Now, who knows a back way to Cathedral Square?"

"I do," said one of the apprentices. "Mother wanted me to be a priest."

"Lead us, please," said Thomas. "As quick as you can."

As quick as they could was a brisk walk, which was slower than Thomas wanted but as fast as the smiths could manage over any serious distance. There were more people out now, even in the side streets. Several times they had to push their way through mobs of people, and once a group of Church supporters blocked their path, entirely. Thomas shouted for his troop to advance and brain anyone who tried to stop them. The Church supporters fell back but yelled and spat at them as they went past.

It was nearly noon when they reached the street behind the law court. It was filled with people. Thomas stopped the troop. "Listen close," he said. "The students are on the steps of the Church courts. That's to the left and twenty yards in. If we can get there, they can get out."

"What do we do?" asked Grayson.

"We push our way through to them," said Thomas. "If people try to fight us, we brain them. Don't stop pushing forward, and don't stop moving. Got it?"

"Going to make a wedge again?" asked Marcus.

"It works," said Thomas.

"Right," said George. "Smiths first, then."

The street was wide enough for them to march ten across if they wanted to. Thomas set them six abreast so everyone else could get out of their way. They began pushing forward, telling people to move and shoving back anyone who refused. A couple of times people tried to fight. George punched the first man and he fell like a tree. Two of the apprentices grabbed the second one and together threw him against the wall hard enough that all the fight was knocked out of him. The rest of the people got out of the way until they reached the square.

"Oh, my word," said George. "There's thousands of them."

"Doesn't matter," called Thomas, who couldn't see around the corner. "Can you see the students?"

"Aye," said George. "Right here."

"Then keep pushing. We need to get through."

They rounded the corner and waded into the crowd.

The noise hit Thomas first; a wave of it that made talking nearly impossible. Thousands were singing and shouting There were people playing horns and drums somewhere, though Thomas couldn't tell where. He couldn't even see the square for all the people in it. His world was reduced to the people that pushed and shoved at them.

One voice rose above the cacophony. "Let them through!"

George craned his neck to see. "It's a preacher."

"And he wants us there why?" asked Marcus.

"Let them come!" called the preacher. "Let them hear what the Archbishop has to say about their king's plan to allow witches to roam free through the kingdom!"

"Head for the stairs," said Thomas. "Slow and steady."

They made their way through the now-silent section of the crowd. They could hear singing and prayers from other parts of the square where folks had no idea what was going on in front of the Church courts. The people around them glared but made way. Several muttered threats and insults as the group went by, but no one tried to stop them.

When the last of the people parted before them, Thomas could see the mass of students shoulder to shoulder on the wide porch of the Church courts. There were nearly two hundred of them and their numbers were completely dwarfed by the massive crowd that surrounded them. Thomas marched his own troop up the stairs and called up, "Make room for some more!"

"Thomas!" Graham called from the middle of the line. "What in the name of the Four are you doing here?"

"Getting you out," said Thomas. He turned to look into the square. Thousands of people filled it, jammed together until folks could barely move. Some wore the Church's colours. Others carried banners proclaiming "The High Father Above All!" and "God before King!" and "Death to the Witches!" They were singing, playing pipes and beating on drums. Preachers stationed throughout the square shouted to their followers. And around the edges of the square, in front of every building were Church cavalry, fully armoured, lances pointing to the sky. There were hundreds of them. Thomas shuddered.

"Thomas Flarety!" the Fencing Master's voice filled the air. "Get over here!"

"Keep together," said Thomas to his company. "When we go, we're leading."

"We're not going to go," said Graham. "Not without the rest."

"Who's missing?"

"The lawyers went inside two hours ago."

"What?" Thomas was appalled. "Did you hear the king's proclamation?"

"We did..."

"Do you know what it means? You should have gone after them then!"

"*Thomas!* Here! *Now!*"

Thomas shook his head in disbelief and worked his way through the ranks of the students to Master Brennan. The man's bald head was practically glowing. He glared at Thomas. "What are you doing here?"

"Getting you out," said Thomas. "There's a street to the side there. We can leave through it."

"We're not going anywhere," said the Fencing Master. "Not without the lawyers."

Thomas swore. "Did you hear the king's decree? Did the Master of Laws?"

"The Master of Laws was inside when it was proclaimed," said Master Brennan. "And watch your language."

"The proclamation that declares witchcraft non-existent automatically renders the writs for proof of lawful incarceration void," said Thomas. "If witchcraft doesn't exist, the accused can't be charged with it, therefore their incarceration is automatically unlawful, and no writ is necessary."

"Just because the king says it doesn't exist, doesn't mean it doesn't really," said the Fencing Master.

Thomas stared at the man in surprise. "As far as the law is concerned, that is exactly what it means."

"Well, the Church must disagree, because they're still in there."

"Then get them out," said Thomas, keeping the words slow and even. "Now."

"Don't you give me orders, boy," said the Fencing Master. "We wait until they come out, and then we all leave. Not before."

"Give them a hymn!" yelled the preacher from his box. "Show them our loyalty to the High Father!" The preacher started in on an old battle hymn and the mob took it up with a will, roaring it out with more volume than tune, and making it nearly impossible to hear anything else. The Fencing Master stopped talking and craned his neck toward the Cathedral.

"Have you sent anyone in after them?" Thomas yelled.

"I have not," the Fencing Master glared at Thomas. "The Master of Laws said to wait, and wait we shall."

You stupid son of a... Thomas forced himself to take a deep breath. "The Archbishop is going to give his response to the king's proclamation. When he does, what do you think is going to happen to us?"

"Well, that depends on his response, doesn't it?"

"The streets are already a mess of people," said Thomas. "They're already fighting. This entire square is a riot waiting to happen and there's *cavalry* surrounding it! We need leave. Now!"

"You don't give orders here." Master Brennan's tone was unyielding. "Get your company and get in the ranks. Now."

Thomas opened his mouth to argue further, but the bells of the church began pealing. The square fell silent, and for a moment it seemed as if everybody held their breath. The cathedral doors opened and the Archbishop stepped out, followed by a host of priests and Church soldiers. The people went wild. The Archbishop sketched a blessing over them all and let them cheer for a bit. Then he raised his hands for quiet. Throughout the hushed square, the preachers stepped down from their boxes, and criers in Church livery took their place.

The doors to the Church courts opened. Thomas spun in place, staff at the ready, but it was only another crier. The man walked forward, saying, "May I be let through, please?"

"Clear the way!" shouted the Fencing Master. "Let him through!"

The students shuffled, creating a path down the middle of their ranks. The crier walked through and stopped on the stairs.

The Archbishop lowered his arms and began speaking. The criers took up his words, until they echoed through the square.

"We have heard the words of King Harold Plastine!" called the Archbishop and the criers. "We have heard them and found them deeply disturbing! We have prayed and sought guidance from the High Father, and we have realized that there can be only one conclusion!

"The Banished have taken control of this kingdom!"

The crowd roared in horror and anger. People began yelling and crying. A few near the students charged up the stairs and were pushed back. The Archbishop raised his arms and he and the criers began speaking again.

"Do not despair!" the Archbishop and criers declared. "For though the very highest levels of the kingdom have been infected by the wickedness of the Banished, it can still be stopped!

"Even as we speak, our troops are marching through the city! And as they march they are calling on all loyal sons of the Church to rise with them! And now, we are calling on you!

"The king must be brought back to the High Father! He must be made to repent his folly! He must be brought down, so that he will take the road of obedience that the High Father has set out for him as he sets out for all the kings of the world!"

The people roared again, louder and uglier, with a dangerous edge to it.

"We need to get out!" said Thomas "Now!"

"Hold your tongue and hold your place!" snapped Master Brennan.

"Let all those who defy the High Father's will be laid low!" called the Archbishop and his criers. "Let them be chastened and let them be made to understand that the will of the High Father is supreme!"

The crowd cheered, the Archbishop waved his blessing and turned away. The criers stepped down. The one on the Church court stairs walked quickly back to the courthouse. The students watched him go, eyes wide and worried.

"Close ranks!" Thomas yelled. "Close ranks and stand ready!"

The Fencing Master grabbed Thomas's elbow and spun him around. "You don't give orders! You hear me?"

"Obey the Archbishop!" screamed the nearest preacher. "Obey him and lay the students low! Lay them all low! Now!"

The mob howled and surged up the stairs.

"Defence!" screamed Thomas even as the Fencing Master's hand closed on his collar and yanked him off balance. Thomas flailed and tried to pull himself upright. Behind them, the door to the Church courts swung wide open. A company of Church soldiers, swords and shields at ready, stood in the doorway.

Thomas moved, locking the Fencing Master's elbow and driving his boot into the side of the man's knee. Master Brennan yelled in pain and lost his balance, his hand pulling away from Thomas's cloak as he fell. Thomas spun and ran to where his own company stood. Then the crowd was on them.

The mob slammed against the students like a storm wave against sticks on the beach. Some students lost their footing from the impact, and several were pulled into the crowd. The students swung their staves hard, cracking wood into flesh and bone. Those around them began yelling and crying in pain. The nearest attackers tried to back off, but the weight of the people behind drove them forward into the staves. Dozens were beaten to the ground and trampled on.

Horns sounded from all corners of the square.

The preacher screamed and the people charged forward again. The students lashed out, breaking heads and arms, crushing shoulders and sending men and women to the ground. Still the people attacked, and more students were pulled out of formation and into the roiling mob around them.

"What now?" demanded George.

"We're getting out of here!" Thomas shouted back. "Spread the word!"

The crowd attacked with fists and sticks. Some had knives. The students smashed at them with their staves. There were swirls of motion around the troop where the students who'd been dragged out of formation were being beaten and kicked. Thomas swore, knowing he could do nothing for them.

Horns sounded again from all sides, and Thomas realized it was the Church's cavalry blowing them. *If they come at us we're dead.*

"Thomas!" Thomas turned and saw Eileen pointing behind. The soldiers were marching out of the Church courts, shields high and swords at ready.

"Get down the stairs!" Thomas screamed, pushing himself to the front of the formation. "Form up at the bottom! Spread the word!"

The students yelled the orders to one another. Thomas shouted, "Now!" and began swinging his staff. A man in front of him fell and Thomas stepped forward over his body. The mob surged around the students and for a moment Thomas wasn't sure they'd be able to go anywhere. Then the formation lurched forward, driving people back or crushing them underfoot. From all sides, yells of pain and outrage, battle cries, and the sound of fighting filled the air.

The Church soldiers spread out, making a wall of bodies and steel. Several times they clashed with the retreating students. Several students fell, crying in pain or lying still after the soldier's swords cut into them.

When the students reached the bottom of the steps, the mob surrounded them on all sides.

Which protects us from the soldiers, Thomas thought, *if it doesn't kill us.* "Everyone stay in formation! We're leaving!"

Voices rose in protest.

"My brother's in there!"

"We can't leave them behind!"

"We're leaving!" Thomas screamed. Thomas smashed his staff onto a man's head, knocking him out of the way. "Student Company behind me! Everyone follow!"

They drove toward the side street, only twenty yards away. Their staves crushed skulls and their boots trampled anyone who fell in front of them. George walked beside Thomas, laying about him with his stick. There were cries from students as well, as more were pulled from the ranks and into the mob. Thomas kept driving the troop onward, knowing the mob would take them all if they stopped.

"The soldiers are coming!" someone yelled. "They're coming down the stairs!"

"Keep moving!" Thomas screamed, not sure if he could be heard at all. "Keep moving or we're all dead!"

Twenty yards became fifteen, fifteen became ten. Thomas's arms were exhausted. He kept swinging, kept stepping forward, knowing that only the movement kept them from being overwhelmed.

Ten yards became five, and then there was no one in front of students anymore, only an empty street. Some of the students began running, dashing away from the chaos and violence behind them.

"My company and smiths against the wall!" Thomas yelled. "Everyone else stay in formation and keep moving! Stay in formation!"

Some listened, though not all. Thomas caught some that tried to run and shoved them back. Others dashed away. Slowly, the last of the formation trickled out of the square. George worked his way over to Thomas. "What now?"

"Rear guard," said Thomas. "Ten wide. The company and your smiths. Get them ready."

The last of the students pushed their way out of the square. The crowd followed, keeping their distance from the staves of the students.

"Form a line!" Thomas shouted. "Block the street! Michael! William! Rally the others! Keep them together!" He ran and took position, George right beside him. The Student Company and the smiths fell in behind them, forming two lines across the alley and swinging at the mob. "Anyone seen Master Brennan?"

"He went down on the stairs," yelled someone behind Thomas.

"What now?" asked one of the smiths.

"Keep going!" said Thomas. "Back away. Slow and steady!" The students behind him were mostly bloody and bruised with torn clothes. All of them looked scared and angry. Thomas called back to them. "We walk, slow and steady! When I shout "Go!" we run! When I shout "Stop!" we turn and brain anyone who is following! Got it?"

"Aye," said a half-hundred voices behind him.

"If we break, we die, so stay together!"

Thomas could hear the preachers screaming at the mob. The weight of the mob's numbers pushed the people forward, but the street was too narrow for them to overwhelm the students. Thomas kept students moving slowly backwards, smashing anyone who came near with staves and iron bars for another half-block.

"Go!"

The troop turned and ran, their formation dissolving as the faster passed the slower. The mob roared and ran after. Thomas forced the last two ranks to stay back and keep together. He let them run for a block. "Stop!"

Most of the students pulled to a halt and turned. Some kept going. Thomas couldn't blame them. The frontrunners of the mob were close behind. "Attack!"

The students and smiths swung their weapons and men fell to the ground, unconscious or crying in pain. Thomas kept them attacking until the crowd's momentum was stopped and there was space between the groups.

"Go!"

Three more times they did it, and each time, fewer people followed. On the last time there were no more than twenty, and the students beat them all down or sent them fleeing. No one was close enough to pursue.

"Get in formation!" Thomas ordered. "Everyone form up and get ready to march!"

The students milled about until they got into something resembling order. Thomas had them assemble into rows of five and did a quick count. Seventeen rows and two extras. *Eighty-seven,* Thomas realized. *Plus the Student Company and the smiths. Out of more than two hundred.*

He looked for members of the company. Marcus was missing. So were Jonathan, Bruce and Mark. Thomas cursed in his head. "We're marching back to the Academy! We're taking the back streets, and with luck we'll get there without having to kill anyone else."

"You... you think we killed people?" said a young man Thomas didn't know.

"Yes," said Thomas. "And we hurt a lot more, and they're going to be coming for us, so we need to get back to the Academy before they do. Who knows this area?"

"I do," said one student, coming forward.

"Name?"

"Percy, Captain."

"Percy, you're leading us. We need a route back to the Academy as fast as you can, without taking us down any major streets, can you do it?"

"Aye, Captain. I think so."

"Good. Get to the front."

They followed Percy through the streets at a fast walk. Some were limping, others cradled hurt limbs. Most of the faces had blood on them. No one complained or asked the company to slow down.

All round them they heard chanting and fighting. Once a troop of city watchmen came down a side street towards them, looking as beat and battered as the students themselves were. The watchmen stopped and let them go by.

When they were away from the cathedral, another student whose parents lived in the area took over, leading them down more side streets. A third took over in the next neighbourhood.

"We're nearly there," said Thomas. "So hold together!"

"What do you think happened to everyone else?" asked Eileen. "The other students, I mean."

"A lot of them ran once we broke free of the square," said Thomas "The rest... were probably killed."

Eileen went pale. "By the Four."

"Aye."

They walked on in grim, exhausted silence. Cries of battle and the sound of mobs came from all around. When they entered the student quarter, Thomas practically collapsed in relief. He forced himself to take the lead instead.

"There!" shouted someone. "The Broken Quill!"

"Thank the Four," muttered Eileen.

"Let's stop for a drink!" called someone else, eliciting a ragged round of laughter.

"Nearly there!" called Thomas. "Only a few blocks to the Academy."

They were halfway down the block when a troop of Church cavalry rode out of the street ahead of them, blocking their way.

Oh, by the Four, no. Thomas turned and looked behind. More cavalry poured out of the street on the other end of the block.

"We're trapped," said Eileen.

"They'll kill us," a student moaned.

"Keep moving!" snapped Thomas, his eyes on the Broken Quill.

They did, and Thomas could feel the students panic rising all around him. The cavalry on either end of the street stayed where they were. Thomas waited until they were in front of the Broken Quill and called. "Stop!"

"You lot!" shouted one of the cavalrymen as Thomas ran to the door and pounded on it. "Weapons down and surrender! You're under arrest."

"You have no authority to arrest us!" yelled Thomas, more to buy time than anything else. "We are the King's Students!"

Marcus and Fenris, clubs in hand, opened the door and stepped outside. They looked up the street, then down it, then at Thomas.

"Have you brought us trouble, Thomas Flarety?" asked Marcus.

"Lots of it," said Thomas. "They'll ride us down and slaughter us if you don't let us in."

"We don't like people killing our customers," said Fenris, stepping out of the way of the door. "It's bad for business."

"Get inside," said Marcus. "Fast."

"Go!" said Thomas. "Closest first! Walk and wait your turn! Anyone who runs or shoves gets brained! Now move it!"

The students did as they were told, though most were practically shaking with desperation. Thomas ran out to the middle of the street, yelling, "My company, take the lines! We're in last!"

There were only eight of Thomas's company left, including Eileen, and they spread out as best they could while the cavalry on either end of the block readied themselves to attack.

There's no way to get everyone off the street, Thomas realized. *Not in time.*

The Church cavalry could only fit three horses across in the space, and the riders were practically rubbing their ankles against one another. Someone shouted an order, and the cavalry at one end of the block began moving forward. Thomas looked the other way and saw that the other troop was staying where they were, waiting to be the anvil to the first group's hammer.

The students on the line raised staves and swords. The ones at the door saw what was coming and began shoving their way inside the building. The moving wall of men and horseflesh and steel gained speed.

We're all going to die unless...

Thomas raised his hand, opened it, and sent lightning out to smash into the first horse and rider. The explosion rattled the windows around them. Man and horse both convulsed and fell, taking down the horses on either side. Thomas heard the bones of the horses snapping as they fell. The animals started screaming. The men behind pulled hard on their reins and wheeled their horses around.

Thomas looked to where the other cavalry squad was standing. He raised his other hand and waited. None of the men retreated, but none rode forward either.

And that's as good as I'm going to get.

"Get inside!" Eileen yelled, shoving at the others. "Everyone, inside! Now!"

Thomas, his arms raised in either direction, slowly walked backwards towards the Broken Quill. Behind him, he heard the students scrambling inside. On either end of the street the Church cavalrymen stared with amazed, horrified expressions. The man and horse he killed lay in the street. The two wounded horses screamed shrilly as they kicked and flailed. Their riders, trapped beneath the weight of their steeds, were yelling for help.

"Everyone's in!" Eileen grabbed Thomas from behind. "Come on!"

She pulled him inside. Fenris and Marcus, standing by their stools just inside the door, were staring at him. Their normally-impassive faces were wide-eyed with shock. Eileen pushed Thomas out of the way and she and Michael pulled the door shut, locking it and putting the heavy bar into place.

Thomas's eyes slowly adjusted to the gloom of the room. Every one of the students who weren't in his company was staring at him.

"The king..." began one. "The king said there's no such thing as witchcraft."

"There isn't," said Thomas. "There's magic."

27

Thomas didn't give them time to think about what he'd said. "Mark, take three and secure the back door," ordered Thomas. "Kevin, take three more and go upstairs. Make sure all the shutters are closed and locked."

"We do not allow customers in the kitchen," said Fenris.

"Not the time," said Thomas. "Mark, go! Is there another way out of here?"

"Aside from the doors and windows?" asked Marcus. "The chimney, I suppose."

"The chimney it is," said Thomas. "We need to get word to the Academy, we need reinforcements and we need them now."

"And you are telling me this, why?" asked Fenris.

"I wasn't. Eileen?"

"Over the roofs?" asked Eileen.

"Worked before," said Thomas. "Is the fire lit in the chimney?"

"No," said Eileen.

"Thank the Four."

"Who goes?" asked Eileen.

"You do," said Thomas.

"Not without you."

"I have to stay here with the company."

"You're the cause this whole mess!"

Thomas turned. Keith, bloody and filthy, stood in the middle of the floor. A dozen students, all Traditionalists, surrounded him. "You're what this is all about! You're a witch!"

Of all the people... "Not the time, Keith!"

"Yes, it is!" Keith stomped forward until he was face to face with Thomas. "We're trapped in here because of you! You're the reason the Church is going after the king! You're the reason they've been preaching against witchcraft!"

"That's not why," said Thomas. *What would Henry do?* "It's to do with the war in..."

"Master Brennan should have thrown you to the Church guards!" yelled Keith. "You brought the wrath of the Church down on the Academy! We're all going to die because you sold your soul to the Banished!"

Thomas punched Keith hard on the side of the jaw. Keith's head went sideways and he spun, falling backwards over a chair. The students of around Keith raised their weapons, but none moved. Behind them, George and the smiths stepped forward, and Thomas heard the scrape of George's blade leaving its scabbard. Keith's troop looked behind and saw the big men with the iron bars.

Thomas drew his rapier.

"Anyone who does anything stupid I will run through," Thomas said, keeping his voice cold and hard. Thomas caught a glimpse of movement just beside him and raised his other hand, holding it in the position he used for casting lightning. "Don't."

"We will not," said Marcus, sounding as calm as ever. "But we do not allow fights in our tavern."

"You may consider yourself banned for a week," said Fenris.

The absurdity of the statement nearly made Thomas laugh. "I promise to leave as soon as possible." He looked down at Keith, unconscious at his feet. *I didn't think I could hit that hard.* "You lot," he said to the students around Keith. "Was he leading you?"

"Aye," said a young man in fencing armour with dirty yellow hair and blood spattered on his face. "I'm Carl, his Lieutenant."

"Carl, the Church soldiers are going to come charging in here and try to kill us. You and your troop can either go out there and deal with them, or you can be on our side. Decide. Now."

Carl looked down at Keith. Then he did a slow circle, taking in the bloody, bruised students that filled the room. "We're with you."

Thank the Four. "Take your take your troop and secure the windows upstairs. And look out in the street while you do it. I need to know what they're doing."

"Yes... Captain."

"And take him with you," said Thomas, pointing at Keith. "Tie him to a chair in one of the rooms upstairs. We'll deal with him later."

Carl called for the other seven left of his troop, and together they dragged Keith up the stairs.

Thomas let go of a breath he hadn't realized he was holding and faced the bouncers. "Marcus, Fenris, would you please send for Madame Blossom?"

"No need!" snapped Angeline Blossom, pushing her way through the students. "What in black pits of the Banished is going on here? Why are there boys with swords in my kitchen?"

"We're under siege," said Thomas. "How much would it take to light the place on fire from outside?"

"What?"

"A great deal," said Marcus. "The roof is slate, the walls are stone, the shutters are solid. If they break through the shutters or pour burning pitch down the chimney, it's possible. Otherwise, not."

"Good."

"You still haven't told me what's going on!" snapped Angeline Blossom.

"We were attacked by a mob and by cavalry, and had to hide."

Angeline stared at him. "You're serious?"

"Yes."

"And you ran in *here*?"

"It wasn't a matter of choice," said Thomas. "Can you get everyone some food and something to drink? The Academy will pick up the bill."

"We don't run tabs," said Angeline. She looked over the crowd of bleeding, bruised and exhausted students in her tavern. "Usually."

"It will be paid," said Thomas. "I swear it."

"Heard that before," said Angeline, though her tone wasn't as harsh. "This all of you?"

"All that's left," said Thomas. "There were two hundred of us, before."

"Two hundred!" She did a quick head-count. "By the Four..." Angeline's brow furrowed and her jaw set. "Right then. Food and drink for everyone. You'll eat what's in the kitchen, mind, and no special orders, hear?"

"I promise," said Thomas.

"I'll get the girls roused and send them down. And see what we have for bandages."

"Thank you."

"Aye, well, wait until I send the Academy the bill." She shook a finger in Thomas's face. "And don't get my tavern burned down, hear?"

"Yes, ma'am," said Thomas. "I'll try."

Angeline stomped off to the kitchen, shouting for her cooks and barmaids.

"Not going to tell her about the magic, then?" said Fenris.

"I'll leave that to you," said Thomas, his eyes on the students that half-filled the room. Those not securing the building had collapsed onto the benches. All of them were exhausted. Most were hurt, some badly. And most of them were staring at Thomas with looks that ranged from fear and hostility to amazement. Thomas sighed and headed for the stage.

"Now what?" asked Eileen, falling in behind him.

"We send someone for help," said Thomas. "Go look up the fireplace and tell me how high it is."

Eileen did. Thomas climbed onto the stage and called, "Listen up! I don't know how much time we have, so pay attention! Yes, I have magic. No, it is not witchcraft. There is no such thing as witchcraft. Yes, I can throw lightning and do some other things. No, it will not be enough to hold off the Church troops when they attack. We need to get someone out of here to get reinforcements, quick."

"The chimney's capped," called Eileen. "There's no way we can get out there."

Thomas swore and looked to Fenris. "Any other exits?"

"A balcony on the top level at the back," said Fenris. "You could possibly reach the roof from there. With a ladder."

"George," said Thomas. "Take Eileen and check it out."

George nodded, and he and Eileen followed Fenris out of the room.

"For the rest of you," said Thomas. "Anyone not badly hurt, help reinforce the doors and set up the tables as barriers. Fenris says they can't burn us out so they'll try to smash their way in. We need to make sure all the shutters upstairs are tightly shut and barred, all the doors are locked and blocked, and that we have another layer of defence in case they get inside."

"Who put you in charge?" said one of the students.

It was more of a grumble than a challenge, but Thomas answered it anyway. "Sir Walter Deehan, advisor the king. His orders were for me to find you lot and bring you to safety."

"Sir Walter?" said Graham Silvers, rising. "He told you to come get us?"

"Yes," said Thomas. *And how do you know him?*

"Good of him," said Graham. "Right, then. Thomas is in charge by order of the king! Everyone get up and get working!"

Thomas blinked in surprise then shrugged it off. *As long as they're listening.* "Carl! Where are you?"

"Here!" shouted Carl from upstairs. "They're still closing the shutters."

"Good. What's going on outside?"

"The cavalry hasn't moved," said Carl.

"What about in the alley?"

"Freddy took those windows," said Carl. "Freddy!"

"Here!" said a lanky, dark-haired student, coming out of another room.

"What's happening in the alley?"

"No one's come down it," said Freddy, "but both ends are blocked, now."

"Cavalry?"

Fred shook his head. "Foot soldiers."

So, if need be, we could fight our way out the back. "Good enough. Let's get this furniture moved. Everyone who's not badly hurt, help. Now!"

As they worked Thomas did the rounds of the room and discovered that he had the remnants of six companies with him. He put the smiths under George's command then divided the companies up into four groups. One he gave to Carl, the next to Graham, and the other two picked their own captains from their groups: Avery, a short man with dark hair and a growling temper; and Horace, who was tall, strong and blond.

"If I may suggest?" said Marcus, "the last time this happened, the students built their first barricade of tables just inside the entrance, then a line of tables across the width of the room, there," he pointed to a place a quarter of the way down the room. "A final ring of tables around the stage."

"The last time?" Thomas eyebrows went up of their own accord. "When did this happen before?"

"Fifty years ago," said Marcus. "The Lord Mayor declared that too many students were engaging in drunken debauchery and banned them from all drinking establishments. A hundred students barricaded themselves in against the city watch."

"Did it work?"

"They lasted two days, I believe, until my grandmother managed to open the back door. When they were forced back to the second line of defence, they lost control of the kitchens and began sobering up. They were about to surrender when the king repealed the law."

Thomas stared at the man. "You're joking."

"Not at all," said Marcus. "According to my grandfather, the students paid for all drinks and damages, which made it a rather good couple of days for us."

"Two days..." Thomas looked at the exhausted, bleeding students. *If that isn't enough, nothing will be.* "Right then, we do it your way. Everyone listen up!"

They were still moving the tables into position for the first barricade when George and Eileen came back. George looked pale. "They've got crossbowmen at one end of the alley."

Thomas swore. "Either of you hurt?"

"We're fine. But they came mighty close."

"Thank the Four," said Thomas. "Help with the barricades."

"They're moving outside!" called Carl from upstairs. "They're bringing in foot troops!"

"Keep building the barricades!" Thomas shouted. "My company, Graham's company to the front door! Everyone else, have your weapons ready but keep working!"

Thomas went to the front door and opened the grille. He leaned against the door to peer as far to the side as possible, and had George lean on the other. Thomas saw foot soldiers with armour and shields advancing on the Broken Quill, six across and five lines deep with four wagons coming behind them. He told George.

"Same on this side," said George.

"Can't see what's in them."

"Barrels, I think," said George. "And some sacks. And furniture."

They watched as the soldiers with shields formed a circle around the front door. Behind them, other soldiers began unloading the wagons, forming crude walls around the entrance of the inn.

"Dammit," said Thomas. "They're making their own barricades."

"They're planning to keep us here a while, then," said George. "Otherwise they'd just try to knock in the door."

"So why aren't they trying to knock in the door?" asked Thomas.

"Maybe they're too busy," said Graham, behind them. "If there's still fighting out there, they may not have enough men to take us. So they're blocking us in."

"Do we have enough men to take them?" George asked. "Maybe we can make a break and run for the Academy?"

Almost as if in answer to his words, a row of crossbowmen took places behind the barricades, their weapons trained on the door.

"We'd lose a lot of people trying," said Thomas. "And if the cavalry is still out there..." he shook his head. "Better to wait."

Thomas kept a dozen men on the door and went back to helping with their own barricades. Within an hour they were finished. The tables were solid and thick enough stop a crossbow bolt. With luck, they'd give the students enough protection to mount a defense if the door was breached.

I hope it's enough, thought Thomas. *I hope we don't even need it.*

Angeline and her barmaids tended to the injured and brought stew for everyone. Thomas wasn't hungry but forced the food down anyway and made everyone else do the same. He checked on the wounded and was pleased to see that no one's life was in danger. The injuries were mostly bruises and broken bones, and a few knife wounds. Thomas ordered the badly injured ones to sit on the stage, away from any potential fighting.

Keith woke soon after he was tied to the chair and started yelling at the top of his lungs. Thomas sent George and two of the smiths up to tell Keith he could either be silent or gagged. Keith was quiet after that.

Thomas had the company leaders divide their troops into squads of eight and seven, and set rotating watches of the front door, back door, and upstairs windows. Thomas's company took the first watch so the others could rest.

Then there was nothing left to do but wait.

Thomas had never heard the Broken Quill so quiet. The students that weren't on watch sat still for the most part. Some slept. Most stared into space or talked quietly with one another. A few went into the private rooms, and when Thomas went to check on them, he heard them sobbing. He left them alone for a time, and then sent up members of his company to talk to them.

It was sunset when Father Alphonse arrived.

He came in a coach, and got out at the barricades. The soldiers had to help him climb over. Eileen, on watch at the front window, saw it all and shouted it down to Thomas.

Thomas hadn't thought he had the energy to be more scared, but Alphonse's arrival made him want to lock himself in one of the upstairs rooms and hide. Instead, he called George to the front door and the two of them stationed themselves on either side of the grille.

"What can you see?" Thomas called from the centre of the room.

"Nothing different on this side," said George. "The barricades are still blocking everything."

"Alphonse is coming over them on this side," said Thomas. "They're helping him down now."

Eileen ran down the stairs, rapier in hand. "What do we do?"

"Maybe we can bargain with him," said Graham, behind them. "Agree not to leave the Quill for the rest of the war."

He doesn't want a bargain, Thomas thought. *He wants me.*

Father Alphonse took his time, once he was over the barricade. He straightened his robes and spoke quietly to the troops before walking up to the door. Behind him, a dozen crossbowmen sat ready to fire.

"I see you there," said Father Alphonse. "Thomas, how are you?"

"Well enough," lied Thomas. "Yourself?"

"Very well, thank you. And your friends?"

"Again, well enough."

"So many of them were taken in the square, I was worried," said Father Alphonse. "There were close to fifty bodies, last I counted. And at least as many in the cells."

Thomas felt his jaw tighten. "What do you want?"

"To tell you what's happening in the city, of course. May I come in?"

"No."

Father Alphonse tried to look disappointed, and leaned on his stick. "It is rather hard, standing here, talking through a grille like this."

"Too bad."

The Inquisitor shrugged. "As you wish." His next words were loud enough to reach the windows upstairs. "I just thought you should know that the people have risen up against the king. The city is in flames, and even now the king's troops are being forced back to the palace. We expect victory within the next few hours."

"You're lying," said Thomas.

"Believe that, if you like." Father Alphonse kept his voice loud. "I wanted you to know that we will accept your surrender. All you have to do is put down your weapons, swear your allegiance to the Archbishop, and hand Thomas over to be tried for witchcraft. Then you may walk away."

"You know the king declared that there's no such thing as witchcraft?" said Thomas.

"The king is corrupt," said Father Alphonse. "He will return to the teachings of the High Father's Church when our army is at his door." He smiled. "And when your fellow students have surrendered, I will personally supervise your confession."

Thomas hands began trembling, and his stomach roiling. His legs threatened to give out. Thomas managed to say "Go away" and shut the grille before it happened.

"Remember!" shouted the Inquisitor. "Throw down your weapons, swear allegiance to the High Father, and give us Thomas. Otherwise, our troops will storm this building, and we will kill you all!"

Thomas leaned against the door, wishing fervently for Father Alphonse to die on the spot.

"He's getting back in his carriage," called a student upstairs. "He's heading away!"

Eileen took Thomas's hand. "Now what?"

"Get everyone together," said Thomas. *And hopefully I can figure out something to say.*

Thomas went up on the stage. "Did everyone hear what he said?" Some shook their heads. Others went to tell them, but Thomas spoke first. "The gist of it is that the Church troops will only accept your surrender if you drop your weapons, pledge allegiance to the High Father, and turn me over to be charged with witchcraft."

No one said anything, though many cast wary glances at one another. In their faces Thomas read fear, exhaustion and pain. Some looked like they were ready to give up. Others had their jaws set in mutinous expressions, as if they could defy the Archbishop through sheer force of will. Others looked guilty, as if they had at once thought of surrendering Thomas and immediately realized how awful they were for thinking it.

"Don't just sit there," said Thomas. "Discuss."

"Who said we wanted to surrender?" asked one of them. "We're fine in here."

"We're fine in here for now," corrected another.

"We have food, we have drink and they can't burn us out. We're good!"

"It doesn't mean they can't smash their way in eventually," said a third.

"Thomas can stop them!" said another. "With lightning!"

"I can stop some of them," warned Thomas. "But the magic is exhausting and lightning would make me pass out after two shots."

"Can't you just make them all vanish?" asked a lanky one near the front.

"If I could do that I'd have done it in the square," said Thomas.

"Then what good is magic?"

"I've been trying to figure that out since last summer," said Thomas. "Near as I can tell, it annoys the Church, so that's something."

He was rewarded with some chuckles from the group.

"He get us all killed!" shouted Keith from upstairs. "We'll all die because of him! They'll kill us all because he's a witch!"

"He's got good ears," said Graham.

"And big mouth," said George, rising to his feet and heading for the stairs. "I'll be right back."

"He's right, unfortunately," said Thomas. He saw read the relief on the faces of the students who wanted to say those very words but hadn't. "As long as I'm here, they won't accept your surrender, so if they break in, they'll kill you all."

"Are... are you asking us to turn you in?" asked Carl.

"No!" said Thomas. He stopped then, and sighed. "Not yet, anyway. But it's something we might have to consider if it starts to get bad." He looked at the bloody, exhausted students that surrounded him. "Or worse, I should say."

"It won't get worse if you're not here," said Graham. "So you'd better leave."

Thomas's eyebrows went up. "And how am I supposed to do that?"

"You're the smart one," said Graham. "Think of something." He jumped up beside Thomas on the stage. "The soldiers are going to break in eventually. When they do, we'll only be able to hold them off for so long. Especially if they bring in crossbows. Now, I know we can fight until reinforcements come, if we know they're coming. I also know that, if reinforcements don't come, we're going to have to surrender eventually. And we can't do that with Thomas here."

The students muttered back and forth amongst themselves. Graham let them for a short time. Then he raised his voice. "So I say we find a way to get Thomas out and send him to get some reinforcements while the rest of us sit here with food and wine and the glory of holding off the Archbishop's army! Sound good?"

There were thoughtful faces in the crowd, then nods of agreement, then calls of "Aye" and "Yes" and "Why is he still here, then?"

"There you are," said Graham, grinning at Thomas. "Since you botched rescuing us the last time, you get to do it again."

"Fine," said Thomas. "But you're in charge until I get back."

"Fine," said Graham. "Now hurry up and get out of here so I can run up your tab."

The students chuckled at that. Thomas sent them back to their posts or to their rest. He wandered through the building twice, from the cellars beneath to the rooms that Madame Blossom and her staff kept on the third floor, trying to figure out a way out of the place. Nothing came to mind. Madame Blossom and her barmaids brought out more stew for dinner. Thomas took his and sat on the stairs. George and Eileen joined him. For a while they just ate, watching the students. Most were lying down, trying to get some sleep. Others talked in quiet groups, or stared into space.

"So," said George. "How *do* we get you out of here?"

"You're asking me?" Thomas said around a mouthful of stew. "I've been through the place twice and I have no idea."

"The balcony is no good," said Eileen. "The alley is blocked."

"I could go out the front door," said Thomas. "That might surprise them enough that I'd get away."

"Probably not," said George.

"What would Henry do?" asked Thomas.

"Burn the place down and run out the back?" said George.

"No," said Eileen. "Henry would have brought archers."

"Or cavalry," said George. "Where is he, anyway?"

"No idea," said Thomas. "I haven't seen him since this morning."

"I hope he's all right."

Me, too, Thomas finished the last of his stew and looked around one more time, contemplating the ceiling. The attic above had only two windows. One looked over the street and the other was above the alley, and they were too small to climb through, anyway.

Could we go through the roof?

Thomas went to Fenris. "Can you take me up to the attic again, please?"

Fenris took him through the kitchen door and up three flights of stairs to the family and the barmaids' quarters. There were five rooms. "Too bad you didn't install windows on the sides as well," said Thomas. "We'd have been able to go out and get help."

"It is a failure we will regret, I'm sure," said Fenris without cracking a smile. Thomas rolled his eyes and tapped against the sloped ceiling. They had plastered over it, but Thomas could feel wood right behind. "How thick are the roof slats?"

"No idea," said Fenris. "They've been plastered since well before my time."

"I don't suppose there's a trap door that leads to the roof for cleaning the chimney, is there?"

"We put a ladder on the balcony."

"We'd need to break through to get out." Thomas sighed. "How much will Mistress Blossom charge us for doing that?"

"A fair amount, I should think," said Fenris.

"Less than what it will cost if the Church gets impatient and burns the place down," said Thomas. "What's on the other side of it?"

"Five more roofs," said Fenris. "Then an apartment building on the corner. It's two stories higher than this one, with windows overlooking the rooftop."

"Which will be perfect if we can get through to the roof," said Thomas. "I'll send up George and the smiths. They're the strongest, they can probably break through the fastest."

"Try to do as little damage as possible," said Fenris. "This is my room."

Which means he'll have no place to sleep. "Thank you, Fenris."

"Just get them out safely, Thomas," said Fenris. "We like you lot, you know. We'd rather not see you dead."

Thomas went back to George and Eileen. "George, can you follow Fenris upstairs and see if you can break through the roof? Take some others with you."

"Right," said George, getting up and calling for the other smiths.

"The roof?" Eileen said. "Will that work?"

"Don't know," said Thomas. "Don't have a better idea, though."

Eileen leaned into him and rested her head on his shoulder. Dropping her voice to a near-whisper, she said, "You're not going to let them take you, are you?"

"Not without a fight," said Thomas, making his voice as quiet as hers. "But I'm not going to let anyone die for me either."

"Do you think they'll surrender?"

"If things get bad enough," said Thomas. "As long as the doors hold out, they'll be fine, but once the soldiers break through..."

"We have the barricades."

"They'll bring in crossbows," said Thomas, "And then we're done for."

"Aren't you cheery," said Graham, coming up behind them. "We'll hold them at the door."

"I know you will," said Thomas, putting on a smile.

"And you won't be here to see it anyway because you'll be off getting help." He sat down beside them. "How is that going, by the way?"

"We think we can break out of the roof," said Thomas.

As if in answer, there was a THUD from above loud enough to shake the walls. Every student in the room looked up. A second THUD, and half of them struggled to their feet.

"It's all right!" called Thomas. "It's us doing that. Not them."

There was another THUD, then silence. Thomas waited for more, but none came. Soon George stepped out of the kitchen and came over.

"Too loud," said George, who looked mighty annoyed. "We can break through, but anyone outside will hear us."

Thomas swore and thought hard. "Is there any way to do it quietly?"

"Not quickly," said George.

"Captain!" a student ran out of one of the upstairs rooms. "They're coming up the alley! Dozens of them!"

"Everybody up!" Thomas shouted. "My company at the back! George and the smiths with me! Everyone else to the door and barricades!"

They ran for the kitchen, with Marcus walking behind.

At Fenris and Marcus's suggestion, the back door had been barricaded with barrels of wine, each weighing well over five hundred pounds. The students at the back were on their feet, waiting.

"They won't get through," said Marcus, who had followed Thomas in. "That door is six-inch thick oak bound in iron, and triple-barred. They won't get it open without an axe."

Thomas ran out to the common room. "Upstairs! Are the troops bringing axes?"

The moments it took him to come back were some of the longest Thomas had endured. "No axes I could see," came the reply. "Just swords and shields!"

"Keep watching!" Thomas ran back to the kitchen. He arrived just as the Church soldiers began pounding on the door –with the pommels of their swords by the sound of it. Thomas waited for the sound of breaking wood. It didn't happen. The barrels that blocked the door didn't even shake under the pounding.

But maybe they're making enough noise. "George! Go upstairs and get working. As long as they're banging on the door, knock holes in the roof."

"Right!" George ran for the stairs, taking two of the smiths with him. Thomas watched for a short time longer, then turned to his company. "Smiths, go take a break. My company stay here. If you hear wood breaking or smell smoke, call for help. I'll send someone to spell you in an hour, otherwise, got it?"

"Got it," said Michael.

Thomas walked back to the common room. "Why is the back door so thick?"

"It's a favourite for thieves and those who try to sneak out without paying for their drinks," said Marcus. "There hasn't been a successful break-in, or out, since our grandfather changed it."

"Good thinking."

Thomas told the students what was happening. Most relaxed, though no one put their weapons away. Thomas stayed on his feet and in the middle of the room, listening to the hammering from the back door and above. Both went on for the better part of a quarter hour. Then the men at the back door gave up. A moment later, the roof work fell silent.

"They didn't get through," said Eileen. "Not as quickly as that."

"I know," said Thomas. "We'll have to wait until the next attack."

Thomas's company were coming back in from the kitchen when the student watching the front from upstairs called out, "They're coming! And they've got a battering ram!"

28

Thomas and Eileen ran for the front door, the rest of their company behind them. Avery and his company had ringed the door and manned the barricades. Marcus had returned to his stool and was looking quite unconcerned.

"How thick is the front door?" Thomas asked.

"As thick as the back."

"Same reason?"

"That, and other incidents."

"Will that be enough?"

"Depends how big the battering ram is," said Marcus.

Thomas yelled, "How big is the ram?"

From above there was the sound of steel sticking into wood, and a yelp of surprise. A moment later Carl came running down the stairs, shouting, "We're all right! We had to open the shutter to get a good look. They shot at us. There's six men holding the ram, three to each side."

"Ah," said Marcus. "That will dent the door, but not break it, I should think."

The first hit of the battering ram shook the door and echoed through the room. The students at the barricades tensed.

The battering ram hit again. Then the men wielding it found their rhythm and set up a steady beat, pounding hard against the door with each stroke.

"If I might suggest," said Fenris from the kitchen door. "Boiling water poured out the shutter slats of the window above the door has worked well for this sort of thing in the past."

Thomas stared at him. "Someday, I'm going to have to hear all the stories about this place."

"There are many," said Fenris. "I'll fetch the kettle."

The battering ram kept smashing at the door. The door rattled with each hit, but stayed on its hinges, and didn't buckle or break.

"Look out!" said Fenris, coming out of the kitchen with a kettle big enough to make tea for everyone in the room. He held it easily in one hand by its towel-wrapped handle. "Hot kettle, out of the way please."

The students cleared a path and Fenris went upstairs. The ram struck the door a dozen more times. Then came the splash of water, and screams of pain. The banging on the front door stopped. From above came more thudding as George and the others got in a few more strikes before they, too, fell silent.

Fenris came down the stairs, swinging the empty kettle in his hand. "They left," announced Fenris. "And were none too happy, I might add."

"Think they knew that wasn't going to work?" asked Eileen.

"I wonder," said Thomas. "Maybe they're just planning to keep us busy all night so they can exhaust us before their real attack."

"We need to get out of here," said Avery.

"I know," said Thomas. "We're working on it."

"Well, work faster," said Avery.

"They're coming to the back door again!"

Thomas swore, and headed for the kitchen.

Two hours and four more false attacks later, George came back downstairs. He was covered in plaster dust and splinters. "We're through," he told Thomas. "Sorry it took so long. Whoever made this place did it to last."

"Can we get out there?" Thomas asked.

George nodded. "I think so. Roof is wet and slippery though. I wouldn't want to walk on it."

"Neither would I, but since there's no choice..." Thomas headed for the kitchens and the stairs up.

"I'll come, too," said Eileen. "It's better than sitting around here."

They went up the back stairs. The temperature dropped as they went closer, and not just from the cold wind Thomas felt coming in. Angeline was standing by the door to Fenris's room, glaring. "You tore a hole in my roof."

"We did," said Thomas.

"It's going on your bill."

"I know," said Thomas. "Of course, you have to let me go out so I can get the money to pay it."

"I've heard that one before," grumbled Angeline. "Just be careful. I don't need you falling off the neighbours' roofs. It won't do a thing for our reputation."

The hole in the roof was big enough for even George to crawl through, though it would be a tight fit. Thomas put his head out and looked. The cold was refreshing, after the close air of the tavern. There was no wind to speak of, and no scent of water on the air. *At least we won't have to deal with rain.*

It wasn't much of an escape. The roof was steep—expected in a town where winter meant large quantities of snow and spring and fall meant weeks of rain—and ran down to a common gutter between the buildings, then up to the next equally steep roof, which was covered in tiles as well, though Thomas couldn't tell if they were slate or clay. Either way, they'd be slippery. Getting down it would be easy enough, but climbing the next one would be nearly impossible. And if there were any rotten spots in the roof next door, or any of the shingles were loose, whoever was climbing would be almost certain to slip and fall. *Thirty feet down at least. That's broken legs if I'm lucky.*

"We'd need rope," Thomas said. "Otherwise we'll fall off if we slip."

"We could cut a hole through to the next roof," said one of the smiths.

"Too noisy and too close to the Church troops," said Thomas. "Better to go over."

He turned his eyes away from the roof to the sky. The clouds were low and thick.

Father Alphonse said the city was on fire. In Frostmire, when the city had been burning, the glow of it had reflected on the low clouds, turning the sky ruddy orange and dirty yellow. Thomas searched the sky on both sides, and could see a few clouds lit from below with orange light, but nothing to suggest the entire city was on fire. *He lied, of course,* Thomas thought. *At least that's something.*

Thomas pulled his head back in and asked Angeline, "Do you have any rope?"

"A fair bit," she said. "What for?"

"For getting over the roof and getting your money," said Thomas, heading for the stairs. "What else?"

Back down in common room Thomas took the stage. "We've gone through the roof," he said. "It's wet out and steep, but I can make it. Not by myself, though."

"Take George," said Eileen.

"Take Eileen," said George in the same moment.

The laughter that received was far more than the moment deserved, and Thomas could hear the tension in the sound. He smiled himself and tried to think of what to say.

"Take both," said Graham. "And go quickly before something else happens."

In the dim light of the fire the bruises and blood on the students stood out against their skin. Thomas could see the inner lights of each of them, shining faintly in the dim light of the room. Most of them were tinged with red. *If I don't get help, they're all going to die.*

"I will," said Thomas. "As soon as it gets dark. And I'll be back as fast as I can. I promise."

"They're coming again!" shouted the front watcher. "Lots of them, this time!"

"Posts!" Thomas yelled as he ran up the rest of the stairs. "Everyone to their posts!" He dashed to the front room and looked out through the slats on the shutters. What he saw made him swear and run back down. "Everyone on your feet! This is it!"

"This is what?" asked George. Around him, students were shaking one another awake and grabbing at weapons.

"There's at least fifty of them, and they've got bigger ram," said Thomas, drawing his rapier. "Twelve men carrying it on ropes. Everyone on the barricades and windows!"

"You're supposed to be leaving!" said Graham, whose company was on watch at the front door. Carl, beside him, nodded.

"I know," said Thomas. "Everyone get to your posts! Now!" The rest of the company formed up at the front door. Thomas looked to Marcus and Fenris. "You probably shouldn't be here if they break through."

"We aren't intending to be," said Marcus. "We will keep the kitchen door shut and claim to be prisoners, should it come to that. Would you like us to send the others from the kitchens out to you?"

"Please," said Thomas. "And thank you for helping us."

"Our pleasure," said Fenris. "Do try not to get killed."

"They're taking down one side of the barricades to let it through!" shouted the student on watch.

"Get ready!" Thomas yelled. "Is everyone at their post?"

"Yes, Captain!"

"The Academy and the king!" cried Graham.

Every student in the room raised their voice. "The Academy and the king!"

The ram slammed into the door with a BOOM that reverberated through the room and shook the door on its hinges.

"How long do you think the door will hold?" asked Jonathan.

"No idea," said Thomas. "George?"

"Maybe ten blows," said George. "If that."

BOOM!

"We could open it first," said William. "Time it to the battering ram."

"And then what?" demanded Jonathan. "Get them all drinks?"

"I don't know!" snapped William. "I was just thinking about saving the door!"

"Well, think about saving us!"

"We could charge their barricade," said Michael. "If they're attacking, we might be able to break their line."

"We could drag in the ram," said one of the smiths. "If it's just a log on ropes, we could grab it and pull it in."

BOOM!

That could work, thought Thomas. "Michael, spread the word through the room so they know what's happening. When the door opens, we charge. George, have your smiths brace the door."

The smiths piled against the door, pushing on it and one another.

BOOM!

Thomas waited, counting under his breath.

BOOM!

About ten counts between hits. Thomas kept his voice low and said, "George, get the bar off."

George pulled the bar off the door and the smiths pushed even harder against it.

BOOM!

The door shook and moved, but only a little.

"On my call, everyone gets off the door," Thomas said. "George, open it when I say! My squad and Carl's attack from either side of the door. You and you," he pointed at two smiths, "Get ready to grab the front of the ram when it comes in and pull it off its ropes. Try to pull it to the ground. We'll kill the men holding it. Understand?"

"Yes, Captain!"

BOOM!

"Smiths away! Grabbers ready! Squads ready! We go through in twos!"

Eileen stood right behind him and the remains of the his company lined after. Carl's squad lined up opposite, leaving enough space for George to open the door.

...Five, six, seven eight, nine, "NOW!"

George hauled the door open, and the end of the log the men were using as a ram swung through, pulling the men holding it off balance. The smiths caught it on either side, pulling the ram forward and making the Church soldiers stagger. Two more smiths grabbed right behind them. Thomas thrust out, stabbing the closest soldier. The other troops outside tried to snatch the log back, but had to let go of the ropes and the end of it tumbled to the ground. Inside, two more smiths caught it and the six dragged it into the Broken Quill.

"Charge!" shouted Thomas. "The Academy!"

"The Academy!"

Thomas and Carl rushed out and the rest of their squads followed. Five Church soldiers fell in the first moments of the fight.

Maybe we can take the barricades!

Even as he thought it the Church soldiers rallied. The ones who had held the ram scrambled away over the barricades. The other Church soldiers advanced. Steel clashed and the soldiers, using their shields, pushed the students back. Past them, Thomas caught a glimpse of crossbow men on the intact part of the barricade, and saw the open part of the street filled with troops.

We can't win this. "Back! Everyone back!"

Carl fell with a sword in his gut as the words left Thomas's mouth. The student behind Carl hit the ground a moment later, screaming and bleeding from a hacked-open leg. Thomas tried to grab him but the Church soldiers forced him back. Thomas cut and stabbed with his blade, trying to keep the soldiers back long enough for the others to get back inside.

He was nearly at the doorway when the crossbow bolt slammed into him.

It caught Thomas high in the chest, just beside his shoulder. His dagger flew out of his hand as he spun and slammed back against the doorframe. Thomas heard someone scream his name and then a large hand grabbed his cloak and yanked him inside. He stumbled and fell. George dragged him across the floor as a pair of smiths slammed the door shut. The rest of the smiths piled against it, pushing with all their weight. The door was hit hard from the other side and jolted in its hinges.

"Take him!" George shouted, and Eileen and Graham grabbed Thomas's arms and hauled him to the barricades. Thomas yelled in pain as the bolt, still in his chest, grated against the bone and shifted as they pulled him.

George charged forward and slammed the bar into place on the door. "Smiths! Pick up that ram!" he shouted. "Jam it against the door!"

Eileen and Graham stopped pulling Thomas's arms and the pain in his chest went down from unbearable to just excruciating. They propped him up against a table and Eileen knelt in front of him. "Thomas! Can you hear me? How bad is it?"

"I can hear you," he said through gritted teeth. "I don't know how bad it..."

He ran his hand up to the bolt and touched it. The pain flared worse and everything went red.

"Thomas!" Eileen's voice broke through it. "Don't you pass out! You hear me?"

"Get Madame Bright!" yelled Graham. "Now!"

"You have to heal yourself," Eileen said. "Can you do that?"

"I don't know," said Thomas. He looked at the hole in his chest. Blood soaked through his armour and the padding beneath it. "It's bad."

"It is," said Graham.

Thomas looked away from the injury. "Who… else was hurt?"

"Carl's dead," said Graham. "Greg had his leg cut and fell. Michael was stabbed in the stomach."

"Michael?" Thomas looked around. "Where?"

"Here, Captain," said Michael. He was still standing, though barely. One hand was against his stomach. "Sword got through the chain mail."

"How bad?"

"Not deep," said Michael. "Hurts like mad, though."

"Get him to the rest of the wounded," said Thomas.

"Thomas!" Eileen sounded exasperated and scared. "Worry about yourself!"

"Oh, the Four protect us!" said Madame Bright, kneeling beside him. "That's a nasty one."

"We need…" the world started spinning. Thomas shook his head, trying to make it stop. "The bolt… out."

"You'll bleed to death," said Graham. "I've seen these before. The artery is right underneath there."

"I can't heal it with the bolt there," Thomas said. "Pull it out. Now!"

"You don't want to…"

"George!" Eileen's voice rang through the tavern. "Here! Now!"

George came at a run. "What?"

"Pull the bolt out. Fast."

George hesitated, "Thomas, should I…"

"Do it," Thomas managed through gritted teeth. "Hurry."

George knelt, put a hand on Thomas's chest, and grabbed the bolt. The world went red again and Thomas heard a sucking sound. For a moment the wound hurt less. Then the air hit it and Thomas yelled in pain. Blood gushed out of the wound.

"Heal yourself!" Eileen yelled. "Do it!"

Thomas slapped his hand over the wound. Blood slid through his fingers and down his chest. Thomas began chanting the healing spell—five words, over and over. White light flared from his hand and poured into his body. The pain of it drove his voice higher and louder, until he was screaming the words through clenched teeth.

Then everything went black.

29

Thomas came to his senses on the stage with the other wounded. He was propped up against the wall. His armour and shirt were both gone, and bandages wrapped his chest and shoulder. Pain pulsed in his chest in time with his heart, but nowhere near the agony it had been before. It took Thomas several tries to focus his eyes. When he finally managed it, he tried to push himself to his feet. A hand on his good arm stopped him.

"Don't do it, Thomas," said Angeline. "Not with a wound like that." She held out a bowl and spoon. "Lucky you're not dead, the way you were bleeding. Open your mouth."

Thomas tried to protest, but the moment he opened his mouth the spoon went in and the broth on it was too good to resist. He let her feed him the whole bowl. The warmth of it spread through him and gave him strength. "Is Graham around?"

"He is," said Angeline. "I'll see about getting him."

She went away. Thomas lay his head back against the wall and closed his eyes. *I'll just rest for a moment.*

"Thomas?"

Thomas blinked awake. Graham, Eileen and George were all kneeling front of him. All three looked exhausted. Eileen put her hand on his. "How are you?"

"Hurting," said Thomas.

"You should be worse, with a wound like that," said Graham. "Dead, in fact."

"You're the second to say so," said Thomas.

"Guess your magic worked," said Graham. "Good thing. The Inquisitor will be very annoyed if he doesn't get to torture you before he hangs you."

Thomas's eyes were focusing better, now. He looked around the room, saw weary students lying behind the barricades. There were no more wounded than the last time, at least. "How are things?"

"The same, mostly," said Graham. "The front door cracked a bit in the last attack."

"The last one?" Thomas tried to comprehend that. "How many have there been?"

"They've been coming at us all night." Graham grimaced. "We drove off the last two attacks with boiling grease. Probably left some nasty marks. They'll be back again soon, I expect."

Thomas started to bring his feet under him. "Where do you need me?"

"Right where you are," said Graham. "Get sleep. We'll need you if they get through the door."

Thomas wanted to argue, but the idea of sleeping seemed so good that he couldn't think of anything else. "All right."

"We'll look in on you when they're done."

Thomas nodded, closed his eyes, and slept again.

"Morning!" Graham's voice echoed through the room. "Those on duty stand down! Next group, to your posts!"

Students stirred themselves from sleep and groaned wearily as they stumbled to their spots behind the barricades. Thomas pushed up to his feet without thinking and, to his surprise, managed to stay standing. His chest was crusted with dried blood, and the wound still throbbed, but not nearly as much.

He spotted the company and Eileen by the front door. He stepped off the stage and headed for them.

"Captain!" Jonathan saw him first. "You're supposed to be resting!"

"I was," said Thomas. "I'm better."

"Not enough to fight," said Eileen. "Get back on the stage."

"I can do more than just sit there."

"Thomas!" Graham's voice rang out across the room. "What are you doing up?"

"I'm better," called Thomas, heading for him. Thomas wobbled a bit as he walked, but he managed to keep upright. "Where do you need me?"

"Sleeping on the stage," said Graham.

"Well, I'm not going do any more of that."

"Then go upstairs," said Graham from behind them. "Take over watch at the front window. Eileen, help him up the steps, then get back here."

"Right," said Eileen. She grabbed Thomas's good arm and put it over her shoulder. Together the two of them manoeuvred back to the stage. Eileen helped Thomas back into his armour, then up the stairs. The student in the front window stepped aside to let Thomas take his place. As soon as he was gone Eileen wrapped her arms around Thomas, and put her head on the uninjured side of his chest. "Oh, thank the Four."

Thomas wrapped his good arm around her. "Don't thank them too hard," he said. "I barely made it up the stairs."

Eileen kissed him. Passion and desperation pushed her lips hard against his. He pulled her close and kissed back just as hard. Tears streamed down Eileen's face. "I thought I'd lost you."

"Not yet," said Thomas. "We're still all right."

"For as long as the door holds," said Eileen. "We'll be fine." She kissed him again and hugged him tight. "I've got to get back downstairs."

"I know."

"All right." She hugged him once more and left. Thomas leaned against the wall, peering through the slats of the shutters. Morning light was shining down on the street, reflecting off the helmets of the Church soldiers beneath them. *I hope they're all freezing.*

The Church soldiers shifted in their positions, passing loaves of bread to each other. One soldier came by with by with a bucket that steamed, and poured hot mulled wine into the soldier's cups. The scent of it reached up through the slats to Thomas. His stomach growled in response. *Too much to hope that breakfast will be any time soon.*

Thomas tried raising his arm, then moving it back and forth. It worked, but not well. *Doesn't matter, since I don't have a dagger anyway.*

How long until the next attack, I wonder?

It came a quarter of an hour later. Below, commanders shouted and troops began dismantling the barricades on one side. Thomas leaned as far as he could but couldn't see what was coming. In desperation he cracked open a shutter and peered out.

By the Four. Thomas stumbled out of the room to the railing as fast as he could.

"They've got another ram!" he yelled. "A big one!"

"Everyone up!" shouted Graham. "Thomas, back to the window and shout out what's happening! We'll send someone up with a boiling kettle as soon as we can. And if you see someplace where your magic would be useful..."

"I'll use it," promised Thomas. "Just hold the door." He got to the window and looked out again. "They're moving the barricades!"

Graham's voice rang up from down below. "How many?"

Thomas opened the shutter a crack again. This time a crossbow bolt slapped into the wood, driving its point through just above his head. Thomas swore and ducked, pulling the shutter closed. "At least a hundred!" He called. "The ram is as big as the one that nearly got through the last time!"

"Smiths to the door!" Graham ordered. "Eileen's company stand by! Thomas, can you do anything?"

Thomas reached for the shutter and tried opening it. Three more crossbow bolts smacked into it. "Not without being skewered!"

"Right! Everyone ready!"

Thomas peered through the shutter slats. "The ram is past the barricade! They've got shields up to protect them from grease!" The men below moved into position and started swinging. *Here we go.*

BOOM!

The first hit shook the whole building.

BOOM!

Thomas tried opening the shutter again. More crossbow bolts slapped into it.

BOOM!

I'll go downstairs if they break through. He peered through the slats again.

BOOM!

"The troops are on either side of the door!" Thomas yelled. "They're waiting for the door to—"

BOOM-CRACK!

"Stand ready!" shouted Graham. "Everyone stand ready! We need to keep them out!"

I need to surrender. The thought frightened Thomas more than the battle had. *If I don't surrender they'll kill them all.* "Graham! Graham!"

"Not now!" yelled Graham.

Thomas headed for the stairs. "Graham I have to..."

BOOM-CRACK!

From somewhere outside came howling.

Henry?

Thomas ran to the shutter and tried to peer out again. New sounds came from outside—men fighting and horses screaming and above it all the unearthly howl that was the battle cry of the White Wolves. Thomas's eyes went wide. He pushed the shutter open, looked, and slammed it shut. A pair of crossbow bolts stuck into the wood but he didn't care. He ran for the balcony. "The White Wolves are out there!"

"The Wolves?" Eileen was by the front door, weapons in hand. Her eyes were wide and her voice filled with disbelief. "What are the Wolves doing here?"

"Saving us!"

CRACK!

"CHARGE!" shouted Graham as the door split apart and the big log bracing it tumbled to the ground. "Keep them out!"

Graham and eight others rushed forward. The first two soldiers died in the doorway. The next got a step inside before he died. Then two more charged in, shields up to protect their faces. They were cut down in seconds, but it made room for the next two behind them, who were pushed in by the two after that.

"Push them back," Graham screamed. "Don't let them get in!"

Thomas ran down the stairs, strength surging through him at the thought of rescue and the sound of the battle. Thomas knew it wouldn't last. *So long as it lasts enough for Henry to get here.*

Six soldiers were through the door now, with others pushing them forward. The students were getting slowly driven backwards to the barricades of tables behind them.

"Now!" yelled Graham.

"The Academy!" Eileen and the Student Company charged, driving into the soldiers at the door. The soldier's line wavered, and more of them fell, but they didn't back up.

"Smiths!" shouted Graham. Eileen and the company ran for the barricades as George and the smiths charged forward. Instead of weapons, they had tables held out in front of them like shields, ramming them into the soldiers hard enough to send them stumbling back. The soldiers' line broke apart. Eileen and the company ran back at them. More soldiers died, but the others rallied and once more the students were driven back.

"Fall back!" Graham yelled. "Fall back to the barricade!"

The students and smiths rushed backward, leaping over the tables and chairs. Most made it. Others fell, screaming as the soldiers cut into them.

"Hold them!" Thomas shouted, running forward and climbing over the second line of barricades. "Henry and his knights are coming for us! Just hold the line!"

More Church poured into the building. Outside, horns blared, and there was a roar of charging horses and the smashing of heavy bodies against armour and shields. The students cheered wildly, and the soldiers redoubled their attack.

The battle along the barricade grew furious as the soldiers tried to break the student lines. Students fell wounded and were pulled away to have their place taken by others. One of the smiths fell back, dead, and Eileen jumped up into his place, fighting beside her brother.

"Surrender!" shouted one of the Church soldiers.

"The Academy!" screamed Graham, and every student roared it back.

Thomas stepped forward to take the place of one of the fallen, and thrust his rapier into one soldier's eye. The man fell and another took his place. This one used his shield to keep the point of Thomas's rapier away and cut with long strokes that forced Thomas to stay back.

One of the Church soldiers jumped over the barricade and the body of the young man he'd killed to get there. He hacked on either side of him, forcing the students back. More soldiers jumped over, forcing the line apart.

"Retreat!" Graham yelled. "Second barricades!"

Thomas broke off his fight and jumped over the second barricade. His legs gave out halfway over and he landed badly, ending up on the floor and jarring his aching chest. He gasped in pain and scrambled to get out of the way as the others came over the barricades.

Outside the howling grew closer, and more horns blared.

Thomas staggered to his feet and stumbled back. The barricades were crowded and there wasn't room for much more than stabbing across the tabletops. The student's rapiers were designed for point work, but the soldiers' shields took the brunt of it.

The soldiers pushing into the Broken Quill now outnumbered the students. Only one line of barricades remained, and there was precious little chance they could hold it if they were driven back. Thomas tried to peer past the Church soldiers to the door, but could only see more soldiers.

A score of voices rose up in howls just outside the door, and a moment later the first of Henry's wolves fought their way inside. The Church soldiers, now caught between two enemies, fought desperately. The floor grew slippery with blood and bodies soon littered the room on all sides of the barricades. The Knights of the White Wolf kept coming, implacable and unstoppable. Henry's voice rang over the sounds of battle. "Enough! Surrender now, and I'll let you live!"

Some surrendered, throwing down their weapons and begging for mercy; others fought until they were surrounded, and died under a dozen blades.

The students jumped the barricades and cheered the Wolves, clasping hands and thanking them. Thomas staggered through the crowd, looking for Eileen. Everywhere there were bodies and the crying, screaming wounded. Henry's hand closed on Thomas's shoulder, making him yell in pain.

"Sorry," said Henry, letting go. "We need to leave. Fast."

"Thomas!" Eileen had a cut on her cheek and another on her arm, and blood spattered over the front of her armour. She threw her arms around him, kissing him hard and squeezing him. Thomas winced and squeezed back just as hard. "Thank the Four," she said. "I thought we were all dead." She let him go and rounded on Henry. "And as for you..." She reached up and kissed Henry on the mouth.

Henry pushed her back. "We have to leave. Now."

"But..." Thomas realized he was exhausted and probably not being clear. "The students..."

"Henry!" George descended on them like a blood-soaked mountain. "About time. I'd nearly given up."

"So has the king," said Henry. "*Everyone! Shut Up!*" Henry's bellow reached the rafters. "We are leaving! Wounded, Healthy, everyone! Hurry up before reinforcements arrive. Sir Patrick!"

"Here, my lord!" said the big knight who had helped them all in the north.

"Take twenty Wolves and circle the Academy. As soon as you see us trying to break the line on the Academy gates, you hit them from the flank." He surveyed the students and the barmaids, who were scrambling to get the wounded bandaged. "Go faster! We're leaving!"

"Leave the worst ones here," said Angeline Blossom. "We'll take care of them and hide them from the Church. You get the rest to safety."

"Right," said Henry. "Anyone who can't walk, stays! Hurry!"

Eight bloody, broken students were laid on the stage. Another ten who were almost as badly hurt insisted they could go, and leaned on their fellows to walk. Twenty more lay dead on the ground.

Fifty of us left, Thomas thought. Graham yelled and prodded the last of the students to get in line. Fenris and Marcus began pulling bodies out of the room into the street outside.

Henry looked over the room once more then went outside to give orders to the Wolves. Thomas followed him. The sun was high and shone down on the blood-soaked streets. There were bodies everywhere. Most were Church soldiers, though here and there Thomas could see one of the White Wolves lying dead on the ground. Most of the knights were re-mounted, now, and sat in a bristling ring of steel around the entrance to the Quill.

Thomas caught Henry just before the other could mount. "How bad is it?"

Henry sighed and leaned on his horse. He looked tired and battered, which Henry never looked. "It's very bad," said Henry. "The King is holding the inner city. The Archbishop controls the outer city. The king's supporters barricaded a dozen places, but none of them are able to break out. We're the only knights left outside the walls and we've been playing hide-and seek with the Church cavalry all night."

"What about the magicians?"

"What magicians?"

"I found a spell that multiplies magicians' power," said Thomas. "I gave it to Robert and Sir Walter. They were going to get all the magicians together and help."

"There's been no magic, Thomas." Henry mounted. "We have to go."

Why aren't they doing anything? They've had a day and a night. They should have done something.

The students began filing out of the Broken Quill in two bloody, exhausted lines. The smiths followed. There were only a dozen of them left. George came up to Henry. "The smiths want to go back home. They said they'll go on their own, but they want to get back to their families."

"They'll die in the streets," said Henry. "They're better off with us."

"I know, but they want to go."

"I have to reach Sir Walter," said Thomas.

"What?" said Henry. "No."

"We have to!" Thomas pointed at the students. "Look at them! How much longer are they going to last? How much longer is the city going to last? I need to get to Sir Walter and get the magicians together before the king has to surrender!"

"Sir Walter is inside the city walls," said Henry.

"Do you know where?"

Henry glared down at Thomas. "Yes, I know where."

"Can you take me there?"

Henry's jaw clenched, and for a moment Thomas was scared he was going to refuse. "Sir Patrick!" Henry shouted. "New plan. Twenty Wolves are coming with me to deliver Thomas to the king. You use the rest and you get this lot to the Academy."

"I want to go with Thomas," said Eileen.

"And me," said George.

"Of course you do. Three horses! Fast!"

Thomas looked back. Eileen and George had followed him out, the rest of his company hard on their heels.

"Where are you going, Captain?" asked William. "What's going on?"

"He's coming with me," snapped Henry. "You lot get back to the Academy and wait for orders."

"When will he be back?"

"As soon as I can," promised Thomas. "Just get to the Academy. They need you."

"Get on," said Henry to Thomas. "We've got a ways to go."

The knights brought three horses in bloodstained armour and White Wolf livery. Thomas tried not to think about what must have happened to the riders as they mounted. Henry shouted orders and twenty White Wolves packed together in a tight formation around Thomas and Eileen. George picked up a shield from the ground and mounted the third horse, taking his place with the other knights.

"Ride!" said Henry, and led them into the city.

"Henry, where did..." Thomas realized it was a stupid question and rephrased it. "How did the White Wolves get here?"

"The king sent all over the country for troops months ago," said Henry. "Just as we were coming back. He figured the Church was going to try to seize power."

"You didn't tell me?"

"I didn't know. I found out yesterday morning when he summoned me to the castle."

Thomas looked at the grim knights around him. "And John sent the Wolves."

"They're loyal to me," said Henry. "It was probably better for him to move them out of Frostmire, anyway. They arrived two days ago." He looked at the sky. "Three, I should say. We've been up all night." They turned onto a main thoroughfare. There were corpses lying on the cobbles and nearby Thomas could hear the sound of fighting. "It's been a long, bad night and it's going to be a worse day." He sighed. "I thought you were dead. All of you. Then I heard the Quill was under siege and took a chance."

"Thank the Four you did," said Thomas.

"What happened to your chest?"

Thomas looked at the bloody mess on the front of his uniform. "Crossbow bolt. Healed it."

"Lucky."

It took an hour for them just to reach the city walls. Somewhere, a single bell rang out the second hour of the morning. Twice they dodged singing mobs of Church supporters and once Henry's scouts galloped back, warning of Church cavalry. Henry led them down the twisting side streets and through a dozen turns before he brought them back on their route.

Ahead, the sounds of fighting grew louder and louder. "Brace yourselves," said Henry. "This is going to be ugly."

A barricade five feet high, made of wagons, barrels, crates, and furniture encircled the old gatehouse. The king's flag had been raised in the middle of it, and the people inside were yelling, "For King Harold and Criethe!" as they fought.

Hundreds of townsfolk were in the square, charging the barricades. They were armed with knives and sticks and homemade spears. The ones who hadn't reached the barricades yet were singing a battle hymn. The men and women behind the gates—burghers and tradesmen and workmen, reinforced by the king's guards—were barely holding them off.

"The Archbishop's letting the people fight each other," said Henry. He spat. "That way he keeps his troops fresh until he needs them."

"Henry!" One of the Wolves called from the back. "Cavalry coming! Fast!"

Henry swore. "Thomas, Eileen, stay in the middle and stay out of the fight! Wolves, we have to reach the barricade! Charge!"

The Wolves howled and galloped out of the side street, swords hacking and steel-shod hooves trampling through the Church supporters. The defenders behind the gates saw the Wolves charging and cheered. The people on the ground tried to fight back, but they were barely armoured and no match at all for Henry's knights. The Wolves cut through them like a jagged knife, leaving a trail of bloody, broken bodies behind them.

"They come!" shouted one of the Wolves.

"Back line wheel and charge!" yelled Henry, his voice pitched high to be heard over the battle. Ten of the wolves turned their horses and charged at the cavalry, George among them. In front of Thomas, the Wolves broke to either side, clearing a lane to the wall. "Thomas, Eileen! Get over the wall!"

Thomas kicked his horse forward, Eileen beside him. He reached the wall and the king's men on the other side held out their hands. Thomas reached out with his good arm, kicked his legs free of the stirrups and let them haul him over. The soldiers grabbed Eileen's hands and pulled her onto the wall. "George!" she called. "George! Come here!"

One of the Wolves sounded a horn and the entire company wheeled away and out of the square, taking George with them. Eileen screamed his name until a soldier pulled her down from the wall. Thomas grabbed her and pulled her close. "He'll be all right. He's with Henry. He'll be fine."

Who are you?" the soldier demanded. "What are doing here?"

"Thomas Flarety. Here to report to Sir Walter Deehan." said Thomas. "Where is he?"

"In there," the soldier pointed through the gate. "The old custom house, just inside."

Thomas grabbed Eileen's hand and they ran, dodging men and women with makeshift weapons heading for the wall. The guards at the gate ushered them through and into the middle of an army, standing ready to attack.

"Thomas?" The surprise in Sir Walter's voice would have been funny, under other circumstances. The man was sitting on horseback, surrounded by a dozen other knights. Thomas ran to him, Eileen dogging his heels. "Sir Walter. Where are the magicians?"

"What?"

"The magicians. What did you do with them?"

Sir Walter stared down at Thomas, then whistled loudly. Two of the king's messengers rode up. "Give them your horses," he ordered. "Quickly."

The messengers dismounted and helped Eileen and Thomas into their saddles. Sir Walter wheeled his horse and set off at a brisk trot. Thomas and Eileen kicked their own beasts into motion and followed. Six other knights followed them. Thomas urged his horse faster until he was alongside Sir Walter. "Where are the magicians? What's happening?"

"We're losing," said Sir Walter. "Badly. Too many people are dying. The Bishop's forces outnumber ours and when they breach the gates and overrun the inner city, the king will have no choice but to surrender."

"But the magicians—"

"The Archbishop has sent terms for the king's surrender. He must swear fealty to the High Father, restore women to their proper places in the kingdom, and hand over all witches to be cleansed of their sins. Probably by fire. Look."

Thomas looked. A dozen bodies lay around the fountain. Most wore normal clothes, and had makeshift weapons. "They were inside the gates. Just supporters, no troops. They marched up to the palace walls and we had to drive them back."

"Why aren't you using the magicians?" Thomas demanded. "They could have helped."

"They're more help where they are."

"And where's that?"

"The old watchtower. The king wanted them in one place to show his good will, should the need arise."

"But..." Thomas was flabbergast. "You saw what Robert and I did. And that was just two of us. There are seven—"

"The king gave the order," said Sir Walter. "I followed it."

Thomas swore. "Did you at least leave them the spell books?"

"No. The king took them to the Royal Library. The easier to hand them over when we surrender."

We can't surrender. Thomas remembered the small cell where the Inquisitor had held him before; remembered what they had done to Charles and the others. *I can't surrender.* He looked down and saw more blood on the streets. Thomas wished he could wipe away the fighting and drive the soldiers off the streets and wash all the blood from the cobbles until the city was clean and sparkling. "Where are you taking us, Sir Walter?"

"The palace," said Sir Walter. "The king ordered you be put there if you survived."

"Take us to the old watchtower instead."

Sir Walter's eyes narrowed. "The king wants you in the palace."

"The king wants to win the war," said Thomas. "Since he can't have both, which do you think he wants more?"

Sir Walter hesitated.

"What have you got to lose?" Thomas demanded. "Let me talk to the magicians! We can help. I know it. Please!"

Sir Walter considered a moment longer. Then he kicked his horse to a gallop. "This way."

The old watchtower had been built before the city walls. Heavily fortified and eighty feet tall, it dwarfed the buildings around it. It had been used to spot attacking pirates on the seaward side and bandits on the landward side. Now it was mainly for watching for incoming storms. The guards at the door snapped to attention when the troop reined in their horses in front of the tower.

"Which floor?" demanded Sir Walter.

"Second," said one of the guards. "There's been some yelling, but they haven't tried anything."

Sir Walter pushed the door open and led them inside and up the stairs. The second floor was a mess hall, with chairs and tables and a fireplace that send a small amount of heat into the room.

Around the central table sat the magicians of Hawksmouth, arguing.

They were all fairly normal-looking in the daylight. The one with the deep voice was a long, thin man, with short dark hair and a neatly trimmed beard. Beside him sat a young man with the same build and hair. Next to them were two matrons, both stout and both looking quite annoyed. On the other side of the table were Robert the baker and a fat man who was sweating and red, despite the relative cool of the room. A tall woman in a rich green dress rounded out the group.

"It is not seemly," the tall man was saying as they entered. "They can't just keep us here for no reason!" He glared at Robert. "You said the king needed us!"

"He does," said Thomas. "Come to the battlements. Now."

"Thomas!" Robert jumped to his feet. "Thank the Four!"

"What is going on?" demanded the rich-looking woman. "Why are we prisoners?"

"Sir Walter?" said Thomas, starting up the stone stairs to the next floor.

"Do as you're told," barked Sir Walter. "Now!"

The seven magicians rose and followed, their steps slow and sullen. Eileen followed behind, urging them upward.

The third floor of the tower had bunks in it. The fourth floor had barrels of arrows and crates of supplies. The fifth floor was empty and had only a ladder leading up to the roof. Thomas went up, shoving open the trap door and causing the men above to jump and swear.

"Who are you?" demanded one burly fellow, his hand on his sword.

"Servant of the king," said Thomas, pulling himself out of the trap door. The roof of the tower was circled with battlements, and from it Thomas could see the entire of the city. "We need you to clear the roof."

"What?"

Thomas turned in a circle as the magicians came up the ladder. He could see the ships in the harbour, and the rough, cold spring sea on the other side of the breakwater. The sky above was still clear. There was moisture in the air, though not the heavy promise of rain.

Sir Walter came up last. "Now what?"

"Now we stop the fighting," said Thomas. "Everyone join hands."

"What do you mean, you foolish boy?" said one of the matrons. "Our magic can't stop anyone."

"It can if we work together," said Thomas.

"Now, look here, boy," began the deep voiced one. "You've gotten us dragged into—"

"SHUT UP!" Thomas shouted, startling them all. "The king is losing the war. The Church will burn us alive. And the only way we can stop it is to stop the fighting so shut up and do as you're told! Now everyone hold hands!"

"What... what are we doing?" asked the boy as the magicians took each other's hands. "Are we going to kill people?"

"No," said Thomas. *I hope.* "Everyone take a deep breath and let it out slowly."

Six of them did at once. The tall man looked ready to argue but the rich woman prodded him with an elbow and he breathed deeply as well.

"Good," said Thomas. "Another. And another. Now everyone close your eyes and think about your magic. Envision it passing through your body, travelling out your left hand into the right hand of the person beside you. The person beside you will feel the magic flowing into them. And don't let go. No matter how powerful the magic gets. Understand?" Thomas took Robert's left hand in his right, and the rich woman's in his left, completing the circle. One by one the magicians closed their eyes, and when they had all shut them, Thomas closed his own. It took him a few moments to remember the words. *I hope I have this right.*

"Let the circle's magic be brought together. Let it be subject to our will, and guided through my body. Let it be directed where I will, and let it be bent to my purpose."

He closed his eyes and willed his own magic to flow. He heard the rich woman gasp in surprise and felt her start, but she didn't let go of his hand. Around the circle, others gasped as magic flowed from one body to another. It moved slowly at first, but quickly gained speed, moving faster and faster until it was impossible to tell whose magic was whose.

The magic began growing stronger.

Thomas felt the power begin to vibrate. Not the deep, rhythmic vibration that he'd felt in the stone circle last summer, but something higher, faster. The magic made his entire body shake, and its power kept growing. Around the circle he heard the other magicians exclaiming in wonder.

"Keep your hands joined," said Thomas, praying it wouldn't interrupt the spell. The vibrations of the magic threatened to shake Thomas's teeth loose. The power racing around the circle began to heat up.

"How much longer?" asked the boy, through what sounded like gritted teeth. "It's starting to hurt!"

"I know," shouted Thomas. "Just a bit longer!"

The burning stayed, but grew no hotter. The vibration grew no stronger. The magic stopped growing in strength. Thomas opened his eyes.

In the middle of them was a cyclone of magic.

The light that spilled from it threatened to blind Thomas, even as he realized that he was probably the only one that could see it. It was whirling so fast that Thomas was sure that touching it would send him flying. He couldn't see past it to the magicians on the other side of the circle.

"Now what?" cried Robert, fear in his voice. "It's burning!"

"Now," said Thomas, looking up to the sky, "we clear the streets."

He had done weather magic before, in Frostmire; a small snowstorm that covered their escape from an ambush. Just as it had then, Thomas felt his consciousness expand, becoming one with the air around him. He felt the currents of it, tasted the water that it held. He could see every eddy and whorl of wind as it slipped through the streets of Hawksmouth. Thomas let his consciousness expand even more, until he could see the entirety of the city. He saw every building, every street. He could see the mobs attacking barricades across the outer city. He could see the troops the king had led out, carving a path to the end of the block where hundreds of Church cavalry and infantry waited just out of sight. He could see the frenzied mob outside the Academy walls pounding at the gate, nearly ready to burst through. Everywhere there was fighting, and bodies lay in the streets. The cathedral had been turned into a fortress, and the Church had a thousand more troops waiting there.

It will be a bloodbath, Thomas realized. *No matter who wins, there's going to be too many dead.*

"Sir Walter!" called Thomas, fighting to say the words as his focus expanded even further. "Tell the king to pull back. Tell him it's an ambush. Tell him to wait and to follow the storm."

"What do you mean?" said Sir Walter. "What storm? There's hardly even a wind."

"There will be," said Eileen, and Thomas could practically hear the smile in her voice. "Thomas is calling one."

There was a moment's silence. Then Sir Walter turned and ran for the ladder, and Thomas was away in the clouds again, calling the winds to him.

The first to come was a small breeze. It zipped around corners and gusted into faces, catching people by surprise. Thomas followed it, directed it, and found that he could control where and when it blew. He increased the power of it, and called other breezes.

The defenders inside one barricade near the docks were nearly overwhelmed. Their royal flag was still standing, but a mob backed by trained infantry was about to overrun them. Thomas sent the wind there, making it howl through the ranks of the attackers. He made it whirl around the barricades a dozen times, driving the mob back. Then he turned his attention to the Academy.

The students were lined up behind the creaking gate. Many of them Thomas recognized from the Broken Quill. What remained of his own company stood in the front rank, rapiers ready. They were tired and bloody and not one face had any hope left in it.

Outside the gates, the mob sang and yelled for joy.

Thomas sent the wind first, strong enough to drive the mob backwards and blind them while he turned his attention to the bay. He made the wind speed up, pulling freezing salt water into the sky above Hawksmouth; more and more of it until it grew dark with towering grey-green clouds. Thomas felt the different temperatures of the air, felt how it became much, much colder as the clouds went higher. He also quickly learned that, if he sent the water high enough, fast enough, it made hail.

Rain first, Thomas decided, and brought a deluge down on Hawksmouth.

The first drops spattered around them. Thomas redirected it, keeping it from the tower. His consciousness flew on the wind and he found Henry's knights, battling Church cavalry in the streets. Thomas brought the rain down hard on the Church lines, the strength of it enough to bow the heads of the knights and horses alike. He brought the wind up again, lashing them backwards and taking shingles off roofs nearby. The Church cavalry struggled to hold their line. The blasts that blew around them grew to hurricane strength, racing up and down the streets and pushing the pelting rain hard enough to sting the flesh of the men fighting.

Henry's knights managed to pull back, and as soon as they were free, Thomas reached for hail. The water from the ocean had gone up hard and fast, and the windstorm that lashed the city had sent it high into the sky again and again.

When he released the hail on the Church's cavalry, it came in stones the size of Thomas's fist.

Horses panicked and their riders fought to control them as hailstone after hailstone crashed down. The foot soldiers fared no better, and were soon holding their shields above their heads to protect themselves. The wind roared higher, driving the Church troops back.

And at the other end of the block, The White Wolves stood in the calm and dry, watching the Church troops retreat. Henry shouted an order and the Wolves advanced forward at a slow walk, following Thomas's storm. The Church knights tried to form a line, but the wind drove them back, the rain blinded them, and the hailstones battered their bodies and their animals. With no other choice, they retreated.

Thomas found the king's forces and gave the men they were fighting the same treatment. The king stood, dry and amazed, as the Church troops and their followers were beaten bloody by the hail, knocked down by the wind, and near-drowned by the rain.

He saw Sir Walter reach the king and tell him what was happening. The king passed orders and his troops rallied together. His knights harried whatever Church cavalry tried to weather the storm. His infantry followed after the Church soldiers, inflicting damage whenever they could. And from above, fist-sized hail and freezing rain and howling winds battered the Church's forces.

Then Thomas turned the force of the rain against the men and women at the Academy gates.

In a quarter of an hour the people around the Academy had dispersed. In a half-hour, the streets of the city were empty of everyone but soldiers as the force of the storm drove people under cover. Thomas let the rain wash the streets, carrying puddles of blood into the drains and sewers and the harbour.

The Church's soldiers tried to regroup. Thomas made the winds blow harder, the hail come down larger, forcing them back farther and farther, rendering the cavalry useless as their panicked horses tried to bolt away from the hail that slammed down on them.

Thomas was impressed that they still managed an orderly retreat.

Slowly, surely, he drove them back toward the cathedral, until all the Church's troops were crushed together in the square. He kept the wind blowing hard and the rain pouring on the city, washing the streets free of blood and keeping the mob under cover.

The king reached the square, his horse coming to stand side by side with Henry's. Both men looked exhausted and grim. The king shouted, "Surrender and lay down your arms!"

The Church's men stayed where they were.

Thomas brought the full force of the storm down on them. More horses panicked as hail smashed down, rain blinded them and wind threatened to knock them over.

"If you don't surrender," yelled the king, "we'll bring down lightning next!"

Oh, you shouldn't bluff like that. Thomas reached up into the clouds and found the lightning waiting. *Lucky, your Majesty. Very lucky.*

Thomas unleashed the lightning, sending bolt after bolt down onto the cathedral's spires.

It was enough. Soldiers threw down their weapons and shields, and dropped to their knees. Others dashed into the cathedral. Horses went mad and bucked and fought, stomping the soldiers around them.

Thomas cast his thoughts into the clouds. The hail stopped but the storm was not going to give up easily. He spread it out, letting it douse the surrounding countryside as it lost its strength. Rain even fell on the roof they were standing on, quickly soaking them all to the skin. Thomas made sure the storm would blow itself out and let the weather go. All his senses snapped back into his body and he was standing on the roof again.

The magicians around Thomas looked stunned, but no one seemed ready to collapse. All seven gaped at him with a mixture of wonder and shock. The tall man looked horrified as well, and Robert was grinning ear to ear. "That was... amazing."

"I could feel bits of the storm," said the fat man. "I could feel myself as part of the storm."

"We could *feel* what you did with it," said the tall one. "It was... frightening."

"It didn't touch us at all," said one of the matrons. "I thought surely it would, but..."

Thomas walked to the battlement and looked out. The sun was breaking through, reflecting off a thousand wet walls and puddles, making the city shine.

"Did... did we kill anyone?" asked the boy.

"We stopped the fighting," said Thomas, knowing it wasn't an answer.

30

It was after dark and Thomas was still awake when Henry, George and the rest of the White Wolves rode up. The other magicians had talked until the exhaustion had set in. Then they'd all gone to the bunks on the third floor. Thomas fully expected to pass out, but even when the trembling took him he couldn't sleep. He and Eileen ate instead, raiding the tower larder for bread and smoked meat and tea. Then they sat outside the door on the steps, wrapped tight in their cloaks, too tired to speak, leaning against one another for comfort. Eileen dozed once or twice, but started awake at each sound.

The streets were quiet and dark and still slick with water. The wind from the ocean smelled fresh and cold, as if the rain had washed away the smell of the harbour as well. The sky above had cleared and Thomas could see the stars.

When they heard the sound of horses' hooves on cobblestones, they both jumped to their feet, swords in hand. The Wolves came into sight Eileen ran out to them. George practically jumped off his horse to meet her. Eileen hugged her brother so hard that George complained his armour was going to bend. He didn't let her go, though.

Henry didn't dismount. "The Archbishop is holed up inside the Cathedral. The king wants you to get him out."

Of course he does.

The streets were deserted and dark. The bodies had been cleared away, and the rain had done its job, rinsing the streets of blood. *At least I did that much.*

The kings troops surrounded Cathedral Square. All the buildings were occupied with soldiers, and his knights blocked all the streets leading in. The king himself was on the courthouse stairs where the students had been only days before. Sir Walter stood beside him. Thomas dismounted and bowed. "Your Majesty."

"Thomas," said the king. "You saved the city."

"Yes, your Majesty."

"And my army. And possibly the kingdom as well. Thank you."

Thomas bowed again.

"The Archbishop barricaded himself inside the cathedral with three hundred men while the others were surrendering," said the king, pointing. Thomas looked. There were bodies on the steps of the cathedral, and blood had trickled down the stairs to make pools on the cobbles. All the cathedral's windows had broken panes, and the door had fresh scars from whatever the king's men had used as a battering ram.

"As long as the Archbishop is in there, he's a rallying point," said Sir Walter. "Everyone who believes the Church is more important than the king will be ready to fight for him. And the Mother help us if other countries get wind of it. We need to end this tonight."

"If you kill Archbishop Culverton, you'll make him a martyr," said Henry, who was still sitting on his horse. "And if you burn down the largest church in the country, how bad do you think the riots will be then?"

"I am open to suggestions," said the king. He walked down the stairs to Thomas. "Can you break down the door?"

"Not by myself," said Thomas.

"Get the others," said the king to Sir Walter.

"Have you tried talking to them?" Thomas asked. "Can't you convince them to come out?"

"We've tried," said Sir Walter. "They aren't speaking to us."

Thomas's mind flashed back to the Archbishop's visit, and he nearly smiled. *I know this isn't what he meant, but...* "Maybe he'll speak to me?"

"You?" Sir Walter looked horrified. "They'll kill you out of hand."

"The Archbishop said I could go to him at any time," said Thomas. "He said he would guarantee me safe entry and exit."

"That was before the war!"

"Absolutely not," said the king. "We need you to break open the doors."

"No, you don't," said Thomas. "The others can do it. Just give them the spell books."

The king frowned and chewed his lip.

"Please," said Thomas. "I might be able to end this."

"And if not?" asked Sir Walter. "If he kills you as you walk towards the door?"

Thomas didn't have an answer to that.

The king stared out at the cathedral for an inordinately long time. The cold damp air started to creep under Thomas's cloak and armour, and sent a shiver up his back.

"Try it," said the king at last. "Thomas, come with me and I'll give you our terms. Sir Walter, send over a messenger. Tell them Thomas will negotiate on our behalf."

"No," said Thomas, making both men turn to him in surprise. "With respect, your Majesty, say that Thomas Flarety is suffering a spiritual crisis and seeks the guidance of the Archbishop."

An hour and a half later, Thomas walked across the square alone, without armour or weapons. Henry had dashed back to their apartment and returned with his dress uniform. Thomas had cleaned up as best he could and changed clothes while the king and Sir Walter peppered him with what they wanted him to say, to look for, and to do.

The square was silent, save for Thomas's boots clicking on the wet cobblestones. He was far too aware of the men with crossbows stationed on the battlement above the cathedral door and peering through the broken windowpanes. He could see their inner lights, glowing faintly red.

Please, don't let any of them have itchy fingers.

Thomas walked slowly up the wide stone stairs and stood before the immense wooden doors. He had time to study the scars and dents in the smooth oak from the king's battering rams, the puddles of blood on the stairs and the corpses of the men that lay there before the door opened. A rough voice said, "Step in."

The inside of the cathedral was very different at night. The stained glass let in little light, and the shadows thrown by the few torches made the giant space oppressive. Thomas stood and waited as the soldiers shut the door behind him with a dull noise. They shoved a large bar across it, the scrape of wood against wood grating on Thomas's ears.

The soldier searched Thomas for weapons, then said, "This way."

Thomas followed him. Barricades had been hastily erected inside, using barrels and crates of food and whatever else they could scrounge. The soldiers were spread out, their numbers small in the large building. Some talked to each other in low voices. Others sharpened weapons. Most slept. Those still awake stopped talking and watched him as he passed. They looked tired and hopeless, even more than the students had been at the Broken Quill.

He spotted Cormac, Ethan and Anthony, sitting together. They wore Church colours and were spattered with blood and dirt. Their faces were bruised and cut, probably from the hailstorm. They stared at him, hatred in their eyes. Thomas stared back for a few steps then deliberately looked away.

The soldier led him up past the altar to a door set behind. He knocked and then pulled it open. "Through here."

"Thank you," said Thomas.

The chamber was small and cosy, with a cheerful little fire crackling in its fireplace and two comfortable chairs. The Archbishop was sitting in one, a cup of tea in his hand.

Thomas bowed low. "Your Grace."

"Thomas Flarety," said the Archbishop. He managed a smile, but it was strained and tired. "You are welcome here."

"Thank you."

"Please sit." Thomas did. The Archbishop took a sip of his tea. "Can I assume your spiritual crisis came at the behest of the king?"

"In part," said Thomas. He held his hands to the fire, letting the heat sink into them. The flame danced yellow and orange, and the logs glowed red and white where the heat had burned them to ash. "And I should say that if I'm not out by tomorrow morning, the rest of the magicians will break through the door and the king will send in his army."

The Archbishop nodded. "Of course."

There was a knock and the door swung open. Father Alphonse stepped inside and smiled. "Thomas! This *is* unexpected."

"Father Alphonse." The Archbishop's voice was cold. "You are not to be part of these proceedings."

"But surely Thomas has come here to give his confession," said Father Alphonse. "I should hate to miss it."

"He has come here to negotiate on behalf of the king," said the Archbishop.

"I've come to do both," said Thomas, catching them by surprise.

The Archbishop recovered first. "Given Father Alphonse's previous actions, I would not expect you to be comfortable in his presence, or to believe that I am speaking in good faith with him here."

"It's all right," said Thomas, turning his eyes back to the fire. The flames quivered back and forth, but never settled into a pattern as they ate their way through the wood. "Would you close the door, Father Alphonse?"

The Chief Inquisitor looked dubious, but the Archbishop gestured for him to do it.

When he heard the door click shut, Thomas held out his hand. A turquoise blue ball of light appeared in his palm. The Archbishop gasped and Father Alphonse stumbled back in shock. The ball of light swirled gently above Thomas's hand.

"I want to tell you," said Thomas, "everything that's happened to me since I decided to walk home last summer."

The men were silent, staring at the ball of light. Eventually, the Archbishop raised his eyes to meet Thomas's. "Walk? Hawksmouth to Elmvale? That's a very long way."

"Yes, it is," said Thomas. He let the light fade away. Then he began talking.

Thomas told them how Bishop Malloy had manipulated Thomas's father with his power, and how Thomas had seen through juggler Timothy's tricks and later watched him die under his wagon. He spoke of discovering his own magic, and the fight on Ailbe's porch that made him and George killers, and the chase to Hawksmouth. Then of Bishop Malloy's raids on the students and the riot they caused, and the race to the Bishop's summerhouse; of the stone circle that gave him power, the battles they fought, and how Benjamin had died saving Eileen's life.

Then Thomas described Bishop Malloy's useless blood sacrifice, and how he had pulled the magic from the Bishop's body before running the man through with a rapier. And how, when Thomas released them, the small magics of those who died became part of him.

"You confess to murdering Bishop Malloy?" said Father Alphonse.

"No, I confessed to killing him," said Thomas. "Don't interrupt."

The Chief Inquisitor opened his mouth to retort, but the Archbishop raised a hand. "Fetch us some tea, please, Father Alphonse," he said. "And perhaps some biscuits. I'm sure Thomas will wait until you return before he continues."

Thomas waited. Father Alphonse brought the tea and poured it. Thomas sipped at it, and began speaking again.

He started with Eileen's arrival in Hawksmouth and the attack that led to his interrogation. He told of the journey to Frostmire and the snowstorm he'd called and how he first fought the enemy's magic on the frozen plains. He spoke of Frostmire castle, and how Cormac and the other young Lords taunted and abused Eileen and the dance and the bloody battles that made Eileen a killer, too.

Thomas told them of his kidnapping and how the magic was drained from his body, and of how Eileen had burned a man alive to rescue him. Then of the march to Frostmire castle and the death of Richard Antonius, and their return home.

The Archbishop sent Father Alphonse for some wine and bread. Thomas ate ravenously.

Then he told them of everything in the past few weeks, up to the moment he'd walked in the door.

And when he was done, Thomas sank back in his chair and waited.

"That is..." the Archbishop looked for the proper words... "Quite a story."

"It is indeed," said Father Alphonse. "All that you left out is how you pledged yourself to the Banished to gain your powers."

The Archbishop gave Father Alphonse a look clearly meant to silence him, and then asked. "Why did you tell it?"

"Because I need you to understand why I'm here," said Thomas. "The king asked me to break down the Cathedral door and let his troops in. I asked him to let me talk to you instead."

"How very noble," said Father Alphonse.

"I'm broken," Thomas's words came out soft. "Ever since Bishop Malloy. I don't sleep at night. When I do I dream of fire and blood and everyone I love being killed. Eileen... She's so angry at everything and George," Thomas shuddered, remembering George's anguished face as he pounded his fists against the table. "My friends are broken. We've all killed so many people, and it's broken us all, and I want it to stop."

"Then give yourself over to us," said Father Alphonse. "Surrender yourself and let us..."

"Torture me?" snapped Thomas. "Hang me? Burn me? And what about everyone else that has magic? Will you leave them alone once you have me?"

Father Alphonse shook his head. "Thomas, witchcraft must—"

"There is no such thing as witchcraft!" Thomas was on his feet without any memory of standing up. "There's never been any such thing! The Church didn't even call it witchcraft before the last war! If I surrender to you, how many other people are going to be broken? How many will have to kill someone or die?"

Thomas turned to Archbishop Culverton. "I can make this stop." The words came out harsh and loud. "I can make it stop if you'll listen to the king's demands, or I can make it stop by killing you all, and *I don't want to kill anymore!*" He stood, swaying, a moment longer, then collapsed in his chair.

Father Alphonse started forward, but the Archbishop stopped him with an upraised hand. He poured more wine in Thomas's glass and held it out.

Thomas took it with a shaking hand and drank. When the glass was half empty, the Archbishop asked, "What does the king want from me, Thomas?"

Relief coursed through Thomas like a river. He put down the glass. "He wants freedom of belief and worship for all four of the gods. He wants you to refute the Church of the High Father's claim to supremacy over the throne, and to allow him peace to rule as he sees fit, without any interference." Thomas's lips curved up, though it wasn't a smile. "And that includes the removal of all the powers of arrest and interrogation of the Inquisitors."

"That is preposterous!" snapped Father Alphonse. "The Inquisitors are the protectors of the Church!"

"Be silent," said the Archbishop."

"I will not! The king would gut—"

"Enough!" The Archbishop's voice was sharp, and Father Alphonse stilled his tongue. "And what do *you* want from me, Thomas?"

"I want you to honour the king's declaration and profess that there is no such thing as witchcraft. I want Father Alphonse to stop hounding my friends and me. I want Lords Cormac, Anthony and Ethan turned over to the king. And I want you to let the king's negotiators in here and bring this stupid war to an end."

"We should not listen to him," said Father Alphonse. "We should hang him on the church steps and let that be our message to the king."

"And then the king will bring down this building, and all of us will be killed and war will rage for years," said Archbishop Culverton. He put his hands on the arms of his chair and pushed, groaning as he rose to his feet. "My word, old bones are not suited to late nights." He straightened slowly, rubbing at his back. "It must be getting on to morning, I should think. Will you give me your arm to lean on, Thomas?"

"Of course," said Thomas, rising. The Archbishop put his hand into the crook of Thomas's elbow.

"I will walk beside you to the door," said the Archbishop. "And you may tell the king I will see his negotiators, and that I will declare there to be no such thing as witchcraft, and for all followers of the Church to loyally serve their king, in the High Father's name." Thomas's own legs nearly buckled in relief. It took three deep breaths before he could steady himself, and he realized that the Archbishop was holding him up. Father Alphonse was staring in horror, his mouth opening and closing in wordless rage. Archbishop Culverton smiled at Thomas. "Come. Your young lady will be waiting, I am sure."

The first bell of the morning sounded as Thomas stepped out of the Cathedral. A shout went up from the king's men. Thomas was halfway across the square when Eileen shook off Sir Walter's restraining hand and ran forward. Thomas stumbled to her, hugging her tight while she cried. George and Henry descended on them moments later.

"We've won," said Thomas. "Tell the king. We've won."

EPILOGUE

By late spring, the trees on the Academy grounds had spread their leaves, the grass had risen and turned green, and the warmth of the sun had everyone in shirtsleeves under their robes. Thomas and Henry leaned against the wall beside the gate, watching the other students passing through it.

Thomas kept expecting to see more faces he knew.

Fully a quarter of the Academy's students had died in the fighting. The king had come to the Academy to praise their courage and offer his condolences to their families. There had been funerals and special church services and weeks of mourning.

The Broken Quill had painted their door black in memory of the students who died there.

But the Academy was still the Academy, and in three hundred fifty years it had not missed the spring exams once. And so for the past month the Academy had been a gripped in furious, studious activity. Students exchanged class notes and held study groups and quizzed one another. The library filled up with young men and boys pouring over their books and snapping at anyone who interrupted them.

And on the week of the exams, Eileen sat in a room with two hundred prospective students, and listened as the Headmaster read the Royal Decree announcing that the Academy would once more be open to girls and women. Then Eileen sat down and become the first girl in two hundred years to write the Academy Entrance Exam.

Now, Academy classes were on a break. The students were spending most of their time in the taverns and theatres, worrying about how they had done on their exams. Thomas, with a confidence born of hours of study, knew he'd passed everything. Henry was sublimely unconcerned. Eileen had been a wreck for a week, pacing and swearing and trying unsuccessfully to distract herself.

Today was the day they were posting the results. It was also the day Thomas had promised to demonstrate lightning to the Master of Sciences.

Once magic was declared legal and Thomas had admitted to having it, he had been deluged with requests for demonstrations, lectures, and papers explaining how it worked. He'd refused them all during exams, but now, with nothing else on his plate, had to give in. The Master of Sciences was determined that, if magic was a natural force, it was a measurable one, and therefore Thomas needed to submit to being measured.

"Here they come," said Thomas.

Eileen was wearing her green dress and bodice with her white blouse. She'd declared once she'd written the exam that she'd not wear the robe until she knew she'd been admitted. Claudine was with her, practically skipping with excitement. Since the declaration had been made, the Academy grounds were no longer off-limit to girls, and Eileen had invited Claudine as her guest. George and Linda followed right behind, with Linda leaning on George's arm and laughing as they walked. George was carrying a large basket with him.

"Did they pack a picnic?" asked Henry. "Please tell me they packed a picnic."

"Looks like," said Thomas. He left Henry behind to kiss Eileen and take her hand. Claudine took Henry's arm and together they all walked through the gates.

As the six of them walked across the commons toward the crowd a student, perhaps a year older that Eileen and possessing a shock of sandy blond hair and several more inches of height than Thomas, fell in beside them. He kept his head down and looked at the ground. Thomas waited for him to say something, but the young man was silent until they were nearly at the commons. Then he blurted. "I start fires."

Thomas blinked in surprise. "What?"

"Fires," said the young man. "I start them."

"Well, don't do it in the library," said Henry. "They get upset about that."

The light dawned on Thomas. "With magic?"

"Aye," said the young man. "I start fires with magic. That is, I *can* start fires with magic. When I want to."

"That's wonderful!" said Thomas. "Can you control it? Enough to light a candle or something?"

"Aye, I can do that," said the young man. "A candle is easy." He stood straighter. "I never told anyone before."

"Can't blame you," said Thomas. "What's your name?"

"Brandon," said the young man. "Is... there any way for me to have magic like yours?"

"I can teach you some things," said Thomas. "But magic is only really powerful if a group of magicians work together. Would you like to be one of the king's magicians?"

Brandon looked wary. "Can I stay at the Academy?"

"I did," said Thomas. "And I'm the head of them."

"I'll do that, then," said Brandon. "I'll do that today, if I can."

"Tomorrow," said Thomas. "I'll introduce you to Sir Walter. He's in charge of us."

"Another one," said Henry, as Brandon headed away. "Impressive."

"There's a thousand of us here," said Thomas. He faltered. "Eight hundred now, I guess. It makes sense that some would have magic."

"Good day, Thomas Flarety," said the Master of Sciences, a large man with a bushy beard and eyes shining with excitement. "I hope this will be suitable."

This turned out to be an archery butt, set on the far side of the commons, about twenty yards away. Thomas nodded. "I would suggest no one stand near it. And we should have buckets of water standing by, to put out the fire."

"Excellent ideas," said the Master of Sciences. "Should have thought of that myself. Of course, I've never dealt with magic before."

It took a while longer for the buckets of water to be in place, and the students to be pushed back far enough that Thomas judged it safe. Half the student body had turned out to watch the event, at it took a fair bit of convincing to get them to move. Then the Master of Sciences and his professors insisted on standing equidistance from each other down the short length of the field, to see if they could measure the speed of the lightning's passing.

"Right," said the Master of Sciences. "Everyone cover your ears. Thomas. When you are ready!"

Thomas was amazed at how nervous he felt. *It would be just perfect to not have this work, this one time. I can just see it happening.* Thomas took a deep breath, raised his hand and willed lightning to hit the target. There was a clap of thunder, and the archery butt exploded in a flaming mass of hay and wood.

The students stared in awe, and then began cheering.

"You're their favourite new trick," said Henry.

"Wonderful," said Thomas. "That's not going to make life harder at all."

"Amazing!" said the Master of Sciences, "Absolutely incredible! Can you do it again?"

"I could," said Thomas. "But after two, I tend to pass out, and given that they're posting marks today..."

"Of course, my boy. Of course. Not to worry. But another day, perhaps? We've been trying to see the true power of lightning for years and having you cast the lightning would make it much safer, I think, than standing out in a thunderstorm waiting. Much drier, too. We just need a way to measure the power of it..." He wandered off, muttering to himself.

"Eileen! Eileen!" William was running toward them from the library. "They're posted!"

The words electrified the crowd. Students took off at a run toward the library and the large posting board that was put there every spring.

Eileen stood frozen in place. "He means the marks, right? Just the marks?"

"Oh, no," said Henry. "They post the names of the admitted as well."

Eileen's fists went to her mouth and she began shaking. Thomas held out his hand, but she didn't move until George pushed her from behind. "Well don't stand there like a lump. Go see!"

Eileen stumbled forward, catching Thomas's hand to regain her balance. She didn't let it go. She started walking toward the board, slowly at first, then faster and faster until she was running across the grounds with Thomas beside her.

A crowd several hundred strong surrounded the boards. Students pushed their way forward to see their marks, only to be pushed aside moments later by others. Shouts of joy mixed with groans of disappointment and cries of despair. Eileen, Thomas's hand still firmly in hers pulled up at the back of the crowd. "How do I get through?"

The students in front of her turned at the sound of her voice. They tapped the ones in front them on the back. "She's here!"

Word spread through the crowd. The young men began moving out of the way, until Eileen had a clear path. She let go of Thomas's hand and started walking forward. The students on either side followed her movement, craning their necks to watch.

"They're listed by grade," said Thomas, following her. "Then by last name."

"Here!" said Michael. He and the other ten survivors of the company were standing in front of the New Admissions list, resolutely facing out. "We haven't looked yet," he said, stepping aside. "No one has."

Eileen took his place in front of the board. One hundred twenty-five new students were admitted to the Academy every year, and five pages with twenty-five names each were nailed to the board. Eileen put her finger on the bottom name on the last page and ran it up. Then she did the same with the second last, and the middle page. Her hand started trembling as she went to the second page, looking at the higher and higher scores beside the names of the boys who would be attending the Academy.

A third of the way up the page of the highest scoring new students, Eileen's finger stopped. She stayed there a moment then, in a voice they could barely hear, said, "I'm in." She turned, her eyes meeting Thomas's. For the first time in months, Thomas saw nothing in them but joy. "I got in."

Eileen ran forward and jumped into Thomas's arms. "I got in!"

The Student Company let out a cheer, and Thomas squeezed Eileen tight while she laughed and cried with joy.

It took a nearly an hour before Eileen could break free of the crowd. Half the students congratulated her, then the Master of Rhetoric and Professor Dodds, then the Headmaster himself. When the last hand was shaken, Henry pulled the bottle of wine from George's basket and declared it time for lunch. The six sat together on the common, surrounded by the company, sharing the food and wine and laughing. The students peppered Eileen with advice and Claudine declared that she would be taking the exams next spring.

When the last of the food and wine was gone, Henry announced that he would buy them all a round at the Broken Quill, so they could properly toast Eileen's victory. The students cheered and as a group they all walked to the gate. Eileen held Thomas's hand and leaned on his shoulder.

"I can't remember when I've been this happy," she said.

"Thomas," George's voice came out half-choked. He pointed. A carriage stood on the other side of the gates. John Flarety and Lionel Gobhann were standing in front of it, and Magda Gobhann and Madeleine Flarety were inside, peering out the windows. All four looked worried.

"Oh, by the Four," Thomas barely breathed the words.

Henry looked at the carriage, then at Thomas. "What?"

"Our parents," said George. "They've come. All of them!"

"Really?" said Henry, who sounded like he was enjoying himself way too much. "You stopped a war two months ago. How frightening can this be?"

"I have to tell my parents about the magic," said Thomas.

"I have to tell them I got into the Academy," said Eileen. "I mean, they knew I was trying, but..."

"If you're going to worry about anything," said Henry, "worry about explaining what you two have been doing since exams ended."

Eileen spun around and raised a warning finger. "My parents don't need to know *anything* about that! *No one* needs to know anything about that!"

"If you don't want anyone to know," said Henry, "then you should really learn to be quieter."

Eileen swung a fist at him and Henry dodged out of the way. Thomas caught her other hand and pulled her to him. George opened his mouth to say something to Thomas but just then Madeleine Flarety spotted them. "Thomas!" His mother raised an arm and waved. "Thomas!"

Thomas looked at his parents' concerned expressions, then at Eileen's furious face and George's baleful glare. He began laughing. He took Eileen's hand in his and pulled her forward. "Come on. All of us."

Hand in hand, with Henry and George beside them, Thomas and Eileen walked through the Academy gates to face their families.

www.ingramcontent.com/pod-product-compliance
Lightning Source LLC
Chambersburg PA
CBHW021957010726
47494CB00003B/782
9781897492840